ETERNITY IN AN HOUR

Eternity in an Hour
Eternity Book One
By Matthew Merendo

Published by Less Than Three Press LLC

Edited by Amanda Jean
Cover designed by Natasha Snow

First Edition May 2017
Printed in the United States of America

Digital ISBN 9781684310135
Print ISBN 9781684310142

To Poppy,
Without you, Tristys and Rami would still be
waiting

ETERNITY IN AN HOUR

MATTHEW MERENDO

Pronunciation Guide

Coquels	co-KELLS
Cyræa	sir-RAY-uh
Quell	KELL
Quelles	KELLZ
Quellys	kell-WISS
Raàmidon	RAM-ih-dawn
Spàlor	SPAY-lore
Tristys	TRISS-tiss
Ystan	WISS-tn

To see a World in a Grain of Sand
And a Heaven in a Wild Flower:
Hold Infinity in the palm of your hand
And Eternity in an hour.

-William Blake, *Auguries of Innocence*

CHAPTER ONE

Ramidon eś Harys, his eyes pinned to the firebird flying above the forest, didn't see the body before he tripped over it. It was male, about the same age as Rami, maybe a bit younger. It had blond hair, thick but brittle from malnourishment, and it had on nothing but a pair of breeches. Its bare shoulders and back were blistered with sunburn. Most importantly, Rami noticed as he bent to get a better view, it was still breathing.

"Can you hear me?" Rami asked. He moved closer to the boy's ear and asked again, louder, but there was still no response. He nudged him a few times, pushed tentatively once and then twice on his shoulder, and the boy finally spoke. It was more of a groan, really, but it was something. He was definitely still alive.

He must have floated across the Coquelai to land on the beach. He was still clinging to a splintered plank, a dark hardwood Rami hadn't seen before. After the groan, he tried to roll over, but his arms were wedged beneath the wood. He coughed and pushed weakly against the board, trying to pull his right arm free, but he wasn't strong enough and fell back to the sand.

Rami, who had been dazed by the shock of the half-dead stranger, sprang into action. He lifted the plank just far enough off the ground to release the boy's arms and rolled him onto his back. The boy's eyes were closed, and his face wasn't sunburned, but his lips were as dry as the Quellusian Dead Stretch. He needed water, and he needed it fast.

He looked across the bay to Telia's small cottage. It wasn't too far away, maybe half an hour, but he needed water now. Rami considered. He hadn't used his magic in years, ever since the episode at the Altar, and he hadn't hurt anyone since then, either. But this felt different. If Rami didn't Touch a little bit of Water-magic now, this guy could die. And wouldn't the guilt from that be just as bad as the guilt he's had since the accident at the Altar?

Probably not, but he still had to help. He hadn't Touched the quell in twelve years, but he could still feel it, still See it all around him. Actually getting it to do anything was a bit more difficult. He opened the stranger's mouth and concentrated. He even used his free hand to massage the air—he knew that had no real effect, but it made him feel a little bit better. Half a minute later, the quell finally listened. Water began to coalesce just above the stranger's mouth, taking a second to fall.

After the first few drops, the stranger licked his lips and then strained in the water's direction. Rami pulled more quell through; more water coalesced, falling quicker. He drank longer than Rami thought possible, only stopping because of a coughing jag. Once the hacking settled down, he lay motionless on the sand.

Rami wasn't moving, either. He was a bit woozy from Touching quell again, and he was trying very hard not to fall flat on his face. Luckily, since he was already kneeling, he wouldn't have far to fall.

Quell-high aside, he wasn't entirely sure what to do with the person on the ground. He didn't look any better now than he did before the water. Should Rami give him more? Should he take him to Telia, who'd be able to help a lot more than he could? Should he just leave him? Pretend he'd never stumbled across an unconscious guy on the beach who smelled surprisingly good, considering he'd been adrift at sea for who knows how long?

No, he couldn't do that. He had to do something, but water obviously wasn't enough. He'd take him to Telia. She'd know what to do. He lifted the stranger into his arms—his back was so sunburned that the skin felt like a fire—and made a beeline for Telia's. The guy was tall, taller than Rami, but he weighed next to nothing. Even if Rami hadn't trained with the Physical Services, carrying him wouldn't be a problem.

Just a few seconds into the run, the stranger started to twist in Rami's arms. Rami gripped tighter. The struggling ceased, and the boy opened his eyes. Rami nearly dropped him. He had never seen eyes like this before! It wasn't the color, exactly—although the hues did seem to shift slightly, a little darker now, now a little lighter. It was the colors! They were different. One eye had the whole Bluewood in it, the other every shade in the Greenwood. Nobody in the Coquels had two different-colored eyes. No one. Yet here in his arms...

"What's your problem?" the stranger asked weakly, without aggression. His voice was melodic, deeper than Rami had expected from a body this thin, and the words seemed to last a second too long, the syllables a tad drawn out. This was Cyræan, not Quellosian: the length made sense. So did the eyes.

The stranger was smiling now, joking despite the situation, and he lifted his head from Rami's shoulder. "You never stumble across a half-dead boy before?" Despite himself, Rami smiled back, about to respond, but the stranger's eyes closed, the smile melted from his face, and his head fell back to Rami's shoulder. Rami walked quicker.

Rami nearly tripped twice on the way to Telia's. When he reached the path to her door, he walked by it, all because he couldn't take his gaze from the stranger's face. He wanted to see those eyes again, but they never opened.

CHAPTER TWO

Tristys had to pee. It was the first thing he knew, even before he opened his eyes. The second thing he knew, once his eyes were open, was that he wasn't in Spålor.

For one thing, Spålorians didn't break their new slaves by letting them sleep in the most comfortable bed Tristys had ever felt. Strangely enough, the bed looked like a rock. An enormous white rock. A rock that molded to Tristys's body and felt softer than the blanket he had covering him, but still a rock.

After examining the bed, Tristys let his gaze work its way through the rest of the room. It was small, the rock bed taking up most of the space, and dimly lit by short sconces on the walls. Someone had hung a few tapestries; they were so close to the sconces Tristys had to bury the vague fear the whole place would go up in flames. The two windows in the room were open and unbarred—more indications this wasn't a slave-camp. The moons were full. Back home, they always reminded Tristys of two sponges that had soaked up too much light from the sun. He was comforted to see they looked the same here, wherever here was.

There was a woman in the room, too. Tristys hadn't noticed her at first, since she was asleep in a chair in the corner. Her gray hair curled around her pudgy face, and her head had drooped so low her chin rested on her chest. She was breathing heavily, slow and deep, and the rhythm nearly lulled Tristys back to sleep. But he really had to pee and that won.

"Excuse me, lady?" he asked too quietly. He tried again, too loud this time. She jumped up, jerking back her head. It hit the back of the chair, and Tristys winced, but the white rock just absorbed the blow. The woman didn't even flinch.

She was wide-eyed now, apparently surprised that Tristys was awake. Her mouth was moving, opening and closing, but she wasn't saying anything.

"I'm sorry," Tristys said, holding his hands out to calm her. "I didn't mean to scare you, but I really need to pee." He had thought about asking her where he was, or how he got there, or what happened next, but when Nature called, Tristys answered.

Unfortunately, the woman was less than helpful. She ran out of the room before he could ask another question. She hadn't even had the decency to take him to the nearest relief hole. No matter. She'd left the door open, so he'd find it himself.

As he started to get out of the bed, he quickly realized he was still weak from his ordeal. He had trouble remembering specifics. He remembered everything about his capture by the Spȧlorians after running away from his home in Paru. He remembered the slavers, Tăd'kūnun and Vun'gor, and he remembered Vun'gor's animal companion, the enormous feline t□s named Va'kūnga. He did not remember getting off the ship. There was a storm, a terrible storm, then nothing. His memory was absolutely blank, just a hazy feeling of terror.

"I see you're feeling better." The voice was deep, deeper than Tristys's, with a strange accent and a unique vibration. It flowed over him like a river.

Tristys turned his head to see a boy in the doorway. He was young, probably younger than Tristys himself, with jet-black hair. He wore it spiked. He had on a tight blue shirt, sleeveless, that showed off his well-developed body. His complexion was flawless, his skin tone olive. Tristys had never seen someone so attractive, even when he used to stalk the Paruan army recruits with his friend Rylin. And he had seen quite a few attractive guys doing that.

First thing's first, thought Tristys as he admired the boy's bicep, which curled to bring some sort of strange yellow food to his mouth. "I have to pee." He started to get out of the bed again, but the blankets had wound around him and even that little bit of exertion tired him out. "Really, really bad," he added, since the boy hadn't done anything at all to help. He was still standing in the door, leaning against the frame and eating the weird yellow thing.

He pushed himself off the door frame and side-stepped closer to the bed. He even moved like a river, without a single sharp movement. "Bathroom's down the hall, first door on the right."

Tristys wasn't entirely sure what a bathroom was, so he asked a question. "What exactly is that you're eating?" He could have asked something more important, but he couldn't help himself. The most beautiful boy in the world repeatedly putting a long, thin object in and out of his mouth? Please!

He could figure out where he was later.

"This?" He held it up. "It's a banana."

"Right, of course." Tristys finally managed to yank the last cover off his legs and threw it to the side with the others. "Well, whatever it is, I like the way you eat it." He punctuated his come-on with what he hoped was a seductive look. Since he'd never really seduced anyone, he wasn't entirely sure he did it right.

He needed more practice. The banana-eater looked confused, not turned on. He crinkled his nose. "What? Why would you like the way someone eats something?"

Tristys rolled his eyes. He didn't have time to explain. "Look, I really need to pee."

"I told you, down the hall, first door on your right."

In the hallway outside the first door on his right, Tristys hesitated. This didn't look like a way out of the house, and if these people had their relief holes dug right inside the places they lived, opening this door was going to be very unpleasant. They obviously hadn't heard the old Cyræan adage *Don't poo where you pray.* He pushed open the door and held his breath.

But that was pointless. This room wasn't a relief hole, though he had no idea what it was. There was only one small window for ventilation. More sconces lit the room, which had virtually no furniture in it. Just some more strange things made of more white stone. But the square thing attached to the wall at waist's height was hard to the touch, so it wasn't the same stone as the bed.

There was another bit of square stone opposite the first. This one wasn't very high, though, and sitting on the ground. The last thing in the room looked like a chair, but it had a hole in the middle. Anyone unsuspecting would fall right through, so Tristys wasn't sure how successful a chair it really was.

In any case, this wasn't a place he could relieve himself, so he left. He wandered down the hall, hoping to find a way out of the house. Sure enough, at the end of the hall was a door that opened onto the outside, and Tristys ran the little bit of grass to the beach and did what he had to do.

As he was heading back to the house, Tristys noticed the windows that looked into the room he had been. The kid inside had finished his banana, and now he was bent over Tristys's bed, doing something to it. Was he fluffing the pillows?

"Hey, what are you doing?" Tristys asked without realizing it.

The boy jerked straight and turned to face Tristys. "I was fixing your bed, obviously." Tristys wasn't sure, but he thought there was a bit of blush in his cheeks.

"I see," Tristys said.

He stood at the window, not moving and not saying anything, and the boy stood inside, not moving and not saying anything. Finally, the boy broke the silence. "Are you coming back in here, or are you planning on floating back to wherever you came from tonight?"

That wasn't very nice. "Maybe I will leave," Tristys said, without the slightest intention to leave.

"Do you want some food and water before you go? The nearest town is at least a twenty-minute walk, and I doubt someone like you could make it that far without help."

And that was downright rude! He turned

sharply away from the window and huffed the entire way back into the room. The boy had moved to the same chair the old woman used earlier, and he had the nerve to be reading a book now!

"I'll have you know, kiddo, that I could easily fend for myself if I had to. In fact, I was in the process of running aw—moving out on my own when you stupid Spàlorians captured me!" Tristys had no idea why he said 'you Spàlorians' when this was obviously not Spàlor, but he wasn't about to correct himself. At least not in front of this guy.

"Don't call me 'kiddo'," the kid said. He didn't even look up from his book. "I'm almost certainly older than you."

"Give me a break," Tristys said, one hand on his hip. "You look like you're eighteen at most. Maybe seventeen! I'm twenty-two."

"Yeah, that's what I thought." He turned a page.

"What's that supposed to mean?" Both hands were on his hips now.

"I'm twenty-four, that's all." He finally looked up from his book, staring Tristys directly in the eyes. Tristys had never seen someone with purple eyes before. "Also, I don't know why you think we're Spàlorians, but I can assure you we are not." He stared a second longer, his lips pursed, and they turned into a slight grin as he added, "Kiddo."

"Well, what am I supposed to think? One minute I'm on a ship heading for a life of sex slavery, and the next I'm lying in your bed, tangled up in your blankets."

"Oh, this isn't my bed," he said, his nose back in the book.

Tristys deflated. "It isn't?"

"Nope. It's Telia's, the woman who let me know

you woke up. She's an old family friend, and I was just visiting when I found you washed up on the shore like a beached whale. I carried you here then, but now I'm thinking perhaps I should've pushed you back into the Coquelai." He turned a page, and Tristys twitched. "After all, that's what I'd do with a beached whale."

"Are you calling me a whale?"

The kid—no, he was a guy—looked up and smiled so wide his eyes shut.

"That's it, I'm out of here!" It was a threat, of course, and it seemed to work: the guy put the book down and stood up.

He pulled another yellow fruit from a pocket and tossed it to Tristys. "Here's a banana for the road." He sat back down.

"If you pick that book up, I swear to the two moons—"

He pursed his lips, but he didn't pick up the book. Tristys considered it a win.

After another second, he sat down on the bed. "If this isn't Spálor," he said while staring at the floor, "where is this?"

"We're in the Coquels. It's an archipelago in the Coquelai, east of where you come from."

"In the ocean?" Tristys asked. "I don't think anybody even knows there's land in the ocean."

"They don't. We keep it a secret."

Tristys was silent for a second, letting this information process. Besides the Offlands and Spálor, Cyræa was supposed to be the only other land. That was what he had learned in school. That was what everyone in the entire world thought.

"There are lands farther east, too. Not islands. Huge countries with forests and deserts and mountains." He took a second, looking at Tristys.

He seemed genuinely concerned, which was just as surprising to Tristys as this news of other lands. "It's a big world out there."

"But everyone speaks Cyræan?"

"No, just you folks from Cyræa speak that."

"You're speaking it," Tristys said. He felt a bit more comfortable now, and he liked to contradict.

"Yeah, but I learned it in school. I took it as a language requirement, mostly to avoid the nasty professor who taught Spàloric."

"So you don't normally speak Cyræan?"

He answered, but it wasn't in any language Tristys understood.

"Okay, I get it. I get it."

Neither said anything. They looked at each other for a few seconds before that got too uncomfortable. The guy picked up his book, and Tristys started to admire the tapestries, but those got old very quickly.

"I'm thirsty," he said at last. He wasn't really, but he had to say something, and he'd already used the relief-hole excuse.

"What happened to the whole 'I'm out of here!' thing you had going on a second ago? I was a fan of that idea."

"I'm too thirsty to leave," Tristys said. He was always rather good at exaggeration.

"Well, I can fix that pretty quickly." The guy picked up a glass on the table beside his chair and handed it to Tristys. "Here's more proof you're not in Spàlor," he said, grinning. He held a hand above the glass, snapped his fingers, and water fell from just beneath his palm into the glass, which Tristys quickly dropped from surprise. It shattered on the floor.

"I should have figured that would happen," the

guy said. Tristys heard the comment, but he was in a state of shock. What had just happened? What was going on? Where in all the Two Mothers' creation was he?

"Are you okay, kiddo?"

That snapped Tristys out of it. "Don't call me kiddo."

"You started it." He was grinning again, and Tristys hated to feel melodramatic, but that grin made it hard to breathe.

"I hope the cup wasn't important."

"Nah, Telia has a friend who works with Earth-magic. He'll whip up another few to replace that one." He sat back down in his chair and reached for the book again, but Tristys lunged and yanked the book off the table.

"Don't even think about it!" he said. "You have got a lot of explaining to do!"

The guy sighed heavily. He was good at exaggeration too. "I thought you said you were leaving."

"I'll leave after you explain what you just did."

"You promise?"

Tristys said nothing.

"Well." The guy put his hands on his thighs and pushed himself out of the chair. "Just the chance is reason enough to give it a shot, I guess." He picked up the broken pieces of cup on the floor and then headed for the door. "Follow me, kiddo."

"Don't call me kiddo!" Tristys shouted reflexively.

"Oh, right. Forgive me?"

Tristys scowled. "Unlikely. I still haven't forgiven you for the beached whale comment!"

The guy laughed this time, a full-throated, infectious chuckle. "I'm Rami," he said as he walked out the door.

Okay, take note, Tristys told himself. *Rami must be the Coquellian word for 'nice ass'.* As he watched Rami strut down the hall, he didn't think he'd have a hard time remembering.

~~*

His name was Tristys. Tristys of Paru. After they'd settled into Telia's small spare room, Rami had asked him his name. He'd been stalling, waiting for the Cyræan to offer it so he didn't look too interested, but he'd finally caved. What was it about this guy?

They were sitting in cottonbloom chairs. Rami thought the material was a bit much, since you sunk so far into them you had to yank yourself out again, but Tristys seemed to like it. He kept bouncing in them, pushing himself off the ground and seeing how far he could compress the bloom.

"You're not going to break it," Rami said when it seemed like Tristys would never stop.

"Does this ever get old?" Tristys asked. He stood up and threw himself backwards into the bloom. His butt nearly touched the floor. "I don't think it will."

Rami had to do something or they might be bouncing in blooms all night. "So, what do you want to know?"

That got his attention. He plopped once more into the bloom and looked expectantly at Rami. "What's your name again? You just told it to me, but I—"

"Rami."

"Rami," Tristys said. "Rami, Rami, Rami." He emphasized or drawled out a different syllable each time, like he was tasting it to see which flavor was the best.

"It's Rami," Rami said again. "Ray-me."

"Ray-me." Tristys nodded once. "Got it." He smiled again, and Rami's gaze was momentarily distracted. He'd been having a hard time not staring at the shifting blues and greens of Tristys's irises. Currently, the right one was navy and the left one was phenomenal. He had to stop looking at his eyes!

"I really can't get over these chairs," Tristys said. He wasn't bouncing again, but he was shifting like he wanted to. "They look like plants."

"They are."

"I'm sitting in a plant?"

"More or less," Rami explained. "They're cottonblooms from the Whitewood in Quellos, which is one of the islands here. They're preserved with Life-magic, so they don't wither."

"What island is this?" Tristys asked. Rami had expected a question about the Life-magic; perhaps this guy was a fan of non-sequiturs. Or maybe his brain just had trouble handling so much information at once. Or both.

"We're on Quelles, the island of Water." Tristys looked like he wanted more, so Rami continued. "It's the roundest of the islands, as well as the most southwestern."

"I see," Tristys said, nodding his head slowly. "And how exactly did I get here?"

Rami had been wondering the same thing since he found him. "I'm not really sure. I just found you on the beach—"

"If you say anything about whales, so help me—"

Rami smiled, but he didn't say anything about

a whale. "You were on the beach, half-dead, so I brought you to Telia, since she Touches Life-magic. She healed you. You were badly burned and dehydrated."

Tristys said nothing. His eyes were focused on a spot on the ground, and his mouth hung open slightly. Rami found himself staring at Tristys's teeth, which were perfectly white and almost perfectly straight.

"All I remember," he said finally, closing his eyes and his mouth, "is the boat."

"The boat?" Rami knew there was a slave ship, but what else was he supposed to say?

"Yeah, Vun'gor's ship."

"Was Vun'gor your slaver?"

"Yes, he was." Tristys thought a minute, obviously remembering something. "He was my friend, too, though. Something happened, I can't remember." Now his brow was furrowed, and he was shaking his head. It was the first time at least a hint of a grin wasn't on his face. "There was a storm, and someone was shouting..."

"Your slaver was your friend?"

"After a while, yes," Tristys said wistfully. He wasn't looking at the floor anymore, but he wasn't looking at Rami, either. In fact, Rami had the strange feeling that Tristys would have preferred being on the ship still instead of here in the Coquels.

Rami wasn't entirely sure what to say. He wanted to comfort him, but he had nothing to offer, and he certainly couldn't give him a hug. Not with that smile. Definitely not with those eyes. It was bad enough he had to look at them from a distance.

He finally settled with a question. "How did

you end up with the Spálorians anyway?"

"They captured me."

"Yes, I gathered that," Rami said. This guy was infuriating. "Did they raid your town? Paru, right? That's one of the bigger towns in the panhandle, isn't it?"

Tristys looked impressed. "It's the biggest, actually. But no, they hadn't done anything to Paru. It's too well defended. Most of the whole Cyræan army's there."

"Then how—"

"I was running away from Paru," Tristys said. His eyes were back to the ground. "Things got out of control, and I had to leave. They burnt down my house, and I was afraid for my—"

"Wait, wait," Rami interrupted. "Who burnt down your house? And why?"

"I don't know." He held up his hands in defeat. "Random Paruans, I guess. Probably Kitadyn and his family. I'm sure they had something to do with it."

"Who's Kitadyn?" Rami asked. "And you never told me why they burned down your house."

"Kitadyn was my best friend." He hesitated, obviously not wanting to answer the why. "And they did what they did because I'm diverted, and they found out. That was the worst of it, the arson, but they did so much more before that. They bullied me, and they beat me up, and they destroyed crops. The arson thing was the last straw. I had to leave."

Rami had stopped processing after 'diverted'. There was no Coquellian word for 'diverted'; it was the Cyræan word to describe men who were attracted to other men. It was the most heinous offense to the female-worshiping Cyræans, but here in the Coquels, things like that didn't matter. To most people, anyway. For Rami, though, things just got much worse.

It got even worse when he remembered the banana.

"Wait, so all that banana stuff. You weren't actually interested in the fruit at all, were you?"

Tristys blushed. Rami tried not to notice how good it looked with Tristys's pale complexion. "No, that was my inept attempt at flirting."

Rami nodded. His breaths were coming too quick, too short, and he felt as if his face were on fire. He had to calm down. Just because this kid had gorgeous eyes, and just because he had literally fallen beneath Rami's feet, and just because he happened to like men... all that didn't mean anything. In fact, it meant nothing at all as long as Rami didn't let it.

"Are you okay?" Tristys asked. He leaned closer to Rami, and Rami took a step back.

"I'm fine, I'm sorry." He wiped his forehead and wasn't surprised to find he was sweating. "I just can't believe people treated you like that. Nobody cares here in the Coquels."

"Must be a nice place," Tristys said. No smile.

Rami had to get it out. "I'm not like that, though."

Tristys was taken aback. "You care?"

"No, no!" Rami said quickly. "Of course not! But I'm not—you know—diverted, if that's what you want to call it. I have a girlfriend."

Tristys looked relieved. "Oh, I figured. Nobody in Paru is like that, either. I'm used to being the only one."

"You're not the only one," Rami said. He had no follow-up, though he was so lost in his own mind at this point he barely noticed the silence.

Tristys broke it. "You know, I know you're supposed to tell me about your magic now, but I'm exhausted."

"Yeah, it's very late," Rami said, immediately trying to look tired. "We can talk in the morning."

"I'll be here," Tristys said. "Am I sleeping in the same bed as before?"

Telia was probably already asleep in the second bedroom. "Yeah, that's fine." Rami stood up and stretched. His shirt rode up a little too high as he extended his arms, and a bit of his stomach showed. Tristys's eyes got wide, and Rami quickly dropped his arms. He wasn't shy about his body, but he hated the way Tristys's reaction made him feel.

"Where will you be sleeping?" Tristys asked nonchalantly.

"Probably on the floor in Telia's bedroom. That's where I've been sleeping the past few nights."

"You know, if you wanted, you could sleep in the bed with me. Has to be more comfortable than the floor."

"It would be," Rami said at once, "but no, thanks. I'm good on the ground."

"Suit yourself," he said as he walked out of the room.

Rami followed him down the hall and into Telia's room, and he built the makeshift bed he'd been sleeping on: a few cottonbloom petals for comfort, two pillows, and a blanket pushed up against the side wall.

As he was fighting with his blankets, Tristys spoke suddenly. "Thank you."

"What? What for?"

"For saving me. I don't know anyone back home who would have done the same thing."

"Don't mention it, kiddo. It's nothing I wouldn't have done for any other beached whale I found on the shore." Rami waited for the flurry of outrage, but Tristys had already fallen asleep.

CHAPTER THREE

Rami woke up first. He always rose early. Plus, Tristys still had some healing to do; Telia's Life-magic wasn't perfect.

It was the first of the week. He hadn't wanted to stay at Telia's this long. He had planned on being back to Ramidalé by month's end. Of course, there was no real reason for those plans; he just liked having goals in mind. He worked better that way.

But obviously he wouldn't be back to Ramidalé by the end of the month, so there was no reason to rush. He tried to go back to sleep, but it was futile. The sun had started to rise, and a shaft of light had skirted the curtains to fall directly on his eyes. He stared for a while at the dust particles, but it was no use. He got up.

His sleeper-pants had twisted around his waist—he always tossed and turned while he slept—and his mouth felt like a desert. There was the aftertaste of banana, too, and though it was his favorite fruit, he didn't like the ghost of it in his mouth. He shuffled to the kitchen, careful not to wake Tristys, and poured himself a glass of water. Telia had finally agreed to get quell-plumbing installed in the house last summer; he had threatened never to visit again if she didn't. It had been an empty threat, but she'd listened.

He sat at the table for a second, but the light

peeping through the curtains was too tempting. Sunrises were one of Rami's favorite things; they were half the reason he was a morning person. He took his glass of water and headed outside.

The beach was deserted. He'd expected it to be. Telia lived far enough away from Lower Ramidalé that she avoided most unwanted visitors. He never understood why more people didn't come this way, though. It was his favorite part of Quelles, possibly his favorite spot in all the islands.

He loved it so much that he and his family had named the thin, pointed piece of land that jutted far out into the Coquelai after him. There wasn't a damn thing special about that piece of land. It was just more beach, indistinguishable from the rest of the southwestern shore. Same sand, same waves, same little red crabs that liked to pinch the feet of beachgoers. But that little piece of beach had pushed itself out, got battered eternally by waves and storms, and still managed to stay put. It was inspiring.

It was also the best place to watch the sunrise, even better than the mountain vistas of Morningsview, high in the Westerwards of Quellas. The sun was rising now. To the ancient peoples who first lived on the islands, the sun was the Painter of the Sky. It made sense, when you saw views like this, the Painter's palette buffing the blue with deep purples and oranges.

"It's beautiful," Tristys said. He was behind Rami, still on Telia's porch. He had wrapped one of the cottonbloom coverlets around his shoulders, and his eyes were still puffy from sleep.

"I know," Rami said, turning back to the sunrise. Tristys bunched up the cottonbloom and tiptoed onto the sand to stand next to Rami.

"Back in Paru, we didn't really have sunrises." Rami looked at him askance, and Tristys chuckled. "We had them, obviously. We just couldn't really see them. There was always so much smoke in the sky, either from brushfires or military maneuvers. Sometimes, it was from actual battles."

"I can't imagine living in a place that didn't have this," Rami said. The sun was peeking over the horizon now, and the bright orange light was making Rami squint, but he kept watching.

"Oh, we'd have a sunrise on occasion. It was always a big deal. It meant the fires had stopped, or the battles had calmed down, or at least the wind was blowing in a new direction, you know?" He wasn't looking at Rami, but he smiled. It wasn't a happy one. "But by evening, the wind would have shifted back, or the Spàlorians would have started attacking again. It always ended the same."

Rami crinkled his brow. "You're not a morning person, are you?"

That elicited a genuine laugh. "I'm not, can you tell?"

Rami nodded. "Did I wake you?"

"You did, but I don't mind. I can fall back to sleep in a second." He started walking back to the house, making sure his blanket didn't hit the sand. "Besides, I'd have missed the sunrise if you didn't wake me, right?"

"Right," Rami said, still feeling guilty. He'd tried to be so quiet. "No sunrise without me."

"Right." Tristys smiled, and it seemed genuine. "No sunrise without you."

He was alone now, and he faced the sea again. He was hungry, but he decided to stay outside for a few more minutes. The purple in the clouds was different than it had been, heavier and darker. A storm was coming. It would be here soon, and Rami wanted to enjoy what he could of the Painter's masterpiece before the rain washed it away.

~~*

On his way back to the bedroom, the older woman whistled at Tristys. She was in the kitchen, and he turned slowly, unsure what to expect. He couldn't remember her name—Talia or Telli or something—so he nodded acknowledgment. She repeated something in her language then motioned for him to come and sit at the table. He listened.

She turned back around and continued what she had been doing, but a moment later she put a plate on the table in front of Tristys. It held three pieces of a dark brown bread covered in an even browner paste. The women stared expectantly at Tristys, and when he didn't really react, she started to mime eating motions. He wasn't sure if he should be flattered at her assumption he didn't know how to eat or warmed by the meal she made him.

When he tasted the toast, he chose the latter reaction. It was delicious. The bread itself had the slightest hint of the long yellow fruit he'd eaten with Rami. The dark brown glaze, though. He had never tasted that before in his life. It was rich and sweet and probably the best thing in the world. He ate all three pieces in seconds. The woman, who had been watching him the whole time, unwrapped more bread.

The front door opened then shut again. Tristys turned in his seat to wave at Rami as he walked by the kitchen. Rami waved back but didn't stop walking. A split second later, he back-stepped to the doorway.

"What are you doing in there?" he asked.

"Eating," Tristys said. "She makes some tasty toast, you know."

Rami grinned as he pulled out another chair and sat at the table with Tristys. "I know. I've been eating Telia's food since I was a baby."

"You're still a baby," Tristys said at once. He wasn't even sure why; it made no sense and was totally random. Something about this guy just made Tristys catty.

Telia—Tristys almost had the name right!— had been watching them, and she said something in her language, to which Rami responded, also in her language. They laughed, and Telia turned back around to pull out more bread.

"What was that about?" Tristys asked.

"You're a nosey one, aren't you, kiddo?"

"Are you ever going to stop calling me that?" He also wanted to ask if his next round of toast was done yet, but he tried to stay patient.

"Probably not, since you like it so much."

"Back to annoying Rami, I see." Rami nodded emphatically, popping one of the pieces of toast Telia had just set down into his mouth.

Tristys took a slice of his own, ignoring Rami when he tried to slap his hand away. Between the two of them, they went through another four helpings of toast. When they declined a fifth, Telia looked relieved. She said something in her language, picked up a small pouch on the table, and left the kitchen. Tristys heard her close the door on her way out. He and Rami were alone.

He gave Rami a questioning look.

"She's going to get more banana bread," Rami said, grinning.

Tristys smiled, but he said nothing. Without bread or an old woman between them, the silence got awkward pretty quickly. Tristys tried not to stare at Rami, but that was a daunting task. He was, after all, very easy on the eyes. Finally, Tristys couldn't take the silence.

"So," Tristys said, his eyes drilling holes into the table, "now what?"

"What, 'now what'?"

"Well," Tristys said, squirming, "what now? I mean, I'm here. So now what? Do I try to get home? Do I stay here with you? Do I travel the world? Now what."

Rami didn't answer for a few seconds. He looked concerned. He licked his lips once or twice before sighing and putting his hands flat on the table. "I'm not sure," he said at last.

"What are my options?"

"I'm not even sure you have any options. If the authorities catch sight of you, you'll be exiled. If we try to get you back home and we're caught, we could both get exiled. If—"

"Wait, wait, hold up a second," Tristys said. "What is all this talk of exile? Who's getting exiled where and why?"

"The government here doesn't like foreigners." Rami's voice became distant and smooth, as if he were giving a well-prepared speech or lecture. "As a group, foreigners tend to wreck things, so the country always reacts badly to them. There are very strict bans on immigration. Also on citizens leaving the Coquels, because we don't want people to know we're here. It's bad enough the Calerelacians found out about us and—"

"What could foreigners do that's that bad?" Tristys asked.

"Well, the Calerelacians, for instance. When they made contact and started trading with two of the islands, everything got so thrown out of whack that it led to the biggest war we've ever had. Whole islands were almost destroyed."

"The foreigners almost killed entire islands?"

Rami hedged. "Well, no. We killed our own islands. When the wars started, the Calerelacians backed off."

"But you blame the foreigners."

"Right," Rami said, slowly, in a tone belying the illogic.

"And because of that, I'll get exiled?"

"Yes, you will. Thrown right back into the ocean." Rami's eyes narrowed, and he grinned and bit the side of his lip. "Like a beached whale."

Tristys smacked him on the shoulder. "I hate you, you know that?"

"Sure do, kiddo." Rami laughed. "Sure do."

Silence again, but this was different. Tristys was thinking, only taking time out to stare at Rami and wish him naked once every few minutes. Rami, too, seemed preoccupied, though Tristys didn't know his subject matter. Tristys, though, was still trying to answer the now-what question.

"Would you want to go back to Paru?" Rami's voice was soft, almost afraid. Tristys thought it was adorable. "I mean, I can't imagine a war-torn country being that splendid, but your family is there. And it's all you've ever known, I guess."

Ever since he'd woken up here, he hadn't given much time to contemplate what had happened, what he'd left behind. This was so different than it had been when the Spàlorians captured him. At least in Spálor, he knew how to get home. He had the hope of seeing his family, of escaping, of being set free. And now he was here... and he didn't even know where here was. It was too much.

"Until now, I mean," Rami continued quickly. "Now you know me, and I imagine if you want to stay, we can—"

"I think I'm going to retch," Tristys said. He didn't wait for a response. He darted outside, across the short distance to the beach, and to the water's edge, where he heaved onto the shore. Rami had caught up with him, a hand on his back.

Rami had brought a cup with him, and after they sat down a few minutes later farther down the beach, he filled it with fresh water and handed it to Tristys. Tristys hugged his knees, his head resting, and looked at the sand as waves rolled onto the shore and then back out. His feet were bare, and he enjoyed the pull of sand sucked from under his toes. Ironically, having the ground ripped from under his feet helped him to remember that he had ground under his feet in the first place.

"Are you okay, kiddo?" Rami asked finally. He was next to Tristys, sitting in almost the same position, though his hands were drawing patterns in the wet sand. He didn't look at Tristys while he talked to him.

Tristys's smile was weak. "Yeah, I'm fine." He swallowed deeply and tried to focus on the way Rami's hand had felt on his back instead of the way his stomach and head were still churning. "It's just strange, you know, to think that I can never go home. I'll never see my mom or my sister. Or the rest of my family." His eyes were looking out to sea, squinting and searching the horizon. "It's just weird."

Rami nodded and pulled his hand from Tristys's back. "I don't think the—what?—six helpings of banana bread and chocolate helped."

"No, probably not." A breeze blew in from the ocean. It smelled nothing like the breezes back home. The sand here was different, too. Whiter, cleaner, finer. No wars. No brutality. No hateful stares or painful words. But no Rylin, no Nylit, no family at all. But did he even have a choice?

"I don't know what I want," he said at last. Rami hadn't broken the silence; he must have known Tristys was lost in his thoughts. "But at this point, I don't think there's anything I can do about it. I don't want to put you in danger trying to escape home." He looked at Rami and added, "Especially when I'm not even sure I want to escape."

Rami nodded as if it made perfect sense. "We'll take it one day at a time, okay? I don't have to leave Telia's for a few weeks. We'll figure something out by then. I have a friend who's related to some pretty important people in Imidalé. Maybe I can have him petition to get you citizen—"

When Rami stopped mid-sentence, Tristys shot him a quizzical look. His eyes were wide, and Tristys followed his gaze to the sand around them. No, to the water around Tristys. To one of the waves rolling back to the ocean, which had somehow managed to become stuck in time, lifted slightly off the sand and frozen, with just the smallest bit of vibration, around Tristys.

He panicked.

"What's going on?" he shouted, standing up immediately. The water rose with him, stayed for just a second, then crashed back to the sand, flowing out to sea like any wave would. "What was that? What did you do?"

"I didn't do anything!" Rami shouted back. But he didn't look panicked. Water had just tried to attach to Tristys, and he was only mildly perturbed. "I don't understand it, but I think you're Fingerprinting."

"Finger-whatting?" Tristys asked. He kept twisting his head around, twirling in a circle, watching the water at his feet to make sure it didn't freeze again.

Suddenly, Rami's expression shifted. His eyes narrowed, and he licked his lips before speaking. "Have you been lying to me? This is important. Tell me the truth."

Lying? About what? "What are you talking about?"

"Are you really from Cyræa?"

"Of course I am! I was born in Paru, raised in Paru, and captured in Paru! So were my parents, and their parents, and their parents' parents." He stopped a second. "Well, without the captured part."

Tristys caught Rami holding back a grin. "The quell doesn't Touch foreigners, Tristys. And it's Touching you right now. Look."

It had begun to rain. Hard. Water was pouring in sheets so thick that Tristys had trouble seeing Telia's house in the not-so-far distance. His pajamas were soaked within seconds, before he had even noticed it was raining.

"What are you talking about?" he shouted again, louder, with more frustration than anger. "I'm not doing anything."

"Look, Tristys! Look how wet you are! I'm barely misted!" He was right. His clothes weren't soaked, not even damp. "You're calling it to you!"

Tristys was back to angry. He wasn't doing anything, and he would be damned by the Two Mothers if he was going to let this guy from some imaginary place tell him otherwise! "I'm not doing a—I don't know what—"

In a matter of seconds, Tristys felt everything drain away. Something squeezed his anger, his confusion, even his energy from him like water from a crushed sponge. He swayed slightly, tried to regain his center, but failed. His eyes rolled to the back of his head, and like a sponge dropped into a sink, he crashed into the sand.

CHAPTER FOUR

Telia's Life-magic came in handy a second time since Tristys's arrival. Telia came back from the store just as Rami was carrying Tristys's limp, bedraggled body into the house. She thought he'd drowned. But after a cursory inspection, she declared simple quell-exhaustion and assured Rami, who made her repeat herself dozens of times, that he'd be fine once he woke up.

Even Rami knew the signs of exhaustion—fainting, bodily twitches that started in his center and radiated outward, and that certain tinge of color that depended on the quell in question (blue, for Water-magic, in Tristys's case)—but his paranoia made him stay by Tristys's bed for most of the day, placing a hand in front of his mouth every few hours to make sure breath still moved. Much to his relief, it always did.

After his last inspection, Rami had gone into the kitchen to find Telia at the table, eating a bisiberry pie she had just made. He helped himself to a piece and sat across from her.

"It's coming down out there now as fast as it was around Tristys when he Fingerprinted earlier," he said after he swallowed his first bite. It was, as expected, delicious.

Telia glanced out the nearest window. "Yes. We haven't had a big storm in a few days, though. The plants were starting to worry."

"I'm sure. Droughts are scary." Of course, in a land that could create water out of thin air, droughts were never really a threat.

"He's still alive?" Telia asked as she cut another slice of pie. "I shouldn't have another piece, but I'm going to. My weekly splurge."

"Yeah, he is. Still breathing."

"A few more hours, that's all. He's sleeping off the exhaustion. Don't fret."

"I'm not worried." A large peal of thunder shook the house, and Rami involuntarily jerked his hands to his ears. He'd hated storms when he was a kid, and some habits died hard.

"I can tell you are, dear. Don't forget how long I've known you. You only drum your fingers like that when you're worried." She nodded at his right hand. He had, indeed, been drumming his fingers, though even he wasn't aware it was a nervous gesture. She was good.

"Well, I'm not worried about his waking up," Rami confessed. "I'm worried about what I'm going to do with him once he does."

"He Fingerprinted, right?"

"Yes, I think so." Rami's brow furrowed in frustration. "I'm not really sure, because it wasn't a normal manifestation, and he's not Coquellian, right? And no foreigner before has ever been able to commune, so I don't know why the magic would have Touched him. But I can't exactly send him off to the Altar with a few bananas, some toast, and a good push in the right direction."

Telia laughed. "No, of course not. You'll have to go with him."

Rami blinked back his surprise. "What?"

"I said you'll have to go with him. He'd never make it to the Altar alone. It's on the other side of

Quelles! Not to mention the fact he sticks out like a sore thumb here."

It's the eyes, Rami thought. He said, "You seriously think I should take him to the Altar? I'm just going to march in and say, 'This here's my Cyræan who speaks with eś. He's going to attune now, so move over!' The high priest hates me as it is. I can just imagine—"

"Oh, Liana is an old friend of mine. I'll give you a note to take to her, and if that doesn't work, I'll give you some of this pie. It's delicious, and she loves bisiberries."

"I don't think a pie is going to be enough, Telia. He's foreign, remember?"

"Just trust me, dear. She's like a cat: curious by nature. You bring her a foreigner who speaks with Water and she'll forgive whatever it was you did to make her hate you so much."

Rami had his doubts, but he'd humor the old woman for a second. "What if she turns him in to the authorities?"

"She won't. I told you, she's like a cat. What do they hate more than anything? Being told what to do. You know, she and I once tried to run away to the Offlands together. We were tired of Coquellian luxury one week. We were in Quellos, so I'm sure you understand. I think we got as far as southern Quellys before we gave up. That island is dreadful. People should be exiled there instead of the Offlands."

Had to be another one of her stories. Rami wasn't sure how many or how much of them was true, but they were always entertaining. He almost pressed her for more details, but the image of Tristys asleep in the bedroom kept him focused.

"I don't know, Telia. Even if Liana lets him go,

it's like you said, he sticks out like a sore thumb. Even if I teach him the language and dress him in real clothing and find a way to cover up those eyes, people will still know something is up with him. He carries himself differently than we do."

"Take him through the Bluewood. You can follow the Rockaways, sleep in the caves along the way. It'll be rough compared to civilized traveling, but you've always liked to camp out."

Rami thought for a second, trying to calm the rising panic. She was right: trekking through the Bluewood would avoid most people, thereby keeping Tristys safe from exile. But it would also mean spending weeks alone with him. Having to sleep next to him. Having nothing to do and no one to talk to except him.

"I don't know if that's a good idea, Telia." He laughed awkwardly, tried to make a joke. "We'd be alone together the whole time."

Telia's face contorted in a strange grin, her eyes narrowed and as mischievous as Rami had ever seen her. "I am rather certain that neither you nor he will mind spending so much time alone together."

Rami was dumbstruck. Was she really suggesting what he thought she was? Was he really blushing? "He may not mind," Rami said without looking at her, "but I would. I can't even spend more than a minute with him before I want to run away screaming."

"Right," Telia said, still wearing her lewd face. "And that's why you cradled him in your arms and rushed him here for me to heal—"

"I didn't—"

"Twice. And why you've been checking his breath every ten minutes for five hours. And why you've been pacing the house."

"I don't—"

"And why you've looked at him so carefully that you can tell he holds himself in a strange manner. And why—"

"I get it," Rami said brusquely. His face had become a blank slate, wiped clean of any emotion, his usual defenses sprung into place. "But what you're implying—you're wrong."

Telia's smile shifted into concern. She put a comforting hand over his, stopping his fingers from drumming so quickly the taps nearly blurred into one. "Rami, I have known you since you were just a baby. We've always thought—"

"You've always thought wrong," he said simply. He stood up, subconsciously intending to go check on Tristys again. It was his fault, that stupid boy's fault, that Telia brought this up. "I will take Tristys to the Altar. I will teach him Quellosian on the way through the Bluewood. Once we arrive—"

"Rami, you're upset. You always get so formal when you're upset. Please, just—"

"Once we arrive," he said more forcefully, "I'll give him to Liana. After that, I will leave, and I will never see him again." His eyes narrowed slightly, the first hint of emotion on his face. "Then you will see how wrong you are."

"Rami, sit down here. You're getting—"

"And then I will return to Ramidalé Proper." The distance in his voice, in his look, in his body language shifted Telia's concern to worried panic. "I have told you before not to bring this up, Telia. I expect it from people like Gawen, but not from someone like you."

He started to walk away, but he stopped and

turned around at the last minute. "Please write your note for Liana. Leave it on the table." The last thing he saw as he left the room was Telia's hand still resting over the ghost of where his own hand had been.

~~*

When Tristys awoke, it was the middle of the night. It took a while for him to remember where he was and what had happened. Something about Fingerprinting, Rami had said, but what that meant, Tristys had no idea. Maybe Rami was still up and he could ask...

But Rami wasn't in the room. In fact, he wasn't even in the house. Telia was there, asleep in a cottonbloom chair. She wasn't covered, and the air in the room was chilly, so he took one of his own blankets and tossed it over her. She looked upset; even in the darkness, Tristys could see freshly dried tears on her cheeks. Surely she couldn't be this upset over his latest health issue, could she? Something else he'd have to ask Rami.

With nobody awake in the house, Tristys had nothing else to do but go back to sleep. He took a banana fruit from the kitchen and used the strange knob on the counter—Rami had called it 'plumbing'—to fill a cup with cool water. But even after the snack, even after a full-blown fantasy that involved Rami confessing his undying love, Tristys still couldn't fall asleep.

He was afraid. Here he was, lying in a stranger's bed, in a foreign country, with no way home. In a foreign country that would exile him in a second if they found him. In a foreign country with crazy magics that apparently didn't like him much. Afraid was an understatement.

He twisted one of his remaining blankets around his legs, up his torso, and through his arms, which was a habit he'd started as a child and still hadn't grown out of. He liked tightness, the feeling of being bound. It made him feel safe. Though the chains he'd worn after he was captured, before Vun'gor let him roam the ship, hadn't made him feel very safe.

But why was he thinking about that? He wasn't a slave now; he never was one, really. And no matter what these islands and their people threw at Tristys, nothing could be as bad as Spàlorian sex-slavery, right? He just had to keep looking at the positive things—not a slave, still alive, not dead—and take things one day at a time. He'd figure something out.

In the meantime, Tristys thought as he sighed and turned on his side, he'd just keep tightening his blanket.

~~*

Tristys wasn't even fully awake when Rami started bossing him around.

"Get up," Rami said, his voice flat. Tristys opened his eyes, but the sun was shooting through the window directly onto his face. He squinted, still couldn't see, and gave up. He rolled over.

"Get up," Rami said again, more forcefully. "We're leaving today."

Tristys opened his eyes again, far enough away from the shaft of sunlight that he could see Rami darting around the room, tossing this and that into several large cinch-sacks. He hesitated a second before finally looking at Tristys.

"I mean, if you feel up to it." He sounded almost apologetic, but his voice quickly grew distant again. "Fingerprinting usually doesn't leave too heavy an exhaustion after, since you're not actually manipulating the quell."

Tristys tousled his hair, scratching an itch and squinting a bit to clear his eyes. "As usual, Rami, I have no idea what you're talking about." He took a moment to decide how he felt. "But I feel fine. A little tired still, but fine."

"I figured," Rami said, back to throwing things in sacks. "You look fine, too."

"Well, I had no idea you felt that way about me!" Tristys said. "You look pretty fine yourself."

"I meant you're no longer blue in the face. You're back to being forward, though. I'll take that as a good sign."

"I don't know where we're going," Tristys said, tossing the blankets aside, "but I'm pretty sure we don't need the skin from the banana I ate yesterday."

Rami stopped his frantic packing and stared at him. "What?"

"You just put the banana skin in the bag." Rami started digging. "No, the blue bag, right after I said you were fine."

Rami huffed as he pulled the skin out of the bag. "It's a peel, not a skin." He slammed the trash in a garbage receptacle near the bed. "Can't you at least pretend to clean up after yourself?"

"I'm sorry, next time I intend to faint after your magic runs amok with me, I'll be sure to tidy up first." Tristys was awake now, and he was feeling feisty. He wasn't about to let Rami guilt-trip him about the night before, especially when he had no idea what had happened.

Rami looked a bit abashed, which was enough for Tristys. "Is there anything I can help you do? Do you have another bag I can toss things into?" He let a light grin play across his face. "I think I see a few seed pits from that bitter red fruit you love over there on that table."

Tristys expected some witty remark, some sharp comeback, something, but Rami just kept packing his bags as if he were alone in the room. A few minutes later, when the blue bag was so heavy it made Rami's bicep bulge deliciously, Rami finally spoke.

"Be outside in ten minutes," he said, and then he was gone.

~~*

Lower Ramidalé was unlike anything Tristys had ever seen, even in his imagination. It was hard not to stare. It was also hard to stare, because Rami was in such a rush that Tristys had to move too quickly to get a good look at anything. He was mildly annoyed, but it was hard to get really angry when you were surrounded by houses made out of mushrooms.

Yes, mushrooms.

After Rami had walked out of the bedroom so coldly, Tristys had spent a moment trying to think if he'd done anything wrong. As far as he could recall, he hadn't. This made him mad, as he hated unjust attitude. When he finally left the house, after saying an awkward goodbye to Telia, he'd met Rami head on, determined to give him as hard a time as Rami gave Tristys that morning.

But Rami didn't give him any time at all, really. They walked—no, almost ran—in silence from

Telia's house through a sparsely forested path before breaking into what Tristys assumed was Lower Ramidalé. And from that point, the only thing Tristys felt was awe.

Yes, he'd had the best rest of his life while sleeping on a rock with pillows made from plants, but even that was mundane compared to this town. The only city he'd ever known back home was Paru, where every building looked like all the others, sitting rigidly in grid-based perfection, and it was stifling.

Here in Lower Ramidalé, though, everything was free. No two buildings looked the same, and if there was any sort of order to the planning, it was too subtle for Tristys to see. The first building Tristys saw he mistook for a tree—it wasn't really a mistake, though, because the building actually was a tree. And the two or three trunks around it were buildings, too. A series of enormous vase-like flowers turned out to be an inn, a decaying stump was the entrance to an underground market, and a hollowed-out boulder housed a store where you could buy clothes. When Tristys saw the same fruit Rami had eaten that night—only a thousand times bigger—he nearly choked.

"That's that fruit you like, isn't it?" Tristys said, momentarily forgetting that he was trying to give Rami the cold shoulder.

"It is," Rami said, without looking at Tristys or slowing down his speed.

"The ones we ate weren't that big." Tristys craned his neck so his gaze could reach the top of a particularly gigantic mushroom. "Does everything here get that big?"

"No."

Tristys sighed. Oh, right. Rami was being

weird today. "Care to explain?"

"Not really, but if it will get you to quit talking, I will."

Rami paused, as if he wanted Tristys to say something, but Tristys stayed silent.

"That's just a regular banana, but whoever lives there used Life-magic to make it grow so big. And Death-magic, probably, to keep it from decaying."

"So you people grow things really big and then live in them?"

"Mostly it's just the people here in Lower Ramidalé, but yes, we do."

"Strange," Tristys said, mostly to himself.

Rami heard him, though. "It would be more strange, I think, if we could do it but chose not to simply because it was out of the ordinary."

Tristys nodded, already allowing the conversation to slip back into silence while he stared at magically enhanced mushrooms and fruit. If the rest of the Coquels was half as accepting of the unordinary as Lower Ramidalé was, Tristys had a feeling he'd like it here.

~~*

Lower Ramidalé was not a large town, and Rami had them back into the forest as quickly as Tristys's legs could carry him. The forest slowed Rami's pace, and Tristys was thankful. Even without running a marathon, the heat was nearly unbearable; it clung wetly to Tristys's light clothing, wound its way through his hair, and licked every stretch of bare skin. The canopy prevented most of the sun's light from reaching the ground, and Tristys mouthed his thanks again—he couldn't imagine what this trek would be like in direct sunlight.

Just as he had through Lower Ramidalé, Tristys spent most of his time staring around him, jerking his head right and left and up and down, trying not to miss anything. The ground was a mess of decaying leaves, most of which were covered by brilliantly colored fungus, and the heavier shoes Rami had given him before they left now made sense. Vines crept along the trunks and through the lower branches of the trees; one particular species wrapped itself so tightly that it killed whatever supported it. The flowers sported colors that Tristys hadn't ever seen in Paru, and he actually got Rami to laugh when he pulled one with enormous petals off its stem and wore it as a hat.

Everything smelled here, too, and every step brought something new to Tristys's nose: now the cloying scent of a fruiting flower, now the nauseous odor of a decaying rodent, now some unscented fresh air that sneaked through the canopy. When he bent down to take a whiff of a peculiar pitcher-shaped bloom, a small green lizard leapt out of it and landed on a nearby leaf. Instead of running away as Tristys thought it would, the lizard cocked his head and stared.

"You better be careful," Rami said through a suppressed chuckle. "Everything isn't as friendly as that lizard."

Tristys scoffed as the reptile finally skittered away. "You think that was being friendly? You're even more socially inept than I thought!" He meant to jest, but the accusation came off a little too serious. Perhaps he was angrier than he thought.

"What's that supposed to mean?"

"Nothing. I just don't get you." He wasn't going to bring up the mood swings from Telia's house, but now that the opportunity presented itself, Tristys thought he'd take it. "It's just one minute it seems like we're friends, and the next minute it's like you can't stand the sight of me." Rami still looked perturbed, so Tristys tried to lighten the mood with flirtation. "You're as cold sometimes as you are hot all the time."

His comment did something to the mood, but it didn't lighten it.

"I told you, I'm not that way." He wasn't looking at Tristys again. "You have to quit implying that I am."

"I never said you were."

"Yes, you—" Rami stopped, as if realizing that he was, in fact, wrong. "Just quit it, okay?"

"Fine." Tristys was sticky with sweat, and he'd had enough of Rami's odd behavior. For someone who wasn't "like that", he certainly protested a lot. And Tristys was tired of that, too.

They traveled in silence for a while. It wasn't too rough to get through, considering this was a jungle, but Rami did have to hack down a few vines here and there. He looked good wielding a hatchet, the sweat glistening off his bare biceps, but Tristys tried not to gawk... too much. Tristys was surprised, since there were so many plants, that he didn't see more animals; aside from the lizard and all the bugs, the forest was deserted.

"I wanted to get us through Lower Ramidalé quickly," Rami said suddenly, just as he finished hacking through a particularly thick vine. "We can go back and sightsee later, but I didn't want anyone asking questions. I told you, officially speaking, I should be turning you in for exile right now, not taking you to the heart of the island's magic."

Tristys had never asked for an explanation, but he liked getting one. He smiled. "And what are we going to do once we get to the heart of the island's magic, anyway?"

"We're going to see if you can attune." The hatchet broke through the vine with a sharp crack. Before the ends fell to the ground, Rami grabbed one in each hand and held one out for Tristys. "Here, rub the sap on your arms and legs if you want. It'll cool you down a bit, and it keeps away the insects. Keep it away from your face, though. It burns if it gets in your eyes."

Tristys did as he was told, and the sap really did cool him down. He wasn't so sure it kept the bugs away.

"We have to keep you a secret, though, for as long as we can. Which means you're going to have to blend in." After sapping himself up, Rami took up his hatchet again and hacked away at another vine. "And that's going to be difficult," he said, "considering your eyes are so spectacular." He started, perhaps surprised at his own words. "I mean, almost nobody in the Coquels has two eyes that are different colors. And nobody in the Coquels has eyes that change hues like yours do."

Tristys couldn't resist. He sidled up next to Rami, put a hand on his wrist, and batted his eyelashes furiously. "Why, thank you for noticing." Then he added, somewhat more seriously, "In Cyræa, pretty much everyone has eyes like mine."

"Must be a nice place to live." Rami's voice was soft, almost unintelligible, but Tristys heard it.

Noticing his eyes, wishing he lived where Tristys came from... more hot-and-cold Rami. "But enough about that. We need you to blend in, so the first thing we have to do is teach you how to speak Quellosian. There won't be too much interaction at the altar, but you'll have to be able to answer a few questions, at least."

From that point on, Rami spoke no Cyræan at all. Their progress through the forest slowed down considerably, because Rami had to use a lot of gestures and facial expressions to get Tristys to understand what he was saying. For Tristys, this experience was just as bizarre as a walk through a town made of mushrooms and flowers. A few days ago, he had no idea that there were more languages than Cyræan and Spálorian; now, he was learning Quellosian. What next?

Not surprisingly, a person who's speaking a language you don't know doesn't make for a very exciting conversation partner, and Tristys quickly grew tired of listening to this strange language, even though it did feel somehow familiar to him. After a few hours, he started to pout; he became angry when he realized Rami was enjoying himself, saying who knew what to Tristys who couldn't say anything back.

When the two entered a clearing left by the collapse of a dying tree, Rami's amusement fell from his face. He was looking at the sky—the first of it they'd seen in a few hours—and even Tristys could tell it was going to rain.

"We have to hurry," Rami said, once again in Cyræan. "It's going to rain sooner than I expected."

"Finally, I can understand you again!" Tristys said, ignoring the urgency in Rami's voice.

"Have you ever heard the expression 'when it rains, it pours'?"

"No," Tristys answered, already growing bored with another language lesson.

"It originated here on Quelles. So unless you want to be drenched and frozen in the morning, we need to get to Rockaway before the rain starts."

"Oh, Rockaway! I love it there!" Tristys said with exaggerated enthusiasm. He was still bitter about the past few hours of Quellosian. "My family and I spend the winters there. It's so warm!"

Rami rolled his eyes. "Rockaway Labyrinth is a system of caves that goes from the south of Quelles, which is where we are now, to the east of Quelles, which is where we want to go."

"So we're going to crawl through caves to get to the Altar?"

"No, there are lots of unpleasant creatures in the caves," Rami said. "Besides, the caves are pitch black, and neither you nor I manipulate Fire-magic. We'd get lost and starve to death before we found our way out."

"So you only do it with water?" Tristys asked, changing the subject in his usual way.

Rami hesitated. "Yes, you could say that." The monotone suggested there was more to the statement than Tristys understood, but he didn't push it.

Rami sped their pace, and the Quellosian lessons ceased. For once, Tristys didn't mind. There had been a noticeable change in the forest: flowers that had once been open and lustrous had turned inward or shut their blooms completely, and fewer animals were calling to each other in the treetops. The sundry smells were gone, too, replaced by something something overpowering.

It wasn't a scent or smell, not exactly. It was more like a nasal feeling, a vibration that registered only to Tristys's nose: it felt like rain.

After Rami cleared the last of the vines in their way, Tristys could see a clearing ahead. Just beyond stood the cave they'd be sleeping in. It was a welcome sight, considering the bruised gray of the sky. Lightning flashed, though the bolt remained hidden, and several seconds later a dull boom of thunder roared from the way the two had come. The cave was pallid gray, its craggy face flaking off in geometric patterns. Light penetrated only a few feet into the cave; farther than that was a blackness so complete that Tristys had the irrational urge to refuse to enter.

"Don't worry," Rami said. "It's safe this close to the mouth. And if you're scared of the dark, I'll be lighting a fire once we get inside."

Rami wasn't mocking him for once, so Tristys swallowed his fear. "I thought you said you can't use Fire-magic?"

"I can't," Rami said blandly. "I brought flint and tinder."

Something made Tristys want to laugh, but he stifled it and started walking towards the cave. Rami, who was ahead of him, took the hint and entered the cave first, stopping just where the light began to fade into darkness. Almost immediately, Rami got to his knees, opened one of his packs, and built a small mound of tinder. It lit after just a few strikes from the flint, and as Rami nursed an increasingly large fire, Tristys no longer wondered why he'd been putting dry sticks in his bags throughout their journey.

Just as Rami stood up, a bright flash lanced across the cave's entrance, accompanied by a clap of thunder rolling rockily to its conclusion. That, apparently, heralded the deluge. Rain began to pour from the sky, heavy walls of it that made visibility nearly zero. It felt as if some god—not Tristys's gods, or course—was sitting above the cave and emptying bucket after bucket over the edge.

"You weren't kidding when you said it pours."

"Of course not." Rami was smoothing out two blankets he'd laid near the fire. He'd put them so far apart, though, they were against either side of the cave and separated by the roaring flames.

He patted out one last wrinkle on the purple blanket and, satisfied with the bed, sprawled across it. He extended his arms far above his head and twisted his body, almost writhing in pleasure from the stretching, and his shirt rode up just a bit along his torso. Tristys caught a glimpse of chiseled abdomen before turning away, his desire overpowered by an unexpected rush of guilt.

The rain brought a drastic decrease in temperature. Tristys shivered, the sweat earlier still lingering on his body and exacerbating the chill in the air. He grabbed the edge of his blanket and pulled it closer to the fire before sitting down. He wanted to say something, since the silence was starting to deafen him, but he had no idea what to say, so he simply sat, cross-legged, on the unbelievably soft yet painfully drab blanket while Rami fidgeted through another one of his packs.

"Here," Rami said finally. He handed Tristys a plate of bread with some cheese on it, a banana, and two pieces of some other fruit Tristys had not yet tried. "If you put the cheese in between the bread and find a stick with a twigged end, you can set the sandwich on top and toast it. It's pretty decent. Watch." Rami followed his own instructions, and within a few minutes, he had something he called a grilled cheese.

That was too much work for Tristys, though, so he opted for cold cheese on bread moist from the humidity in the air. He peeled his banana in silence, refusing to look as Rami ate his own. He tried the other thing Rami had given him, some fruit with strange seeds on the outside, but he didn't like them.

"I'll give you some water now," Rami said, his voice soft and almost gentle, "if you promise not to drop the cup again."

Tristys rolled his eyes, and Rami handed him an empty cup to hold while he filled it with water from a canteen. Tristys drank it quickly, draining a second cup as soon as Rami refilled it. He wanted another, but Rami ignored the hints.

"The meals will be better at the Altar," he said, almost apologizing. "We've got to ration what we have now."

"You picked that fruit from right outside," Tristys accused. "And you can make water from the air!"

Rami scrunched up his shoulders. "True, but we don't really have time to forage in the forest. And I prefer not to commune with quell if I don't have to."

There was definitely something up with Rami and his magic.

"Besides, we should spend all our free time teaching you Quellosian. It won't take us long to reach the Altar, and you need to pass as one of us."

"We're going to need a lot longer than we have, I think."

"We can practice a bit now," Rami said. Those

words ushered several hours of discussion about, as well as several one-sided conversations in, Quellosian.

Tristys learned that the language wasn't called Coquellian because it had originated, like the people of the Coquels, on the island of Quellos, before there were seven islands unified under a single name. He also learned that, despite his worries, he was actually picking it up quickly. His mouth apparently knew how to make most of the strange sounds in the language, like the clicking tongue, the trilled 'r', and the guttural 'n' and 'h'. By the end of the lessons, Tristys could have simple conversations with Rami—very, very simple, but conversations nonetheless.

"You'll be ready to go in no time," Rami said. His eyes were heavy, and he'd been yawning through most of the last few conversations they'd had about favorite colors and hobbies and family members. "We've got probably another week before we get to the altar, and I think maybe a day or two after that should be more than enough time to get you ready if we don't do anything except walk and talk. Think you can manage that?"

Tristys was skeptical, but Rami had been such a good sport over the past few hours, he couldn't let him down. So he said yes... in Quellosian.

"I'm impressed," Rami said, smiling the first true smile Tristys had seen all day. He stretched again, showing less skin this time, and yawned before lying down. He didn't say good-night, and though Tristys waited a few moments, apparently he wasn't going to.

Tristys, his arms and chin resting on his knees, stared out the cave at the rain. It hadn't let up at all, still cascading from the sky in silver sheets of cold. It felt like he was sitting behind a waterfall, which probably explained why he was thinking of home, of the times he and Kitadyn and Rylin would sneak to the Kysim Cliffs, hiding behind the waterfalls and making up fantasies about leaving Paru and living together in one of the big cities closer to the center of Cyræa.

He'd thought up his own fantasies over the past few days, daydreams that mostly involved a life of leisure lived safely in Rami's arms, and for those first few days, he actually thought it was possible. But now? Not so much.

Something had changed. Tristys had no idea what, but something was different. Those first few days, he and Rami had laughed together, teased each other, shared smiles. Tristys didn't have much experience, but he knew flirting when he saw it. But ever since that day on the beach, ever since he had pulled the magic or whatever it was, Rami had been different. He hadn't called Tristys 'kiddo' once since then, hadn't looked him in the eye. Tristys wasn't even sure they'd laughed at the same thing since then, either. Rami had to be mad about something, and the only thing that had changed was the quell.

Tristys stood up and shivered. He was still cold, but he didn't want to sleep so close to the fire. He grabbed the edge of his blanket and pulled it away, closer to the cave's entrance and farther from Rami, since he didn't want to intrude. But a second later, he pulled the blanket in the opposite direction, further into the cave but closer to Rami. Not so close that Rami would notice the next morning, but closer nevertheless. *After all*, he thought to himself before drifting to sleep, *a boy can dream.*

CHAPTER FIVE

Several hours later, Tristys awoke to the sound of Quellosian chanting. Rami was tending to the remains of the fire, packing up the salvageable pieces of wood and stamping out the last of the cinders. He never acknowledged Tristys, just kept on reciting words in Quellosian. Tristys recognized a few of them, and he wasn't positive, but he didn't think they made any sense together. Rami also had the hiccups.

"If you're going to keep chanting like that, can you at least drink something? I retain information better without hiccups." He said it a bit more snappishly than he'd intended, but it wasn't his fault: he really wasn't a morning person. "How long did we sleep? I feel like I just went to bed."

"We slept for quite a few hours," Rami said as he packed the last of his belongings. "The rain's stopped, and I want us to get"—he hiccupped again—"to the Rockaway Trib before nightfall."

"Drink, dammit!" Tristys shouted. Rami looked as surprised as Tristys felt by the outburst, and it took him a second to kick into action. He pulled a canteen from his pack and took a few swigs until the hiccupping stopped.

"Happy now?"

"Just a tad," Tristys said. He started gathering his own belongings, which consisted basically of the pillow and blanket. He rolled them tightly into a form more suitable for travel, shoving them into a waterproof bag before approaching Rami. "Turn around," he ordered. Rami shot him a skeptical look, but Tristys ignored it and waited the second it took Rami to do as he'd asked. He opened the pack strapped to Rami's back and shoved his sleeping accoutrement in it, pushing down so hard Rami nearly fell over. Rami squealed; Tristys laughed.

"All right then," he said as he shifted the weight around until it balanced out. "Let's go."

"Lead the way." Tristys gestured to the entrance of the cave in a motion as fluid and smooth as he could, trying to imitate Rami. Rami didn't catch the poke, and Tristys was too groggy to explain it.

The night rain had revivified the jungle. Everything seemed bigger and brighter and louder today than it had yesterday. Tristys even noticed more animal life this time: small furred things jumping through the lower tree branches, multi-colored birds with trailing tail feathers, and some sort of lizard with odd horns protruding from its face. The bugs were in rare form, too, and when Rami cut through another one of those bug-repelling vines, Tristys lathered himself up, just in case Rami was right.

"Why's it called Lower Ramidalé?" Tristys asked suddenly. He'd been musing on the town ever since they'd left it.

"What do you mean?"

"Well, is there an Upper Ramidalé somewhere?"

"No," Rami said, simultaneously hacking at another vine and batting an enormous bug off his shoulder.

"Why isn't that place just called Ramidalé, then?"

"Because Ramidalé is in the north. It's the capital of Quelles." Rami acted as if Tristys should have known this already, which of course made Tristys angry.

"Why didn't you say that a second ago when I asked in the first place?"

"Because I'm trying to cut our way through a forest without getting us hopelessly lost." He was tense, and his words were sharp. "We're in the densest part of the jungle," he added, stopping to scan the area, "and few people have been through here. There's no reason to be here, really. Unless you're escorting a fugitive, I guess."

Tristys couldn't be sure, but he thought he heard a smile. Which made no sense, considering how cold Rami had been the past few days. But then again, even over those past few days, there had been moments of... something. But this was getting ridiculous! Hours of cold shoulder seasoned with the occasional genuine smile or laughter. It was confusing, and Tristys hadn't done anything to deserve it.

"There is an Outer Ramidalé," Rami said quietly, several minutes later.

Rami offering information? It wasn't a marriage proposal, but Tristys would take it. "Oh yeah? Is that by the big Ramidalé or the lower one?"

"The big one. It's actually a bit to the west." His voice rose, as if he were expecting a reaction. "It's entirely underwater."

Tristys decided to humor him. "Underwater?" He wasn't really surprised. When people lived in overgrown fruits, an underwater city didn't seem that far-fetched.

"Yeah, underwater. It was made by the best Water-practitioners the Coquels has ever known. And only the best are allowed to keep up with its maintenance. My father is on the team, so he goes there all the time."

Tristys had the feeling Rami wasn't too happy about his father's going there all the time, but he wasn't sure why. "Don't you get to see him often, then?"

It was barely perceptible, but Rami started hacking a little bit more forcefully. "If you manage to attune at the Altar, you can see Lower Ramidalé for yourself." He gave the most forceful slash yet, and two vines fell to the forest floor. "That is, if you can convince everyone, including the officials, that you're Coquellian."

There was no smile, no rictus, no inflection, nothing. No way to tell what, exactly, Rami had meant by his words. Would Tristys go alone? Meaning Rami would leave him after the Altar? Was the reference to his nationality a veiled threat? Or a joke? Or both? Or neither? Why did this guy have to be so confusing?

"It's a cool place," Rami said. "I've only been there once, but I think you'll like it." And he smiled.

Tristys felt like every single mood swing Rami'd had was condensed into the last two statements. All he could manage in reply was, "Yeah, maybe one day I'll go there." Rami nodded, seemingly satisfied and unaware that Tristys was upset. The two started walking together again in silence—no small talk, no flirting, no Quellosian lessons—and Tristys started to wonder if you could go deaf from a silence this loud.

~~*

A few hours later, Rami stopped so suddenly that Tristys nearly bumped into him. They'd been traveling all day, with only two short breaks, and the sun had already passed its zenith. The forest was stifling. Tristys felt as if he were drowning, just about to faint, but he said nothing to Rami. Rami'd said nothing in return, and Tristys had finally learned to drown out the silence with the forest's cacophony. When Rami finally did speak, Tristys took a moment to realize he was being addressed.

"Take our belongings and go sit in that clearing over there, okay?" Rami shrugged the packs from his shoulders and gave them to Tristys. "Don't move, or you'll get lost, and I'll never be able to find you again."

"Wait, you're leaving me here?"

"Yes."

"In this strange jungle with ferocious creatures?"

"Yes." Rami was grinning now.

"Why?" Tristys hated the hint of real fear that crept into his voice. He also hated that Rami already had his back to him and was walking away.

"I'm going to Saloris. It's a small town just a bit north of here." He seemed finished, but Tristys kept staring, refusing to let that be all the explanation he got. "I need to get a few things, you'll be fine."

"But the ferocious—"

"Like that lizard, you mean?" His grin was an all-out smile now, and it was driving Tristys crazy.

"You said—"

"Most things here are more scared of you than you are of them." He was walking away again.

"Why can't I just come with you?" The hint of fear was turning into a much stronger sensation.

"Because you can't," Rami said, turning to face Tristys. "You don't know the language well enough. You'll stick out like a sore thumb." He turned around again. "And we cut off sore thumbs here."

"You people cut off your thumbs just because they're sore?" Tristys said, intentionally misunderstanding.

"No, of course not. I just—"

"Then why did you just—"

"I just meant that if people realize you're a foreigner—which they will!—somebody is bound to do something about it."

"Like cut off my thumbs?"

Rami gave his characteristic scowl. "I won't be gone long. There's a book in my pack, the blue one. Read it."

"I can't read your—"

"Just do what I say." As he walked away, the last thing he said was, "Read it!"

"I don't—I really don't like this, Rami!" Tristys shouted. He knew how he sounded—immature, childish even—but he didn't care. He didn't want to be left alone, especially not in a strange forest.

"You shouldn't yell," Rami said, peeking his head through some undergrowth. "It'll attract the ferocious beasts." He wriggled his eyebrows and disappeared. Tristys threw a nearby mushroom, but it was too late.

He waited a moment or two, but Rami never returned. He waited a few more moments for some army of ferocious beasts to emerge and eat him, but that never happened either. He leaned against a tree whose trunk was twice as wide as his shoulders. The bark was cool on his skin, even through the light fabric of his shirt, and he closed his eyes and tilted his head back for a moment. Between the sights and sounds of the new forest and the Quellosian lessons with Rami—and Rami's presence itself—Tristys had managed to keep his mind off home, but alone like this, he had a hard time not traveling back to Paru.

He missed his family. He hadn't seen his eldest sister, Nylit, in years, since before she had moved to the capital. He missed her most. But he missed his mother, too, and his father, and his brother Evynn who had died in the war. And even Keltyn, his younger brother who treated him as badly as the rest of the town once they found out Tristys was diverted.

And the town! He missed Paru, and that alone was such a strange feeling, considering the reason he ended up here in the Coquels—and on that Spàlorian slave-ship before—was because he ran away from it. He didn't miss everything. He was glad to be out of the shadow of the chapel, an enormous, gaudy stone edifice that stood over everything like a cruel captor. He didn't miss the people, either, who treated him as if he were an animal at best and an abomination at worst. But he did miss the town itself. It was where he'd grown up, where he had played and slept and worked. He missed his old house, most of all, but even that was gone now, burned in the arson that had led to his life-changing decision.

But that was what he'd done: he'd run away. And he'd ended up here, in the Coquels, in an unbelievable forest with incredible magic and gorgeous guys. Or at least one gorgeous guy. He had to let go of his past, let go of the life he led in Paru, and learn to live here in the Coquels. He opened his eyes, pushing off from the trunk behind him. He ran a hand through his hair, which needed both a wash and a cut.

"Time to learn this language," he said out loud. He wasn't prone to talking to himself, but now was a special circumstance. "After all, I'm a Coquellian now." He paused, trying on the statement as if it were a new pair of pants. "I'm no longer Cyræan." Still a bit uncomfortable, but it'd probably stretch once he wore it a bit longer.

The book had nothing on its cover. Bound in blue leather, it was larger than any book he'd seen in Cyræa. The pages were thick, and they had two columns of text: on the left, simple words in Cyræan, and on the right, some foreign script Tristys assumed was Quellosian. The letters looked similar to the ones he knew, with the addition of several characters and some unfamiliar accent marks. He knew what most of the Quellosian words were from his conversations with Rami over the past few days, so now he could learn how to write them. After a few hours, he already felt a lot more comfortable than he'd expected with the new script.

Just after he'd read his first full sentence in Quellosian, Tristys looked up from the pages to find Rami standing several feet away, staring. He held several bags, two in one hand and one in the other, with the slightest hint of a smile touching his lips. But it lasted only a second: his face blanked before a slight red rose to his cheeks. He looked cute when he blushed.

"You were so caught up in your reading," he

said, "you didn't even notice when I said hello."

Tristys wasn't that into the book, and he said as much. "I don't think so. I would've heard you."

The faint blush deepened, and for the first time ever, Rami seemed flustered. "Oh, well, maybe you didn't hear me because I was too far away, or maybe—" He stopped abruptly when Tristys's laughter bubbled up out of his silence. "Anyway," he said forcefully, "can you write a novel in Quellosian yet?" His words sounded composed, but he still wore the slight blush. Adorable.

"Not yet, but I bet I could read one." It was an exaggeration, but he did feel a lot more comfortable with the language since picking up the book. So comfortable, in fact, he wondered if there weren't some sort of magic to it. He was going to ask, but then he got distracted by Rami's shirt.

It had several buttons undone at the top, and Tristys could see quite a bit of Rami's chest. Once he noticed, it was hard not to stare.

"That's good," Rami said as he shifted on his feet. "I'm glad you like the book. You can read more later, but right now we have to start moving again. I want to get to the Rockaway Trib by nightfall."

At the moment, a shaft of sunlight pierced the canopy above and alighted directly on the bit of bare skin Tristys was trying not to stare at. The irony caught him immediately, and he started to laugh.

"What's so funny?" Rami asked, looking indignant. "The Trib isn't too far away from here, actually, and you of all people shouldn't be laughing about it. I don't know what's going to happen when you try to cross it."

"No, I'm not—it's not about the—" Tristys gave up. There was simply no easy way to tell someone you were laughing because even the sun can't help but stare at his body. "Never mind. What's the Rockaway Trib?" Rami's worry was contagious, and Tristys felt his good humor evaporating. As if the air here needed any more moisture...

"It's a river," Rami said, continually shifting his weight. Tristys still hadn't gotten off the ground, and he could see Rami was impatient. "It's really more like a stream. A very wide stream, perhaps, but it's not very deep. Usually you just walk across it. It comes up to my waist."

Tristys stood up. "Well then, what's the—" He gasped when Rami suddenly reached out and brushed Tristys's butt. He shot around and stared at Rami wide-eyed.

"What? There were leaves stuck to you, that's all!" he shouted, holding up his hands in innocence. Tristys cocked an eyebrow. "I told you, I'm not that way."

"Right, of course not." He paused with significance. "But what's going to happen at this river, if we can just walk across it?"

"I said I can walk across it. I didn't say anything about 'we'."

"Rami, please. I may be scrawnier than you, but I'm taller than you are, too. If you can walk across it, then—"

"Do you remember what happened the last time you let Quellesian water touch you?"

Tristys thought back over the past few days. It was the beach. But he didn't really remember what happened on the beach. "Not really, since I fainted right after I touched it, and we never really talked about it." Come to think of it, they never really talked about magic, either. Tristys would have to ask more questions later tonight. "What happened?"

"I think you Fingerprinted."

"Rami, I don't know what—"

"Fingerprinting is quell's way of telling us that we can commune with it. Usually, the Fingerprinting is insignificant: dirt sticks to Earth-practitioners or flames will lean toward Fire-practitioners. Sometimes, though, it's much worse. People die."

"I don't really want to die," Tristys said, already much more worried than he had been.

"And usually when people Fingerprint, they don't actually commune with quell. That's why Fingerprinting is usually so small. But you, you were obviously communing."

"I wasn't communing anything!"

"Not on purpose," Rami said. His voice had that distant, soothing tone Rami got when he was explaining or lecturing. Tristys hated it. "But you did. That's why you fainted. You pulled too much Water-magic too fast. I'm afraid if you get near the Trib that will happen again."

"So when we cross this I'm going to faint?"

"Perhaps. Or you could die. That's what happens if you pull too much quell. You die. It happened to Ramis the Betrayer during the Great War, when he saved Ramidon II's life after he—"

"Save the history for later, okay? Imminent death is not a topic I take lightly." Academic digressions were simply not an option at the moment. "So you think I'm going to die trying to cross this?"

"If you pull too much quell, yes." Rami had something up his sleeve—Tristys could tell, because Rami was grinning, and even Rami wasn't sadistic enough to grin at someone's imminent death—but he wasn't budging with it yet. Tristys wanted to sit down, since his knees felt flimsy, but he settled for leaning against the tree again, just in case Rami decided to start off in a rush.

"Rami, if you really think I'm going to die—"

"Of course I don't. That's why I stopped in Saloris. I got something that I hope will help." He lifted the two bags in his hands.

"It better be something pretty damn miraculous," Tristys said, "because I really don't want to die today." He bent down and stuffed his language book back into Rami's bags and picked them up. He held the old packs out to Rami, but at the last minute he pulled them back. "You're carrying those," he said, motioning to miracle bags. "I'll get these."

Rami cocked his head curiously. "Thanks," he said after a beat. "Let's go, then!" He started off, almost bouncing on his feet. "After all, we have a bit of a walk before your death." He turned his head and grinned so wildly his eyes shut.

"You know, Rami, one of these days..."

"One of these days what, kiddo?" The grin was still there.

"I don't know, Rami. Just one of these days..." And Tristys was grinning, too.

~~*

When Tristys caught sight of the Rockaway Trib for the first time, he couldn't even blink. Its shallow waters were clear enough that he could see, even from this distance, the riverbed. Rami hadn't lied about its depth but he'd greatly misrepresented its width. Tristys could barely make out individual trees on the other bank, a massy blur of green the only indication that the tributary was a stream rather than a sea. The water, an unbelievably deep, transparent blue, coursed slowly uphill. Wait, uphill? Tristys looked again, harder. He squinted. Yes, uphill.

"Rami," Tristys began tentatively, "is this stream flowing up into the mountains?"

"It is." He stood, hands on his hips, next to Tristys; he too had his eyes on the Rockaway Trib, though his gaze held less awe and more calculation. He hadn't yet opened his bags from Saloris and revealed what they contained. The anticipation was driving Tristys crazy.

"Does all water flow uphill here?"

"Only on Quelles, but nowhere else." He gave a slight nod of his head, as if he'd finally decided on something, and bent to his knees to start unpacking his bags from Saloris. "We think it's the island's way of showing off."

"Makes sense," Tristys said, even though it made no sense at all. Rami had just about finished unpacking the bags, and the miracle that he had to save Tristys's life was a small black box with a spigot on one side and something that resembled a giant, crumpled blanket. It wasn't a blanket, though: the fabric was glossy, and he imagined it would feel cold and hard, perhaps slippery, if he touched it. "What is that?"

"It's a raft."

Tristys had seen rafts, and whatever Rami had pulled from the bags was definitely not what he'd seen before. "Are you sure?"

"Of course I'm sure."

"It looks like a wet blanket."

"At the moment, it is."

Tristys, who often liked to feign confusion for a joke, genuinely had no idea what Rami was talking about. "You said it was a raft."

"It is. It's a piece of quell-work. It's going to blow up—"

"It's going to blow up?!"

"Not like that. It's going to inflate, and you're going to sit in it, and I'm going to push you across the Rockaway. It's got Air-magic woven into it, so it'll repel water. It's waterproof."

"Oh." Tristys wasn't very sure, but Rami seemed convinced. And he'd know better than Tristys did... "And you think that'll keep me from Fingerprinting or whatever and then fainting or dying?"

"That's the idea. I'm hoping since you won't actually touch the water, it won't try to leave its Fingerprints on you."

"Think it'll work?"

For the first time, Rami looked unconvinced. "I'm not sure." He'd been spreading out the crumpled blanket, and he was now trying to connect the spigotted box to it. "If it doesn't and you start to Fingerprint again, I'll just push you faster."

"How sweet!" Tristys said, clapping his hands together and batting his eyelashes. Rami wasn't paying attention, so he'd missed the exaggeration.

"I know there's a button or a switch or something around here," Rami mumbled to himself. "I don't know why they hide the damn things." After a few more seconds, Rami was rewarded with the sound of rushing air. The blanket—no, it really was a raft!—started to inflate. Tristys still wasn't impressed.

"Why didn't you tell me about this before? This is just a fancy boat, and we're talking about my life here!" He wasn't actually mad—in fact, he was a bit touched that Rami had thought ahead to protect him.

"Well," Rami said as he stood up, "no reason in particular. I just liked watching you squirm." Rami sure grinned a lot lately, Tristys thought.

"I hate you," Tristys said simply. "Let's get this thing in the water. I think it's done. It stopped getting bigger, anyway."

"No, let me get it into the water. You stay away from the edge." He lifted the raft easily with both his hands and headed to the edge of the Trib. "Grab the bags and throw them in here." Tristys complied wordlessly. "Now," Rami said, "get in."

Tristys had the urge to complain or tease, but his nerves were kicking in, so he stayed quiet. He kept hearing Rami's words—you'll die, you'll die, you'll die. He did what he could to shut the voice up, but he still heard the slightest whisper. He got into the raft anyway.

As he expected, the material was cold, almost like a lizard's skin. He pressed a palm to the raft to steady himself as he sat down, and the reaction was instantaneous: his skin felt excited, as if someone were rubbing hundreds of feathers along his palm. He pressed a bare arm to the raft, felt the same thing. He found his voice.

"Rami, I think it's touching me?"

Rami's head shot up. "The quell?"

"No, the raft!" Tristys had both arms pressed to it now, and the sensation was incredible. "It's like it's tickling me or something! Can a raft do that?"

"So you're ticklish?" Rami asked.

"Yes, very, but not the point!" The thought of Rami tickling him quieted the voices a little bit but not entirely. He turned around to face Rami, whose face was contorted by the exertion of pushing the raft and what appeared to be amusement.

"You're fine," he said, grunting a little. Apparently pushing a raft with Tristys and their supplies across the forest floor was a bit much even for Rami. "It's probably the quell in the raft, not the tributary."

Something in Tristys's mind clicked. "Wait, there's quell in this raft! That's what Printed or whatever on me at the beach! What if I start to manipulate this or it starts to do it to me or—"

The raft stopped moving. Rami bent forward, his face just a few inches from Tristys's, and he put his hand on Tristys's shoulder, and it felt the same way the raft felt on his skin. "Calm down, kiddo. The quell here is centered, so it can't do anything unless it's loosed. And besides, Water-magic Touched you. This raft has Air-magic in it." He squeezed Tristys's shoulder. "You're fine. I've got you."

Genuine care. It shocked Tristys, shocked him both out of his panic attack and back into his past, to the last boat he'd been on with the slaver Vun'gor. Vun'gor was the only other person, besides Tristys's family, to show any concern for him. Vun'gor hadn't let anything happen to him— nothing he could control, anyway—and Tristys suddenly knew Rami wouldn't, either.

He took a breath and turned around, resting his back on the edge of the raft. He could feel Rami close behind him. "Well, onwards then!" he shouted, pointing a finger toward the coursing water just in front of them.

"Onwards!" Rami echoed. As Rami pushed the raft, he leaned farther into Tristys, and their skin was nearly touching. If Rami didn't mind, Tristys sure didn't, either. He titled his head back, just a little, and sure enough, Rami's face was right there. He expected some sort of flinching, some pulling away, but all he got was a wiggle of Rami's eyebrows and a quick "Hey."

Their eyes met, only for a second, but Tristys felt some sort of spark ignite between them. He felt the raft lift off, and even though he knew it was probably floating on the tributary now, he felt as if he and Rami had somehow left the raft behind, were spinning into space together, leaving the Rockaway and the island of Quelles and everything else behind. Rami's lips parted, his tongue darted out to wet them, and Tristys licked his own lips, waiting for the kiss he knew was about to come.

"If your head bumps my chin," Rami said, "I'm going to drown you in this river."

All at once Tristys fell, dropped out of space and back into the raft. There was no malice in Rami's words, but it definitely wasn't what Tristys wanted to hear. He scooted up just a little, the fear of death by quelling a bit too much to resist.

They were almost entirely on the Trib now. Tristys cinched his eyes. He didn't want to see any jets of water careening toward him, signaling the end of his short stay in the Coquels. He gripped the raft's rim, tried to focus on the tickling sensations, and bent his head. He counted to ten. No waterbolts striking him in the face, no shouts from Rami, no feelings like he had on the beach before he passed out. Nothing.

And the raft had stopped moving, too. "You can open your eyes," Rami said. "It works."

Tristys opened his eyes. Rami was in front of him now, standing in water just past his knees, a tow-rope dangling in his hands. He had taken off his shirt. He looked better than any warrior Tristys had ever seen in Paru. His arms, his smooth chest, his eight-pack abs. The sweat and humidity licked his tan skin, and his pants rode low along his waist. Tristys's eyes had widened to the point that they actually hurt, so he snapped them shut.

Maybe Rami hadn't noticed...

"Don't worry," he said, "I'll turn around now."

When Tristys opened his eyes, he wasn't sure which made him happier: the satisfied smile that had spread across Rami's face when he saw Tristys's reaction... or the fact that Rami's backside looked just as good as his front. He did know, however, that he'd use the rest of the trip across the Trib to figure it out.

~~*

The entire trip across the Rockaway Trib took nearly an hour. Rami had to move slowly, and he had no trees to shade him from the sun. Consequently, he often splashed water on his upper body to cool off. Each time he did this, Tristys watched avidly—gawked, even—partly because he couldn't help it and partly because he suspected Rami wanted him to. For the first time he could remember, he and Rami chatted idly, discussing irrelevant topics like the bizarre weather of the forest and what lay beyond the mountains in the distance. It was nice.

The other side of the tributary looked pretty much exactly like the first side. Rami pulled the raft onto the bank and offered Tristys a hand to help him out.

"Thank you," Tristys said.

Rami nodded. "One sec, okay? I'm dying here."

Tristys wasn't sure what Rami was talking about, but it quickly became clear when he headed back into the Rockaway and dived completely beneath the surface, breaststroking through the shallow water. A few seconds later, he emerged with a splash, and water ran in rivulets along the sharps lines of his face, down the plains of his pecs, through the ridges of his arms and abs. Now Tristys was the one dying. And he had a feeling Rami knew it.

"That's much better," he said.

"Yeah, much." Tristys hadn't been this hot and bothered since the last time he and Kitadyn had wrestled each other.

"We have to hurry now," Rami said, already pulling their supplies from the raft. "Look at the sky. It's going to rain again." Sure enough, the sky had the same lightly bruised look that it had the day before.

Tristys remembered the walls of rain, how cold the air had become. He had no desire to try to go through that without the shelter of a cave and the heat of a fire. He bent down to help Rami get their supplies.

"No, leave the raft. It's not important. Plus, I don't want you to get near the Trib. After all that work to get you across, you know?"

Tristys did know. "Thank you," he said, "again. I don't know another person in the world who would have done that for me." He thought of

Vun'gor. "No one left in the world, anyway."

"No worries, I would have done it for anyone." Rami was standing up now, not doing anything but looking at Tristys. "I mean, I'm a sucker for any beached whale in need."

Tristys lunged at Rami and smacked his bare shoulder. "You're a jerk, you know that?"

Rami's only response was a grin.

They quickly got back into the rhythm they'd had yesterday. Rami hacked a path through the forest, and Tristys followed. They interspersed Quellosian lessons with more chit-chat. Mostly chit-chat, actually. And mostly Rami.

"Gimme a banana," Tristys said after a particularly enticing conversation about the best type of food in the islands. "Now I'm hungry."

"You ate two of them a little bit ago!"

"You're the one that brought up the island cuisines," Tristys accused.

"My mistake then." Rami tossed the larger of the bags to Tristys, who barely caught it. The thing was heavy! "There should be some more in there. You dig it out, I'll keep going. Don't get too far behind!"

The forest had become thicker over the past hour or so, and the bits of sky they'd seen had become increasingly foreboding. Tristys approved of Rami's hurry. What he didn't approve of, however, was this bag. It had to be magical. He couldn't find the bananas. He found everything else, but no bananas.

"Rami, wait up. I can't find the stupid things." He bent over, putting the sack on the ground and rifling through its contents with both hands. He'd been in the forest now for almost two complete days, and he'd grown accustomed to the various croaks and chirps and screeches, but the low, deep-throated rumbling was a new one. It sounded so familiar but somehow out of place. Was that thunder?

There they were! He pulled one out of the bag and lifted his head to call out to Rami. "Rami, did you put these things—"

His voice caught in his throat. The rumbling wasn't thunder. It was purring. And it was coming from a cat, an enormous feline with eerie yellow eyes and deep, almost impossibly black fur. It looked almost identical to Va'kūnga, Vun'gor's tös, without the tufted ears. It sounded like Kūnga, too, which explained the familiarity. But this was definitely not Vun'gor's cat, and it definitely wasn't purring. It was growling.

"Rami?" Tristys squeaked. He had the irrational urge to laugh. To think, all that trouble getting across the Trib, only to be done in by a silly little cat. It wasn't little, really. In fact, as it pulled back to pounce, Tristys realized just how big it really was.

"Rami!" He shouted again, louder this time. The noise angered the cat, who growled louder. It wiggled its rear end; Tristys stood up.

A second later, the cat leapt. Tristys raised his hands, a poor shield against unsheathed claws and yellowed fangs, but before the cat landed Tristys heard a guttural scream from behind him. Almost simultaneously, a torrent of water wider than Tristys materialized in front of his face and fired itself at the cat, intercepting the pounce. Both the water and the cat fell to the ground. The cat hissed, but the water, instead of absorbing into the dirt, picked itself up and began to pelt the cat. Arrows of water formed, several to each side of the cat, and they too joined in the deluge. As the cat batted them away, they reformed and restruck. After a few seconds, roaring in frustration, the cat fled into the woods. The water followed.

Tristys turned. Rami was curled over, one hand resting on his thigh to support his sagging body. His breaths were ragged, shallow gasps, and his head hung as if his neck were broken. It was Tristys's turn to pounce, this time with less grace but more compassion than the cat.

Rami's skin was ice. "Are you okay?"

"I," Rami breathed, looking at Tristys through eyes whose whites had turned blue, "I'll be—" His eyes fluttered in their sockets, and he smiled that smile Tristys loved. "I just know—know that—cats don't—don't like water."

"No," Tristys said through heavy tears and manic laughter. "No, they don't." But Rami didn't hear him, couldn't have heard him, because he'd already passed out.

CHAPTER SIX

Rami wasn't dead. At first, he seemed to be: no movement, no heat, no breath. Tristys had no idea what to do, so he just sat on the ground, hovering over the limp body in his lap. But Rami started breathing again, and Tristys's tears turned into sobs. He held Rami tighter, squeezed him to his body, before letting him go, worried that the extra constriction might impede Rami's labored breathing.

Though he had suffered exhaustion himself, he had no idea how to treat it; after all, he'd only been on the receiving end of treatment the first time. The sky had grown darker, and Tristys felt the first drops of that night's rain. They'd never make it to the cave this time. Tristys dragged Rami, who weighed a lot more than he looked, to the nearest tree. He propped himself against the trunk, for the second time that day, and waited.

They spent the entire night against that tree. Rami never stirred, and Tristys barely slept. The rain fell as forcefully as it had the night before; not only was it cold, but it stung as it hit his prone body. Shivers wracked Tristys's body, and he considered getting the blankets from the packs, but he decided against it. They'd get soaked, and that'd be worse. Plus, he didn't want to leave Rami even for a second.

The next morning, Tristys awoke as shafts of

sunlight pierced through the trees and hit his eyelids. For a brief second, he forgot where he was and why Rami was nestled in his lap. Then he remembered, and he panicked. Was Rami still alive?

Yes, he was. His skin was still too cold, though not as cold as it had been last night, and his skin wasn't tinged blue. Those were good signs, Tristys thought. He squirmed a bit to readjust his body, and his legs, which had fallen asleep at some point, started to wake up. Pinpricks started to dance along them, and he couldn't help it: he started to cackle at the sensation. He tried to stay quiet, but it didn't work.

His laughter helped, though. Rami must have heard it, and he stirred. Tristys resisted the urge to shake him awake; if he needed sleep, he'd have it. But he wanted to make sure he was okay, to know if there was anything else he could do to speed his recovery. Waking him up, though, was probably not a part of the process.

A few minutes later, Rami woke up of his own accord. He was too fatigued to speak much; his major contribution to the conversation was a smile or a nod. He never even tried to move from Tristys's lap—not that Tristys would have let him if he had tried. They shared a small breakfast, but they kept conversation to a minimum, since it tired Rami out. By evening, Rami wanted to move to the nearest cave. After much convincing, Tristys reluctantly agreed.

They didn't get more than a few hundred feet, though, before they had to quit. Rami was still too exhausted to hack through the jungle, and Tristys was too weak to wield the hatchet, support Rami, and carry the supplies they needed to survive. So

Tristys chose the biggest tree, tried to weave a quick blanket of vines to protect against any rain, and he and Rami settled down for another night in the forest with no fire. Rami argued against sleeping together of course, but Tristys insisted, so they cuddled like spoons, shivering in sync with the pelting rain that came a little after sundown.

The next several days saw Tristys and Rami repeating this process, each day getting just a little bit farther. The only real difference was Rami's increasing chatter. And he chatted a lot, both in Cyræan and Quellosian. Tristys's vocabulary increased exponentially, along with his knowledge of Quellosian grammar and punctuation. He learned some common expressions, some silly idioms, and the origin of the language, too.

And he learned a lot about Rami's friends and family. Telia, for instance, had been a long-time family friend. She'd even lived with Rami and his family before Rami had joined the Physical Services—which was a career path for people who wanted to hone their bodies rather than their magic—and moved to Imidalé, the capital of the island of Quell, to train. While he had been gone, she'd apparently had a falling out with his family and moved to Lower Ramidalé. He came to visit when he could, and though he'd asked both his parents and Telia countless times, nobody would tell him exactly what happened between them.

Rami was a bit more secretive about his own past. Tristys learned about his time in the Physical Services, which explained how he got such an amazing body, and his time at Imidaléan University, which explained how he'd gotten such an amazing mind. He heard about Calissa, the girlfriend Rami had had for years. They had met at school when Rami was just sixteen years old, and they'd been dating since just after. She was an amazing quell-practitioner, one of the few people left in the Coquels who had been Touched by more than one of the six quell. She could use both Air- and Water-magic.

Tristys had finally had time to ask Rami about the magic, too. He'd learned that the quell had some sort of effect on lifespan—the average Coquellian practitioner lived to be 127 years old. In Cyræa, people were lucky to live to fifty. Rami didn't know whether Tristys would live to be 127 now, since the quell had Touched him, and neither did Tristys. The only thing Tristys did know, though, was that something had happened when Rami saved him from the jungle cat. Perhaps it had happened before that. In either case, Rami was different: he had agreed now to open up a little, to lower his walls just a bit and let Tristys in. Tristys liked it.

This was the sixth night since the cat attack. Rami was almost entirely better, but since they were no longer near the mountains, they'd continued to sleep with no fire, huddling for warmth. Tristys knew that would come to an end soon. They were just a day or two away from the Altar, and he had no idea what the Altar would bring. He licked rain from his upper lip and jerked his head sharply to shift some bedraggled hair from his eyes. Rami was with him, spooned in his arms, and he pulled him closer, tighter than he had on any other night. He felt Rami's hands circle his wrists, felt him pull Tristys's arms tighter around his body. For the first time, Rami held him back.

~~*

"Why do you keep doing that?" Tristys shrieked suddenly. For a second, Rami thought Tristys was genuinely freaked out, but then the grin spread across his face.

"Doing what?" Rami asked.

"Staring at me! You're always staring at me lately." Tristys gave him a pointed look before kneeling next to the extinguished fire. The sun had lowered on the horizon—or Rami assumed it had, since the trees blocked his view—and the temperature had already begun to cool. They'd light a fire now and keep it going as long as they could; it died quickly once they fell asleep, though.

"Please," Rami said, refusing to look away, "don't flatter yourself. I was zoned out, not staring at you." He was lying; he actually was staring at Tristys. He found it hard not to, these days. The kid had some sort of pull over him, no doubt. He'd had some pull over him since they first met but ever since that day with the cat...

"Right, of course you weren't." Tristys picked up the pile of dishes they'd dirtied for dinner. "In any case, you won't be able to zone out while looking directly at me any longer. I have to go clean these now." He held up the dishes. There were a lot of them tonight; this was their last night in the forest, so they'd decided to celebrate with an overblown, three-course meal. A six-leaf salad topped with sour-root sap, then grilled cap-head mushrooms imbued with a sweet pink sauce, and finally a dessert salad made with pretty much every fruit or berry Tristys could find. They'd eaten over an hour ago, but Tristys said he needed time to digest before he did the dishes.

Tristys had done virtually everything since the attack. Rami was much better now, but Tristys still insisted that he rest. Rami feigned an argument, but he didn't really mind. He liked having someone take care of him. It was a nice change from the self-sufficient life he'd led since he left the Altar so many years ago. After more than ten years of non-stop effort to tone your mind and body, a few days' worth of lounging in a forest was a welcome respite. But he did feel a little guilty when Tristys had to leave his sight, especially for cleaning. He'd be near water... not to mention that damn cat could still be around.

"Be careful," Rami said. "Don't fall in." He tried to sound flippant, but just sounded worried.

Tristys stopped and turned around to face him, a queer tilt to his head and voice. "I will," he said. "If you hear me scream, just fling some waterbolts my way, okay?"

"In a second," Rami said. He Touched the quell in the air near Tristys, asked it to materialize and shoot a few small bolts at Tristys to tease him. It listened, of course, and Tristys, now with a slightly damp shirt and a much bigger grin, turned away in a huff.

"I'll get you for that later," he said calmly, with total assurance and no further explanation. As much as Rami hated to admit it, as much as Rami fought against it, he was titillated by the possibilities. He smiled.

He was fighting against it less and less now, especially since the attack. For so long, he'd been afraid to touch quell, afraid to embrace his attraction for fear that it would end up in another death. But now, both on the beach that day and here with the cat, he'd used his magic to save someone, someone who was undeniably attractive. Maybe what happened with Tierran had been a fluke...

"Well, that was uneventful," Tristys said. He was even wetter now than he was when he left, and his shoes made funny gurgling noises with each step he took.

"What happened to you?" Rami asked, his thoughts now scattered. "You fall in after all?"

"Yes, actually." He set the dishes, now clean, near the fire. "I dropped your stupid cup, and you always talk about how much you love it, so I went in to get it. It's a lot deeper than the Rockaway Trib is, you know."

"I do," Rami said, trying not to laugh outright, but every step made that squishing noise and it was beginning to be just a bit too much.

"I really hate being wet."

"Tell me again," Rami said.

Tristys crinkled his nose. "What? Have I said that before?"

"No, tell me again. In Quellosian."

"I'm sick of speaking in Quellosian," Tristys said... in Quellosian.

"You're really good at it." Rami started digging around for another book he'd brought from Telia's. . "You need to keep practicing, though. You're good now, but you have to be great to convince people you're a local. Especially with those beautiful eyes you have."

Beautiful? Really? Did he just say that? This is what not fighting so hard leads to! But maybe Tristys didn't notice...

Tristys's beautiful eyes narrowed a bit, almost as if he were concentrating, but he didn't say anything. He didn't say anything about last night, either, when Rami gripped him as tightly as he could and pulled their two bodies so close that there was, he hoped, no space between them. The rain was chilling, but he'd never been so warm.

Two hours later, Tristys was a bit better at Quellosian. Still not great, but better. From where they were settled, they could see just a little bit of the sky. There were stars tonight, the first time since they'd been camping outside of caves. There'd be no rain. The night would grow chilly, but without the torrential downpours of the past few nights, tonight would be surprisingly pleasant for them.

"So," Tristys said, getting up from his log and heading to the pack that held their sleeping equipment.

"Don't tell me you're tired already!" Rami said.

"No, just a little chilly." Tristys's eyes were half-closed and puffy, and Rami knew a lie when he looked at one, but he didn't say anything. He wasn't tired at all. Tonight would be their last night like this, and it wasn't raining, and for some reason, he didn't want tonight to be over already. He knew the reason, of course, but he wouldn't admit it, even to himself.

Tristys wrapped his blanket around his shoulders. He hesitated before sitting down on his log again, presumably because he didn't want to get the blanket dirty, but he finally shrugged and sat. Only Tristys would worry about dirtying a blanket when he's camping in a forest, Rami thought.

"So," Tristys said again, "what happens tomorrow? We get to the Altar, we meet Telia's friend the high priestess or whatever, and then what?" He was sitting on the log in his usual stance, right leg pulled up so that the ankle tucked itself underneath his left thigh. Rami had named it 'the Tristys'.

"We'll see if you can commune with the water quell, and if you can, you'll pass the Trial of Communion. Normally you'd stay after that for training, but I have a feeling Liana will want to skip that part, considering."

"Considering I'm an evil foreigner?"

"Exactly," Rami said.

Tristys was munching on a mushroom he'd washed at the stream. His appetite never ceased to amaze Rami. "Did you do all that, then? The training and everything?"

Rami hesitated. When he had argued with Telia about taking Tristys to the Altar, half the reason was having to spend time alone with him. The other half was having to relive memories from the last time he went there. "Not exactly."

Tristys just looked at him, waiting for more.

"Fine," Rami said. He shifted his position a bit; talking about this always made him physically uncomfortable. "There was an—an incident at the Altar, I guess. I wasn't able to complete the Trial."

Tristys looked concerned, and the worry creased his brow. "But you can still use the magic, obviously."

"Right." Rami's stomach felt ill, and though he blamed that second helping of berry salad, he knew that wasn't the real reason. "But I never got the training, or the experience, or the honor of truly communing with quell."

"Rami, you and your quell saved my life."

"True, I suppose. I can save your life, but I'll always be a failure at that Altar."

"You're not a failure," Tristys said, pulling the

blanket a little tighter and trying to stifle a yawn.

"And you're not exhausted." Rami had heard all this before, from his parents and Calissa and Salice and even Gawen. "Look, I realize you're just—"

"No." Tristys tossed aside the rest of his mushroom and stood up. He walked to Rami and knelt in front of him. "I'm serious, Rami. You're not a failure. You weren't then, and you certainly aren't now."

Rami blushed, another thing he seldom did. Unless he was with Tristys, apparently.

"And you're even cuter when you blush, you know."

Rami blushed harder.

"Like now, for instance." Tristys laughed, tossing his head to push the bangs out of his eyes.

"I still don't understand why Cyræeans have an easier time seeing in the dark," Rami said.

"We're just lucky, I guess. Probably has something to do with my beautiful eyes." He smirked at Rami, and Rami wanted to die from embarrassment.

"So you heard that, eh?"

"I did."

"Well," Rami said, deciding to try a new tactic, "they are beautiful. In that objective, distant sort of way, like a work of art, you know? Like a painting in the—"

"Save it." Tristys had yawned two more times, and he was yawning again, though smiling through it. "You can explain tomorrow."

"Ready for bed, then?" Rami still wasn't tired, but he didn't want to keep Tristys up any longer. He looked as if he were about to pass out as it was.

"Definitely." He was still kneeling in front of

Rami, and he stood up. "At least it's not dreadful tonight like it has been the past few days."

"Indeed," Rami said as he watched Tristys pile up some blankets for their bed. "If we could keep the fire going, we wouldn't need for a blanket."

"I know, right?" Tristys had sprawled out on the blankets, and he was stretching, his arms and legs pushed to their lengths. He looked almost cat-like. Rami kept his waterbolts to himself.

He took his shoes off—Tristys said they smacked his shins while they slept—and sat next to Tristys. He lay down on his side and scooted into Tristys, just as he had done every night prior.

"Uh, what are you doing?" Tristys asked.

"What do you mean?" Rami didn't move away but did turn slightly so he was looking at Tristys, who had propped himself up on an elbow.

"I mean, what are you doing? We don't need that tonight. It's not raining or anything. It's not even that cold." Rami's eyes widened, and his mouth moved as if he wanted to speak, but nothing came out. "I mean," Tristys continued, "we just cuddled for warmth, that's all." Again, Rami's mouth moved, but there simply were no words. "Right?" Tristys asked, more forcefully.

"Right, of course," Rami said, finally finding his voice. It was weak, though, and he felt as if he were about to cry. He fought the tears that sprang from a well he didn't know he had. What had he been thinking, lying down and crawling into Tristys's arms as if it meant anything? "I'll get my own blanket," he said, starting to get up, but Tristys put an arm on his shoulder, gently holding him back.

"Rami, wait." He paused for just a second before starting to move away again, but Tristys held his shoulder more tightly. He looked at Rami, stared right into his eyes, and Rami noticed that same look of concentration, as if he were studying a puzzle. Rami thought about pushing him away, laughing it off like a joke, just his teasing Tristys, but he couldn't move, held motionless by the hand on his shoulder and the terrifying fact that he didn't want to get up, didn't want to pretend it was a joke anymore. Dammit, he didn't want to get his own blanket.

Tristys squinted now, trying to solve the puzzle even harder. Rami had an irrational urge to yell at him, to tell him to open his eyes because when he shut them Rami couldn't see the colors he'd grown to know, but he fought it back. Another few seconds passed, and the silence was becoming unbearable. He wanted to get up but his body still refused to move, and a wave of nonsensical panic washed over him: what if they never moved again?

But Tristys moved. He pushed harder on Rami's shoulder, and Rami fell to his back. He stared up at the star-freckled sky and the two moons—dichromatic, just like Tristys's eyes, though these were white and light yellow—but in a second the sky was covered by Tristys's face, and the moons turned to lidded eyes and Rami felt Tristys's lips—soft, warm, wet, still tasting like the sweet mushroom he'd been eating—on his own. It lasted no longer than a second, the gentle pressure from Tristys's closed mouth, the shock and relief that washed over Rami and made his limbs feel limp and his heart beat faster than it had during any of his training, yet it happened, and when Tristys pulled away, his face hovered over wide-eyed Rami's, looking expectantly, flinching slightly, as if he were afraid of retaliation.

But there was none. Rami didn't want to retaliate. In fact, he wanted to do it again, another kiss, more lips. He wanted to find the mushroom and eat it. He wanted to replace the moons with Tristys's eyes, to reach up and grab Tristys's face, push it into his own and have their lips touching so they'd never separate, but he didn't. Instead, he simply rolled to his side, pushed himself into Tristys so they were spoons, took Tristys's wrists and wrapped them tightly around his body, and refused to let go.

~~*

The next day, neither Tristys nor Rami mentioned what happened the night before. They didn't need to. The haze that had colored their relationship had lifted, like the mist rising from the jungle each morning into evaporation. It was gone. They awoke early and left their clearing quickly, each doing the job he'd grown accustomed to. They talked as they walked, half in Quellosian and half in Cyræan, and they teased each other just as much as they did before, although the jests were softer now, gentler, and always accompanied by a touch. The forest grew thinner as they approached the Altar, and Tristys walked next to Rami.

In the early afternoon, Tristys heard the sound of rushing water. They were close to the Altar. When they crested the path, his hand in Rami's, he lost his breath at the sight. Enormous torrents of water, five of them, shot high into the air, higher even than the trees of the forest. The largest was in the middle, surrounded by four smaller spouts. As majestic as the water was shooting into the sky, it was even more breath-taking on its descent. It swirled and danced, slowed and sped up. Sometimes it hung there, hovering in space as if it had no real reason to fall back to the ground and therefore chose not to. It was even more amazing than the Rockaway Trib flowing upstream. This island really did show off!

There were buildings behind the waterspouts, simple structures that looked nothing like the houses he'd seen in Lower Ramidalé. In fact, these were almost Cyræan in their respect to the traditional idea of a building. The one closest to them was obviously some sort of check-in station, and the door opened almost at once. A girl came out, young and startlingly beautiful. Long hair flowed behind her head, a blonde even lighter than his own. As she ran towards them, she shouted at Rami, and Tristys realized it wasn't just her hair that flowed: every movement of hers was fluid, so fluid he had trouble isolating a single motion, a single shift in direction or force. By the time she reached them, she'd be tall as he was, if not taller.

Rami hadn't said anything in return, hadn't said anything at all since they laid eyes on the Altar, but he looked surprised. When the girl reached them, she wasn't even winded.

"I was worried," she said, throwing her arms around his neck and embracing him. The force of the hug pulled Rami's hand from Tristys's. "You told me you'd be here days ago!"

"We got held up," he said blankly. "I didn't know you were—"

"So this is Tristys? Rami mentioned he'd have a friend." She smiled warmly, and then said the words Tristys knew were coming but hoped wouldn't: "I'm Calissa."

~~*

The time Rami spent with Tristys in the forest, especially after the attack, had been the best days in recent memory. He had spent the majority of his life pushing so much of himself aside, but after the attack, he had finally given up and given in. For the first time, it felt as if he could breathe again. He liked it.

But when Rami saw the Altar again, he felt his breath catch in his throat. Spray from the waterspouts whisked into his face, and everything that had happened here came rushing with it. His time with Tierran. The joy just before and the terror just after the blast. All the shame and regret that he redirected into a promise to change the way he was, since the way he was had caused so much pain. There was too much mist, too many memories, and his breath was gone.

Calissa was the cincher. She was part of the promise, albeit indirectly, that he made to himself the day after the accident with Tierran. He couldn't break that promise, not now, not after everything he'd done. After all, hadn't he changed his name? Hadn't he struggled with himself, trained his body and his mind so that he wouldn't cause any more pain? So that he wouldn't become the Betrayer he was fated by name to be?

"Yeah, I'm Tristys," Rami heard Tristys say. He looked at Tristys. His face was drawn, as if he already knew things had to change. He was beautiful, but so many beautiful things can burn you.

Calissa nodded, but she turned back to Rami. "So what happened out there? I got your message from Saloris a few days ago, and I figured you'd already be here. When you weren't, I got worried."

Tristys looked as if he were about to speak, but Rami cut him off. "Nothing happened," he said quickly. "Tristys really enjoyed the forest, so we took our time getting here. We had a minor incident with a jungle cat, but it was no big deal."

"No big deal," Tristys mumbled. "Right."

"Oh." Calissa still looked worried. "I guess it doesn't really matter, since you're both here in one piece now." The warmth of her smile was intoxicating. "You two have to be tired, even if you did take a leisurely stroll to get here. I can let Liana know you're here if you want to stay outside a bit." She turned to Tristys. "I saw you gawking at the Five Waves. No, don't be ashamed. Everyone does. They're breathtaking, aren't they?"

"They are," Tristys said.

"Do the tourist thing, then. Walk around a bit, get up close and personal. I'll let Liana know you're here and get your room ready." As she walked away, she stopped and turned back to Tristys. "I'm really glad that Quelles is the first island you're getting to see. It's not my home, but I definitely think it's the best." Without another word, she sped off, leaving Tristys and Rami alone.

After a second, Rami said, "I don't know why she's here."

Tristys was thin-lipped. "You told her about me, didn't you?" he said, his gaze pointed at the ground and his voice empty.

"Apparently." Rami couldn't remember what exactly he'd said in his letter. He had written it on the spur of the moment, an impulse, because he had to tell somebody about Tristys but had nobody he could trust more than her. He'd sent it as soon as he sealed it, so he didn't have time to second-guess himself.

"You don't even remember what you told her?" Tristys looked worried now, and the pitch of his voice had gone up to match it. "Who knows who she could've told! Should I pack my bags for the Offlands now or later, do you think?"

"No," Rami said. He had to resist the urge to put an arm around Tristys's shoulder. "She's not like that. She won't tell anyone."

Tristys licked his lips. "Are you going to tell her what happened?"

Rami had no idea what to say. Pretend nothing had happened? Play it off as a cruel joke? Swear him to secrecy? It obviously couldn't continue or happen again, but how do you handle the past?

"Whatever happened was a mistake, Tristys. We shouldn't have done what we did."

"You liked it, you know you did. You can't tell me—"

"Tristys, it was a mistake." He said it forcefully, but he wasn't sure if he was trying to convince Tristys or himself. He looked at Tristys, and it was just as bad as the memory rush a few minutes ago with Tierran. There was the half-healed scratch on Tristys's face from a branch Rami had let go too soon, the smell of Tristys behind him and around him at night, the taste of that mushroom on his mouth. But it was all wrong, all temptation, all Tierran. "It was a mistake."

"Do you deny it, then? Do you deny that you liked it?"

"Tristys, it doesn't matter whether I liked it or not. It was a mistake. We should just be thankful nobody got hurt, and we should—"

"Nobody got hurt?" Tristys said. Rami could see tears mixing with the anger in Tristys's eyes, and he wanted anything, anything in the world to happen, besides those tears falling. "What do you call this?"

"Tristys, you're not—"

"Don't tell me what I am!" Tristys yelled.

"Tristys, please, keep your voice down!"

"And stop saying my name!"

"C'mon, kiddo, just—"

Tristys's eyes bulged, and he jerked towards Rami. For a second, Rami flinched, afraid of a hit. "And don't ever call me 'kiddo' again." All trace of that sadness had evaporated, leaving nothing but the anger. "Ever again."

"Fine, I won't, but you—"

"Guys?" Calissa said softly. She had come back, but Rami hadn't even noticed. How much of that had she heard? "Liana's not ready yet, but Tristys's room is. Rami, I figured you'd be sleeping with me."

What was that supposed to mean? Who else would he be sleeping with? Was she implying—no. No, she wasn't. This was Calissa, not Telia or Gawen. Rami had to keep a clear head and not let the paranoia get to him. And he didn't know why, but he trusted Tristys to stay quiet about the kiss, too. "Of course," he said, trying to keep a level voice.

He turned to Tristys. The tears were gone. But so was something else. He looked... heartbroken. Tristys was right, then. Someone got hurt. Again. And again, Rami had only himself to blame.

~~*

As Tristys followed Calissa into the Altar's introductory buildings, he was surprised to find that he wasn't surprised at all by Rami's sudden reversal. This was not the first time he had been burned by a guy who couldn't handle his own diversion, and if his track record was any indication, it wouldn't be his last. Was he upset? Sure. Was he angry? Definitely. But was he going to break down into a sopping pile of sadness? No. He hadn't with Kitadyn, and he surely wasn't going to with Rami, either. He'd do the same thing he did with Kitadyn: hope Rami came to terms with himself. In short, he'd wait.

In the meantime, though, he had magic to learn. The Altar of Five Waves had, besides the five waves themselves, several stout buildings made of a light gray stone. It was hard to the touch, but it looked like no stone he'd seen before. In fact, it looked like a luxury item they'd had back home during the good times—a sponge. It was porous, and Rami had no idea how it withstood the Quellesian weather. Probably magic.

Inside the building, Tristys stood in a spacious room, well-lit by sconces situated along the walls. The flames looked strange to Tristys: the light coming off from them was unnatural, and the flames weren't flickering at all. "Is that quell stuff?" he asked, pointing.

Rami looked a little pained, but Calissa answered. "Yes," she said pleasantly. She apparently couldn't feel the bad blood between him and Rami; Tristys could, though, and he was shocked it wasn't crackling. "Nothing too fancy, but it gets the job done."

"It's certainly not the firewalls of Malatapia," a female voice said, "but it's actually rather an intricate centering of us." Tristys turned to see the speaker: a petite woman, sitting in a cottonbloom chair in the corner of the room. "And what you call 'quell stuff', my friend, is better known as quell-work." She was correcting Tristys, but her tone was light and playful. "This chair, too, is a bit of quell-work, made from a flower found in the Quellosian Whitewood, which you have yet to see."

Tristys almost told her that he knew that, since he'd been rather intimate with the cottonblooms in Telia's house, but he was still a bit dumbstruck by the woman before him. She was petite, shorter than Rami, but she had long, flowing hair that reached far below her waist. It was dark gray, almost like smoke, and there was a single bright blue bloom above her ear. Her clothes were made of a striking material that refused to stand still even when she did, and the low-cut blouse made Tristys blush to notice it. She wasn't young, but she looked good.

She stood up. "Feel free to gawk," she said, without sarcasm. "I can only imagine how a Cyræan would react to our vision of priesthood." She stepped closer to Tristys and did a quick turn, her dress dazzling with reflected firelight as it moved. "See? No tattoos. No scars. No chastity belts. Just a lot of flowers." She pointed to her hair, which Tristys now noticed had small, blue bell-shaped flowers threaded throughout its length. "We are rather different than the Daughters you are used to."

Tristys still gawked openly. "I can see that," he said. "You'd be executed back in Cyræa just for that top alone!"

She smiled, almost proudly. "Nobody gets

executed here in the Coquels." For being such a small woman, she had a commanding presence; nobody spoke because they knew she'd speak again first. "I am High Priest Liana, and you must be Tristys. Calissa filled me in on the details, and I must tell you, it is truly a pleasure to meet you." She turned to Rami, who had kept his distance, standing a few paces behind Tristys and Calissa. "Ramis." She exhaled a deep breath, and Tristys wasn't sure if he misheard the extra 's' on Rami's name. "It is good to see you again."

"Save it," he said briskly. His arms were crossed and his jaw was set as he stared at her. "You don't have to play the pleasantries with me."

"We may have had our differences in the past, Ramis, but I think—"

She broke off when Rami turned and walked away, shaking his head as he went.

"Ramis was a bull-headed boy, and I see he hasn't changed a bit."

"No," Calissa said, concern on her face. "He hasn't."

"Go to him." Liana gestured in the direction Rami had gone. "I will take care of our guest. He and I have quite a bit to talk about." Her smile was so warm, and her tone so amicable, that Tristys wasn't quite as afraid to speak with her.

Tristys thought Calissa would run immediately after Rami, but she turned to him. "Hang in there," she said. "I'll see you later, maybe for dinner? It'll give us a chance to catch up."

Catch up? What did they have to catch up on? He'd never even met her until a few minutes ago...

"Sure," he said, looking at Liana for confirmation. She nodded, and he repeated himself with more conviction. "Sure!"

Liana put a thin arm on his shoulder and, with a little more force than necessary, guided him down a hallway. They entered another room, very similar to the one they had left, but much smaller. The walls were bare, besides the sconces that lit the room with unnatural brightness, and there was no furniture except for a table and some chairs. Books and maps littered the table.

Liana sat down, gesturing for Tristys to take one of the other chairs. "Judging from your expression," she said, "Ramis has been lecturing you a lot."

"What?" Tristys asked, unsure if he mistranslated something.

"You seem to know that you're going to get a lot of information from me. I remember Ramis had a penchant for pedantry, so I just assumed you'd had your fill of lectures from him."

"Oh," Tristys said, chuckling. "Yes, I guess I have."

"I will try to keep this brief then, for both our sakes. Try not to worry too much about the language barrier. You'll find that relaxing lets the meaning flow a bit easier." She grinned, a bit wickedly, and Tristys had the feeling that she knew something he didn't. Probably something magical.

She took a letter from the table and skimmed its contents. She'd obviously read it many times before. "This came from Telia a few days ago. She's told me about your situation." Her eyes lifted from the page and looked directly at him. They were blue, startlingly so. "It's fascinating."

Back in Paru, Tristys had been the center of attention once people found out about his diversion. He'd hated it. People stared, they prodded and poked and interrogated, and they were mean and hateful. Liana's attention right now reminded him of that time in his life, but her eyes were filled with curiosity and a deeper genuine care, so he tried to skirt the discomfort. "Thanks, I think."

"You're aware, I assume, that the quell has never Touched a foreigner before, right?"

"Yes. That's the first thing Rami told me. Right after he told me your people hate foreigners."

She prefaced her correction with a quick shake of the head. "No, we don't hate foreigners. We fear them. For a country as isolated as we have been, foreign interactions can be, and often are, explosive." She was still looking at him, directly at him, and he started to imagine those blue eyes getting bigger and bigger and bigger until he had to look away.

"Yes, it's true that you'd be exiled if the wrong people found out about you. But if it's also true that you've been Touched by eş, then I have a feeling your exile would be—what's the right word?—postponed."

"That's a relief," Tristys said. He hadn't meant to say it, but it slipped.

"It is true then?" she asked.

"What?"

"That you've been Touched by eş."

He wasn't entirely sure what eş was, but he had a guess. "Is that Water-magic or whatever?"

She cringed, just for a second. She hid it well. "Yes, it is. The quell have proper names, but too few people use them nowadays."

Tristys chose to ignore the discussion thread about cultural choices and names. "Then yes, it's true."

Her eyes went back to the letter. "And Telia tells me that you were not only Fingerprinting, but you were actually communing with it."

"I wasn't doing anything to it," Tristys said, perhaps too defensively. Rami had accused him of this, had seemed angry about it, and Tristys didn't want to make Rami any angrier. He didn't want to make any of the locals angry, really.

"No, of course not. How could you?" she asked, but she seemed to be talking more to herself than to him. "How could you?"

She grew quiet. Tristys waited, but she stayed quiet for a few minutes. Tristys got bored.

"What did you call Rami earlier?" he asked, quite suddenly. "You said something like 'Ramis'. I thought I misheard you at first, but—"

"Ramis is his name, my dear," she said.

"His name is Ramidon," Tristys said, for once absolutely sure of something.

Liana thought a moment. "Perhaps I do recall Telia mentioning something about his changing his name. How quaint, though, that he'd change it to Ramidon."

She had that expression that hinted she was about to go off into her head again, and Tristys wasn't about to have that happen. "I'm not following," he said.

"No, I suppose you wouldn't, since you don't know the history of the Great War." She settled back in her chair, and Tristys knew he was in for a lecture after all.

"Hundreds of years ago, the seven islands of the Coquels fought each other. It was a civil war caused by the introduction of foreign trade. The leader of Quelles, a wonderful man named Ramidon II, led a force against the tyrant Bellimar

II, who had instigated the war. He was successful, dealing such a blow to Bellimar that the war would have ended after Ramidon's next attack. But he was betrayed by his confidant, Ramis. Ramis loved Ramidon, but Ramidon rejected that love, and so it grew bitter and angry, and it nearly destroyed the whole of the Coquels."

Tristys spoke his next thought aloud. "Why would anyone name their child after someone like that?"

"Oh, the name is quite frequent in Coquellian history. There are many laudable Ramises in our past, and even the one commonly known as Ramis the Betrayer isn't as terrible as he sounds. In the end, he sacrificed his own life to save Ramidon's, giving him his second most common epithet— Ramis the Redeemed."

Tristys wasn't convinced. "Still, if Rami felt like—"

"It is our Ramis, nobody else, who links his name to the darker side of the Great War. But Ramis is not what we are here to discuss, though I think you'd prefer if it were." Her words were always incriminating, but her tone never matched. She said the last bit with a gentle smile, a twinkle in her eye. "We are here to deal with your Fingerprinting. Quite frankly, if you Fingerprinted as severely as Telia suggested, I'm surprised something else hasn't happened since then."

"No," Tristys said. "I've been fine since that day on the beach. We had the run-in with the cat, but Rami used his own Water-magic to save me. I didn't do anything." He regretted saying those words at once. He wasn't sure why, but he felt as if what Rami did to save him should've stayed between him and Rami.

Liana jerked at his confession. "Ramis can Touch eş?"

He knew it. Him and his big mouth. He tried to turn back time. "I don't know. Maybe. I'm not sure what it was. Maybe he just threw water at the thing. It was probably just that."

Liana's eyes were narrowed, and Tristys knew she wasn't fooled. Should he tell Rami about the slip-up or let it go? "Yes, probably. In any event, I'd like to get you into the alcoves at once."

"I don't know what—"

"Patience, my dear. I'm getting to that." She straightened herself up in the chair, stretching her neck until it cracked. "Ah, my bones aren't what they used to be," she said. "Never get old."

"I'll try not to." Tristys tried to hide his impatience, but he wasn't very successful.

"The meditation alcoves are perhaps the second most sacred places on the islands. They are unique in that they have some sort of heightened connection with quell, some special relationship to it. Whenever quell Fingerprints, it is telling you that it wants to get to know you, wants to share itself with you. But quell is an old-fashioned beast. It wants you to approach it gently, to woo it. To tame it, really. You go in the meditation alcoves to complete the taming. If you do it well, you commune, and you become the quell's master. If you do it badly, the quell rejects you, and you are Untouched."

"So I just go in this room and sit?"

"You can sit if you'd like, or you can stand, or you can lie down. You meditate. What exactly meditation means, however, is left for you to decide."

Tristys hated just sitting around. He wasn't

about to say that, though.

"After you are done meditating, when you feel ready, there is a Trial you must complete to commune successfully. Without completing the Trial, your relationship with quell is incomplete. I will warn you now, the Trial is dangerous. Lives have been lost."

Tristys got worried. He didn't like lives being lost. He didn't like that his life had almost been lost pretty much every day since he washed up on this stupid island.

"Calm down," Liana said, holding out the palms of her hands. "I will personally oversee your Trial, and I won't let anything happen to you. If you cannot pass, I will rein in the quell to save you."

Great. Another person to whom he'd owe a life-debt. Lovely.

She waited a moment, saying nothing while she studied him. Then she stiffened and stood up, slapping her hands down on the table. "Well, then! Are you ready?"

Tristys hadn't been ready for any of this. For leaving his family, for getting abducted by sex-slavers, for winding up stranded on a strange island where people could control water and look sexy and drive him crazy and threaten his life ten times a day. He hadn't been ready for any of it, but here he was, living it.

"Born ready," he said, and almost believed it.

~~*

Liana led him outside. They walked across the open area between the buildings and the cliffs Tristys and Rami had climbed to get here, passing so close to the waterspouts—the Coquellians called them 'waves'—that he felt their spray striking his face. Their destination was a small building, no bigger than one of the poorest houses in Paru. Inside it was dark, lit only by a single small sconce, and empty. A flight of stairs led down.

"Go," Liana said simply. "Along the way, you'll find small rooms carved into the stone. They are the meditation alcoves. Feel free to enter them if you can. Choose whichever strikes you. You have as long as you need." She bowed slightly, almost imperceptibly, and said "With quell's caress."

He wasn't entirely sure what Liana meant by entering the rooms if he could. Why wouldn't he be able to get into them? Would they be locked? Would the doors be too small or too high up to reach? He had no idea, but he trusted her—after all, Rami brought him here—so he just started walking down the stairs.

He found his answer when he got to the first alcove. The hall was stone. Carved out of the stone on his right side was an entrance, but there was a thick sheet of flowing water barring passage. He put out a hand to touch it, and the water jutted out to meet him, pushing his hand away. It was unsettling, and he kept walking.

He passed four more doors like this, with water barriers. The fifth had nothing blocking the path, and he peeked his head through the door. It, too, was dark, the only light a pale blue emanating from the floor. No, not the floor—the water on the floor. It felt wrong, so he kept walking.

Two doors later, as he passed by another open entrance, he had the same sensation of misting that he'd had walking by the waterspouts on the surface. Without making any sort of conscious decision, he walked fully into the room. He had to step down to enter, and his bare feet touched water at once, halfway up his shins. It was cold, shockingly so, but in a pleasant way. It tingled.

Nearby was a table, which Liana had told him was a place to put his robe. She'd made him take off his clothes entirely, gave him nothing but a robe to wear as he walked through the cave. He didn't like being naked, and he was afraid to take off his robe for fear that somebody who walked by would look in and see him. When he turned around, though, he realized he had nothing to fear: water had sealed the door, just like the entrances to the other caves he'd passed.

He panicked, but only for a moment. He was trapped, yes, but it seemed to be part of the process. And hadn't Liana said earlier to relax, because it was easier to understand that way? Fine. He'd go with the flow so much it wouldn't know what hit it. He shirked his robe, not even bothering to catch it as it fell to the floor. He looked down at it in disbelief. It was floating on the water, but it wasn't absorbing any of it. He picked the robe up and it was completely dry. He bent over and forcefully pushed the cloth under the surface and pulled it out again. Completely dry. Completely, entirely dry. He wondered what the point of the table was, but he set it on top of the wood surface anyway.

Completely naked now and still self-conscious, Tristys wandered the room. It held absolutely nothing of interest. It was entirely empty, save the water, the ghostly light, and the table. The walls were bare stone, and the ceiling was too high to see. He looked for anything to occupy his mind—a design, a unique rock outcropping, even a bug (and he hated bugs!)—but there was nothing. He sighed audibly, mostly for himself, and sat down in the water.

He sat cross-legged, and the water came up to his waist. His entire lower half was tingling, almost as if it had fallen asleep and was just now thinking about waking up. Sleep, though, was a deadening, a numbing, and this was everything but. His legs felt strangely alive, strangely present, as the pinpricks danced along them. He rubbed his legs with his hands, the sensation escalating, and he decided to use that feeling as a focus. He drowned out everything, every coherent thought, until he was that sensation, nothing but pinpricks.

Nothing happened. A few minutes of intense concentration later, and he was exhausted. It was hard to shut yourself up, he realized, and even worse, it didn't seem to do much. With nothing in the room to occupy him, and his body already adapting to the sensation, his mind wandered. His first thought, strangely enough, went to Calissa— how she'd affect his relationship with Rami, how nice she seemed even though he'd just met her, whether he'd feel guilty around her knowing what he and Rami had done in the forest... and what he hoped they'd do again.

That led to Rami, of course. Why he'd changed his name. What had damaged him so badly that he was afraid to accept his own sexuality when, by his own admission, nobody on these islands cared if you liked men or women. Why he seemed so averse to Liana and Water-magic.

Water-magic. Tristys pooled his hands and picked up some of the water in which he was sitting, letting it run through his fingers, enjoying those pinpricks as they twinkled along his hands and arms. Would he know if he communed correctly? Would something happen, or would he just know it, like the way he knew to choose this room? He thought about drinking some of the water, but he ultimately decided against that. Glowing water probably wouldn't go down well, he reasoned. Back home, anything glowing came from Spålor, and that was never good.

Back home. He missed it still, just as he had missed it this entire time. Here he was, sitting in a cave filled with magic water that he could maybe control one day, and he was thinking of his war-torn, sand-drenched home. Should he stay here? Should he try to get back to Cyræa? Rami and Liana had mentioned foreigners, which meant there were more foreign countries. Maybe he should go there. If he stayed here, though, maybe things would work out with Rami and this magic.

That seed sprouted into a long-winded series of elaborate fantasies. He became the most powerful magician in the world, charging home to save his country from the Spålorians. In another, he became the greatest magician in history and told his native land to screw themselves, staying in the Coquels and living luxuriously with Rami, a quiet domestic life in a little house like Telia's, complete with a few children of their own. He had no idea where they got the children, but that was the beauty of fantasies. It didn't matter. He even had one—a short one, albeit one that he didn't really hate—where he and Rami and Calissa lived happily ever after, all three of them together in some sort of strange love affair.

It was at that point that his stomach started to hurt. He was hungry. He hadn't eaten in he couldn't remember how long, and he'd been in this room for what had to be hours, and absolutely nothing had happened. The most notable thing had been a temporary questioning of his sexuality! It was time to go. He'd try again tomorrow.

He stood up, and he was shocked to watch the water rolling off his body, leaving him completely dry. He looked around the room, hoping to see something different, something changed. Nothing had changed. Nothing was different. He put on his robe, the water barrier splashed to the ground and rolled back to join its brethren in the room, and he crossed the threshold.

Before he left, he took one quick glance back into the alcove, to look out over the sea of glowing magic water, with just the faintest hope that something, anything, would be different. It wasn't. With a heavy heart and a mind much more confused now than it had been, he went to find Liana.

CHAPTER SEVEN

Despite everything that happened here, Rami still thought the waves were beautiful. There was nothing in the Coquels, not even the floating city of Zebelli or the firewalking walls of Malatapia, that came close. It had something to do with the sheer naturalness of the Altar's waves. They were pure magic, pure nature, without any human intervention. There was something easy about that, and right now, Rami needed easy.

"I figured I would find you here," Liana said from behind him. He hadn't seen or heard her approach, and when she spoke, he didn't turn around. "You used to come here all the time when you were upset."

"I'm not upset," Rami said, pouting. He was upset, and he hated that she knew it.

She was standing next to him now, her hands behind her back. They were both looking at the wave, the smallest of the five and the one farthest away from the altar proper, the one that Rami had liked from the start. "You still think it's beautiful?" she asked.

He grinned, but there was sadness to it. "Of course." He licked his lips, tasting a little of the spray on them. It was sweet, unlike anything else in the Coquels. When he and Tierran had free time, they'd come here with blankets, fresh fruit, and books. They'd spend whatever time they had talking together, reading passages from their favorite books to each other, talking about what they'd do with their quell once they had it.

Liana didn't look at him, but he sensed she was about to drop one of her bombs. He braced himself. "Tristys told me you can commune with quell."

Yeah, that stung. He felt a quick slice of betrayal before he remembered he never told Tristys to keep that a secret. And if that was the first thing she'd brought up, Tristys probably hadn't told her anything else. Bless him. But just because Tristys told her things didn't mean Rami had to, as well. He stayed silent.

"Ramis, you told us quell left you Untouched after the accident."

Rami scoffed. "Oh, you're calling it 'the accident' now? Last time I saw you, you were calling me a murderer and a blasphemer. Or was that all an accident, too?"

"Ramis, I was upset. You have to understand, Tierran was—"

"I don't want to hear it." He shut his eyes tightly, as if that would block out anything she might say. "I don't want to hear anything about him, and I don't want to hear your apologies."

She stood tight-lipped for a second. Her eyes narrowed. "Can you truly commune with eş?" she asked. "Are you Touched?"

His only response was to pull a thread of water from the wave in front of them and coil it around his arm before letting it drop back to the earth. Her gasp was surprisingly satisfying.

"Ramis, you told us the quell had left you! Why would you lie?" Her face was contorted, her expression torn somewhere between sorrow and anger and confusion. "How could you refuse the Trial? How could you Touch quell without—"

"I never said I used it," he interjected, getting angrier with her holier-than-thou accusations. "I spent my whole life ignoring it, because I knew that it had something to do with my feelings for Tierran, with my feelings for—" He tried to said 'men', but the word simply wouldn't come out. "I couldn't bear that again, so I shut everything off, everything that I thought could—"

"Ramis, you need to—"

"Quit saying my name!" he shouted. He remembered, briefly, Tristys shouting the same thing to him earlier that day. He continued in a quieter voice: "My name is Ramidon now, anyway."

She was shaking her head, pity plain on her face. "You shunned eş, you changed your name, you gave up everything you wanted because of that one day." It wasn't a question, but he felt himself nodding in reply anyway. "Ramis, I don't know—I can't begin to tell you—"

"Please, Liana," he said, fighting back tears. What she said was true. It was easy to ignore when somebody wasn't rubbing it in your face, gloating about it. It wasn't as if he had a choice in the matter, either. He couldn't bear the pain again...

"No, you have to listen to me. You need to know something about Tierran, something I never told you, because I didn't—"

"I told you, I don't want to hear about him." He was shaking his head now, viciously back and forth to block out any incoming noise. His eyes wouldn't focus. If she said that name one more time, he thought he'd vomit.

"Tierran isn't—"

"Shut up!" he yelled, and he ran. Childish, perhaps, but he ran away from her, and when she didn't chase him, he thanked the quell for small favors.

Nothing that had happened was her fault. She'd yelled and she'd accused and she'd condemned, but she wasn't to blame. Only he was to blame, him and the love that led him to betray eş. He'd never let that love hurt him or anyone else again. He ran, because nothing she said would change that... so why bother listening at all?

~~*

When Tristys came out of the stone hallway, Calissa was waiting for him. He was surprised.

"Liana told me she forgot to show you your room," she explained, "so I thought I'd wait here for you." She held up a book that she'd had on her lap. "I've wanted a chance to finish this book on the stormbreakers of Calerelac anyway. It's totally fascinating."

Tristys wondered how long it would take before he could go an entire conversation without uttering the following sentence. "I don't know what—or where, for that matter—that is."

"Oh," Calissa said, looking more sheepish than Rami ever did in the same situation, "I'm not used to hanging out with people who don't know all my pet topics. Sorry." She closed the book; apparently she wouldn't be finishing it now, either. "They're magic-wielders from the nations to the east of us. They tap into some very powerful elemental forces. Stormbreakers control lightning and rain, basically, and they have a penchant for sadism. Very unique."

"They sound creepy," Tristys said.

"They are. This book's about the magic, though, not the breakers." She stood up, smoothing out imaginary wrinkles in the thin blue shirt she had on. "Anyway, I figured you have to be hungry. It's late, but the dining rooms should still be open."

Tristys noticed then that it was dark outside, the only light in the room coming from a small lantern Calissa had brought. "How long was I in there? It wasn't even dusk when I went down."

"Oh, you've been in there quite a while. Something like six or seven hours, I think."

Tristys must have looked surprised, because Calissa laughed at him. It was a fast laugh, with peals that led into each other. He liked it. It was contagious, too, because he heard his own laugh echoing hers, a bit more self-consciously.

"Don't worry," she said. "It happens to all of us the first time we commune."

Tristys wasn't entirely sure he had communed, and he tried to tell her as much while they walked to the dining rooms. She wouldn't let him. She actually seemed offended when he started talking about his experience, insisting that the time in the alcoves is a sacred, private matter, meant only for you and quell to know. He quit talking about magic entirely after that. Instead, they talked about Rami.

"He's something of an odd duck," Calissa was explaining as they ate their late dinner. The cafeteria had absolutely no selection—one entree, one snack, one dessert—but that didn't really matter, since the food was delicious. Some sort of fish baked in a sweet sauce, a mix of greens in oil, and a berry cake. "I didn't meet him until after he'd already been here, so I don't really know what went down. I do know this is the first time he's been back, though."

"And Liana doesn't seem to be a fan," Tristys added through a mouthful of cake. It really was delicious.

"No, she's not. He's not a fan of hers, either. I've tried to find out why, but he shuts down if I mention anything about this place."

"Oh, he shuts down for you, too?" Tristys asked. They'd been doing that all night, comparing facts and features and behaviors of Rami as if they were both equal in his life and should therefore receive the same treatment. Tristys was slightly creeped out by the whole thing, since this was Rami's girlfriend, but Calissa seemed fine with it.

"Totally. You get used to it, though. He has certain no-no topics, and I just stay away from them."

The conversation lulled a second while they both finished their cakes. "After the Altar, then, he did what? The Physique Services or something? At the same time as school?"

"Physical Services," she said, correcting a slight mispronunciation on his part. Calissa spoke Cyræan decently—she and Rami had actually met in the introductory course, though she wasn't as good at it as he was—and she'd been helping Tristys with the language during their conversation.

"Well, Physique Services would apply just as well, considering Rami's body," Tristys said, giggling. He immediately blushed. This was Calissa, not Rylin! They were so similar, though, Calissa and his childhood friend, this wasn't the first time he'd almost forgotten.

"I know!" Calissa said, joining in the laughter. She didn't seem offended at all. In fact, she seemed absolutely tickled. "If only everybody who went to university looked like that, right? Would've been a lot funner for me, I'll tell you!"

He nodded, eyes wide, partly in awe of the idea and partly because he was surprised he was having such a good time with Calissa. He wanted to hate her from the moment he realized she was with Rami... but he didn't. In fact, he liked her quite a bit.

Buoyed by the good humor, he asked something he'd been thinking about all night. "So, I don't know if I'm overstepping my boundaries here, but aren't you and Rami together? And haven't you been together since, like, forever?"

She started nodding before he even finished, and she started talking at once. "Rami and I have a complicated relationship," she said. She'd probably said this hundreds of times, he realized. "Officially, yes, he and I are together, and we love each other. He's more important to me than almost anyone in the world. But, you know," and now she hesitated, "things are complicated."

Complicated how? he wanted to ask, but he didn't. He said nothing, and she changed the subject, and the conversation meandered from Rami, to highlights of the other islands, to a story about her and her best friend Salice during one particularly wild party, then back to the stormbreakers from Calerelac, then back to Rami, and through a dozen other random topics. They didn't realize how long they'd been together until Rami came into the dining hall.

"I'm glad you two are best friends now," he said. Tristys wasn't sure if he was angry, jealous, or just feeling left out. "You've been gone for hours, and I've been sitting in my room all by myself."

Calissa rolled her eyes. "You could've come and found us earlier. We've just been sitting here chatting."

"Not about you," Tristys said at once, and at once regretting it. He was trying to show indifference, to show he was still upset, but instead he just looked like he was trying to cover something up. Sometimes he said the stupidest things...

Rami just looked at him askance, and Calissa grinned. "I was telling Tristys about the islands, places he should see once he gets accustomed to it here."

"Did she convince you to stay?" Rami turned to Calissa. "Pretty impressive for only knowing him a few hours." He was still talking to Calissa, but Tristys couldn't take his eyes away from Rami's gaze directed squarely at him. "He couldn't wait to get back to Paru when it was just us two."

"That's a blatant lie!" Tristys shouted. A few people at a nearby table looked up, startled, and he lowered his voice. "You know I loved—"

"It doesn't matter." Rami waved his hands, dismissing Tristys's words. "I'm glad you want to stay now. Calissa needed a few more friends. Quell knows she doesn't have enough as it is."

Now it was Calissa's turn to object. "Rami, quit it. Why are you acting like this? We didn't mean anything by not coming to get you. We just figured—"

"No, it's fine." Rami wasn't shouting, but his voice was too loud. The people at the other table were staring now. "I'm tired anyway. I'll be in our room, Calissa." He emphasized her name, as if Tristys would accidentally mistake the invitation's intended recipient.

"Whatever," Calissa said, already turning back to Tristys. "I'll be there soon."

Rami left without another word. Tristys and Calissa rolled their eyes at each other, and they made some off-hand comment about how odd a duck Rami was. After that, they tried to get back into stride, but their momentum had vanished.

Calissa took Tristys to his sleeping quarters, and they said good-night. She said she wasn't looking forward to dealing with the pouting Rami, and Tristys said he didn't blame her, but that was a lie. He'd have gladly switched her places, because dealing with the pouting Rami meant he'd be sleeping next to him rather than sleeping alone in a big cottonbloom. He missed the nights in the jungle. Their bed was always hard and cold and wet, but at least he was never alone.

The next morning, Tristys wanted to go back to the meditation alcoves as soon as he woke up. Nobody had left a note or anything like that, and Calissa hadn't said to meet her anywhere the night before, so he left without feeling too guilty. They'd figure out where he went, right?

On the way, he ran into two people. The first was a young boy who said hello, but Tristys ignored him. He didn't even look up from the ground for fear that his eyes would give him away. The second person was a woman. She looked a little older than Tristys, which means she was probably much older than he, considering the effect quell had on the age of the Coquellians. She literally ran into him, her head engrossed in a piece of paper, and she apologized. He said no problem, but he said it in Cyræan. She didn't seem to notice, so he shrugged it off and tried to forget about it.

After those two run-ins, getting to the meditation alcoves was a breeze. It was mid-day; he'd slept quite a bit, and most people seemed to be occupied indoors. So he went to the same alcove he'd chosen yesterday, and like yesterday, he put his robe on the table and sat down in the phosphorescent water, smiling at the strange tingling sensation that traveled along his body.

This was a meditation alcove, right? So he tried to meditate. He emptied his mind of every thought he could. This wasn't as difficult today as it was yesterday, mostly because he had just woken up, so his mind wasn't quite as quick as it usually was. Even still, Tristys could never keep his mind empty for long, and his thoughts began to drift. He decided to try the Cyræan method of meditating, which consisted of chanting the same prayers over and over and over again, sometimes while fasting. He'd never done it back home, but right now, he liked the idea of at least having some guidelines to work with.

That didn't work, either. In fact, Tristys wasn't sure, but he felt like the tingling sensation dulled once he started the Cyræan tactics. Reciting prayers to foreign gods probably wasn't the best idea after all. He liked the focus of the prayers, though, so he decided to use that tactic—the meditative focus—and work with it. Since he was at the Altar of Five Waves, and he was trying to commune with Water-magic, he chose the obvious topic: water.

He sat for what felt like hours, trying to meditate on water. He thought about the Kysim Falls, the rapids near Paru, and the sea that had nearly been his death after the freak storm had freed him from the Spålorians. He considered what water meant here in the Coquels, especially on the island of Quelles, with the constant rain and the crazy rivers that flowed upstream. He went back to those jungle nights, covered in rain (and Rami), how it had felt to let it soak through his clothes, his hair, and even his bones. He thought about single drops, the way they had looked as they'd fallen from the sky, or as they'd careened down Rami's chest as he'd crossed the Rockaway Trib. He tried to keep those kinds of thoughts to a minimum, since this was about Water-magic, not Rami.

He thought about every possible permutation of water he could imagine, and still nothing happened. He just sat there, surrounded by this water that was supposed to be magical, supposed to be talking to him or something, but the only thing it had done so far was glow a bit and tickle. He slammed his hand at an angle into the water, something he always did as a child to make waves, though this time he did it out of frustration. The force created the wave, as he expected, but the wave seemed to move in slow motion. It rose higher than it should have, and it continued to gain height long after it should have fallen back into the pool.

Time seemed to freeze. The wave stood in midair, refusing to fall, the pale blue glow almost pulsing. Tristys stood up, his head now level with the top of the wave. He stared it at, motionless, before he couldn't resist the urge to reach out and touch it. He felt as if some other hand, not his own, was reaching out, index finger outstretched, pausing just a hair's breadth away from the time-lapsed wave. The slightest motion forward, then contact. Skin on water, and the light exploded outward in all directions, carrying small stars of water with it. They diffused through the whole room, and Tristys spun himself around to look, eyes agape, at the galaxy he'd created. When he looked down, he realized he wasn't spinning himself after all.

He was no longer standing in the water. Rather, he was standing on it, on a pedestal the water had created beneath him, lifting him up. Tendrils of water wound their way like vines up the pedestal, and they wove an intricate pattern around Tristys's body once they reached him. Thin strands twisted around each leg, meeting at his pelvis and joining each other to form thicker ropes. They traveled up his midsection, briefly kissing his skin as they went, and split again at his arms.

As the thinner tendrils wound their way to his hands, Tristys felt his arms rise above his head. His eyes were drawn to his hands, which crossed at the wrists with palms facing down. Tristys gasped as the tendrils reared back from his skin and struck, like a snake, at his palms. There was no pain as the tendrils entered. Tristys looked at his legs, and sure enough, those tendrils were moving up his body as they were drawn in through his palms. When the last of the tendrils had entered his hands, time unfroze. The stars fell back into the sea, and like a moon that had come too close to its planet, Tristys crashed to the floor.

~~*

Liana, not Calissa, was waiting for him this time.

"You shouldn't go off alone," she said as soon as he emerged. "Somebody could—" She stopped when she saw his face. It had to be plastered all over it: something had happened.

"Liana, there were stars, and I saw—"

"Hush!" she shouted, a look of horror on her face. "What happens in the alcoves is for you and you alone. It is sacred, and—"

"Yeah, Calissa told me. Sorry, I forgot." He was too excited, though; he had to keep talking about it. "But something happened, and I think—I think I'm ready."

She looked skeptical. "Tristys, I am happy for you, but I don't know if we should rush this. Let's not forget, you are still a foreigner, and we have no idea what to expect."

He pushed his wet bangs off his forehead, which made him smile like a mad person. That alone was a big enough sign! He was wet. The water had actually absorbed into his body. Nothing magical, just what regular water should do. But it hadn't done it last night. He'd left the pool completely dry. But he was wet now. He knew what to expect.

"No, Liana. I don't mean to disrespect you or your learning, but I know. I'm ready."

She thought a moment, obviously arguing with herself. Finally, she sighed. "If you insist," she said. "Traditionally, the Trial is held in front of an audience, including all the priests and all the supplicants." She grinned wryly. "In your case, though, I think it's best that we buck tradition."

Tristys nodded. Audiences gave him performance anxiety.

"Meet me tonight, three after zenith. We'll conduct the trial then." She nodded down the steps that led to the meditation alcoves. "If you follow the stone hallway to its end, you'll find me there."

Tristys nodded again, still elated but already beginning to feel the pangs of self-doubt and anxiety. Why was he so nervous? He knew he'd communed; the quell had deferred to him. He had no doubt.

She could see the excitement on his face, apparently. "You look as if you're about to burst," she said, grinning at his exuberance. "You can tell Calissa, if you want, but I'd keep this away from Ramis."

That shouldn't be a problem, he thought, since Rami wasn't really talking to him. But Liana's words also confirmed something Tristys had suspected since that day on the beach: Rami didn't like Water-magic, for some reason. And Tristys didn't want to give Rami any more reason to be standoffish and mean. He'd keep quiet.

"I won't tell if you won't tell," he said, winking, and Liana rolled her eyes, chuckling as she left.

~~*

Tristys traveled through the stone hallway by running his hand along the wall. There were very few sconces, and he could barely see his own fingers in front of him. He didn't really expect to find anything, but he kept hearing Rami's stories about the creatures that lived in the Rockaway

Labyrinth. Between that and his fears about the upcoming Trial, Tristys was a wreck.

When he'd woken up from a nap, he'd tried to find Calissa or Rami or even Liana to no avail. In fact, he couldn't find anyone he knew all day. He ate another meal in silence and flipped through the translation book Rami had given him during their journey through the jungle, but most of what he learned didn't stay with him, since his mind was preoccupied.

He was early now—it wasn't even two past zenith yet—but he couldn't wait any longer. He figured he'd get as close as he could to where Liana said to meet her, and then he'd work on meditating again. It was strange, not really having anything to do. In Paru, he'd been busy non-stop; these days, he felt more like he did on the slave-ship than he did at home. It wasn't necessarily a bad thing, since he liked those leisure days with Vun'gor.

But he wasn't with Vun'gor now. He was on his way to some sort of test, something that could be lethal, involving water. It didn't take a genius to figure out that he'd probably have to go in some sort of pool, and ever since Tristys's experience at sea after the slave-ship sunk, he hadn't been the biggest fan of large bodies of water. He was nervous, despite Liana's assurances that nothing bad would happen.

He turned a corner in the hallway and had to shield his eyes. It was bright, very bright! The cavern was enormous, by far the largest single enclosed space he'd ever seen in his life. Most of the room, except for a small ledge around the rim, was a pool, and in the center was an enormous fountain. It had to be the central waterspout, the one huge wave that rose high above the others. It was emanating that pale blue light, too. This was it, then. This was eş. He had trouble swallowing. Did spit count as water, or was he just this nervous?

Liana was here, standing on the other side of the room with Calissa. He breathed a bit easier when he saw the two women. Somehow knowing he wasn't alone here made it a bit less... threatening.

"Welcome, Tristys," Liana said. He expected something a bit more formal, but she seemed pretty laid back to be standing above the object of her adoration.

Was there protocol he had to follow? Nobody had told him, so he just nodded his greeting. Calissa smiled, and he waved at her. He tried not to let his awkwardness show.

"I'm sorry I couldn't come to you sooner," Calissa said once he got close to them. "I spent a little time with Rami in the afternoon, and when I came to get you, you were asleep. Then I've been with Liana. She told me about your Trial, and we both figured you'd want a familiar face here."

Wow, they knew him well for barely knowing him at all. "Yeah, you were right. Thank you," he said, looking first at Calissa and then at Liana.

Liana spoke next. "Normally, as I said, this is a performance as well as a trial. There'd be spectators surrounding the pool, and they'd watch you as you struggle to complete the task." She looked around at the empty room. "Obviously, that's not the way it's going to be now. So I'm going to skip all the theatrics, and we can just get to it." She put her hands on her hips and tilted her head at the water. "Hop in."

He knew it was coming, but he still felt a bit of disappointment when he was proved right. Liana had given him a change of clothes, some sort of traditional garb to wear during the trial that turned out to be a long-sleeved shirt and pants made of an extremely thin, dark blue material. He changed now—he made both women turn around first—and then he got into the pool.

The strange tingling returned, heightened by his total submersion and, perhaps, by the proximity to the heart of eş. The pool was deep, very deep, and he dunked his head to see if he could see the bottom. The tingling felt downright creepy on his eyes, and though he had nearly perfect visibility, he couldn't see the floor. He popped his head back above water to say something to Calissa, but before any words came out, the water started churning... and churning fast.

Tristys no longer wanted to do this. He was treading water as quickly as he could, and already the churning was foiling his plans to stay afloat. He started to panic, to flash back to that night on Vun'gor's ship, to the way the water clawed at him, at his face and his lungs and his mind. No, he couldn't do this again, couldn't almost drown. He wanted out. He wanted out now.

He wrestled to the surface, threw his head up and yelled for help. Liana was there, looking concerned, and so was Calissa, but she looked calm, almost pleasant. She smiled warmly, and Tristys fell back beneath the surface of his memories. He suddenly remembered a giant hand—no, a wave!—slapping him, beating him, bruising him until he'd fallen from the boat. It hadn't been an accident, then, after all.

But now was no time to rehash his past. He was going to drown here and now. The surface was too far above him now, the natural light that shone brighter than the pale luminescence of this alien water beyond his reach. He tried to push his way up, but he couldn't beat back whatever kept him down. He called on his body, begged it to listen, but nothing. There was simply no way out of the water.

Then he remembered what was happening. This was a trial. A trial to test his ability to use Water-magic. So obviously he should use some magic to escape. But by now the oxygen had been nearly depleted, his lungs were burning—so much pain. He wanted to breathe, all he wanted was to breathe, and he had to fight to keep his mouth shut, to keep his lungs from exploding and inhaling whatever they could. He called on the quell, begged it to listen, but nothing. There was simply no way out of the water.

He was angry, so angry. He couldn't attune after all, and he was going to die here, since Liana wasn't going to save him. She'd have done something by now, right? All he wanted to do was let the air out of his lungs. He didn't even care about breathing anything back in. He just had to let go...

So he did. He screamed, as loudly as he could. It was primal, and it was magic. He saw those stars again, just for a second, beautiful constellations spread before, behind, between, above, and below him. Then the water was gone, pushed out of the pool by the force of his power, and he could breathe! He could breathe! He could breathe!

A second later, the water came back, a giant deluge that hurt when it struck him, but there was no pull anymore, nothing pushing him down below the surface. He swam, his entire body shaking, to the surface. He licked his lips, tasting the waters of eş for the first time. They were sweet.

Neither Liana nor Calissa had said anything yet, and he turned to them for something, either congratulations or relief that he hadn't died. Instead, they looked bedraggled and a bit beguiled. Their hair and clothes were sopping. Calissa blew the water from her lips, and Tristys had to laugh. "Did you guys decide to join me or what?"

"Usually," Liana said, wiping her face, "the water doesn't come up quite this high."

"Usually," Calissa agreed. The two women, of course, were practitioners of Water-magic, and they dried themselves almost instantaneously. Liana was wet one second and the next she simply wasn't, but Calissa was a bit more dramatic. She shook all over, and as she shook, the water evaporated.

As Tristys swam over to them, Liana said, "This is perhaps an understatement, but you've passed the Trial. Consider yourself Touched." He hoisted himself out of the pool and onto the ledge next to Liana. "Soon, after some lessons, you'll be able to dry yourself as easily as we just did." She handed him a towel.

He wanted to try it, to tell her that he felt like he could dry himself now, but he didn't want to question her words any more than he already had that day. She was, after all, the high priest. Instead, he used the towel—it was rough on his skin, but it absorbed well—and asked a question. "Are you freaking out?"

Liana didn't react right away, instead looking

confused, almost as if she'd misheard. "I'm sorry?"

"I mean, since it worked. And I'm a foreigner. That's a big deal, right?"

She thought a moment, considering. "I wouldn't say 'freaked out'. A bit shocked, perhaps, and you've certainly upset the status quo." He smiled despite himself. He liked being special. "But you are only one foreigner, Tristys, and you won't be leaving the islands again, so perhaps you aren't as foreign as you think." His smile disappeared. "This is only a small event in the greater scheme of things. Everything is only ever a small event."

Now he frowned. He didn't like being belittled, even by a high priest. It might not be a big deal to her, but he'd just communed with a magic he hadn't even known existed until a few weeks ago! He nodded weakly, since both she and Calissa were staring at him.

"Perhaps you ought to go to sleep now," Liana said. "It is very late, and we'll start your training tomorrow. You'll need your rest." She patted his shoulder. It was a strange gesture, almost grandmotherly, and it didn't fit her well. He didn't like it.

"Actually," Calissa said, looking hesitant and unsure. It was a strange look on Calissa, who usually seemed so assured. "I have a request regarding his training."

"Oh?"

"Rami wants to leave tomorrow, to go back to Ramidalé. He made some excuse about his parents, but I think he just wants to get away from the Altar. You know he's not really a fan of this place."

"Or me," Liana said. Tristys couldn't tell if she

was amused, upset, or just impartial.

Calissa skirted a response. "Anyway, he wants me to go with him, and I want Tristys to go with us." Tristys was touched that she cared enough about him to want to take him with her. "He's our responsibility, and I don't think it'd be right to drop him on you so suddenly." So now he was a hassle? And her responsibility? She'd known him two days! "Plus, it'll be easier to conceal him in the forest. He's still a foreigner, even if he is Touched now."

Liana's eyes narrowed as she considered. "And you will train him, I presume? As you say, he is Touched now. He'll need to learn control."

"Yes. Rami won't be pleased, but he'll get over it, and once he does, I think he'll be glad I brought Tristys along with us." For the first time, she looked at Tristys to include him in the conversation. "If he wants to come, of course."

"Yes, of course!" he said at once. He still wasn't too happy about feeling like a nuisance, but the thought of being separated from Rami right now made him nauseated. He shivered. He blamed his wet hair, but it had more to do with the potential abandonment.

Liana said nothing. Calissa said nothing. Tristys was about to burst. He held his breath, and it felt almost as if he were back underwater, in another trial.

Finally, Liana spoke. "Fine," she said. "You are one of the most promising practitioners I've met, Calissa. If anyone can teach a foreigner about our magics, it's you."

Calissa's face lit up, and she bowed her head slightly. "Thank you, High Priest."

"Will you leave tomorrow?"

"Rami wants to. I wanted to stay a day or two, to let Tristys rest, but Rami usually wins in situations like these. He's a bit of a baby if he doesn't get his way."

"I can imagine," Liana said. "Very well."

"One thing," Tristys said, interrupting Liana. "Can we try to keep the magic-and-me stuff quiet around Rami? I don't think he'll take it very well." Tristys remembered how he'd reacted when they left Lower Ramidalé, right after Tristys Fingerprinted the first time, how cold Rami had been. He didn't want that again.

Calissa looked confused, but she agreed. Liana did, too. "I probably won't even see Rami before you leave," she said, closing the debate. She turned to Calissa. "If you don't mind, I have a few things to say to Tristys. I'll take him back to his room when we're finished."

"Of course, High Priest. I'll say goodbye tomorrow before we leave."

"I'd be devastated if you didn't." She watched Calissa leave, waiting for her to go before she spoke to Tristys. "This flower," she said, taking an enormous blue bloom from behind her hair, "is called the aki-éspera. Most plants, in case you aren't aware, only grow if the conditions are right. Put a seed on a stone, and nothing happens." Tristys wasn't entirely sure this was true, but he rolled with it. "The seed of the aki-éspera, though, is different. It will try to grow wherever it lands, no matter what."

She handed him the flower. It was surprisingly light, its petals were soft, rounded and flowing, and the smell hit him like splash of cold water on a hot day, a deliciously sweet scent that was both familiar and new at the same time. Vun'gor would have loved it. "If the conditions are right, the plant turns out like this one. Look at the petals, the way the various blues dance with each other to create a color so unique you'll never find it again anywhere in the world. It's perfect, Tristys. Wouldn't you agree?"

He would, and he did.

"If the conditions aren't right, though, the flowers look nothing like this. They're poisonous. The smell alone can knock someone out. One petal can kill a man. If left unchecked, it destroys everything around it. It's pretty incredible." She paused for a reaction, but Tristys was petting the petals and didn't look up. He was listening, though. "Because of that, almost none grow in the wild still. But we have people who grow them, who nurture them from seeds. Those farmers spend their entire lives making sure everything is just right for the plant. If it's not, they have to rip out the seedling, rip it right out of the ground before it gets too dangerous and ruins everything." She put a hand on his shoulder, her cue for him to look up from the plant. "They don't want to rip it out, of course. But they have to."

Tristys's initial awe of the plant dissipated, and now he was beginning to wonder what this had to do with anything. He continued to look at Liana, though he stroked the petals anyway. They were too soft; it was almost hypnotic. He tried to hand the plant back to her, but she refused. "Keep it," she said. "Let's go to bed."

They walked in silence out of the cavern, back through the darkened hallway, and out into the night. The only light now came from the two moons, but it was more than enough to navigate by. On more than one occasion, Tristys wanted to say something, to ask about the point of the flower story, to talk about magic, to ask about Rami, anything... but it never felt right. Liana wanted silence, and it seemed that Liana got what she wanted.

"This is you," she said when they got to the outer doors of the dormitories. She opened the door and held it for him. He went in, not sure if he should say goodbye or just keep walking. He kept walking.

"Tristys," she said, "the plant's name, aki-éspera, is Old Quellosian. It means 'undying hope'. It's a paradox, of course, because sooner or later, almost all hope has to die." She paused again, and the drama was getting to be a bit much for Tristys. He wanted to shout at her to get to a point, but his Cyræan training to obey got the best of him.

"I told Calissa tonight that she was one of the most promising practitioners I've seen. You remember?" He nodded. "Well, Tristys, you are the most promising one I've met. I said your success tonight was small, but even the biggest tree starts from something tiny. You may think you tripped into the Coquels, found the quell by accident, but if I learned anything in my eighty-plus years, I've learned it's always quell that finds you, not the other way around."

As if that wasn't confusing enough for him, she added: "Be a good gardener, Tristys. Cultivate well, nurture the good seeds and get rid of the bad ones. Don't forget that almost every aki-éspera seedling has to die." She shut the door, but even through the wooden panel, he heard her final words: "And remember you will be the one who has to kill it."

CHAPTER EIGHT

They'd been moving quickly through the jungle, and the speed coupled with his training had left him exhausted. As usual, Calissa forced him awake with shards of ice.

"Why do you both do that?" he shouted, wiping the water from his cheek before rubbing it tenderly. "If I bruise again..."

Calissa laughed. "You won't bruise." A second later, she asked, "Who else has done that to you?"

"Rami," he said without thinking. A second later, he wasn't sure if he should regret it. Hadn't Rami said something about keeping his magic a secret, or was he making that up? It was too early for Tristys's brain to worry about things like this.

"Rami can't use eş," Calissa said, sounding as if she didn't quite believe herself. That answered Tristys's question, though: Nope, he shouldn't have said anything.

"Maybe I dreamed it." He was just groggy enough that it could be believable. She let it go.

"Rami's out gathering food for the day, so we have a bit of stationary time we can use to train." She'd apparently already taken her morning bath, since her hair was wet again. She could dry it instantaneously with her Water-magic, but she always kept it wet. She said she liked the weight it gave to her hair. Tristys, who hated being wet, had tried to understand for hours before finally giving up.

Rami still hadn't returned to his pre-Altar self. He was standoffish and aloof, and he rarely, if ever, spoke directly to Tristys. Quite frankly, it made Tristys feel terrible. He knew he didn't do anything, and he knew he didn't deserve this treatment, but there was something broken about Rami. And Tristys wasn't proud of it, but the broken ones turned him on.

"Avoiding me again, eh?" Tristys asked, trying not to sound too dejected.

Calissa put her hands on her hips. "Come on, I told you he gets like this sometimes. He went an entire semester without speaking to me once because I told him his friend Gawen was good-looking."

"He got over it, obviously." That didn't sound jealous, right?

"He'll get over it with you, too. You just need to calm down a bit. I mean, it's just Rami. I know he's cute, but there are thousands of cute guys here. Like his friend Gawen, for instance." She grinned wickedly.

"Oh yeah? When do I get to meet this Gawen, then?" He didn't really want to meet Gawen—all he wanted was Rami back, even if only as a friend—but he decided to play along.

"Probably in Ramidalé, actually." She picked up an empty cup from the log they'd been using as a table. "Before then, though, you need to fill up this up." She held it out for him to take.

Tristys groaned. "You're killing me with all this, Calissa. 'Touch this' and 'think that' and 'fill this up'. Can't we have one day of rest?"

"Oh, who are you kidding?" she asked. "You love this, and you know it."

She was right. He did love this. It was absolutely... well, magical. On the first day of his training, he managed to move a surprisingly large amount of water from one vessel (a cup) to a second vessel (his mouth) without actually touching the cup. Calissa had been impressed. On the second day, he moved a whole bowl's worth. She'd been more impressed. The third and the fourth, too, were impressive: he drained a small tributary of the River Ramidalé—he only passed out once, and it was so quick he wasn't even sure he actually passed out—and then he was able to empty a bowl as quickly as Calissa filled it, though he suspected she didn't give it her all. It was so incredible, so amazing. To be able to do something that he never imagined he could do, never in a million years. To be doing it now... it was unbelievable.

"Can we at least use a different cup? That one is hideous." It was strangely shaped, asymmetrical, and glazed an obnoxious, sickly green. It was totally irrational, but he hated it.

"Actually, we're not going to use a cup at all. No props today. We're going to try something a little different."

Tristys was confused. "Then why did you just hand me the cup?"

"Oh," she said, smiling, "it's just funny to see your expression when I bring it out. You really hate that thing, don't you?"

Yes, he really did, and he told her so. "So what are we going to do today?"

"Well, so far, all we've been doing is manipulating water."

"Right. But that's what Water-magic is, isn't it? You use water."

"No," Calissa said, shaking her head frantically. "Water-practitioners manipulate water by Touching eş, which—"

"Which is water."

"No, not at all!" This was as close to frustrated as Tristys had seen Calissa in all their training. She sat down. "I guess this is why training at the Altar begins with heavy theory classes." She was talking more to herself than to him at that point, but then she looked his way. "There is eş in everything. I mean everything!" She looked around, nodding at various things to emphasize her point. "You learn to commune with eş, so you can Touch it wherever you are, no matter. Even if you're in the Dead Stretch, you won't die. Not of thirst, anyway."

"Dead Stretch?" Tristys asked. Place-names always distracted him.

"Yeah, it's a desert on Quellus, the island of Fire-magic." She waved her hand as if she were swatting a fly. "Irrelevent! The point is that you can Touch the eş in everything, not just water, and therefore you can get water out of anything."

"Fine, fine." Tristys was excited. This is what he'd been waiting for. He'd finally be able to make his own ice arrows to shoot at people! "Teach me how to make water."

"You don't make water," she corrected, "you—"

"Semantics, Calissa! Semantics!"

"You don't make water," she said more forcefully. "You Touch the eş inherent in everything."

"That's still just semantics to me," he pouted.

"It's not, though. You need to understand how something works before you can use it."

"Wrong again!" he said, pointing a finger at her. "I have no idea how those funny things in the bathrooms work, but I use them."

"The toilets?" Calissa asked.

"Yeah, and the things that make water so you can wash your hands."

"Sinks? They don't make water, they run it by channeling—"

"Irrelevent!" he shouted, mimicking her hand gestures from a few seconds ago.

The little bit of frustration she'd had evaporated with the good humor, and Tristys spent the next ten minutes listening to a lecture about water that wasn't water. To Touch eş, according to Calissa, you first had to be able to See it. She didn't write the word down, but Tristys could sense the capitalization. Seeing eş involved a sixth sense of sorts, being able to connect with a presence of eş that you normally didn't see. He wasn't exactly sure, but he thought this had something to do with the galaxies of stars he'd seen during both his meditation and his Trial. He tried to ask, but as soon as he mentioned the meditation alcoves, Calissa freaked until he shut up.

He'd never seen those stars except on two occasions, and never for more than a few seconds, and never on purpose. When he expressed his reservations, she assured him it would get easier with practice, that Seeing on demand wasn't as easy as you would think. But true mastery of quell only came when Seeing no longer registers on the level of consciousness, when the body and the mind were so in tune with the magic that Sight was as second-nature as remembering to breathe. Tristys felt like he had a long way to go.

Twenty minutes later, Tristys was still trying to See, but all he saw were the stars he got from crossing his eyes one too many times. At one point, Calissa went and got the cup he'd flung off to the side and filled it up with her own Water-magic. "Put your finger in this," she said, "and try again." He did.

It worked. He crossed his eyes for the hundredth time, and a slight blur gave way to the galaxy. He had two sets of eyes, one that saw everything perfectly and another that saw pale blue stars everywhere. They were densest in the leaves and weakest in the rocks, but even in the rocks, they were there. Wherever he looked, they were there. They twinkled, and he laughed, or perhaps he twinkled and they laughed. Perhaps everything twinkled and everything laughed. He couldn't tell.

In a second they were gone, collapsed back into the supernova of his reality. He looked at Calissa, whose smile was so large he knew she understood what had happened, and he crossed his eyes. The stars returned. They disappeared again, though they laughed a second longer than they had the first time. Crossed eyes again: more twinkling. And again: more laughter.

This was a gift, he knew. He'd done the supernatural, the uncanny, the unreal. Nobody at home, not even the Two Mothers themselves, could do this. In a single hour, he'd done more than anyone he had ever known back home had done, had even thought possible. In a single hour, he had held eternity, and it twinkled and laughed, and he had twinkled and laughed with it.

He blinked away the stars that were still there. Water was rushing down his cheeks, more ice from Calissa, perhaps. But no, this wasn't ice—these weren't daggers. These were warm and wet and a little salty. They were tears. He had been crying without even realizing it, and when he did, he broke down, the shock of his power hitting him like the tidal waves he could now control. He was no longer just Tristys, no longer Tristys of Paru. Now he was magical.

He was laughing now, too, laughing with tears running down his face, and a second later Calissa was on him, hugging him and crying with him. He hadn't even realized she'd moved, but she had, and they sat like that for a few minutes. Tristys reveled in his newfound galaxy, and Calissa let him. They finally broke apart, and Tristys felt a bit sheepish over his exaggerated reaction, but it quickly passed. He was magical, dammit!

He stood up, dusted off the back of his pants, and opened his mouth to ask Calissa how to use the stars he now could See, but then he saw Rami. He was standing just on the edge of the clearing, the vines he'd cut still dangling in his hands, his bare torso beaded with sweat. Tristys had no idea how long he'd been there, but he couldn't hold back his excitement. He smiled, started to walk toward Rami to tell him his news. Rami's eyes narrowed, his face stone. He turned away from Tristys to walk back into the forest, and Tristys felt his excitement, his enthusiasm, all his joy, drain out of him like the light from a dying star.

As he cut his way through the forest, keeping one eye open to spot anything edible, Rami tried to drown his thoughts in the drone of the blade-cutter bugs. The weather had been uncharacteristically wet the past few days, and so the sounds of life—particularly those blade-cutter bugs, whose perpetually moving wings sounded like double-edged swords twirling above their heads—was correspondingly louder than usual. And yet Rami still had trouble keeping his own thoughts submerged.

He'd been replaying his visit to Saloris over and over since Calissa had surprised him. He had sent her a message, but all he'd said was that he'd found a bit of a liability and had to take him to the Altar before he could get back to Ramidale. Or maybe he'd called him a friend? Even so, would that be enough to motivate a surprise trip to the Altar? She was fond of the place, though, so she probably needed very little motivation. And he wasn't sure, because he couldn't really remember, but he might have mentioned Tristys wasn't from around here... He should never have sent that letter.

He wasn't upset that she'd come. She was his best friend in the world, and his girlfriend, and most likely his spouse at some point in the future. They'd spent their lives together, and Rami had accepted that, even learned to look forward to it. But what happened in the forest, with Tristys... it had started to change things, to make things feel... right again. To fix what he'd messed up with Tierran. But no, remember Tristys's face when they met Calissa? That was just more pain, caused by his attractions. But that was Calissa's fault, wasn't it? If Calissa hadn't shown up, maybe—

No, this was too confusing for him to worry about now! He had to find dinner, and he'd walked by at least four edible plants and a wounded frog they could've roasted for a bit of protein. Right there was an anaranroot, its small orange bloom peeking out from fallen leaves. The rare flower blooms underground, and the base of its roots is incredibly sweet. They were hard to get to, since the roots themselves were buried deep in the earth. Tristys loved them. A second later, almost against his will, Rami bent down to the ground to start digging.

Tristys and Calissa had certainly become fast friends. It made him uncomfortable, partly because he was afraid of what Tristys could divulge, either accidentally or on purpose, and partly because he was jealous. Yes, jealous of Calissa, because she got to spend time with Tristys when Rami had forsworn him. He hated the way he'd become: mopey and pouting and jealous. He wasn't acting like himself.

But then again, ever since Tristys had arrived on the scene, Rami hadn't really been acting like himself. At least not the self that he wanted, needed, had to be. He'd known Tristys less than a full month, and he'd already done several things he'd vowed never to do—commune with Water-magic, for instance. And the latest: harvesting impossibly difficult underground blooms just because Tristys liked to snack on them. But the scariest thing, and the most infuriating, was that Tristys made Rami wish he hadn't made that vow so many years ago.

He couldn't believe it, but he'd even considered reneging on his promise to himself and to Tierran's memory. That night in the forest, after he'd mistakenly lain next to Tristys and Tristys kissed him... that night had changed everything. He'd gone to bed with silly fantasies, dreams of learning to master Water-magic and spending his life with Tristys instead of Calissa. He had woken with the same dreams, and the whole way through the forest to the Altar had been blissful. He hated to admit it, but his moody behavior lately had as much to do with a renewed refusal of his feelings as it did his anger that he had to renew that refusal in the first place.

He shook his head forcefully. He had long since excavated the anaranroot from the ground, but he had been lost in his own thoughts. He had to get back to camp; they'd be worried about him if he didn't show soon. They'd be hungry, too! He looked at his pack. There was enough food for a few days, actually, but he cringed a bit when he realized that nearly everything he picked was something Tristys loved to eat. He thought about him even when he wasn't thinking about him! It was infuriating! His eyes caught a nearby blackstalk bush. They tasted like curdled strawberry milk, and Tristys hated them. He rushed to the bush and pulled a handful of leaves, stuffing them in the bag. Before he got back to camp, he took them out.

Back at camp, he saw Tristys and Calissa locked in a heated embrace. He thought he'd been stung by a hallucinogenic insect at first, because why would they be twisted together like that? He wasn't hallucinating, though, and an unparalleled fire raged through his blood. In a moment of absurd insight, he wondered if this is what Fingerprinting Fire-magic felt like. He stared, the breath drawn out of him. He'd never experienced jealousy like this before, not once, and it was paralyzing.

Tristys saw him then. He looked up, and Rami saw tears running down his face, and he realized Calissa was laughing, not moaning, and the jealousy melted into embarrassment. But Tristys's face made him realize something else: he wasn't feeling possessive of Calissa right now. No, quite the contrary. He was jealous of her. When he'd thought they were wound together by passion, he'd been jealous that she got to share that with Tristys and he didn't. And that jealousy made him want to sink into the forest. Even after his pep talk, he couldn't shake it.

Tristys was going to say something. Rami couldn't handle it right now, so he turned and walked away, walked quickly back into the jungle the way he'd come. He'd dropped the foodstuffs at some point, hopefully back in camp so they'd at least have dinner. But right now, he needed to be alone.

Once he'd traveled for a few minutes, he sat down. He hadn't hacked vines, so he was surrounded by dense foliage, and he figured he was safe, had time to think, to rebuild the walls Tristys had torn down. He was wrong. A vine fell, and then another, and Calissa appeared where the vines had been. She was winded, a light sheen of sweat on her forehead and bare arms.

He didn't want to see her. He wanted her to leave. "You know, if you had Life-magic, you wouldn't look so tired."

Her left eye narrowed, a tic she got whenever she was upset. He knew it was a sore spot with her. He wasn't a hurtful person, but sometimes even he couldn't stop himself from lashing out. Even Ramidon had had his bad moments, right?

She didn't say anything, just sat down next to him. She handed him a shirt, which he was grateful for, although he didn't thank her. He was sweaty, and night was starting to fall. The temperature had already started to drop. Tonight would be the coldest it had been in a while. A brief thought of how warm Tristys had been when he'd exhausted himself flashed into his mind, but he strangled it.

Calissa put her hand on his shoulder, and he braced himself for another one of her comforting, grin-and-bear-it lectures. "Rami," Calissa said, braiding his name with her usual sigh, "you're a jerk."

Wait, what? That's not how these usually begin. "I'm sorry?"

"Don't apologize to me." She was intentionally misunderstanding his words, and he knew it. "You should be apologizing to Tristys. You're a bigger jerk to him than you are to me."

"I don't think I'm being a jerk to either of—"

She shot him a look, the one where she lowered her head and looked out the top of her eyes. That shut him up.

"Look, I don't know what happened between you two, and I don't—"

"Nothing happened between us!" Rami said, too loudly and too defensively. When had he become so bad at keeping things hush-hush?

"Something happened," she said, "because you're not the type of person to hate someone so thoroughly for no reason." She was watching him, studying his reactions. Sometimes being this close to a person wasn't a good thing. "And you obviously hate him, considering the way you're treating him."

"I'm not treating him any different than I'm treating you." Rami wasn't looking at her.

"You're talking to me, aren't you? You haven't said a word to him since we left the Altar."

That put Rami on the offensive. "He's not talking to me, either. He could say something to me, but—"

"He tried, just now, and you stormed off."

Well, she had him there.

"And," she continued, "he found your bag of food and what you put in there."

Now he was confused. "What I put in there?"

"The blackstalk berries."

How did he know that would come back to haunt him? "I thought I'd taken them all out before—"

"Rami, why would you even pick them in the first place? They're blackstalk berries. Nobody— and I mean nobody—likes them. Nobody."

"I just—I didn't think—he wasn't supposed—"

"You did it to spite him," she said. Her voice had just a bit of accusation in it, but she sounded far more amused than he would have expected.

"Maybe I did," Rami said after a bit of silence that he hoped would somehow get him out of this conversation. "But I told you, I thought I got rid of them all. It was just a spur of the moment thing, because I was on the ground digging out a stupid anaranroot, and I felt—"

"You didn't get them all out," she said, as if that needed clarification, "and now he's back at the camp thinking you're trying to poison him."

Rami chuckled, despite the situation. Leave it to Tristys to overreact. "Blackstalk berries aren't poisonous. They just taste gross."

"Exactly," she said. She was grinning, another one of her characteristic Calissa moves. She always grinned when she'd won an argument. She ended up grinning a lot. "So what's the deal?"

"I told you ten hundred times, Calissa! I didn't

want him to find the berries! It was a—"

"Rami, you know this isn't about the berries."

He looked up from his lap for the first time. What was she suggesting? "Then what is this about, Calissa? Tell me." He took a deep breath and held it.

"I don't know," she said after what felt like an eternity. "Maybe it's about common decency. Maybe it's about the way you're treating some kid who just woke up on an island where he knows nobody and nothing except the fact that he'll never get home again. Maybe it's about the way he cares about you, the way he's tried to hide his excitement over eş because he thinks it'll upset you. Maybe it's—"

Calissa had a penchant for not knowing when to quit. He interrupted her. "Why would he think that?"

She looked perplexed. "I have no idea, to be honest. He told Liana and me after he passed the Trial that he didn't want you to know, because you acted weird to him for a while after he Fingerprinted on the beach."

"Oh, that wasn't because of his Fingerprinting, that was because Telia—" he stopped himself and quickly backtracked. "Telia was harping again about my parents. You know that puts me in a bad mood." Lies, of course, but he couldn't exactly tell her the truth. She looked at him with one eyebrow raised, but she didn't push it.

"Well, he's been working with eş, learning faster than anyone I've ever even heard about, and he's so excited, but he cares enough about you to try and keep all that quiet when you're around. And yet you still turn your back on him." He already felt bad, and she was making it worse.

"Today, for instance. He just learned how to See, and he was so excited he was crying, and when he tried to tell you about it, you ran away."

She really didn't know when to quit, did she? He wasn't sure what to say, what—if anything— would make it better. She stood up.

"He's a good kid, Rami. I don't know what happened, if anything did." She pursed her lips. "So he has a crush on you. Did he make a move or something? So what? Gawen hits on you every second of every day, and you still spend time with him." She paused, presumably for a reaction, but he was still too dumbfounded by the whole conversation. "You're the first person he met here, Rami. He needs a friend, someone besides me, and he needs it to be you." She picked up the machete she'd used to get here and started through the same path she'd already cut. "And that has nothing to do with your glistening abs or your violet eyes."

~~*

When Tristys awoke the next morning, everything was light. It filtered through the tops of the trees, breaking through the mist and the fog and bathing everything in brightness. It hurt his eyes.

As usual, his first thought upon waking up was Rami. His next thought, which he used to cloud the first, was magic. Drowning himself in Water-magic helped make Rami's rejection a bit easier, so he did what he'd done every morning since they left the Altar: he looked for Calissa.

But she wasn't there. Instead, there was Rami. He sat on a log, his head hanging. When Tristys saw him, he gasped; that caught Rami's attention, and he looked up.

"Good morning," Rami said. His voice was quiet and subdued, but he was looking directly at Tristys, something he hadn't done in days. Tristys hadn't even sat up from his resting position yet; he just lay there, open-mouthed. "Calissa's gone to get some food today."

"Why?" he asked at once, snapping out of his daze. "You got more than enough for a few days last night." Then he smacked himself in the head, figuratively. Rami hadn't spoken to him in forever, and Tristys's response is argumentative?

"Yeah, I know, but she was afraid you wouldn't eat it, since you were afraid of blackstalk poisoning." He smiled weakly.

"Oh, right. I almost forgot about the—"

"You know, about the berries, I never—"

"No, don't worry about it. If you—"

"No, really, I didn't want you to think—"

"I overreacted. I know that. They're just berries, and they're not poisonous, and—"

"I didn't want you to eat them, Tristys," Rami said, looking him directly in the eye. Tristys couldn't keep up with the interruptions. "I didn't even want you to know I picked them. I put them in, and I took them right back out. I thought I got them all. I guess I missed a few." He grinned again, the same unspoken apology lacing it.

"Yeah, you did." He sat up. "But if you pick them again, I'll eat them. They're just berries."

"I won't pick them again," Rami said at once.

"And thank you."

Rami's eyes asked the question before he did. "For what?"

Tristys hesitated. "I don't know," he said,

almost blushing. "For taking the berries back out."

"No problem, kiddo." Rami stood up. "Next time I'll be sure to get them all."

As Tristys and Rami smiled at each other for the first time in days, the canopy above them erupted into high-pitched shrieks and screams. They looked up. A small blur of black and white, barely visible from the forest floor, darted along the treetops, throwing itself nimbly from branch to branch as it shrieked at its pursuer. Only seconds behind the blur flew a broad-winged bird of prey. It was moving so quickly its wings looked as if they were going through, not above, the branches.

"That bird is amazing!" Tristys shouted, finally forgetting about Rami. "It looks like it's flying through the trees!"

"It is," Rami said, much more calmly. "At least, its wings are. They're not corporeal." He stopped for a second as the bird almost trapped its prey in talons. "It's a quell-beast, a firebird by the looks of it." The bird did look like it was on fire, now that Tristys looked closely. "It's a young one, too. It's small."

"What's that thing it's chasing?" Tristys had lost sight of it for a moment, but a particularly loud screech from farther down the trees drew his attention. It had hit something, presumably one of its limbs, on a branch.

"I can't really tell, but if it's avoiding a firebird this long, it must be something fast. Probably a taramisk monkey."

"A what?" Tristys said.

"A taramisk—oh, right. No monkeys in Paru. It's a furry little mammal. They're really smart. People keep them as pets."

"Like a dog?" Tristys wasn't paying much attention to Rami. He wanted the thing, whatever it was, to escape. He was trying to send it luck.

"Sure, like a dog." Rami wasn't paying much attention to Tristys, either, but Tristys didn't care. The blur was getting tired. It wasn't really a blur anymore. Tristys could make out the small, furred head, with its black muzzle and white mane and a long prehensile tail with a huge tuft of fur on the end. The bird, on the other hand, was not showing any signs of fatigue, and Tristys didn't think his luck would be enough. A second later, the monkey hesitated, and the bird took the opportunity: it swooped, letting out a vicious cry, and sunk its talons around the monkey's body. Both the monkey and Tristys screamed.

"Do something!" he shouted at Rami.

Rami looked at Tristys as if he were mad. "Do something? What do you want me to do?" He laughed, presumably at Tristys's insane request. "That's a quell-beast. It's not exactly friendly. I can't ask it nicely to put the cute monkey down, you know?"

This was the second animal attack Tristys had experienced in the jungle. His mind worked quickly. The first attacker—the jungle cat—had been afraid of Rami's Water-magic. This was a firebird, right? A bird literally made of fire. Water had to scare it then, just as much if not more than the jungle cat. Rami might not be willing to confront a quell-beast, but Tristys was.

He crossed his eyes: starburst. He thought about the lances both Rami and Calissa had shot at him. He pictured them, asked the stars he saw to help. He pictured the lances bigger, growing larger as he thought about them. He flicked his wrist to fling them, and they appeared just as he'd asked, moving quickly towards the bird. His first volley was just a single arrow, but it was large and it pierced the bird's wing, leaving a small hole in the feathers of fire. The bird cried out, veering slightly to the left, but it held onto the monkey.

Fine, Tristys thought, *we can dance.* He conjured up another volley, more arrows this time, smaller with more of a point. The bird began evasive maneuvers, trying to dodge the arrows by shifting directions haphazardly, but Tristys flung so many darts that the bird didn't stand a chance. Several struck home, and the bird let out a painful shriek. One last volley, aimed at its legs, met its mark. The bird keened as it dropped the monkey. It angled downward to catch it, but Tristys shot a few more warning arrows, and the bird took the hint. It shot sunward, directly up, and disappeared.

Tristys gasped, breathing a quick "I can't believe it!" before running to find the fallen monkey. He forced his way through the dense foliage, snapping the vines with the sheer force of his determination to find the taramisk. It lay on the ground, one of its arms twisted behind its back, blood oozing from wounds in its sides. Its long, thin ears, complete with tufts on the ends, drooped along its head. It whimpered pathetically, eyes fluttering, and Tristys bent to pick it up. It cried weakly in protest, but it made no move to escape. It hadn't the energy.

Rami had come up behind him, put a hand on his shoulder. "Fix it," Tristys said simply. Tears welled in his eyes, and he had no idea why, but this monkey couldn't die.

"Tristys, what can I do?" He was rubbing

Tristys's shoulders, which felt nice, but it wasn't helping the monkey. "I have no Life-magic, and I'm not trained in the healing arts, and even if I was, that monkey is pretty beat up."

Tristys looked at the monkey. Its eyes were closing, the fluttering less fevered, and Tristys despaired. He'd saved the monkey from becoming some bird's dinner, but he couldn't save it from Death's plate after all, and it made him so angry...

The monkey's arm was still angled terribly, and it started to repulse Tristys. He had to move it, to bring it back to a normal position. He heard the monkey's bones cracking, saw it cry out in pain, and he felt blood running over his hands. He got angrier. Angrier that he had to witness this, angrier that he couldn't do anything to help, angrier that Rami couldn't either. He flushed, felt his own blood in his veins. He was so angry he saw stars. There was tingling, and he lost track of everything. It was just him and this monkey, this dying monkey; everything else had dimmed to nothing.

When his sense came back, he knew two things. First, there was no more blood pouring from the monkey, so it had finally died, and second, he was about to faint. Again. He promised himself he'd quit passing out, at least in front of Rami, because after the third or fourth time, it had to start getting old.

CHAPTER NINE

"I think," Calissa said as she placed a wet rag over Tristys's forehead, "he's Fingerprinting oş." She looked at the taramisk monkey sleeping on Tristys's chest, rising and falling with his breaths. "I don't know what else brought that monkey back, Rami."

He nodded. "Yeah, Life-magic would explain it. And you didn't see the monkey after it fell, either. That thing was... it was pretty much dead."

"It's not dead now." The monkey sneezed in agreement, turned to its other side, and placed a paw over its face.

"When is he going to wake up?"

"Tristys?" She looked down at him. His color had come back—he wasn't stark white anymore, which was the tell-tale sign of overloading on oş— and he no longer looked in pain. "Soon, probably. You said it took him a few days the first time on the beach, right?"

Rami nodded.

"Yeah, then this should be faster. The first time is always the worst. And he has his experience with eş and my training. He should be better soon."

Rami sighed audibly, and Calissa checked the dampness and temperature of the cloth. It was best to keep him warm, and the moisture helped with that. She was more worried, though, about Rami.

"What are we going to do about that monkey?" he asked.

The monkey? "What about it?"

"Well," he said, pointing at the thing, "what's it doing?"

She rolled her eyes. "It's sleeping, Rami. It just died and came back. What would you be doing?"

For the first time, he looked away from Tristys, but only long enough to roll his eyes at Calissa. "I know that, but why's it still here? I mean, why didn't it run off or whatever? Is it going to stick around forever now? Sleeping on him like that?"

She grinned. Was he jealous of the monkey, too? "I don't know about the sleeping on him part, but you know taramisk monkeys. They're really loyal once they make a bond, and I imagine resurrection from the dead is a pretty decent bond-maker."

"True," Rami said, trailing off, probably worrying about the ramifications of a new monkey in their lives.

"Hey," she said, "can you do me a favor and go scrounge up something sweet? Maybe some firespice or a bit of torladesh? When Tristys wakes up, he'll be hungry, and the sugar will do him good."

Rami nodded absently, his attention obviously still centered on the monkey and Tristys, but he left and Calissa was alone, which was exactly what she wanted. She needed time to think, and having Rami around always impeded that. He had never been low-maintenance, but he was much worse now with Tristys around. His feelings were so transparent, even more obvious than Tristys's returned affection, but she'd known Rami a lot longer. It had taken every ounce of willpower she had not to shout at them and insist they make out, but if she knew anyone, she knew Rami, and she knew that this would have to happen at his own pace.

She would, of course, be damned if she didn't try to speed things up, though. It would make her life a bit more complicated if he finally admitted to himself who he was—she'd have to find another romantic alibi—but he was such an amazing person, and from what she could tell, Tristys was, too. They deserved each other, Rami especially. He deserved to be true to himself and to find the same sort of happiness she'd once had.

Tristys interrupted her thoughts. He moaned slightly and shifted his upper body. The taramisk, half-awoken from the movement, chirped disapproval, hopped off his chest, and curled itself tightly into a ball against Tristys's side. The moan worried her. He looked pale again, too white. He didn't look pained, which was a plus, but his expression was far from placid. She'd have to try to tap her strange connection with oş again. Maybe it would help.

With more effort than she cared to admit, she forced the white stars in her vision to take precedence. She looked at Tristys, and it took only a moment to find the problem. Oş, and far too much of it, had lodged itself in Tristys, particularly his hands and arms. She prayed a moment, begging for support, and tried to nudge the clots. Nothing. As far as she knew, she was the only person in the entire Coquels who could See a quell but not commune with it. It made no sense.

She did know a bit about healing with oş, though. In every case she'd seen or heard about, healing was a lot of guesswork, a lot of massaging until you found something that felt a little off and then trying to fix that and hoping it was enough. It had never been so conspicuous, so obvious, so blunt. She wondered if Ystan would want to know about this, or if perhaps the Oşiad had any suggestions...

She considered drafting a letter on the spot, but Tristys started to wake up. He looked infinitely better, almost as if he'd never been sick in the first place. He was still groggy, though, and he didn't sit up right away.

"Good morning," Calissa said, even though it wasn't anywhere close to morning.

Tristys ran a hand through his hair and propped himself up on his elbow. That's when he noticed the monkey. He started, his eyes wide, and jumped up. The monkey snorted indignantly, but it didn't wake up.

"That thing was dead!" he said, pointing to it. "Dead dead dead dead dead!"

"I know," she said. "Or rather, I've heard, several hundred times from Rami. *Dead dead dead dead dead.*" She bent over and gave the monkey an exaggerated inspection. "But it doesn't look very dead now."

Tristys bent down with her and poked it. The monkey swatted his hand as if it were a fly. He poked it again. Another swat. A third poke, and the monkey opened an eye, yawning, and grunted once before going back to sleep.

"I guess it is alive," he said.

"Thanks to you." Rami had come from behind them while they had been determining the monkey's dead-or-alive status. He'd found a torladesh bloom, each of its eight red petals almost as large as his head. "You want something to eat? Calissa said you'd be hungry."

"Is that a blackstalk berry bloom?" Tristys asked. He was smiling, so Calissa assumed he was joking. Rami looked thrown.

"No," he said. "It's a torladesh. It's sweet. You'll like it, I promise." He handed Tristys a petal.

Tristys hesitated, but he took it. Then he hesitated again, and Calissa thought he was going to say something, but he didn't. He ripped a piece of the petal and put it in his mouth, tasting. Then he did say something, presumably what he'd been debating.

"It's good, but not as sweet as the fact that you're the first guy to give me flowers."

Calissa rolled her eyes, but Rami didn't say anything, and for a second she thought he was going to storm off again, but he didn't. He sat down on a pile of leaves and said, "I see he's back to normal again. Fast recovery, wasn't it? You want some?" He looked at Calissa, then at the bloom. She pulled off two petals and gave one to Tristys.

"Keep eating. It'll do you good."

The monkey had smelled the bloom, apparently. He'd woken up and was now staring at the petals in Tristys's hand.

"Can I feed this to it?" Tristys asked. He didn't wait for an answer, handing a small piece of the bloom to the monkey, who ate it after a few cursory smells.

"It's a him," Calissa said. "And it appears you can."

The monkey ate every bit that Tristys had given him then looked up and started pointing. These creatures really were smart! Tristys gave it another piece. "I still don't understand how this thing isn't dead. Last thing I remember, it was bleeding in my hands."

"It was all you," Rami said. "I don't really know what happened. You were staring at it, crying, and the monkey started to heal. The blood stopped, and you fainted."

Tristys blushed. "Yeah, I seem to do that a lot."

"When I tried to revive you, the monkey was breathing, totally fixed. So I brought you and it back here, and Calissa took over."

"I think," she said, taking over again, "that you Fingerprinted oş. It's an unusual Fingerprinting, since you actually did something with the quell, but... I have no other explanation for it." She didn't. It was another strange thing with Tristys and her beloved oş. She really needed to talk to Ystan, or at least somebody else in the Ośiad.

"So now what? Do we have to go to the Altar of Life-Magic or whatever?"

"The Altar of Two Souls," Calissa corrected. "And yes, I think that's the best course of action now. It's what I was going to suggest, actually."

"I think we should go to Ramidalé first," Rami said at once. "We're closer to it than to Quellos, and we can take the ferry over once we recoup, get some more supplies, things like that."

Calissa considered. She'd rather go directly to the Altar, where she'd be more likely to meet someone in the Ośiad, but Rami had a point. They were running low on supplies, and she didn't want them to have to fend for themselves in the forest. Gathering for fruits was bad enough. "I think that would be okay."

"That's what I figured," Rami said. "He Fingerprinted Life-magic, so it shouldn't be too risky. It's not like it's Fire-magic or something, you know."

"Right," Calissa said. "That's settled, then. You okay with this, Tristys?"

He looked surprised to be included. "Me? Oh, I'm fine with it. I have no idea what you two are talking about, but I assume it's for the best. So yeah, whatever." He had been chewing on torladesh the whole time, and his words had been mumbled.

"Fine. I may see if Salice wants to come with us to the Altar. I haven't seen her in a while, and I think she'll want to meet Tristys." She thought for a second and decided to test something. "And she'll probably have Gawen with her, and I'm almost positive he'll want to meet Tristys."

She was right. A brief alarm passed across Rami's face, so quickly she only caught it because she was looking. "You think they'll come?" He sounded less worried than he had looked.

"Yeah, I do. We were actually planning a trip to Quellos before I had to postpone for you guys."

"Okay," Rami said, standing up. "I guess they can come too." He offered the last petal of the torladesh to Calissa, but she declined. He took a few steps to Tristys and offered it to him, but he also declined. The monkey, however, did not. He jumped into Tristys's lap to peel off the petal, and Tristys grunted in pain.

"That cannot possibly have caused you any pain," Rami said, his hands on his hips. "The monkey weighs nothing!"

Tristys laughed, caught in his exaggeration. "I was grunting, then, because of the emotional weight of having saved a monkey's life and therefore being responsible for it for the rest of mine, okay?"

"Does that mean I'm responsible for you for the rest of my life?" Rami asked. Calissa assumed this had something to do with the alleged cat attack, which both of them had alluded to but never explained. She'd given up trying to get anything out of them.

Tristys thought a minute then grinned. "Yes, it does."

She expected an eye roll from Rami, but he smiled back. Progress!

"So we're off to Ramidalé, then, right? And I get to meet your friends!" Tristys seemed excited.

Rami nodded, and Calissa thought of something to make Tristys even happier. "It gets better," she said.

"Oh yeah?"

"Yeah." She shot a mischievous look at Rami, who was clearly worried. He probably knew what she was about to say. "You get to meet his parents, too."

~~*

Tristys had been sitting on the same trunk of the same fallen tree for the past three hours. The day had grown warmer and more humid, and the faint sound of falling water had grown clearer as the breeze picked up through the thinning trees. Ramidalé was only an hour's walk away now, and most of that walk would take them through open-air territory along the River Ramidalé. Rami and Calissa had gone ahead, "to make preparations," and promised they'd be back soon. All they'd left him with was a few bananas, an empty cup which he filled with his magic as he got thirsty, and Firebird.

Firebird was the taramisk monkey. He and Rami had agreed upon the name, although Rami'd argued at first whether he had any business naming a monkey that he insisted wasn't his. They'd had a painfully cute exchange, with Rami stating that he had nothing to do with the monkey and the monkey hopping to Rami's shoulder and combing his hair. Tristys had a hard time deciding which of the two was more adorable.

Luckily, Firebird made excellent company, though he apparently never got tired. He had woken Tristys up from a nap—twice—by bouncing on his chest. They had played three games of fetch, eaten twice, and played a game of tag. Now the monkey was sitting on Tristys's shoulder, doing something he apparently loved to do—combing hair, as long as it wasn't his own.

"Make it look good, Firebird," Tristys said. The monkey chirped an affirmative. Tristys had never thought an animal could understand human speech, but then again, he'd never thought a human could control the elements, either. "Needs to be nice for Rami!"

"And my family," Rami said. He and Calissa, both carrying bags, had emerged from the forest. Tristys stood up, a slight blush on his face, and Firebird jumped from his shoulder and ran to Rami, hopping at his legs until he swapped one bag for the monkey.

"Yes," Tristys said, trying to erase the blush, "them too." He gawked at the bags, which Rami and Calissa were now digging through. "What's in the bags?"

"We're in luck," Rami said. "It's Jungleday."

Tristys was tired of waiting, so he headed to the bags and started to pull at an edge. They were filled with lots of clothes in different colors. "And Jungleday is..."

"It's a holiday here on Quelles. And you're in luck because on this holiday, everybody wears—" she paused for effect as she pulled something from the bag, "—these!"

Three masks, two in one hand and one in the other. They were thin, just narrow bands around the eyes, really, but they were elaborately decorated. She gave the pair to Rami, and she kept the third for herself. It was bright yellow, with dozens of blue and green feathers fanning from the top. "I'm always the bird-of-paradise."

Rami examined the remaining two masks as Tristys tried to get a better look. One was a deep black, almost metallic, with fur and whiskers. The other was pale blue, with two pairs of feathered antennae and a long, tube-like appendage that hung from the bridge of the nose. "You can be the bug," he said, handing Tristys the latter mask.

"Why do I have to be the bug?" Tristys said, exaggerating the whine.

"Because you bug me." Rami laughed at his own joke. Tristys scowled.

"And why do you get to be the jungle cat that nearly killed me?"

"Because I'd like to kill you?" Rami said. Tristys kept scowling.

He knew Rami was flirting. Rami had been flirting more and more over the past few days. Tristys didn't mind, of course, but he didn't always know how to react, so he usually opted for scowling.

"Right," Calissa said, digging deep into one of the bags. "Put the rest of this on." She handed Tristys a pile of folded clothes, the same pale blue as the mask itself. "Also, you're the bug because we're going to bend the antennae so they dangle in front of your eyes and hopefully distract people from noticing that you aren't from here."

"My idea," Rami said, beaming. "And technically you're a moth, not a bug."

Tristys sighed loudly. "A moth is a bug."

"It's a type of bug."

"That's still a bug."

"Right, but you should—"

"Anyway!" Calissa said, pausing to make sure Tristys and Rami shut up. "Jungleday is basically just an excuse to dress up and have a party in the streets."

"You'll find," Rami said as he donned his mask, "that most Coquellian holidays are just excuses to dress up and have a party in the streets."

Calissa nodded as she put on her own outfit over her clothes. Tristys followed suit. The costume was light, but the fabric felt nice against his skin. The mask had a string to keep it in place, but the string was strange, and if he stretched it, it bounced back to its original length. It stayed on his head nicely. Rami bent forward to bend Tristys's antennae into place.

"Well, it's not perfect, but it's better than nothing." He flicked one of the antennae with a finger, one eyebrow raised. "Just don't talk to anyone, and if you can manage, walk with your eyes shut."

Tristys just kept on scowling.

~~*

Rami had said he'd get used to it, but Tristys was still afraid. Ten minutes in, and he was still having minor panic attacks if he looked down.

They were sitting in Rami's parents' house, which happened to be one of the highest in Ramidalé. Unlike most of the buildings in the city, they'd taken up residence in a duplex—half in the trees and half in the cliffs. He, Rami, and Calissa were sitting on one of their terraces, and even though Tristys had moved his chair as far from the edge as he could, all he had to do was stretch out his neck to see the ridiculous distance to the ground. He'd done a quick panorama when they'd gotten out here, and there were exactly two trees in the entire visible forest higher than he was. Two.

"Quit thinking about it," Rami said, his feet dangling over the edge. One nudge from Tristys and he'd plummet to his death. Tristys considered. "Salice asked you a question."

"I just asked what you thought of Ramidalé so far. And the whole Coquels, I guess." Salice had been waiting at Rami's house when they'd arrived. She was short and stocky, with dark brown hair cropped close to her head. Her ears were pierced four times on each side. Not a single one of the eight earrings was the same. "I know you haven't been here very long," she continued, "but seeing all this for the first time must be pretty shocking. Cyræa is less... elaborate than the Coquels, right?"

Tristys didn't answer right away. He looked out again from the terrace, across instead of down, to the biggest waterfall he'd seen in his life, more water falling in a second than he saw as a whole year's worth of rain in Paru. The Kysim Falls were a dribble compared to these. The falls were so close to Tristys that he could feel their mist. In the other direction were the jungle, a jumble of green, and two animals twisting around each other above the treetops. They weren't birds, because they had four legs, and they weren't monkeys, because they had wings, and their long, furred tails ended in plumage. They'd wrapped their tails around each other, and now the bigger one was hovering over the smaller one.

Tristys was pretty sure they were having sex, but he got distracted when a person, wearing the same moth mask as he was, floated by. She nodded as she went. Everyone on the terrace nodded back.

"No, this is just like Cyræa." Tristys said, still startled by the moth-lady. "You know, floating people, cats with feathers having sex in the sky, monkeys that stalk you." He looked at Firebird, who was sitting in Rami's lap playing with a stuffed toy Rami had. The monkey wasn't afraid of heights, either. "Sometimes I forget I'm not in Paru, you know?"

Salice was about to say something else, but Calissa's voice interrupted her. "Hey, can someone help me with this?" The call came from the kitchen, where she was supposed to be making a snack. "I've only got two arms."

Rami was entranced by Firebird, and Tristys was afraid to move, so neither one spoke up. They didn't have to, though, because Salice had jumped up as soon as Calissa had asked. "Be right there!" she shouted. Her voice was deep, not as deep as his, but still surprising. "I really am curious what you think of this place," she said before leaving the terrace. "Tell me when I get back?"

"If he doesn't fall over the edge first," Rami said, not even looking up from Firebird. He was grinning, though. Tristys could tell.

But he didn't say anything after that, and Tristys's mind started to wander. Salice had asked him what he'd thought of Ramidalé. How could he answer such a question? There were no words, at least none that he knew. When the three travelers had finally broken through the last of the forest's foliage and Tristys had seen Ramidalé for the first time, he couldn't believe his eyes. The waterfalls were there, of course, enormous walls of cascading water that fell from the cliffs high above the treetops to the pool below.

The city had grown organically around the falls. Buildings were anywhere they'd fit—between waterfalls, along cliff ledges, in treetops—with bridges connecting everything. Most of the bridges were made from wood and rope, but some of them looked to be made of pure water. Tristys had no idea how pure water would support a person, but he assumed it had something to do with magic.

As Tristys had gotten closer, he couldn't stop gaping at everything. People were everywhere, decked out in costumes. Most walked around; some floated. He'd finally tried tying his antennae into a knot on the top of his head, because he kept having to blow them out of his eyes to see, but Rami stopped him mid-knot and reminded him of the risk his eyes posed. So Tristys just kept blowing so he could see everything.

Back on the balcony at Rami's house, Tristys dipped his hand in the waterfall. It stung, cold and hard. He turned to Rami and Firebird, both of whom were still ignoring him, and he flung the droplets on his hands at them. "I didn't even have to use Water-magic to do that!" he said, holding his chin up in faux pride.

"Splendid," Rami said, barely reacting, but Firebird looked less than pleased as he shook himself to get the water off. Even his monkey was dramatic!

Calissa and Salice came back then, hands filled with drinks and cookies. They brought some of the banana bread he'd eaten at Telia's, but this wasn't toasted. He liked it better toasted, he decided. Salice asked the question again, and he rehashed his experience again, for the third time. The four of them spent about an hour chatting over the food. Tristys was the quiet one, still a bit awestruck by the city, even though Salice kept asking him questions, trying to make him feel welcome. Rami and Calissa, he assumed, were too used to him by now to feel obligated.

At dusk, Salice said she had to go, so they walked with her off the terrace, through the house, and to the water-bridge that led to the city proper. As they were hugging goodbye, a man and a woman approached the bridge from the other side.

"Leaving so soon, Salice?" the woman asked. She had her dark hair pinned up in an elaborate pattern and wore a beaked mask as part of her costume. She was about as tall as Tristys, though the man she had on her arm was shorter than both of them. He had on a reptilian mask, complete with fangs. He looked like a fatter, older Rami. Same black hair, same chiseled face. Different eyes, though. Rami had his mother's eyes.

"I am, Dia," Salice said as the couple crossed the water-bridge. Tristys still found something very unsettling about water that allowed you to stand on it without sinking through it. "Gawen won tickets to some sort of production in Coera, and he wants me to go with him. He feels weird on Quellas without one of its own with him."

Tristys had heard about this earlier. Gawen, who was a native of Quellus, the island of Fire, had a loud personality, and he felt unwelcome on Quellas, the island of Earth, because the zeitgeist there had to do with unadorned practicality. Allegedly, Gawen was the exact opposite.

"Well, I do hope you'll come back after you two are done. Bring Gawen with him. It'll be a treat to have the whole gang home again." The woman, Dia, shot a pointed look at Rami, who nodded.

"I'm surprised Gawen isn't taking his latest boyfriend with him to the show," the man said, his voice gruff and unfriendly. "He has a new one every few days, doesn't he?"

"I think he's single right now," Salice said. "He's in a bit of a dry spell."

"Well, do make sure you have another alternative, in the event he meets someone and abandons you at the show." The man said it in a monotone, without the slightest hint of jest or exaggeration.

"I'll be okay, Garidon," Salice said. "But I do have to go. I hate leaving so soon, but I'll be back. I think Gawen and I are going to head out to Quellos with these guys when they leave." She nodded to Rami, Calissa, and Tristys, who hadn't yet joined the conversation.

Dia turned from Salice to Rami. "You are going again so soon?" Her mouth was a thin line of disappointment.

"Not right away," Rami said, stepping forward. "Tristys Fingerprinted Life-magic earlier—"

"Congratulations!" Dia interrupted. She pulled Tristys into a deep hug. She didn't even know who he was, but apparently it didn't matter. "What a way to start your time here on the islands! Two quell, and you've only been here a few weeks!" Or maybe she did know who he was...

"He Fingerprinted, and you came here instead of going straight to the Altar?" Garidon asked. He put a hand on Dia's shoulder, pulling her away from Tristys. "Are you sure—"

"Don't worry, Garidon," Calissa said. As soon as she spoke, Garidon's harsh expression softened. "He didn't Fingerprint, really. I'm not sure what to call it. He used oş, basically, without meaning to."

Garidon looked confused. "I don't—"

"He saved a monkey, Father."

Garidon looked further confused. "I still don't—"

As if on cue, Firebird jumped off Tristys's arm, where he'd been hanging and started hopping at Rami's foot. As Rami explained, he picked Firebird up. "This guy. He saved him from a firebird. Then in some sick twist of irony, he named him Firebird." Rami grinned. Garidon looked hostile.

"He saved a monkey from a quell-beast with Life-magic?"

Tristys sighed. "No, I used waterbolts to save him from the bird. I used... well, whatever I did... he'd been hurt. He was dying, bleeding all over the place. His arm was broken too, I think. Anyway, I—"

Garidon interrupted him, but he addressed Rami. "You should have gone straight to the Altar. Calissa, I'm surprised. I would expect that you'd understand the—"

"It's fine, Garidon. He hasn't shown any

Fingerprinting since the incident, and in this case, it was a blessing, not a danger. If anything else happens, we'll leave at once."

Dia's face lit up. "So you are staying for a while, then?"

Rami nodded.

"That's wonderful!" She took Tristys by the arm, shirking the hold her husband had on her shoulders. "That will give us time to get to know each other. I'm absolutely fascinated by foreign cultures, you know. I read an entire book on the Cyrītsī religion you people believe in. You'll have to tell me all about it!"

"Okay, I'm leaving for real now," Salice said. She'd gotten about halfway across the water-bridge before she got distracted by the drama with Garidon and Fingerprinting. "Goodbye!" she said, waving as she left.

"Oh!" Dia put a hand to her cheek. "How rude of us! We haven't even introduced ourselves, Garidon!" She took a step away from Tristys and stood up, suddenly formal. "My name is Diala eś Loratis, and this"—she put a hand on Garidon's shoulder—"is Garidon eś Harys. We're Rami's parents, in case it wasn't clear."

Tristys chuckled. "It was pretty clear, actually. You look just like him, sir." He turned back to Dia. "And he has your eyes."

"I can't even see your eyes beneath those antennae!" Dia said, craning her neck to try and peek beneath them. "Rami mentioned earlier that they were something else. You'll have to excuse me." She used a hand to lift up both sets of antennae. "This moth costume, I can't believe he let you wear it. Rami loves moths, you know. He wore this costume every year since he was six."

She gasped. "Oh, your eyes are breath-taking! Garidon, you have to—"

"Leave the boy and his eyes alone, Diala." Garidon took a hold of his wife again and pulled her—again—away from Tristys. It was beginning to feel like a strange tug-of-war, one that Tristys didn't really want to participate in. He shot a glance at Rami for help, but Rami had his head down and... was he blushing?

There was a brief, but awkward, silence. Dia came to the rescue. "Well, shall we go upstairs, then? No sense in staying here!" She had a point: They lived far enough away from the main thoroughfare that few people walked by, and the scenery wasn't that great, either.

She put her hands out and started forward, ushering Tristys, Rami, and Calissa back into the house. Garidon followed. "Are you hungry? Garidon and I were talking about pancakes..."

"What are pancakes?" Tristys asked.

Dia stopped and looked compassionate. "Oh, you poor dear. You have missed out on so much."

"What are pancakes?" Tristys asked again, smiling. He had a feeling pancakes weren't quite as big a deal as she was making them out to be.

"A pancake," she said, "is—"

"He can eat pancakes tomorrow," Garidon said from behind them. "I'm tired, Dia."

"So?" she asked. "Go to bed. You don't have to eat the pancakes."

"Diala, I don't think—"

"It's fine, Mother." Rami wasn't blushing anymore. "We're all tired. We can do pancakes for breakfast."

"We just had some snacks, too," Calissa added, "so we probably wouldn't even eat that many."

Dia looked disappointed again, but she relented. "Fine, then. Tomorrow morning, Tristys?"

He really wanted to know what a pancake was, but he wasn't about to disagree with Rami, Calissa, and Garidon. "Sounds good to me," he said.

"I'll wake you bright and early!" she said as Garidon pulled her down the hallway that led to their bedroom. "Sleep well!"

"Goodnight, children," Garidon shouted. He didn't even look at them as he said it, and Tristys had the sinking suspicion that unlike his wife, Garidon was not very fond of foreigners.

CHAPTER TEN

Almost two weeks later, lying in his bed in Garidon and Dia's spare room, Tristys couldn't sleep. Rather, he wouldn't sleep. He didn't want to wake up the next day, because the next day was his departure from Ramidalé. They were going to Quellos, the island of Life-magic, and the Altar of Two Souls. That meant more magic, but it also meant more treks through uncharted forest, more sleeping on the hard ground, and more having to forage for food. He wasn't ashamed to admit that he'd grown accustomed to the civilized life.

Sure, the forests were beautiful, but Tristys was a city boy at heart. He suspected it when he lived in Paru, and after having spent almost two weeks in Ramidalé, he knew it for sure. He loved everything about this city: the dozens of tiers that made no logical sense whatsoever and the houses next to offices next to waterfalls next to walkways that went nowhere. He'd fallen in love as soon as he crossed the first rope bridge that led him to nothing. It existed simply to exist, and it was perfect. In a city so tightly packed, with buildings nestled literally on top of each other, it was as if some builder had simply got distracted and forgot to finish whatever he intended to put at the end of the bridge. Tristys loved it.

He'd worried at first, thinking that he'd get bored of the city after a few days, but that was impossible. There was so much to do here! His new favorite activity was shopping, albeit with his eyes turned down. Paru had stores, of course, but they were nothing like this. They sold necessities and nothing more. You went in, you got what you needed, you left. Here, though, shopping was an art. You could buy literally anything you wanted, from basic food and clothing to musical instruments and elaborate costumes. There were stores that sold 'fast food', which you ate right on the spot without having to take it home to prepare. It was genius!

On his second shopping trip with Calissa and Rami, she'd taken him into a small, squat store next to a restaurant they'd just eaten at. The store was called the Pleasure Chest, and as soon as he realized what the scanty clothing and edible lotions and oddly shaped objects were for, he couldn't get the blush to leave his face. He'd felt silly, so immature for blushing at sex, but when he caught Rami staring at something hidden from his view, Rami had blushed a deeper scarlet than Tristys. He tried to catch a peek, to see what it was, but Rami grabbed him by the shoulders and dragged him outside to wait for Calissa, who came out a few minutes later. She hadn't bought anything, and Tristys sighed with relief, though he vowed to go back at some point to see what had caught Rami's eye.

They'd gone to a pet store next. Pet stores, Tristys learned, were places you could buy animals like Firebird. Tristys also learned that people in Ramidalé were very fond of pets; he'd gone shopping quite a few times over the past few weeks, and he'd been in more pet stores than he thought possible. Firebird wasn't a fan, either, so they never stayed long; he got finicky with the other animals in cages. Rami had insisted they buy a stuffed toy for Firebird in one of the stores—a banana—and the monkey played with it for approximately two minutes before dropping it and jumping to Tristys's shoulder to comb his hair. Tristys made Rami carry the banana out in the open the rest of that day. Come to think of it, he'd never even gotten it back.

He had grown rather attached to Rami's mother, Dia, too. The morning after they'd arrived, she had torn into his room at sunrise to wake him up and drag him down to the kitchen for his introduction to the elusive pancake. There were three stacks of what turned out to be the most delicious, fluffy thing he'd ever eaten already on the table, waiting for him. She'd whispered to him conspiratorially that she wanted him to have his share without the hassle of the others, and with her help, he ate all three stacks.

"Not a problem!" she'd assured him. "We'll make more!" They had spent the rest of the morning making dozens and dozens of pancakes, Tristys getting so good at it he even added his own ingredients—some berries that he knew Rami loved. By the time the others had come downstairs, they had five stacks prepared. They were also covered in flour and batter, but nobody seemed to mind—except Garidon, who mumbled something about looking like children and acting like them, too. But everyone had loved the pancakes. Even Garidon.

He'd asked Dia about her husband on one of their shopping trips together. They'd gone together nearly every day, with Tristys helping to choose their dinners or which outfit looked best with Dia's complexion. "So, out of curiosity, why does Garidon hate me?" he'd asked one day as they ate his new favorite food, flatbread baked with cheese on top. "Is it a foreign thing? Or did I do something wrong?" He was afraid Garidon hated him because he was diverted, but he'd never spoken to anyone about that here, so he kept quiet.

"Garidon doesn't hate you," she had said before she popped another bite of the bread into her mouth. "He just takes a bit to warm up to Tristys's friends. The only one he really likes is Calissa, and I think that's just because she's pretty." She'd laughed to herself, a pleasant little chuckle, but Tristys wasn't sure why that was funny. "He still hasn't even really taken a liking to Gawen, and he's been around for quite a few years now." She paused a minute, as if something just struck her. "You know, when you meet Gawen, I think it'll be good for you. You two may hit it off." She'd winked.

He'd been flabbergasted. "How did you know I was diverted?" He hadn't said a word, unless Rami...

"Oh, dearheart, please. It's not hard to figure out." He must have looked worried, because she had put her hand over his. "Don't worry. Call it mother's intuition. Besides, I'm sure Rami has told you this, nobody cares about things like that here. 'Diverted' is a Cyræan word; we don't even have a translation for that, because it doesn't matter. Whether you're attracted to men or to women, it's all just love here." She grinned mischievously. "Or lust, I suppose, depending."

That conversation had thrown him for a loop. He knew quite well that Coquellians didn't care about his sexuality. He'd seen quite a few same-sex couples walking through Ramidalé, holding hands, sometimes even kissing, and nobody (except him, of course) gave them a second glance.

He hadn't realized, however, that his own predilection was so easy to detect. He wondered how many other people knew, if strangers could tell just by looking at him as easy as they'd know he wasn't from the islands if they saw his eyes. He wondered if Garidon knew. Despite Dia's assurances, Tristys still felt as if Garidon wasn't a fan, and perhaps it had to do with his diversion after all. Maybe Garidon cared? He needed to sleep, but that'd never happen if he kept allowing his mind to wander like this, so he tried his meditation tactics. He emptied his mind of everything, tried not to think about a thing, and just lay there. It would have worked, had he not heard the knocking.

It was so soft he wasn't even sure he'd heard it. Perhaps it was just a figment of his over-exhausted imagination? But no, there it was again—a definite rapping on his door. He glanced at the window. The night was still thick; not even the sun was thinking about getting up yet. But there was definitely someone there, so he had no choice. He threw off his covers and opened the door, his eyes still half shut.

It was Rami. He stepped inside Tristys's bedroom without a word, shut the door softly, and turned to Tristys. For a second, Tristys wondered if he was dreaming. He'd know if Rami jumped him. That was always the giveaway.

But no, Rami just said, "Did I wake you?"

Tristys snorted. "It's pitch black outside! What do you think?"

"I'm sorry," Rami said. Tristys almost

admitted that he hadn't actually been asleep, but he liked seeing Rami squirm a bit too much. "I wanted to show you something, though, and now is the best time to go."

Tristys was torn between his bed and his desire to see what Rami was talking about. "And it can't wait until I get a little bit of sleep?"

Rami was stone. "No."

"Fine, then. Let me get dressed."

"No time," Rami said, grabbing Tristys by the wrist.

"Are you insane? I'm in my pajamas!" Tristys grabbed his thin shirt and held it up for emphasis. The sleep had left his eyes, but it hadn't left his mouth. "And I need to brush my teeth." He smacked his lips.

"What? We don't have time." Rami started to pull him gently by the wrist. "You don't need to brush your teeth. I'm not going to kiss you tonight."

Tristys perked up and latched on to that last word. "Tonight, eh? Does that mean you're planning on kissing me tomorrow?"

Rami let his wrist go. "Shut up and brush your teeth," he said, flopping onto Tristys's bed and burying his hands beneath his pillow. Tristys had to resist the urge to flop on the bed next to him.

Ten minutes later, Rami was at the bathroom door, demanding that Tristys hurry up. Tristys had been ready for a few minutes, but he liked to tease. When he tried to fix his hair for the third time, Rami muttered a curse, grabbed him by the wrist, and pulled. Tristys shrieked the entire way out of the house about his hair, though he did lower his voice when Rami mentioned if he woke anyone up they'd want to come along. If Rami wanted to be alone with him, Tristys wasn't going to be the one to ruin it.

"We better not miss this because of your damn hair," Rami said later as he led Tristys through the forest. They'd left the city via seldom-used pathways that Tristys hadn't explored. "Especially since your hair looks the same as it always does, no matter how much time you put into it." He quit walking for a second to flick Tristys's hair, which had grown even more and still needed a cut.

"You know, Firebird does that all the time." He used his palm to flatten the piece that Rami had flicked. "I think you're spending too much time together. Perhaps you should cut back."

"Eh, what can I say?" Rami asked, continuing the joke. "He's the only male friend I've got that doesn't make me want to jump off the Ramidalé Rises." A second later, he added, "Which, by the way, is where we're going."

Tristys had figured they were going somewhere high. Their path had been consistently uphill, and he could see the face of a mountain not far ahead with a steep path along it. From the looks of it, it was heading away from the waterfalls, but Tristys figured it'd curve back around to them.

He was right. After a few moments on the path, it curved sharply around itself and headed back to the falls. They turned another corner, and Tristys felt as if he were at the end of the world. These weren't mountains that supported the Ramidalé Rises; this was the very end of the island of Quelles, which was shaped like a giant bowl, with walls made of these cliffs. The top of the waterfalls was here, too, an enormous pool far too peaceful, the surface perfectly smooth, not a ripple, not a wave. This was impossible, with the frantic rush of the waterfalls just over the edge, but here it was. This was Quelles.

"Rami, I can't—"

"Wait," he said. "It gets better. Close your eyes." Tristys gave him a suspicious look, but he listened. Rami led him a few steps forward. "Okay, open them."

Tristys listened. He saw the whole island stretched out before him. Everything was there: the pool at the bottom of the falls, the green forest lying like a quilt across his view, each wrinkle a river. He saw the Bluewood, too, patched into the distance. "I've never—"

"Wait!" Rami said again, his excitement making his words come fast. "There's even more. Close them again."

This time when Tristys opened his eyes, he saw water. This was the Coquelai, the vast ocean that he'd crossed to get here. The waters were wild, white spray beating against the rocky sides of Quelles far below. It was another majestic sight, but what took his breath away was what was happening to his left along the face of the cliffs. It was an exact duplicate of the Ramidalé Rises on this side, with one drastic difference: here, the water was rising, not falling, out of the ocean and into the pool that fed the waterfalls on the other side.

"This is why we call this the Ramidalé Rises. It's something of a natural wonder here. No one knows what's going on, really. The best Water-practitioners in the world can't stop this water from flowing into Quelles, and trust me, the best have tried." He moved a little closer to Tristys to get a better look at the Rises proper. "I think it's beautiful, actually. The way nobody can explain it, not even magic. The way it fights everything, even gravity, and wins. There's no reason to it, but it's here anyway. It just doesn't care, you know?"

Tristys nodded slowly, so distracted he barely felt Rami put a hand on his shoulder.

"There's one more thing," Rami said. "Just give it a moment." Rami turned Tristys around so that his gaze ran along the curve of the island's wall. Then it happened: the sun rose. At first it peeked above the far cliff, the first rays striking the pool's crystal surface and reflecting brightly back at Tristys. As the minutes passed, the rays moved along the pool, waltzing with their reflections. Tristys sat down, spellbound, and Rami sat next to him. Their shoulders touched. Neither spoke, but words weren't necessary or welcome. The sun was enough.

Once the sunrise had ended, Tristys finally spoke. "That's the first sunrise I've seen since the morning after you found me." He remembered it so clearly in his head. "Do you remember?"

"I remember," he said. "That was the day I woke you up too early, right?"

"Right." Tristys leaned into Rami, very tentatively. He didn't want to frighten him, but he wanted to feel his presence a little more firmly. "Do you remember what I said to you when you apologized?"

Rami's eyes narrowed in concentration. He nodded.

"You see then?" Tristys said. "I was right. There's still no sunrise without you."

Rami's face lit up and a smile rose on his face. He put his hand around Tristys's shoulder, and Tristys leaned a little bit less tentatively.

They watched the sun glimmer on the pool for a few more moments, and just as Tristys was about to stand up, he felt Rami shift. Rami said something, quietly, almost inaudibly: "How is it so easy for you?"

Tristys didn't follow. "How is what so easy?"

"Just—I don't know." Rami was struggling. He wasn't looking at Tristys, instead devoting all his attention to a small stone he'd picked up off the ground and was now spinning frantically in his hand. "I don't know. Never mind. Forget it."

"No," Tristys said, putting a hand on the stone to stop it. "Why is what so easy?"

Rami looked up then, his eyes bent in his effort to understand, to explain. "It just seems so easy for you. I don't know how you do it, especially since you're not from here."

Tristys bit his lip. "Rami, I still don't know what you're talking about."

"Just—just being you. Being okay with everything. With who you are." A second passed, and he said more quietly, "With who you like."

Understanding dawned in Tristys, and his heart sped up. "Rami, you've only known me for a little bit." He wanted to tread lightly, carefully. Rami was opening up, and Tristys didn't want to scare him back into closing off. "It wasn't always easy, you know? Where I'm from, back in Paru, being diverted is a sin, and people—"

"Exactly!" Rami said, the temporary excitement shadowing his anguish. "People hate you where you're from, hate you for no good reason, and you're still fine with it. You're fine with everything. It makes you who you are, and it makes you you, and it's good." He was shaking his head now, staring back at the stone. "But here, nobody cares, not at all. But I'm—I'm—" He hung his head. "I can't."

"Rami, listen to me." He hazarded a physical touch, taking Rami's face by the cheek and forcing him to look his way. "I'm not fine with it. I wasn't fine with the way people were in Paru. That's why I ran away, remember? When Vun'gor found me— captured me, really—I was running away, because I wasn't okay at home anymore. I felt terrible about myself, about what had happened to my family just because I liked men." He shut his eyes a second, trying to hold the bad memories at bay. All the hate, the mean words, the abuse. The fire. "If I hadn't met Vun'gor, if he hadn't shown me that it's okay, then I don't know if I'd be the way I am today." He opened his eyes. Rami was still staring rockward. Tristys tried to lighten the mood—"I definitely wouldn't be where I am today, right?"—but Rami didn't bite.

"I just—I'm so scared of hurting someone again, Tristys. Of hurting you." He was crying now, muted tears falling down his cheeks, and Tristys wanted to kiss them away, with his thumbs if not his lips. "I can't hurt again. I hurt Tierran, you know? I'm so scared of it. With you, it's good, it's right, but with me, with my name, it's bad. It's not good, at all. So I ignore it, so everyone stays safe, because I'm Ramidon now, not Ramis. Or I was Ramidon, for twelve years I was, but now here you are, and now everything is so—"

"Rami!" A voice from behind them, someone Tristys didn't know and would probably end up murdering in a second. "Dude from not-the-Coquels!" It was a male voice, but it was high-pitched and invasive. The 's' at the end of Coquels sizzled. "Is that you over there?" Tristys felt Rami shut down, like a chicken that'd just had its neck wrung back home. Tristys decided murder was definitely in order.

He turned his head. Salice was heading in their direction behind the owner of the high-pitched voice who'd wrecked the moment. He was tall, taller than Tristys, with a thin, tanned body. He had red hair swept back and up like a flame. This had to be Gawen.

"His name is Tristys," he heard Salice say. "I've only told you that ten hundred times." She hit him on the shoulder. "And you shouldn't be yelling about a foreigner, anyway! Do you want him to get exiled?"

"Please, Salice. Get over it. There's nobody here but us." Tristys saw Gawen do a quick check left to right, just in case. "See?"

Rami sniffled a few times and stood up, dusting off his pants and giving his head a shake. "You made it back in time, I see?" Everything was bottled back up inside, tight. Tristys could tell.

"We did," Salice said. "I practically had to knock Gawen out to get him here, though. He met some guy in Coera and wouldn't leave."

"You should have seen him," Gawen said, walking towards Rami and standing a step too close. "He was gorgeous. Built like a rock. Short, dark hair. Tan skin." Tristys had a sneaking suspicion that Gawen was simply describing his opposite. "Born and bred in the Coquels." Suspicion confirmed. "He was perfect."

"Well, I'm sorry you two had to part," Rami said. He didn't sound very concerned.

"It's okay," Gawen said. "You love 'em, then you leave 'em. You know how it goes." He'd been talking to Rami this entire time, but he hadn't stopped looking at Tristys. Tristys hadn't stopped looking at him, either. He had some sort of design on his face. It surrounded his left eye, stretching down his cheek. It was a faint red, but the sunlight made it stand out.

"What's your design?" He spoke too loudly, and Rami flinched.

Gawen started a bit, as if he were surprised that Tristys could speak. "My tattoo," he said, acting as if Tristys's ignorance were embarrassing, "is a flame. I'm from Quellus, the land of—"

"Yeah, Fire-magic." Tristys cut him off pertly. "I get it."

"Anyway," Salice said, trying to intercept the aggression. "We just wanted to let you know we finally got back. You weren't home, so we figured you'd be here. You always come here before you leave." She said it as if she couldn't quite understand why. She must be blind.

"You know me too well, Salice." Rami smiled, and it was genuine.

"I do." She took Gawen by the arm again. "But we'll see you down at the house. Garidon was up, and he told us we could wait there until we're ready to head to the ferries. As if we wouldn't have waited there anyway, right?"

Rami nodded understanding. "You know my father."

"I do," she said again, though this time she didn't sound as happy about it.

"Will you two be much longer up here?" Gawen asked. Still staring at Tristys, he was. It was starting to bother him. "We should catch up." Finally, he looked away. Now he was staring at Rami.

"A few more minutes, I think," Rami said. "I'll

see you down there."

Tristys and Rami stood while Salice and Gawen left the way they'd come. Tristys kept looking at Rami, to see if he'd let his walls down again, but he was stone. Once Salice and Gawen had disappeared completely, Rami turned around again to face the Coquelai, but he didn't sit down.

"So, where were we?" Tristys tried, but he got nothing. Rami stayed silent, his jaw set and his eyes secured to the ocean's horizon. It wasn't an uncomfortable silence, but Tristys didn't like it, either.

"You ready?" Rami finally asked after a few minutes. Tristys's legs were getting tired, and he had just been about to sit. Instead, he nodded, and Rami led the way back to Ramidale, back to his parents' house.

He said nothing the entire time. When he finally did speak—to say goodnight outside his bedroom—Tristys jumped. The voice sounded foreign, distant, like a stranger, and Tristys hoped the damage Salice and Gawen had done tonight wouldn't send Rami into another personality-changing spiral. When Tristys turned to return the goodnight, Rami had already gone.

"So, your father said something strange to me last night," Gawen said to Rami. They were sitting on the Daléan ferry to Quellos, in a six-person suite near the front of the boat. Tristys, Calissa, and Salice had gone to get snacks, leaving Rami and Gawen to save their seats. Rami would have preferred a suite beneath deck, out of the main thoroughfare, to keep Tristys as hidden as possible, but Tristys loved the view.

"Oh yeah?" Rami wasn't paying attention. Rami rarely paid attention to Gawen.

"Yeah. I don't think he thought I could hear him, but after Salice and I stopped by to let you know we made it in time to go, he looked at Dia and said, 'He's going, too? This just keeps getting better'. I'm pretty sure he was being sarcastic."

"I wouldn't worry about it." Rami had just opened a book he'd been trying to read since before Tristys even got to the islands. Tristys, as it turned out, took up a lot of his time. "He's not the happiest man around, you know?"

"I don't think he likes me very much."

"He doesn't like anyone very much."

"I suppose," Gawen said, letting the conversation drop. Rami wasn't entirely sure why he'd even brought it up, but Gawen had never been that easy to read. He always had a reason to do what he did, but Rami could rarely see it. "At least the weather is gorgeous today, isn't it? The temperature's perfect, the humidity's just right without Water-practitioners screwing with it, and look at that sky! It's utterly fabulous. It's as blue as Tristys's eye." He paused. "The right one, of course."

"The right one is green," Rami said at once, without thinking or looking up from his chapter. He mentally kicked himself. Did he really have to be so obvious?

Gawen looked satisfied, as if he'd been testing him. "So it is. So it is."

Rami had to cover his slipup, and the best way to do that was to get Gawen talking about himself. "Anyway, just ignore my father. That's what I do."

"I still don't think he likes me."

"Who doesn't like you?" Salice asked. They'd just returned, and Salice had entered their group of chairs first. She sat next to Rami at a small table, on which she placed the sandwiches and drinks she had with her. Firebird jumped from his lap to the table and grabbed a sandwich. Calissa came in next, grinning at the monkey and sitting by Salice, and Tristys took the bench across from Rami. His hair had been blowing in the open-air wind all day, and it looked even more disheveled than usual. It fit him, the wildness matching the little spark in his personality. Rami liked it.

"Rami's father."

"Oh, he doesn't like me, either," Tristys said. That was the nicest thing Tristys had said to Gawen the whole day. "I like to think it's because I'm a foreigner, not because I'm diverted."

"How does that make it any better?" Calissa asked through a mouthful of sandwich.

"I don't know," Tristys said, blowing a flapping bang out of his eyes, "but it does."

"Perhaps you consider yourself more intrinsically diverted than foreign, and so hatred based on that would be more hateful?" Gawen said. He blew a puff of a wood cigarette he'd been smoking.

"Maybe," Tristys looked thoughtful. "I've been diverted my whole life, after all, and I've only been foreign for about a month."

"Can we stop calling it diverted?" Salice squealed. The word seemed to bother her; Rami wasn't a fan of it, either.

"I don't know what else to call it!"

"Why do you have to call it anything?" She was calmer now, but her face was tinted a slight pink. "There's no word for being blue-eyed or blonde-haired. Why make a word for liking the same sex?"

"Because that's the only way they can demonize it," Calissa said. "Giving it a name makes it stand out, makes it special, right? And special can be good-special or bad-special. They made it bad-special." Calissa was never more insightful than when she was eating a sandwich.

Gawen didn't care. He was too focused on Tristys suddenly. "You've known you were diverted forever, then?"

"Not forever." Tristys laughed. "I've only been alive for twenty-two years." Nobody laughed with him, except Rami, who cracked a smile, but Tristys didn't notice. "I've known for a long time, though. As long as I can remember."

"How did you know?"

Tristys pursed his lips. "That's a long story. It has a lot to do with my brother, actually."

Gawen leered. "If your brother is half as good-looking as you are, I'd like details."

Tristys blushed, and Rami rolled his eyes. He wasn't actually falling for Gawen's shtick, was he?

"He did look a lot like me, actually." Tristys's eyes seemed unfocused, wistful. "He wasn't diverted, though. No one was, except me and Kitadyn. Kitadyn was my first crush. His parents lived in the panhandle forever, and it showed. He was well-built, tall and dark with dimples."

"He sounds dreamy," Gawen said.

Tristys looked at Rami. "He looked a lot like you, actually." He compared a bit. "You've got a better body, though. And he looked less—I dunno—foreign."

"Definitely dreamy," Gawen said again.

"I bet he didn't have violet eyes," Rami heard himself say. Was he actually trying to one-up some random kid from the Cyræan panhandle?

"No," Tristys said, "nobody has eyes like yours in Cyræa."

"Everybody has violet eyes in the Coquels, though," Rami said.

He looked at Tristys to gauge his reaction, but neither Tristys nor Gawen were even paying him any attention. They were both staring above his head, curious looks on their faces. Gawen's mouth was agog. *Why?*

He turned around and his own past smacked him hard in the face. It was him. He was alive. *He was alive.* Why was he alive? He couldn't be alive, he had to be dead. Rami had killed him, by accident. Why was he—

"But nobody has eyes like yours, not here and not anywhere." His voice was the same, deep and smooth and hot like fire. His hair was longer, but it was the same deep brown, mahogany eyes to match. His face had matured, but that's what happened in ten years.

"Tierran, I don't—I can't—" He couldn't complete a sentence. He'd been thrown back in time, to that meditation room, to an unexpected but not unwelcome kiss that led to the Water-blast that changed his life and ended, he thought, Tierran's. "I thought I—"

"Later, Ramis," he said, silencing him at once. "First, I think introductions are in order. You seem to have found some friends since we last saw each other." His head turned slowly, panning the social vista. "I am Tierran uś Gaweth."

"Lovely. How do you know Rami?" Gawen was no-nonsense, all business. His arms were crossed in front of him, even though he was sitting down.

"He and I met at the Altar of Five Waves many

years ago, when we were both trying to commune with Water." Tierran didn't skip a beat. "And you are?"

"Gawen," Gawen said. "Gawen uś Ratoth."

"Ah, from the island of Fire, like myself. I should have known by the tattoo, yes?"

Gawen nodded, a terse movement. His lips stayed pursed.

Tierran turned to Salice. "And you must be from the island of Earth, correct?"

"Salice aś Saltar," she said.

"And named after the greatest seyan that island has ever seen, no less! May your domes stay as strong as hers!" Rami was watching the proceedings in a state of shock. He dimly noted how formal Tierran was being, with the dramatic introductions and the return to archaic greetings, but he didn't really care. It didn't really register. This was Tierran. Tierran! Everything he'd believed the past ten years was a lie...

"And the beautiful blonde over there?" He nodded in Tristys's direction.

"Calissa eś Temeran."

"And now we have someone related to a great seyan! I am honored to be in your presence." He bowed too deeply, and Calissa rolled her eyes. He wasn't making a very good impression.

"And from what part of Cyræa do you hail?" He was looking at Tristys, directly at him, with a grin somewhere between pleasure and sadism.

"How did you—"

"Oh, let's not be coy. You practically exude strangeness." Tierran squinted, leaned towards Tristys. "And those eyes!"

"He probably heard our conversation," Gawen said, stretching his back and puffing out his chest.

"Tristys looks entirely normal to me."

"Please, Gawen. It was Gawen, right? His eyes are changing colors."

Tristys looked down immediately, and Tierran leaped at him. He put a hand beneath his chin and lifted. "No, never do that. Never hide what you are."

The advance snapped Rami back into action. Words were starting to form again, coherent thoughts, and sentences. "What are you doing, Tierran?"

"Why, I'm going to Cimedalé," he said, still grinning that wry grin. "Just as you five are."

"Now who's being coy?" Rami's words were angry, but Rami himself wasn't entirely sure how he felt. "My entire life, I thought I've—" He cut himself short, before he said what he was about to say. There were too many people around, including his friends. He wasn't ready for that, not yet, not this type of confession so soon. "We have to talk."

"Shall we get a drink, then?" Tierran motioned behind him. "I have a suite in one of the lower bedrooms. The view is astounding."

"Rami, I wouldn't go in any—" Calissa started.

"We'll get a drink," Rami said, already standing up. "Not in your bedroom. That's it."

A few minutes later, they were standing together in as deserted a hallway as Rami could find. It was on one of the lowest levels of the ferry, some of the nicest rooms on board, and so the traffic here was almost non-existent. The walls were glass, and he leaned against it. Out of the corner of his eye he saw an enormous fish, blue and black and green, swim by. He swore it stopped to listen.

This wasn't about the fish. "I thought you died."

Tierran wasn't looking at him, browsing at his surroundings, feigning disinterest or boredom. "I didn't."

"I thought I killed you."

"You didn't."

"Why didn't somebody tell me?" His voice was strained now, the pace of his speech quickened. "They came in, and you weren't moving, and Liana started yelling. I desecrated the Altar, she said. I blasphemed eṣ, I spit on the quell, and I killed you. She told me I killed you, you were dead and it was my fault." Tierran still looked bored. Rami stopped, felt the same overwhelming helplessness and defeat wash over him. "I asked about you, but nobody would tell me anything."

"Well, I'm telling you now I didn't die. I was sick for a very long time, and they said at first they thought I'd drown from the blast you threw at me. Perhaps—"

"I didn't throw it at you!" Rami shouted, trying to quiet his voice at the end. He couldn't see straight; things kept blurring. He kept living the moment over and over again, kneeling in the alcove, the pale blue light, Tierran just inches away leaning in to kiss, to kiss him! And suddenly the blast, the quell shooting out of him so unexpectedly, so against his will, like a warning. "I wanted you to kiss me. That's all I wanted. When you leaned in, I don't know what happened."

"You wanted to kiss me?" His twisted smile straightened a bit.

"Of course, Tierran." Rami paused, couldn't believe he was about to say what he was about to say. "I thought I loved you. Then everything happened, and I thought my feelings were bad, that the quell didn't want me to love you or become Ramis the Betrayer. I didn't know what, but I thought my power and love and your death were linked, and when Liana started shouting—"

For the first time, Tierran actually looked present. Concerned, even. "Ramis, you aren't the Betrayer."

"I know, but he did what he did to Ramidon because he wanted him, and when Ramidon rejected his love, he—"

"I know the story," Tierran interrupted. He put a hand on Rami's shoulder and drew him close. For a panicked second, Rami thought he was going to kiss him, but he didn't get that close. "You know the story, too. It wasn't love that led Ramis to betray Ramidon. That was jealousy. Okay?"

Rami nodded. He was trying very hard to keep it together, to not let his emotions run out in waves from his eyes. He didn't want to cry, not in front of Tierran.

"If anything, Ramis's love saved the day, made him a hero. He gave his life to save Ramidon on the beach after Bellimar almost killed him, right?"

"Right, but Bellimar wouldn't have been able to kill him if Ramis hadn't betrayed him in the first place because he was—"

"Ramis, quit it! This is stupid! You're being stupid!" Tierran turned to the glass, away from Rami. The view was empty, just water as far as Rami could see. Even the fish had grown bored.

"I know. I've always known. Maybe that's why I was so quick to use Water-magic to save Tristys. But I was young, young and scared and traumatized. Even if I couldn't explain it, you were dead! I thought you were dead! Don't you see how much that can screw a kid up? I thought my love killed you!"

"For that, I am sorry, but I—"

"Why didn't you come to me when you got better? Find me or something. Or at least tell me."

"I didn't think you'd want to know. I thought you sent that blast on purpose, remember? You're talking about how much trauma you went through. How do you think I felt?"

Rami had never thought about how Tierran might have felt, because Rami had never thought Tierran survived. But he had a point. "You still should have found me. You've lived all these years thinking I hated you, and I've lived all these years thinking you were dead. And now you're not."

"Right. I'm not dead. So we can go back to how we were." For the first time, Tierran looked invested in what Rami had to say. "Nothing needs to have changed. We're just a little older now. That's all."

Rami's mouth dropped. "Everything has changed, Tierran! I thought I killed you!" The realization of just how greatly he'd changed his own life because of that hit Rami like a blast of Water-magic. "I'm nothing like the boy I was back then, and it's your fault. And you think I can just be with you now?"

Tierran's face dropped. "Is this about the blond, then? Is that what has changed?"

"Calissa?" What did she have to do with this?

"Don't be dense, Ramis. The foreigner. Are you and he together?"

Tristys. He was talking about Tristys. Another blast of Water-magic. Were his feelings for Tristys that transparent that even this stranger could see? "No, of course not." But were they? Were they together? They clearly had feelings for each other. But Rami had spent most of his life pushing that type of feeling aside. And what about Calissa? What would she say? And his family? And Gawen! He could barely keep Gawen at arm's length before—how would he do it now?

It was too much. He was drowning. "Ramis, are you okay?"

Rami bowed his head, tried to take a deep breath, couldn't. "Don't call me Ramis," he said quietly. He leaned against the wall of glass. The cold felt good through his shirt. Water always calmed him.

"Ramis, let's go to my—"

"Please go." His eyes were shut, his arms pressed against the wall, palms flat. "I need you to leave."

"Ramis, please, let's—"

"No!" Rami shouted, pushing off the glass. His arms tingled, almost as if he were calling on Water-magic. "Please, just go."

Tierran started to walk towards Rami, then stopped, a surprised look on his face. Perhaps he remembered the blast of Water-magic from the Altar so many years ago. Perhaps it had to do with the small rivulets of water flowing freely along Rami's arms and hands. He hadn't called them, and he currently couldn't get them to leave.

"Fine, Ramis. But if you ever—"

Rami shook his head. "Just go."

As Tierran left, Rami leaned against the glass again, allowed his legs to give and sunk to the floor. So much had changed because of Tierran, and so much had to change again. He needed a moment before he went back to his friends. Just a moment. That was all. Then he'd go back.

CHAPTER ELEVEN

Tristys knew he wouldn't like Quellos, and he'd been there less than a day. Everything was too fluffy. And too white. The capital of the island, Cimedalé, had a waterfall just like Ramidalé, but the Cimedaléan Falls were trickles compared to the Ramidalé Rises.

Everything he saw in Cimedalé was pale, if not blanched, and everything he touched was soft. When they passed the palace, his shoes literally sunk into the road. Buildings were made from an incredibly pliant, incredibly white wood; there were no doors or windows, just slits in the walls. The wood was so soft you could bend it to walk in or out, tie it up with a sash to open a window. They rushed through the city, staying for only an hour, just enough time to buy supplies for the trip to the Altar. Tristys didn't mind the brief departure. When he said as much to the group, Gawen told him that Cimedalé was one of the most important cities in the Coquels but it had the lowest residential population. Made sense to Tristys.

By the time they left Cimedalé, night had fallen, so they spent the night in the nearby town of Cimeran. It was a quick ferry ride away from Cimedalé, though this ferry traveled via river rather than open sea. The river, Bellimar's Sword, had a huge role in the Great War; it was the sole means by which the instigator, Bellimar, managed to attack the island of Quell so viciously. After Tristys heard that story, he decided he'd look up more information about this Great War as soon as he had some spare time. It came up too often for him not to be curious.

Cimeran was a small town, with just two inns, and Rami shouldered the costs of separate rooms for everyone, even though Gawen offered to save him money by sharing a bed with Tristys. At the time, Tristys had just rolled his eyes and went to bed early. Gawen had gone from rude to seductive in a day, and Rami had been acting strange ever since they disembarked in Cimedalé. He'd told Tristys he had something to say, but he had to say it in private, but they'd never had a chance. Gawen would interrupt them, or Calissa would want to talk about Elerelacian stormbinders, or Rami would walk up to him with a curious expression, rehash that they needed to talk in private, and then leave, leaving Tristys alone. It was infuriating! Tristys had never considered himself lucky to sleep alone, but that night in Cimeran, his solitary room was bliss.

He slept the entire night. At one point, someone had knocked on his door, but he barely heard it through the haze of his sleep. He assumed it was Gawen, who had suggested earlier without an ounce of subtlety and in front of everyone that they sleep together that night... in the romantic sense. Tristys had panicked, had turned across the room to Rami, but he just had a stupid grin on his face. No help in that department, so he brought up some obscure ritual Calissa had mentioned earlier, and that saved him. When she finally quit talking, he ran to his room and shut off the light. He was asleep before his head hit the pillow.

His sleep was restless, and when Calissa bounded in before dawn the next morning, she had to use the water-daggers to wake him. They had just a short walk to the ferry that would take them to the Altar, but he felt weighted down, as if someone had tossed a heavy blanket over him.

The ferry they boarded was different than the previous two: this one was obviously Quellosian, since its wood was softer than anything he'd seen float before. He had half a mind to worry that they'd sink, but he was just too tired.

He slept for most of the ride. He tried not to, tried to stay awake, but it was no use. When he finally did manage to open his eyes long enough to let them focus, he saw his four friends staring at him, waiting for something to happen.

"What gives?" he slurred.

"We're just seeing whether you're going to freak out again," Gawen said, moving to sit on the bench next to Tristys. His crotch was now eye-level with Tristys's face, and Tristys didn't think it was accidental. As always when there was something he didn't want to get caught staring at, he had trouble not staring.

"What are you talking about?" he asked, directing his gaze to the bench opposite Gawen's crotch. Rami got up, though, and sat down there. Now Tristys had a crotch no matter where he looked.

"You flipped out at everything that made any noise," Rami said. "There was a random bird on a tree awhile back, and you threw your pillow at it."

Tristys looked down at where his head had been. "My pillow is right there," he said.

"I got you a new one," Rami said. "I was half-hoping you'd toss that one, too. You look funny when you throw things."

"Shut up," Tristys said, trying to rub a kink out of his neck. He noticed that all the trees along the sides of the river were white. Leaves, bark, everything. "I am so sick of the color white!" he groaned.

"We pulled Firebird away from you," Salice said. "We were moderately afraid you'd toss him off the boat, too." At his name, the monkey lifted his head from its resting place on his paws. When he noticed Tristys was awake, he stampeded over and jumped to his shoulder.

"Thanks," he said, petting the monkey. He'd hate to have lost him.

He was still tired, though, and for the next few hours, he dozed. The weather was impeccable: not too hot, not too cold, a dry breeze in the air. The trees, as it turned out, shed, and Tristys woke up every few minutes to brush off the pollen—white, of course—that landed on him and Firebird, who was sleeping and sneezing by his side. He paid vague attention to the conversations going on—something about Salice's friend who knew the seyan of Quellas, something else about Calissa's foreign stormbinders, and random bickering between Rami and Gawen that could almost count as flirting. Tristys was too tired to converse much, and it seemed like everyone knew that. They left him alone.

When dusk fell, a few dozen torches burst into flames along the ferry. It had startled Tristys the first time it happened on the last ferry, and it startled him again. A few minutes later, the ferry ran aground, jolting Tristys out of a strange dream. When people began to disembark, he got excited.

"Are we at the Altar?" he said. He wasn't sure, but he had a suspicion that traveling made him lethargic. He didn't like it.

"No, not yet. We've got an unexpected stop-over, since the ferry didn't get as far as we'd hoped."

Tristys groaned. "We're sleeping in the woods again?" He'd grown accustomed to beds and plumbing.

"Not quite," Salice said. "We're sleeping in Fleece."

As it turned out, Fleece wasn't a town, not in any organized sense of the word. The Whitewood was so comfortable, people had simply kept congregating in the same area on the way to the Altar, and that town had become Fleece. Like Cimedalé, there were very few permanent residents. It was just too comfortable.

When Tristys finally saw Fleece for the first time, he was underwhelmed. It looked exactly like the forest had, with the sole change being the fallen cottonblooms. There were more of them, and most were larger than the ones that had fallen in the wild. When a small boy, followed by an older woman who looked just like him, came out of one, Tristys realized these were the makeshift homes and buildings of Fleece. These people sure did love their cottonblooms.

"Here looks good," Salice said, dropping her satchel and plopping into a nearby bloom.

"Sleep already? It's too early for that." Gawen threw his own supplies next to Salice's, but he kept standing. "And Tristys has never seen the Whitewood before, right?"

"Nope, never," Tristys said, yawning.

"The whole damn thing looks like this." Tristys

wasn't entirely sure, but he thought Rami was trying to clear a patch of ground. He kept kicking one or two cottonblooms away, but they just rolled back.

"Why don't we let Tristys see that for himself?" Gawen grabbed hold of his arm and started to pull him away from the group. Gawen looked at Tristys and said, "Okay?"

Tristys wasn't sure why, but he already knew he'd go with Gawen, even though he didn't agree so easily. "I really am tired, Gawen."

"We'll make it quick, just a once-around the city limits."

Tristys crinkled his brow, gesturing around him. "What city limits? There's no city here to limit! It's just a bunch of cottonblooms."

"Told ya so," Rami said. He'd finally settled on a patch of ground that was as devoid of blooms as it was going to get.

"Let's go!" Gawen said, jerking Tristys a little. He wasn't rough, just... encouraging. Tristys followed.

"We could see if anyone else wants to—"

"Nope, shush! Let's go." He was still dragging Tristys by the arm, although Tristys was now following him somewhat willingly. "I'll have him back soon," Gawen shouted to no one in particular, "but don't wait up!" Tristys wasn't sure, but he thought he saw Gawen look at Rami when he added the last bit. Was he trying to make him jealous?

The tour wasn't very eventful. Gawen talked a lot, mostly about himself. Tristys learned about Gawen's home in Malatapia, the capital of Quellus, and he heard at least five times how well-connected Gawen's family was, how well-off they were, how stable and secure. Gawen, it seems, wanted everyone to head to his home after Tristys finished at the Altar of Two Souls, but if the group kept touring the islands after that, he'd probably stay behind in Malatapia, and he hoped Tristys would consider staying behind, too. It was an amazing city, with walls made of fire, far too hard to explore in just a day or two, and Tristys wouldn't get bored very quickly. And when he did, they'd have the rest of the island of Fire to explore, if they wanted. And after that? Who knows.

Tristys was only half-listening, and he was half-listening only so he didn't accidentally agree to live as Gawen's boytoy for the rest of his life. Gawen's suggestive glances every time he mentioned exploring were pretty clear, and Tristys had already escaped sex-slavery once, so he didn't want to have to escape it again. Though something told him Rami wouldn't let Tristys get away quite that easy, especially before he talked to him about whatever it was that he wanted to talk about...

Despite the obvious come-ons, Gawen wasn't terrible. He talked a lot, sure, and mostly about himself, but when Tristys did manage to get a few words in edgewise, Gawen listened attentively. And he made Tristys laugh quite a lot, which was impressive. Despite everything, he seemed like a good guy after all. Maybe that explained why the others had put up with him through the years.

By the time they decided to head back to Fleece, night had fallen. Gawen communed with Fire-magic to conjure up some non-invasive light for the trip back to town. It was a small flame at first, hovering near their heads, but it quickly became more animated once Tristys showed his interest in it. It began to zigzag all over the place, through and around and between Tristys and Gawen, and then it split into several smaller flames that danced in the air, always a step or two ahead of Tristys. Then the smaller flames merged again into a larger one, though now it had a decidedly insect-like appearance, and darted along Tristys's arms or fluttered by his neck or breezed through his hair. It never burnt him, though, even when they made contact; on the contrary, it felt good. It was warm, almost ticklish, and when the firebug quit flitting, started to caress his skin slowly, the touch became almost erotic. This disturbed Tristys, but there was light ahead and voices on the breeze, so he thought he could weather the storm.

"That's Fleece up there, isn't he?" he said, batting at the flame. He never hit it, though. He only hit himself.

"Yeah," Gawen said, stopping next to a large cottonbloom. "But why don't we sit here for a bit? I'm not tired yet." He twirled the thin vines of the flower around the fingers of his left hand. His fire was still there, flitting around haphazardly, acting drunk.

"But Fleece is right there," Tristys said. He was tired, but he wasn't that tired, so there wasn't much conviction to his voice. He took a step towards the bloom.

Gawen reached out and took Tristys by the wrist. "Yes, but this bloom is right here." He pulled, and Tristys dropped into the bloom, bouncing when he landed. He laughed. "See? That was totally worth it."

Tristys snuggled further into the bloom, blowing at the white pollen that had burst out of it when they sat down and was now trying to settle back on top of him. "I guess so." For a few seconds, the bloom's softness took him back to those first nights he spent in Quelles, sleeping in Rami's cottonbloom bed, and then those later nights, sleeping next to Rami himself. Perhaps it was willful amnesia, but for a second he forgot he was next to Gawen, not Rami, and let his hand seek out connection. But as soon as Gawen reciprocated, his thumb gliding over Tristys's little finger, Rami's cottonbloom bed—and Rami himself—disappeared.

Tristys tensed. "We really should get back soon." Tristys started to push himself out of the cottonbloom—it was large, and they'd sunk rather far down into it—when Gawen put a hand on his shoulder.

"Relax, I'm not going to jump you." He leaned in as if he were about to share a secret. "Unless you want me to. In which case, we can—"

"No, no. I know you're not, I just—"

Firebird jumped on Tristys's lap. Where had he come from? He'd been with Rami...

"Sorry to interrupt," Rami said, his voice strangely choked. He'd snuck up behind them—probably not snuck up, exactly, but Tristys hadn't noticed him. He quickly shirked himself from Gawen's arm around his shoulder. He felt a blush rising to his cheeks, even though his brain kept telling him he had nothing to feel guilty about.

"You're not interrupting," Tristys said. "We're just sitting here."

"Yeah," Gawen agreed, but his voice was smiling smugly, even if his face wasn't. "This flower is huge. You're more than welcome to join us." He patted the sliver of space next to him. If

Rami took him up on the offer, he'd be sitting in Gawen's lap. Though Tristys was slightly turned on by the idea, jealousy trumped his arousal.

"No," Rami said, and Tristys breathed an internal sigh of relief. He hadn't really expected Rami to say yes—Gawen's offer hadn't really been real, had it?—but still. "You two look fine together." His voice was flat, no sarcasm or venom at all, and that bothered Tristys more than anything. "I want to catch the first ferry to the Altar tomorrow, though, so try not to stay out too late." His eyes narrowed. "Or up too late, I guess."

Rami turned to leave, and Tristys called for him to wait up, but he kept walking. When Tristys started to get out of the bloom, Gawen grabbed his arm. "Let him go. He doesn't care about us, so why chase him?"

"There is no us, Gawen." He wasn't mad at Gawen, just upset at Rami for overreacting. Did he really think there was anything between them?

Gawen didn't respond immediately. He thought about it a second, and then asked, "Do you want to go, then? Do you want to follow him, hoping things work out?"

At least Tristys wasn't the only one who over-reacted. "I don't think I need to follow him around," Tristys said. "He'll get over this. We weren't even doing anything!"

Gawen smiled, his genuine smile that made him that much more good-looking. "No, I don't mean now. I mean forever. Just following him around like a slave, hoping he suddenly quits being Rami, wakes up and falls in love with you."

"No, I—"

"That's what I did." He used the past tense, but there was something in his voice that made Tristys think perhaps he was still doing some following. "Look, I'm not asking you to renounce Rami and never speak to him again. I just want you to sit with me for a while. That's it."

There were no lascivious looks, no mischievous grins. And he had a point—Rami wasn't going to wake up suddenly and be in love with Tristys. And Tristys obviously wasn't going to be sharing Rami's flower tonight, and this bloom he was in now really was comfortable, and Gawen was pleasant company, so why waste it?

Tristys let himself relax. The energy he'd stored to spring out of the bloom dissipated, and Gawen felt the release. "Good," he said. "Now, where were we before he interrupted us?"

"I think you were telling me about your last boyfriend, and how amazing he was in bed."

"Oh, right!" Gawen said and kept on talking.

Rami's soup was absolutely perfect. He dipped his spoon into the broth and brought it to his lips, but he couldn't do it. He let the soup drop back into the bowl, ignoring the small splashes that struck his blanket. He absolutely hated perfect calaba soup. He liked it too warm, a little overcooked, with the thick calaba leaves wilted and soggy.

It wasn't just the degree of perfection of the soup, though. It had been several days since he had seen a ghost on the ferry from Ramidalé, and he had been struggling with the repercussions since. He simply couldn't believe that everything he had done, all the promises he had made, had been for nothing. His love for Tierran hadn't killed him. His magic wasn't some sort of fail-safe to prevent him from turning into the next Betrayer. It had all been a lie – no, not a lie, exactly. A falsehood. An untruth.

Now, after the truth had looked him squarely in the eye on that boat and asked to get back together, Rami was trapped like a fish in the net of lies and half-truths he'd weaved for the past decade. He'd been with Calissa for so long. Was he supposed to just pull her aside and say, *By the way, I like guys*? She had sacrificed so much to be with him; she was intelligent, gorgeous, funny, charming. She could have had anyone she wanted, and she'd stayed with him, despite his obvious disinterest in the physical side of their relationship.

And what about everyone else? His mother and father, Gawen and Salice... he'd been lying to them his entire life. And poor Telia! He'd yelled at her, threatened never to see her again, all because she saw him drowning in his net and tried to help him out of it.

As if his thoughts had beckoned her, Calissa opened the door. "How's your soup? Perfect as usual?" Her hair was pulled back in a ponytail, and she wore a long dress made of a thin, airy material that came from her home island of Quellos. She'd put a long-sleeved shirt over it, which made no sense to Rami since it weighted down the point of the fabric, but he'd long ago given up trying to understand Calissa's quirks.

"Of course." He spooned up more broth and tipped it right back in the bowl, trying his best at nonchalance. "You know Quellos."

"I do know Quellos," she said as she handed Rami a bowl. "Here, I had Gawen boil it a bit. I know you like it burnt."

"Not burnt," Rami said, setting his bowl of perfect soup on the floor by the bed. "Just well-done." He knew as soon as he saw the first wilted leaf that she'd made it perfectly. His perfect.

She hopped onto the bed next to Rami, sinking in and resting back against the headboard. "Wow, this is the softest one yet!"

Rami grunted his reply through a mouthful of boiling soup.

"So, how's life?" Calissa pulled a moonfruit from a shirt pocket and started to peel it. "I feel like we haven't talked in weeks. Want a piece?" She held out her fruit, but Rami declined.

"It has been a while, I guess. But it's been an odd few months." Rami picked up his soup, walked on his knees across the bloom, and sat next to Calissa.

"Guess who I saw today?" she said at once. She'd been waiting to tell him this, apparently.

"Who?"

"Kalen. He was sitting in the common room, reading a book."

"Oh yeah?" Kalen had been a friend of Rami's and Calissa's back during their days at the University of the Coquels. She'd met him in one of her first classes, and for years, Rami thought that Kalen wanted to pursue her, but he never tried anything. "Why's he here? He's too old to be a supplicant."

"No, he's just passing through on his way back home. He was down past the Shield visiting a friend in Thornvale."

"He's from Anamora, right?"

"He was," Calissa said, smiling. "Do you remember when we went to visit him?"

Rami remembered. He'd never forget it, in fact. It was early in his relationship with Calissa. She asked him to go visit Kalen, and he'd said yes, of course, and after that he worried for days before they'd actually gone. Anamora had started as nothing more than a small village for travelers going between Imidalé and Malatapia, but it grew into a romantic getaway because of the Amorai, an enormous lake with violet water that shimmered between opacity and transparency. Huge lily pads, just big enough for two people, floated on the surface. They'd become so characteristic that a common saying in Coquellian culture, 'taking someone to a lily-pad', had developed as a euphemism for sex. He never said it, but he heard it enough... usually from Gawen.

"Of course. I had a great time." He wasn't lying, either. He did enjoy himself. He'd been nervous, because of Anamora's romantic connotations and his obvious lack of sexual desire for Calissa, but when they'd went through the entire vacation, including a moonlit picnic on the lily-pads, without a single mention of sex—not even an innuendo!—he knew Calissa was the woman for him.

"Me too. I haven't gone back since, though." She perked up. "We should go sometime!"

"Yeah, I'd be down for that."

"Why don't we go there after we finish here at the Altar? I bet Tristys would love it there. He has a thing for the color purple, you know." Rami swore she looked at his eyes with a pointed glare.

"He didn't handle the journey here very well," Rami said, choosing to ignore the glare. "I don't know if I want to travel again right away."

"He's doing better already. I think that was oş's

way of Fingerprinting. He'll be okay once he attunes. He'll just need one night's rest in a real bed. Or a real bloom, I guess, since we're in Quellos." She smiled, because she knew how much Rami hated the blooms. Rami smiled back.

Calissa looked at him a moment, judging, and then asked, "So are you better now?"

Rami took a second to process. He'd tried so hard to keep his distress a secret... he clearly wasn't a very good actor. "Better from what?"

"I don't know. Ever since then, you've been quiet." She twisted at the waist so she was facing Rami.

"Have I?" *Deflect!* "Nobody's been around lately," he accused. "It's hard not to be quiet when you've got no one to talk to."

"Rami, only Tristys has been busy. Everyone else has just been wasting time. You're the one that's been banishing yourself to this room.

"We figured you just needed some space to recover," she continued after he didn't say anything. "That's why we've been leaving you alone."

"Recover from what?"

"Oh," she said, "we thought seeing that guy on the ferry threw you for a loop. You looked shaken up when he appeared. What was up with him, anyway? How do you know him?"

Rami kicked himself for asking the question. They were on dangerous territory again. But this was a perfect time, the perfect opportunity to tell her everything, the whole truth, about his past, who he was, what the two of them really were. But he couldn't do it. He still didn't know if he even wanted to do it. But there was no hurry. He had time to figure it out.

"Oh, just someone I hadn't seen in a while." He had to change the subject. "Can you believe this is still hot?"

"I can. I had Gawen boil it for you, remember?"

He raised his eyebrows to agree, since he was right in the middle of another sip. When he put the spoon down, he segued again. "Any idea how much longer Tristys will take meditating before he goes to Trial?"

He dreaded the answer. Life-magic was one of the ethereal quell, distinct from the four elemental ones and much more dangerous to Fingerprint. The elemental trials could be stopped easily by the overseeing priest, but the ethereal ones were much harder to control. Failure was often fatal.

Calissa wasn't looking at him, and she still hadn't answered his question. Something was up. He felt his dread rise.

"Calissa, what?"

"We didn't want to tell you, since you'd been acting strange, and—"

"Tell me what?" Rami was trying to stay calm, but it wasn't working. He ignored his initial impulse to argue that he hadn't been acting strange.

She shut her eyes. "He's already finished meditating."

"What?"

"He finished last night. He's going through the Trial right now. He said that you'd—"

"Right now? Right now?" Rami couldn't stop repeating the question. "Right now, Calissa? Right now! You know he could die in there, right? He gets poisoned, for Gods' sake! And he'll never know that—" He couldn't finish his sentence, choking on his own words.

He might not have any time at all! Here he was, isolating himself for days because he didn't know how to handle the truth, and Tristys could be dying. Tristys, the only person who had ever made Rami regret what he had decided to do after the tragedy with Tierran. A tragedy, Rami now realized, that was only tragic insofar as it had made him stifle his desires and lie for the past decade. The real tragedy was what could be happening in the Altar.

He had to go. He couldn't stay here any longer. He was angry—he wanted to yell at Calissa for not telling him sooner, for having a meaningless conversation about vacations while all this was happening—but that would have to wait. He needed to get to the Altar. He bolted out of the room.

Calissa followed, but he ignored her, beelining for the trees near the shore that held the Trial of Two Souls. He hadn't been to the shore yet, and he muffled the slight gasp that always escaped whenever he first laid eyes on the sea.

Unlike Quellos, the island of Quelles was not an enormous crater with towering walls protecting it from the sea, and its beaches, like the rest of the island, were breathtaking. Crisp blue water crested into white waves that broke on fine silk sand. The rhythm was calming, and the air had a freedom to it that Rami loved. To the north, Rami could see the Riveras Delta, and to the east, a setting sun draping the Quellusian savannas in orange and purple. But right in front of him were two enormous trees, woven into a single trunk and growing out of sand instead of soil.

Tristys was in there, dying. The trees—the Two Souls—were hollow, but the hollow was poisonous, absolutely lethal to anything living. A supplicant had to commune with Life-magic to protect himself, and if he couldn't... But Rami wouldn't think of that, couldn't think of that. Tristys would be fine.

And he would be. He'd mastered Water-magic so quickly, and he'd saved a monkey from the brink of death, hadn't he? He'd be able to handle a little poisoning, even if it was oş itself doing the dirty work. He'd be fine.

He'd calmed himself down a bit, enough to notice that he and Calissa weren't the only ones on the beach. There was an older woman knee-deep in the water, a few groups of people milling about in the surf, another group of Physical Services agents standing farther down the beach. Salice and Gawen were here, too, so they must have known and hadn't told him, either. Salice had her back to a boulder, and Gawen was pacing near the Two Souls. He ignored them all and sat down on the sand, directly in front of the entrance. Rami wanted to be the first thing Tristys saw if he came out. When, not if. When.

He'd tell him everything then, too. No more waiting for the perfect time, the perfect moment, just the two of them. He'd say it all, explain everything, in front of everyone. Then he'd take Tristys to a cottonbloom, and it'd be Tristys and Rami, not Tristys and Gawen, brushing the pollen off each other.

The wait was agony. Nobody spoke. Gawen didn't stop pacing, Calissa wouldn't even look at Rami, and Salice drew in the sand by her side the entire time. Firebird screeched as he ran from person to person, getting nothing but a distracted pat here and there. Rami felt as if he couldn't catch his breath, his thoughts ricocheting between worst case scenarios and perfect outcomes. When Tristys finally came out, it was neither.

He was alive, but he looked terrible. He was so pale he looked see-through, and some of the lesions from the poisoning were still visible, though barely, on his skin. His eyes were half-shut, and he had dirt and sand in his hair.

"I did it," he said, his voice barely there. He was staring straight at Rami, though, looking right at him and at no one else, even though nearly everyone on the beach was moving forward to congratulate him. But he was looking only at Rami. There were cottonblooms in their future already.

Rami stood up to embrace Tristys, but he was too slow. The people from the Physical Services had beaten him to it, but they weren't hugging him. They were... arresting him?

"You are a foreigner," a tall man with short-cropped hair said, "and therefore you are unwelcome here on our islands." His voice was deep but monotone, flat in the formal words of arrest. Everyone had caught up by now, and Salice, Gawen, and Calissa were all shouting. Rami was too stunned to say anything. The guard ignored everyone. "By the authority of Seyan Ystan IV, seyquel of Imidale and the Great Island Nation of the Coquels, you are hereby banished from this island." Gawen made a lunge for Tristys, but the female agent threw up a hand and a blast of Air-magic tossed him aside. Wind shields went up around the agents and Tristys. "Your exile is immediate, and my team will not rest until our lands are pure once again. In his name."

Calissa and Gawen were shouting, bystanders

were whispering, the female guard was shouting back, and Rami was too late after all.

~~*

Calissa was the first to react. A quick flick of her wrist and the windshield protecting the agents puffed out of existence. She blew aside a second and a third, too.

"That magic's so weak even Kyssan the Plunger'd laugh at you," she said. Her voice startled everyone around her, especially the agents. She'd used oş to magnify it. The woman tried to put up another shield, and Calissa blocked it again. "I wish you'd quit doing that, you're just wasting time."

"Well you," the woman said, "are wasting our time." She looked to be in her early thirties, with an over-sized scarlet bouffant and too much rouge and lip color to match it. "The foreigner must be handled."

"The foreigner," Calissa said, looking at Tristys, "is our friend." He looked stunned. He was barely able to stand on his own, and Calissa had the feeling that if the two burlier agents let him go, he'd fall to his knees.

"That is your own mistake," the woman said. The sneer on her face matched the one in her voice.

Calissa didn't miss a beat. "Perhaps, but your mistake is thinking that we'll let you take him without a fight." Calissa had no intention of actually dueling these people, but she wanted to test the waters and see which of the agents were Touched. She only felt the woman's oş stir. That was good.

"Fighting the Physical Services is a huge—"

"I don't want to fight you. I want to fight the judgment." Calissa took a moment to look around her, to make sure she had support. Rami looked dumbfounded, almost resigned, as if he'd given up already. Salice was practically growling and her fist looked as if it were about to hit someone's face, and Gawen had his fireflies dancing around him already. She gave him a pointed look. This was delicate business, and anything that seemed aggressive would ruin it.

"I'm sorry, miss," the fourth guard said. He was older, and he looked down as he spoke to her. "There is no contesting an exile."

"We've wasted too much time already!" the woman said. She appealed to a shorter man who had his back turned to the group. He'd been that way since this started, and it had been driving Calissa crazy the entire time. He had magic, too, but he was shielding it from her. All she could see was his stupid ponytail, twisted into Calerelacian knots. How pretentious! And ironic, considering the man wearing a foreign design was about to exile a foreigner.

"She is right," the man said. He hadn't even turned around to address the woman. His voice was distorted, unnaturally deep. "We must go." He nodded to the two guards holding Tristys, and they started to pull him along. Calissa scanned her support quickly. Salice was angry but useless. Gawen's quell was too offensive—Fire burned— and Rami had obviously checked out long ago. It'd be up to her to fix this.

She sent the yellow stars she saw to work. A windshield erupted around the agents, locking them in a small circle of ground. She'd clarified the oş so light and sound could pass through.

"You did not just commune against agents of the Seyquel!" the woman shouted, banging physically on the windshield. She'd already tried to blow it away with her own magic, but that was as futile as the pounding.

"Don't bother," Calissa said. "You won't budge my shield." The woman tried again, again to no avail. "I'm one of the strongest practitioners of iş in the islands." The woman banged a third time on the shield, even more violently than before, and Calissa looked at Gawen. She winked.

A second later, the woman recoiled from the shield, letting out a little yelp and nursing her slightly scalded fists. "My friend is a pretty good practitioner of uş, too."

All the agents looked angry, even the older man. The ponytailed guy still hadn't turned around, though. Calissa was tempted to ask oş to turn the man around for her, but she resisted. She was incredibly out of order right now, so she had to tread carefully.

"You better have an incredible excuse to—"

"Do you know anything at all about this person you're trying to exile?" Calissa asked.

For some reason, the woman continued to speak, even though she obviously wasn't in charge. She hadn't done the arresting. "We know he's a foreigner. That's all we need to know."

"And did you give any thought to the situation in which you're arresting him?" Calissa had one shot at getting Tristys free passage through the Coquels, and that was Ystan. She just had to get Tristys to him.

For once, the woman didn't shout back right away. "It doesn't matter, he's a foreigner!"

"He may come from Cyræa, but he's got something of the Coquels in him. If he didn't when he was born, he does now."

"What are you—"

"He's been Touched by both eş and oş. Why do you think he stumbled out of Two Souls? You all were too caught up in your orders to think about what you were doing. Look at his face! You can still see oş's marks."

"Is this true?" the man who'd done the arresting said.

"Of course. Just ask Red there. She'll be able to feel the quell in him."

The man nodded at the woman, who tilted her head. A second later, she looked sick. "It's true," she said. Her eyes were closed.

The leader looked upset, too. "This changes things," he said, "though to be honest, I'm not sure what protocol to follow here." He and the woman, along with the older man, conversed a bit, leaned into each other so they could talk quietly. After some heated words, they straightened up. "He'll come with us to Imidalé, where we'll address the seyquel himself."

"And we'll go with you," Gawen said. Calissa was just glad somebody else had finally spoken up. She couldn't stand her ground alone the whole time.

"Not possible. No way." It was the female agent again, and Calissa considered giving her a separate soundproof windshield. "Under no circumstances will a group of civilians accompany an exile. It would be absolutely—"

"Let them come," the ponytail said. His voice sounded less distorted, deep without the strange timbre, and it gave Calissa the strangest feeling, almost like déjà vu, although she'd obviously never been in this situation before.

"Turn around," she said slowly. "You sound just like—" Before she finished, he turned around, and she was right. She couldn't believe it, but she was right. This was Fal. Here in the Coquels again!

She lost her composure. She knew she shouldn't question him now, she'd have time on the journey, but the surprise was simply too much for her. She asked oş to do a few things all at once: she dropped the windshield around the guards for a second, just long enough to pull Fal to her. With Fal close, she popped another shield up, this one around them, but she changed the magic so that the shield was impermeable to both sound and light. They were in private. Fal lit a small uş-light so they could see each other. Just like he always had.

She intended to yell, to rage, to scream, but when she finally spoke, she was quiet. "I can't believe it's you." But it was him. He smelled the same, a rusted floral that drove her crazy. She thought she'd gotten over this, but there it was again... Desire.

"It is," he said, his voice still so familiar. "It's me."

"You're supposed to be in Calere. You chose the magic, remember?" It had been so many years, but the rejection still stung.

"I know." He still hadn't looked at her.

Calissa felt tugs on the shields she'd put up, most likely the stupid woman again. She ignored them. "Well, what happened? Why aren't you—"

"I couldn't stay away. I did go, for a few years. But the pull, oş... I just—I couldn't stay away."

She understood that, at least. She couldn't

imagine leaving the islands, leaving oş. But there was a time when she couldn't imagine leaving Fal, either.

She had to ask, even though there were disturbances again on her windshield, this time physical banging. That had to be Gawen or Salice or Rami, but she ignored them. "Why didn't you tell me you were here?"

He was already shaking his head. "I didn't think it would be wise, Calissa." He shut his eyes. "You made a choice, too, don't forget."

"I know, but Fal, we were—" A small flame snaked under the shield, twisting into a question mark before evaporating. Gawen. She had to focus. "It doesn't matter. It's in the past."

"Cal, I never meant—"

Before he could finish, she dropped the shield around them. She gave no warning, though, and Gawen, who had been pounding on the outside, fell on top of her. "Dammit, Gawen!" He was good-looking, but he wasn't the lightest person in the world.

"Sorry, sorry!" he said, jumping to his feet and lending her a hand. "We just wanted you out of there. We were bored." He smiled sheepishly.

"My apologies," Fal said, "but we must be on our way. Calissa and her friends will accompany us to the capital." He swung his ponytail around to play with it. "Calissa, remove that shield, please."

She did so, and promptly felt a tingle above her. Sure enough, an enormous drop of water hung above her head for a split second before it dropped, and the female agent let out a whoop.

Calissa was drenched. She could have fought back, sent an even colder, bigger drop at the woman, but didn't. For Tristys.

CHAPTER TWELVE

Tristys hadn't eaten in hours. He was still exhausted from his Trial, and his head hurt. At least the scars had finally gone away! They'd been all over his body, and he was afraid they'd be permanent. But they were gone.

The journey to Imidalé wasn't really a journey, just a single boat ride across the Coquelai. Tristys wasn't allowed to talk to anyone, though Calissa did assure him everything would be okay. He wasn't even allowed to hold Firebird; Calissa had to lock him in an Air-shield to stop him from throwing things at the servicemen. They came straight to the Palace, and a new pair of guards brought him here, to this room, to await the seyquel.

The room was lavish. Circular in shape, it had sconces along the wall with more of those flames that didn't flicker and weren't hot. The walls, covered in elaborate geometric patterns of twirled rope, were dyed dark blue, almost black, and the carpet was the exact opposite, a light blue that grew steadily lighter until bleaching white in the center of the room. Tristys had no idea how they kept it clean.

The guards had told him nothing before they left, so Tristys had sat on a chair near the far wall. But his eyes hadn't left the carpet, whose plush pile was downright seductive to someone as tired as Tristys. He decided to lie down, just for a minute.

He slipped his shoes off and slid from the chair to the floor. Just as he expected, the carpet was ridiculously comfortable. It had to come from Quellos! He lay on his back, stretched out and twisted side to side, letting the bones crack both ways. He tossed his arms above his head, dug his hands into the tufts, and then bent his knees to dig his toes into the carpet, too. He loved the friction of the motion on his soles. It was pure bliss.

"You know, I was curious to see how a Cyræan would greet a seyquel," a man said in heavily accented Cyræan. It was high-pitched, soft and rhythmic, with a lilt of amusement floating through it. Tristys hadn't heard him come in, and he lifted his head to peer through the two pyramids of his knees in embarrassment. "I can't say I expected it to be quite like this, though."

Tristys jumped up, devastated, but the man was smiling, his small, dark eyes set beneath thick gray brows. He had a round face, clean-shaven and slightly wrinkled, with a head shaved to match. He was short, wearing a thin white shirt and baggy brown pants cinched with a rope belt. He looked like every other Coquellian Tristys had seen. This was the seyquel?

"I'm sorry, sir," Tristys said, unsure whether to speak in Cyræan or Quellosian, which honorific to use if any. "I didn't hear you coming, and I just—"

"Please, please, no worries." Ystan walked directly up to Tristys and put a hand on his shoulder. "It is truly a pleasure to meet you, Tristys."

"You know my name?" Tristys hadn't told anyone his name; none of the agents, not even the one with the ponytail who seemed to know Calissa, asked.

"You'll be surprised, I think, by how many people already know your name. News travels fast in the Coquels."

Tristys didn't really consider himself news, but then again, if the situation were reversed—if Rami had landed on the shores of Cyræa—that would be news. It made sense. "I don't know if I should bow or kneel or what. I'm still getting the hang of etiquette. I don't even know how to act around normal people here, let alone kings."

"I'm not a king," Ystan said, "and this isn't Cyræa. We have very few rules and regulations here, you'll find."

"Really?" Tristys found it hard to believe. How could a country function without rules? Isn't that why Cyræa had so many in place?

"Yes, really. We have laws, of course, but they're very basic. Don't kill, don't steal. Treat people the way you want to be treated. You know, the obvious ones." He scratched a red spot on his cheek. "And as far as etiquette, well, we had that in the past, but not now. People treat me just as they treat each other."

Tristys felt how wide his eyes were and tried to rein in his excitement. "That's amazing," he said. "So the Coquels really is perfect, then?"

Ystan chuckled. "No, far from it."

"How do you figure?" Tristys had already forgotten his initial reticence to speak with the leader of an entire country. "You guys have magic. You guys live to be twice the age of everyone else. Everybody is nice to everybody else, and you're all gorgeous and intelligent and perfect."

"Oh, not everyone here is gorgeous and

intelligent, Tristys. You've been here for too short a time to notice, but you'll find that even the most perfect person has his flaws." He grinned. "Same goes for countries."

"Perhaps, but—"

"Do you mind," Ystan said suddenly, "if we carry the conversation to the chairs? I'm not as young as I once was, and I just followed a friend all around the city. Quality time, she said, but now I'm paying for it."

Tristys agreed, of course, and he followed Ystan to the group of chairs on the other side of the room. Why they skipped the chairs that Tristys had been sitting in earlier was unclear, but Tristys didn't argue.

"Now then," Ystan said, "as I was saying, there aren't many rules here, Tristys, but there are some. Like the banishment of exiles."

Tristys felt his breath leave him. What was he saying?

"That's a good example of an imperfection, actually. We Coquellians, it seems, are only nice to each other. To foreigners, we're cruel and merciless. They're sent away without a second thought, straight to certain death, because of innocent traders that landed on our shores hundreds of years ago, starting a war they didn't intend."

Tristys wasn't really in the mood for a philosophical discussion on the nature of Coquellian perfection. "I'm sorry, are you telling me I'm about to get banished?"

"What I am saying is that we exile foreigners at once."

"So I am leaving?" Tristys had stopped breathing.

"Of course not," Ystan said. "You are as safe here on these islands as any other Coquellian."

"I don't understand. I was born in Cyræa, I lived there my whole life. My parents were born there, and their parents, and their parents' parents, and... well... as far back as we can remember."

Ystan looked smug. "I have no doubt. But more to the point, I have no doubt that you are Coquellian."

"Sir," Tristys said, not quite sure how else to clarify this, "I assure you, I'm from Cyræa. There's no chance I—"

He was serious now, all the lightness gone from his face. "There's no chance, Tristys, that you are not Coquellian, if quell has Touched you. The Coquels are in your blood somewhere, if quell is in your blood." A smile lightened his face. "Which, Calissa assures me, it is."

Tristys considered a little display to prove it, but there was nothing challenging in the way the seyquel had said it, and he didn't want to seem pompous. Instead, he asked a question. "But I thought you Coquellians never mixed with anyone, right? Forbade your citizens from leaving, exiled foreigners, all that stuff." Tristys had learned something from his history lessons with Rami after all.

"True, but just because we forbade our citizens from leaving doesn't mean they've always listened. Laws are made to be broken, as they say."

Tristys had never heard 'them' say that, not in Cyræa, but he nodded anyway.

"Now, those laws haven't been broken in a very long time, mind you. But about five hundred years ago, I'm almost sure they were."

"Great War?" Tristys asked, smiling.

"Yes, actually." Ystan looked surprised. "How did you know?"

"Just a guess," Tristys said, still smiling.

Ystan took it in stride. "It was a terrible time, just dreadful. So many deaths, and virtually every island saw attacks. It's never been verified, but people almost certainly fled. The wards were up, but they were weak, often left unchecked."

"But if there's no real proof—"

"You are the proof," Ystan said simply. It was final, his way of closing the conversation.

"Okay then." Tristys dried his palms on his pants. He wasn't sure what else to say or even how to process what he'd been told. He'd been through so many changes over the past month, but this shook him to the core. This was about him, not his location or his situation. This was about him.

"Now, I think the best—"

"I'm sorry, sir," Tristys said. He couldn't take a deep breath, and the edge of his vision was going black. "I think I need a minute." He shut his eyes and pinched the bridge of his nose, which usually helped him in these situations.

"I have a better idea," Ystan said. "Why don't I take you home?"

Tristys stopped. Home? His head swirled. Could it be this easy? And if it was, could he take it?

Ystan caught his mistake at once. "Not home. To the inn with your friends, rather."

Tristys felt strange, torn between devastation and relief, followed quickly by guilt. Shouldn't he want to go home, back to his family? But then why was the relief just slightly stronger than the devastation?

"Shall we go then?" Ystan stood up, but Tristys didn't move, too lost in his own thoughts. He barely felt the hand on his shoulder guiding him through the palace, didn't see any of the people staring or whispering on the trip to the inn, couldn't remember the name of the inn he entered. Tristys couldn't even remember standing up.

~~*

Word really did travel fast in the Coquels. After Ystan dropped him off at the inn, Tristys slept from that evening to the next morning. He woke up late and found a piece of paper on the nightstand – a letter from Ystan, with the seyquel's official seal, granting him citizenship and freedom from exile. He wanted to show Rami, but everyone had already gone down for breakfast. Tristys splashed some water on his face, changed his clothes, and headed down, Ystan's letter secured in his pocket.

The common room was overflowing. There were no empty tables, and people were standing everywhere. When Tristys got to the bottom of the stairs, all conversation stopped. People started whispering and pointing, and Tristys had to fight the instinct to turn and run back to his bedroom. This was how it had started in Paru. He couldn't go through this again.

Rami's voice pulled him out of his flashback, and he scurried to their table, where Rami and Gawen made room for him to sit against the wall. Even still, the stares and the whispers were too much. Within minutes, curiosity got the best of some of the onlookers, and they started to approach the table. It was too much for Tristys, and they ended up going back to their rooms before they finished breakfast. Nobody minded.

They tried to go down for dinner later that day, but the same thing happened. They hadn't left their rooms since then, and that was three days ago. This was mostly due to Tristys's desire to avoid any more onlookers, but that wasn't the only reason. He'd been pardoned by the seyquel, he'd attuned to two quell, and now nobody knew what to do next.

Currently, they were sitting in Tristys's room. He was on the bed with Salice, while Gawen had stretched on the floor, throwing a ball for Firebird. Calissa had left earlier in the day—she had been mysteriously absent since they got to Imidalé—and Rami had pulled a chair into the room. He'd been reading a book the whole morning.

Rami was still acting strangely. One minute he wouldn't leave Tristys alone, and now he acted almost as if he wasn't even here. He'd been waiting right outside the Altar when Tristys had his Life Trial, but he'd barely spoken a word since then. He'd been reading the whole day, but Tristys had caught him staring a few times.

Gawen was another one. He'd flirted so hard in Fleece, but after that, nothing. They'd talk, they'd hang out, but no more flirting. It was like hanging out with Salice or Calissa. Tristys had never wanted anything to happen with Gawen—and he still didn't—but he'd be lying if he said he didn't miss the flirtation.

Tristys turned to Gawen. He was bouncing a bright green ball against the wall. Originally he'd been playing fetch with Firebird, but even Firebird had grown bored of that. Now the monkey was lying next to Gawen, his head resting on his hands and eyes following the ball as it bounced. He looked as bored as Tristys felt.

"So I'm going stir-crazy," Tristys said to no one in particular. "And I'm no longer that interested in Gawen's ability to bounce balls."

"Tell me about it," Salice said.

"I'm surprised nobody made a lewd ball joke. I was waiting for it."

"The boredom has dulled my sense of humor," Salice said. "Forgive me."

"You're forgiven." Rami didn't even look up from his book.

"Can we do something?" Tristys asked. He was whining, but he couldn't help it. This was bad.

"I've wanted to go back to the zoo here," Salice said. "It's so much better than the one back in Coera."

"What's a zoo?" Tristys asked.

"It's a place"—thunk—"where they keep"—thunk—"a bunch of animals in cages." Gawen tossed the ball again, and Tristys shot a blast of Water-magic at it on the return trip. It veered under the table. Gawen wasn't pleased. "So you can hit moving targets now, I see. Lovely."

"I could always hit moving targets. How do you think I saved Firebird?"

"If you think you can handle all the people staring at you, Tristys, we can take you to the zoo. It's a lot of fun." Salice sounded hopeful.

He thought about it. Perhaps if he put on a hat or something, nobody'd notice him. "Sure," he said finally. "Anything is better than staying in this—"

"I was supposed to take him to the zoo," Rami said suddenly. He'd put his book down, spine up, and he looked angry.

"Oh," Salice said, looking back and forth between Rami and Tristys. "I had no idea."

"Neither did I," Tristys said. What was Rami playing at now?

"He didn't even know what a zoo was, Rami, but you had plans to take him there?" Gawen was sitting up now, petting Firebird.

"I hadn't really told him yet." Rami picked up his book again. "But I was planning on it soon."

Everybody just stared at him.

"You know what?" He started flipping through the book as if he were trying to find where he'd stopped. "Don't worry about it. It's fine. Take him."

"Rami, you can come with us," Salice said. "It's not like we were going to go without you. You'll know more about the animals than any of us, anyway."

Rami hadn't mentioned the zoo to him. Was he going to? Why hadn't he? Did he have secret plans that Salice had now ruined?

Tristys didn't have time to mention how mad he was. Just as he was about to say something, someone knocked on the door. This happened often the first day or two, but Rami paid the innkeepers to direct visitors to a fake door. Tristys intended to ignore it, until he heard Ystan on the other side.

"Tristys, it's Ystan." He knocked in time to his words. "I had to promise the innkeeper a tour of the Palace to get him to tell me which room you were in, and—"

Ystan stopped when Tristys opened the door. He was smiling, an almost embarrassed grin that made his bald head look silly. "Thank you, thank you," he said, bowing slightly with each repetition. "I almost certainly avoided detection, so your secret should stay safe."

"Thank you," Tristys said, waiting to see what else the seyquel would say. The exaggerated secrecy was cute, but it made Tristys nervous. Why would the leader of the Coquels come on his own to see Tristys? This couldn't be good.

Apparently everyone else was waiting for the same thing. After a quick silence, Ystan stepped into the room and shut the door. "So Tristys," he said, overly casual, "I may have made a slight misstep this afternoon."

Great. "What exactly does a slight misstep mean?" Tristys asked. Could a slight misstep get him exiled or send him home? He wasn't sure which one he feared more.

"Well, you see, I have a friend, and I may have accidentally mentioned your presence here. She wants to meet you."

"That's it?" Tristys said. "You just want me to meet your friend?"

Ystan hesitated. "Yes," he said, drawing out the syllable, "but when you meet her, you'll realize Tyspal is not your average person."

"Tyspal?" Tristys asked in a bare whisper. A woman shimmered in his mind, tall with long brown hair that curled unless straightened with heat. "Her name is Tyspal?"

"Yes, Tyspal." Tristys saw pale skin, thin lips, an upturned nose.

"Oh." He barely heard his own voice over the lullaby, over the woman asking what he wanted for dinner, over the woman telling him the fire wasn't his fault, and even if it were, she'd love him anyway.

"If you're not busy, I could take you to the Palace now and introduce you two." Ystan looked around the room, but nobody objected. "You won't have to stay long. Tyspal tires quickly."

Tristys nodded absently, stood up and put on his shoes. He said goodbye to his friends, snuck out of his room, and left the Roseate Windwyrm so he could go to the palace and meet his mother.

~~*

It wasn't his mother. He knew it wouldn't be, but when he saw the old woman buried beneath blankets, his heart sank. Tears welled in his eyes, and he choked back a sob. He was so foolish and naive!

"Tyspal," Ystan said, far too loud and far too slow. Was she deaf and dumb? The room was dark, and Tristys had trouble making out any details besides the woman's stature. She was very small, almost withered. "This is Tristys, the boy I told you about."

Her head moved, but that was the only indication that she was even still alive. Until she spoke.

"I told you not to speak to me in that manner," she said. Her words were slow, pauses punctuating each phrase, and her voice broke often. She spoke in Cyræan, and Tristys realized Ystan had been speaking Cyræan, too. "My arms and legs may no longer function, but my ears are perfect."

"I'm sorry, Tyspal." His voice still had a slight edge, a gentle loudness that said he didn't quite believe her.

"Leave us," she said simply. She still hadn't

moved.

Ystan nudged Tristys farther into the room. He bent close to his face. "Humor her," he said, so quiet even Tristys had a hard time hearing. "She's old, and she doesn't have long. Tell her what she wants to hear."

What was that supposed to mean? What could an old woman want with Tristys? He wanted to ask, but Ystan turned and left as soon as he finished without giving Tristys a chance to respond.

"Come closer," Tyspal said. "My ears work well, but my eyes are bad, and I want to see you."

He moved closer, a few feet from the bed. He could see her more clearly now. She was old, perhaps the oldest person he'd ever seen. She had only a few wisps of hair left on her head, and canyons riddled her face, her two eyes craters. Tristys recoiled.

"Closer!" It was as much of a yell as the woman could muster, so Tristys moved to the side of the bed. "There, there you are. Those eyes, it feels so good to see them again." Her eyes were sunk in her face, but Tristys could still see the eyes themselves. They were likes oases in the desert of her face: both blue, but one several shades darker than the other. Dichromatic eyes, just like his. And she was right, it felt good, despite the eroded geography of Tyspal's face.

"It's nice to see your eyes, too. I haven't realized how much I've missed them." He was surprised by how choked up he felt. He blamed his mother's dichromatic blue eyes.

"Please," Tyspal said, her face making a movement—a twitch—for the first time, "do not speak that language to me. I loathe it."

Tristys hadn't even realized he defaulted to Quellosian. "I'm sorry, Tyspal. I didn't realize—"

"So you know my name, boy?" Her breathing was ragged, and her sentences took forever to finish. Listening to her was the most uncomfortable Tristys had been since he'd arrived on the islands.

"Ystan told me," he confessed. "It was my mother's name."

"Did your mother die in the war, boy? Like my father died? And my brother? And my lover? Did she die in the war?"

His mind raced immediately to Evynn, the brother he'd lost to the Spáloric conflicts. "No," he spat, "my mother still lives in Paru. She's fine." The mere suggestion made him angry.

"For now," she said. Her eyes darted away, rolled into the back of her head, and for a second Tristys thought she was dying. "Eighty years," she said once her pupils returned. "Eighty years now, boy."

He wasn't following. "Eighty years?"

"Since I've spoken to another Cyræan, seen another Cyræan. It has been eighty years. Can you imagine what eighty years feels like?"

He couldn't. "You're eighty years old?" He couldn't believe it. The oldest Cyræan he'd heard of was fifty-something.

"No!" She didn't have the strength, but she'd be shouting now if she could, Tristys knew. "I'm ninety-nine!"

Tristys was flabbergasted. "How did you—"

"Nineteen, I was nineteen when I left, when that Two-forsaken king landed on the beach and bewitched me with his empty magics. I was so stupid, so tired of the war and the death and the fighting."

"Ystan brought you here?" he asked, but she ignored him.

"I thought I could save our people. He promised to teach me his magic, to mobilize an army, to raze Spàlor and stop the fighting once and for all. But he lied. He brought me here, and he used me. I was no better than a Spàlorian sex-slave! I remember wishing I'd had that fate instead, because at least they didn't have these evil magics prolonging their lives, saving them through disease just to damn them with age." She was talking too much and too fast. Her breaths were ragged, deep and angry.

Tristys was mortified. "Ystan did that to you?" He pictured the little bald man with the silly grin. Tristys had felt strange around him, as if he had some sort of secret just beneath the surface, but he couldn't picture him in this new light.

Tyspal's head jerked, and her mouth twisted into a weak rictus. "Ystan? Ystan? Of course not Ystan! The king before him, Derascan. Ystan has been my only salvation, but even he is guilty now. He keeps me here, refuses to return me to Cyræa. My only wish has been to see my home again, and now my wish is to be buried there, and still he refuses me."

Tristys felt terrible, but what could he do? "Tyspal, I don't know what—"

"What you can do for me?" Her eyes were gleaming now, almost crazed. Tristys was unsettled. "Don't you see? Eighty years, and I thought my life was a waste. But now here you are, and I know. My life is not a waste, because I can save you."

"Save me? I don't know what—"

"From the magic! Don't you see? You must leave! They will keep you here, keep you alive with their foul spells, but the magic is not yours. It will heal your body but your body will age. Look at this, look at me! Look at me!"

When he finally understood her furor, words began to pour from his mouth. "Please, Tyspal, don't worry about me. I'll be fine, I have—"

"No, you must leave! You must not die like I died!"

"Tyspal, you don't understand, I can use their magic, quell has Touched me, I'm not—"

She gasped audibly. Tristys was afraid she'd break. "You can use the magics?" It was the loudest whisper Tristys had ever heard.

Tristys nodded, afraid. The look in her eyes was worse.

"You are Cyræan, boy! I see your eyes, I see Cyræa in your eyes!"

"I know, but I can—"

"And now you have power, so much power! And yet you stand here still, befriending spineless kings in a country full of cold-hearted egocentrics."

"Ystan isn't—"

"You can save us!" She was actually shouting now, a deep-throated hacking cough punctuating her words instead of breaths. "You can save our country! You can save us all!"

"I don't—I don't really think I—they hated me there, and here I—"

"Listen to me, boy." The blankets near her moved for the first time, and she raised a shaky hand to point at him. Her fingers were gnarled and twisted. "Listen to me. Your power, you can do what I could not. Do not let me die here in vain, thinking my life has been a waste!" Spatters of blood riddled the white blankets in front of her. Tristys began backing away.

"Do what I could not, boy! Do not let me die like this! Do not let us die in vain!"

He turned around now and ran out of the room, throwing the door open and sprinting down the halls of the palace. He didn't quit running until he reached the Roseate Windwyrm. The wind screamed in his ears, but all he could hear was the oldest Cyræan in the world crying for him to save her.

Chapter Thirteen

Ystan's private guards let Calissa pass without a single question despite the late hour. She'd been to see Ystan often enough over the past few days that they'd grown accustomed to her visits. Security was never that serious an issue in the Coquels, so she wasn't that surprised.

This would be the last time she would visit Ystan, at least in the near future. They had intended to stay in Imidalé for a few more days at least, but Tristys—and therefore Rami—was insisting they leave at once.

She wasn't really clear on the circumstances. She'd been out when he got home, having dinner with Fal, and when she'd finally returned to the Roseate, they'd had the entire suite cleaned and all their belongings, even Calissa's, packed. All she could gather was that Tristys had met a friend of Ystan's, someone from Cyræa, and it had upset him. He wanted to leave the city, and nobody really needed to stay, so they'd agreed. Without even asking Calissa.

Everyone wanted to head out as soon as Calissa got home, but she stalled. She had to talk to Ystan. She claimed she'd left something with Fal and had to get it. They hadn't asked what she'd left, and she hadn't told them. So they thought she was going to see Fal again, while they were having drinks and another dinner before they started the trek through the Mauvewood.

Ystan's quarters were composed of several concentric circles. Ystan was in his library, which happened to be the innermost circle. The room wasn't very wide, just big enough to fit a few chairs, a bar, and a fireplace, but the high ceiling allowed the bookshelves to reach three times the length of a person. They were filled, too; it was an impressive sight.

Ystan was in the middle of pouring himself a drink when Calissa opened the door. The guards must have let him know she was coming; he was pouring a second glass. "Hello, Calissa," he said, corking the bottle. "I'm a little surprised to see you here this late."

"Well, your friend upset Tristys to the point that he's insisting we leave the city." She took the drink he handed her and sat in the chair next to his. He'd started a fire, even though it wasn't cold. "So much for your plans," she added.

Ystan grinned as he sat down. "You never were one to beat around the bush, were you?" He sipped his liquor.

"No," Calissa said. "And I tried everything I could to keep him here in the city, but he wouldn't budge. Rami backed him, obviously, and Gawen and Salice don't care. So it looks like we're leaving."

Ystan thought a moment. "You'll be going with them, so you can still observe." He thought another moment. "And it may turn out to be to our advantage. Get him to more Altars. If he attunes to even one more quell, it'll prove my point." He sipped again. "Though even then, I don't think the other seyan will listen to me."

"What exactly is your point, Ystan?" Ever since

she'd arrived in Imidalé, he'd been hinting at something, but he never fully explained himself.

Ystan downed his drink. "I don't want to worry you, Calissa. I know how deep your connection to the quell is."

"Just tell me," she said. She was being curt, but she had to get back to the Roseate. And she had an idea what he'd be saying, anyway.

He was thin-lipped. "We're losing it, Calissa. The seyan, the experts, they won't admit it, but we're losing it."

Ystan obviously expected her to be surprised. He put his hand on her knee when he told her, for comfort, but she didn't need it. Nobody had told her, but she had figured it out herself. She spent her life with oş, studied it, loved it, worshiped it. She hadn't been around when people attuned to three or four quell each, but she knew about it. You didn't have to be a genius to realize that now, when people never attuned to more than two, something was wrong.

"And you think Tristys is the solution?" Tristys was amazing, and his connection with quell was inspiring, but she had trouble picturing him as anything close to a savior.

"Not him specifically, but he's a clue. If he communes again, that is. If he doesn't..." Ystan shrugged. "But if he does, we have to find out why. That's the key."

Calissa was nodding. It made sense. But then again, it didn't. The only thing that differentiated Tristys from anyone else here was his foreign blood, but the quell specifically refused to touch anyone without Coquellian blood in them. So was the very thing the quell rejected now the thing it wanted?

"I'll keep an eye out," she said.

"Get him to another Altar." Ystan stood up and headed to the bar. "Get him off this quell-forsaken island, at least. He won't attune to anything here."

Calissa left quickly after that, lost in thought. Beyond the obvious worries, her loyalties were being tested now. Should she rush to the Order and tell them about Ystan's theories? They wouldn't be surprised either, but did they need to know? And should she tell Tristys, let Rami know? Tristys already had so much to worry about, did he really need to feel as if he were an entire country's only hope?

She'd had a feeling something was wrong with the quell, but to have it laid out for her like this, to have it voiced aloud, shook her to the core. She wanted to run to Fal, to jump in his arms as she would have so many years ago, have him comfort her until their affection settled into discussion and ended, as always, in a heated argument that devolved into uncontrollable laughing. He was staying in an inn so close she could see the lights from the palace doors. It would be so simple, so familiar, so reassuring.

So wrong.

She went home instead.

~~*

Like the Bluewood and the Whitewood, the Mauvewood was a forest made of trees that were not green. It surrounded Imidalé, and to get anywhere from the city, you had to go through the Mauvewood. But unlike the Whitewood, Rami didn't mind the purple trees and the moisture in the air. It felt like night-swimming.

At the moment, he had a kink in his calf, and he was leaning against a trunk to work it out. He hadn't worked out in weeks, and it was starting to show. They hadn't even gone very far yet, had just barely left the city limits, and they were trying to decide where to go. Gawen was trying to walk in a straight line without wobbling. He'd had a few too many drinks while they were waiting for Calissa.

"He's not Fingerprinting right now," Salice said again, "so it doesn't really matter where we go. I haven't seen my parents in a while, so I think we should go to Quellas." Calissa rolled her eyes. Salice noticed. "Just because you don't like the island doesn't mean everybody doesn't!"

"I don't like it much," Gawen slurred. "Too many trees."

"Every island's got trees!" Salice shouted, exasperated. "Look at all these trees!"

"I know. I don't like this island very much, either." Gawen let out a single, raucous laugh. Rami had forgotten how giddy liquor made him. Now he remembered.

"Speaking of trees," Tristys said. He'd wandered quite a few steps away from the group and was barely paying attention to the discussion. "In Cyræa, we have trees. Just a few where I'm from." He picked up a leaf from the ground and ran it along his hand. "But they're green, you know? All green." He dropped the leaf. "And now I've seen white trees and blue trees and even a few green trees, so you'd think purple trees wouldn't faze me." He was by Rami now, and he bent his head the whole way back to look up the trunk. "But I'm a bit fazed."

"It's just a stupid tree," Gawen said, stumbling. "In Malatapia, the trees are on fire."

"Everything's on fire in Malatapia," Salice countered, her nose crinkled in distaste.

"And that's just how we like it," Gawen slurred. He was bent over, hands on his hips.

"The color is so vibrant, even this late at night. It's unbelievable." Tristys pulled a leaf off a low-hanging branch and held it up. Moonslight struck it. "This is my new favorite shade of purple."

Rami cracked a grin at the little bit of jealousy that flared in him. "What was your old favorite shade?" he asked, letting the grin widen.

Tristys tore his eyes away from the purple trees to look at Rami. He was still wide-eyed. "Unimportant," he said at last, and his head shot back up to the trees.

"Guys," Calissa's voice held just a hint of annoyance. "Let's focus. Where are we going?"

Now was his chance. "Why don't we go to Anamor?"

He'd been planning this move for a few days, ever since Calissa had mentioned the resort back at the Altar of Two Souls. He'd wanted to tell Tristys how he felt since he'd seen Tierran, but he had waited so long. Now he felt like he couldn't just tell him on the spur of the moment one day. When he told him, it had to be perfect. And Anamor was a resort town built around romance. It'd be perfect.

"That's the opposite direction of Quellas," Salice said, but there was no argument in her tone. She'd give in.

"And there's no Altar there," Calissa said. Her hands were on her hips and her face was set. She'd be difficult, which surprised Rami. He figured she'd be the first one to jump on board. "I think we should go to Quellus. It's the closest Altar."

"You just said a few days ago you wanted to go back to Anamor!" Rami checked himself. He didn't want to look too invested. Play it cool.

"What's Anamor?" Tristys asked.

"I meant we should go at some point when we have some spare time, not right now!"

"What's Anamor?" Tristys repeated.

"Well, we have some spare time right now," Rami countered. "It's like Salice said. He's not Fingerprinting. Spare time."

Tristys threw a twig at him. "What's Anamor?!"

"It's a town not far from here," Rami said, throwing the twig back. "It's something of a vacation resort—"

"For lovers!" Gawen shouted from the ground. He'd given up trying to stand and was now lying on his back with his head in a mound of flowers. He giggled.

Rami ignored him. "The town's on the shore of the Amorai, which is an enormous roughwater lake. You'll like it, I promise."

Tristys nodded. "Okay, sounds good, as long as Calissa's okay with it."

"I'm not, but I suppose it's on the way to Quellus, so it's not a total waste. We just can't stay there too long, okay?"

Rami didn't need to stay there too long. He just needed one night. "That's fine," he said. "Let's go."

"Nobody asked if I'm okay with it," Salice said. Was she serious?

"Oh, you'll get over it," Gawen said, waving a hand in the air and sitting up. He blew a leaf off his shoulder, but more spit came out than air. "The only reason you don't like Anamor is because you're alone and it's all about lovers." He exaggerated the last word, then he pointed at

Tristys. "You! I'll show you what I mean when we get there."

Rami wanted to argue the last point, but he let it slide. Gawen probably wouldn't remember anything in the morning, anyway.

The sour expression had melted from Salice's face. She looked as if she were about to cry now, which was a strange expression on her. She was usually so hard. "You know, Gawen, sometimes you can be such a jerk."

She waited for a response, but all she got was a flick of the wrist before Gawen fell back onto his back, head in the flowers again.

Salice stomped to Gawen, and Rami thought he might have to pull her off him if she went off. But she didn't. She bent down, put his arm around her shoulder, and helped him up. "Let's go if we're going," she said. "I'm tired and he's drunk."

As they started out, Rami looked behind him to make sure Tristys was still following. He was, but his head was tilted back again, staring at the trees. He stumbled over a rock, caught himself on a nearby tree, and still didn't watch where he was walking. Just like Tristys.

"I guess it'll be nice to get back there again," Calissa said, finally relenting. "Lot of memories."

"Indeed," Rami said. She was right, there were a lot of memories there. And as Rami glanced again at Tristys, he vowed he'd make a lot more.

~~*

Anamor was a lot bigger than Tristys had expected. There were no real roads or paths, just buildings spread across the shore. In a way, it reminded him of the towns he'd seen in Quelles:

every building looked different. But in Quelles, the buildings were shoved right next to each other, and here they were spread out. One building made Tristys shriek in alarm, but Rami just laughed and assured him it was meant to be on fire. Gawen told him all the houses in Malatapia looked like that, and when Tristys asked if they could not spend the night there, Gawen tried to snort, but it was cut short by a hiccup. He was still a little drunk.

The Amorai glistened just beyond the buildings. It was huge. The water was smooth, but it looked slightly odd, as if the moonslight was reflecting back at odd angles and blurring his sight. He shook his head, closing his eyes tightly, and when he opened them, the water looked normal again. He also realized how tired he was. His eyes stung.

They argued about where to spend the night. Gawen insisted on the Blazing Beacon, which Tristys quickly vetoed again, and Salice wanted the Puffball, which Rami rejected. Firebird kept wandering over to an inn shaped like a giant tree. Calissa didn't care where they slept, and even after she mentioned they could switch inns every night if they wanted, they still couldn't agree. Finally, after too long of an argument, she just went to the nearest inn—the Bellimarin, an asymmetrical mushroom smaller than most of the other inns— and announced that she was staying there, and they could go with her or keep arguing. Everyone followed.

The next morning, Tristys emerged from his bedroom wiping sleep from his eyes to find breakfast waiting for him. It was more of a lunch, but he wasn't going to split hairs. Everybody else had already eaten, but there was plenty left for him. And it was still warm.

"So," Salice said as she tossed yet another bitterberry muffin at Gawen. He'd been refusing food all morning, claiming starvation as the best cure for a hangover. "There's an air-dancing show later tonight over at the Purple Host. I saw a poster for it down in the bar when I got breakfast. I thought maybe we could all go."

"I don't know, Salice," Gawen said. "Loud music, crowds of people, all that movement. The mere thought is making me nauseated."

"No, all the poison that liquor left in your body is making you nauseated," Rami corrected. "Now give me that muffin if you aren't going to eat it. They're too good to waste." Gawen threw it at him.

"You need to eat, Gawen. Your starvation theory has never worked." She chucked another muffin at him. It landed in his lap and stayed there.

"Shows how much you know," he said. "It always works."

She shook her head in resigned disagreement and turned to Rami and Calissa, who were sitting at the table together. "How about you two?"

"We were going to walk around town a bit, I think." Calissa looked to Rami for confirmation. "We had talked about coming here back in Quellos, so I just figured..."

"Yeah. Sorry, Salice." Rami's mouth was full so he didn't say anything else.

Salice was visibly disappointed. "I figured you'd want to go, Calissa. You love air-dancing."

Calissa shrugged. "I do, and normally I'd love to go, but—"

"Right, fine." Salice turned abruptly to Tristys. "Well, how about you? What's your excuse?"

Tristys thought a moment. Salice was slightly abrasive, and Tristys had never felt as close to her as he did to the others, but his only other option was staying in the inn with a recuperating Gawen. He shot a glance in his direction, and even though he just saw the back of Gawen's head, he imagined that lascivious grin on his face. Not today! "No excuse, actually. I'd love to go."

"Oh," she said, taken aback. "Really?"

"Yeah, really." He offered a friendly smile.

She lit up. "Okay, then." She stood up, brushing muffin crumbs onto the table. "Well, go get ready. It starts at six past, and we slept in. And you take forever to get ready."

"I wasn't really finished eating, though." He popped another of the dried fruits he'd discovered that morning into his mouth.

"I'll pack you a bag of pineapple. Go!"

"Fine, I'm going, I'm going." He took a second to crack his back before getting up, which received a glare from Salice. Just after he left the room, he stuck his head back around the corner. "By the way, what's air-dancing?"

"Get ready!" Salice shouted, and he jerked his head out of view.

A second later, he jerked it back into view.

"Are you sure nobody else wants to come?" Before he could get an answer, a bitterberry muffin hit him in the forehead. He pulled away, and though he was tempted to see if he could persuade at least Rami to join them, he didn't try. He didn't want to waste any of that dried fruit he liked so much, and with the way Salice had been chucking muffins all morning, she couldn't have many more left.

~~*

There was only one public arena back in Paru, and it paled in comparison to the Purple Host. This one was built of a deep purple stone, rough to the touch and porous, with a dome of darker rock. The ground-level entrances were near the top of the structure, so the builders had either done a lot of digging or they'd used a natural depression. The central performance area was sunk even farther into the ground, and tiers with various types of seating wrapped around the whole perimeter.

They were early, largely because Salice had made Tristys trot the whole way, but much of the seating was already taken. Tristys saw a few empty chairs nearby, but when he made a break for them, Salice just shook her head and walked in the opposite direction.

Tristys followed her to the other side of the amphitheater. When she finally led him to a table-and-chair setup in one of the highest tiers, she mentioned something about having reserved this earlier. "So what's air-dancing, anyway?"

A horn blew, a deep sound that shook his stomach. A breeze picked up—had to be Air-magic—and sped into a brisk wind as it blew down the tiers, carrying the sound so thes note rang first behind him, then all around him, then down in the center of the amphitheater before shooting into the sky.

"You're about to find out." Salice settled back in her seat and took a long swig from her cup.

At the far end of the depressed stage, a door opened. From it emerged a young woman, strong-looking despite her small frame, with her hands cupped in front of her. Her hair, worn free and so long it nearly touched the ground, was a pale blonde. As she walked closer to the middle of the stage, Tristys saw that small twisted braids, dyed black, had been woven throughout the blonde.

She was barefoot. Her only clothing was a thin dress with loose sleeves, pale blue and shimmering. Despite the heavily draped fabric, the dress seemed to hang above her, as if she wasn't really wearing it but hovering just beneath it. She was halfway to the middle of the stage and the train still hadn't fully emerged from the door.

She stopped, stood stiffly, and bowed her head. On cue, music started. He recognized the horn from earlier, softer and subdued, and the resonating sounds of more horns and the light tiptoes of woodwinds, as well as instruments Tristys didn't recognize: a heavy, percussive thumping; the tinkling of what sounded like hundreds of bells; and something rich and full-throated that moved in waves rather than distinct notes.

The woman was floating now, just barely off the ground, and spinning slowly in place. She had uncupped her hands, letting them hang at her sides, and loosed her sleeves, which were just as long as the train. As she spun, everything—including the train—twisted around her legs. It reminded Tristys of the way he preferred to sleep.

But a second later, the music crescendoed and the dancer shot into the air, far higher than even the highest seat in the amphitheater. She threw her arms to the sides, and her sleeves streaked through the air, shimmering along impossible angles. Her train—which wasn't a single piece of material as Tristys originally thought but rather hundreds of narrow strips—began to weave itself into the same intricate pattern as the braids in her hair. When it finished, it flipped itself up, flipping the dancer down, and bursting free from the pattern only to twist itself into something new.

The performance took Tristys's breath away. The dancer continued these impossible feats with just her Air-magic, in time with the music. She was the only person on the stage, and yet she wasn't dancing alone: her train, her sleeves, even her hair became partners, weaving in and around each other with uncanny ease. They wrapped forcefully around her neck, her arms, her legs. The music grew loud and violent, sharp and aggressive, and Tristys gasped.

This wasn't just a dance, this was a story. She was enslaved, shackled by something. Tristys felt the present slip away, felt himself fall into shackles on a ship that sailed to a land Tristys loathed. As the dancer fought against her fate, struggling against the cruel masters of her dress, Tristys battled through his own memories, realizing how much he'd pushed aside and how lucky he'd been to find kindness, even love, in the master he'd had.

By the time the dancer took her final bow, Tristys was raw and torn open. He was crying, but they were tears of happiness, of thanks, of every emotion he'd bottled up since he'd landed on the islands. The dancer left the stage, and the music grew subdued again, still dignified. Tristys felt as if the orchestra played it just for him.

Everybody started clapping. People jumped to their feet. Tristys stood and wiped a tear from his eye before he started to clap. After a few minutes, when the noise had settled to the unintelligible drone of hundreds of conversations at once, Salice put a hand on Tristys's shoulder.

"You okay now?"

"Yeah yeah, I'm fine," he said, shutting his eyes to push away the last bit of tears. He wasn't ashamed, but he didn't really want to explain his reaction, either. But he didn't have to.

"If I had known they were doing the Voelora, I wouldn't have brought you. Or I would have warned you, at least." She was sincere, and for the first time, Tristys noticed how full her brown eyes were. "Give me your cup. I'll get us more beer, okay?"

When she got back, she told him there were still two performances to go. She assured him that neither was about slavery, though, so he tried to relax. The beer helped.

After a few minutes, the next dancers took the stage. There were two of them this time, a man and a woman, dressed in the same material as the first had been. Their dance told a story, too, but Tristys found himself less enthralled. It was a simple story, common even in Cyræa, with a boy meeting a girl and falling in love. Since he wasn't so emotionally invested, he could sit back and enjoy the beauty of the performance without getting battered by the story. It was nice.

The final performers of the night were another couple, though this time it was two men. They were dressed differently than the others. Their hair was short, cropped close to their heads, and they had very little clothing on, just knee-length pants and sleeveless, open vests. They were nicely built, but Rami was better.

"This is a little different than the last two," Salice said as the music started. "There'll be more than Air-magic going on here."

"That explains the lack of flowing costumes, I

bet."

"Sure does," she said, dropping the conversation and sitting back in her chair.

There was indeed more than Air-magic. The couple floated just off the ground, and when the music crescendoed, half the pit erupted into flames and the other half flooded. Almost at once, cords of fire and water threaded themselves around the dancers, fire to the taller one and water to the one with the nicer body. The men began to move, dancing much closer and much tighter than the previous couple had. It was violent, full of thrusts and lunges, with abrupt, stiff motions. The choreography seemed more about weaving the Fire- and Water-magic than it did dancing on the air. The flames kept changing colors, from red to orange to blue, and even the water fluctuated between shades of blue and white. The music was tribal, with a relentless, grinding beat, and Tristys realized that this wasn't dancing, this was sex.

Indeed, every motion, every gesture, was erotic. At one point, the flames and the water shot through each other without mixing, twisting one around the other but remaining entirely separate. At another point, the flames engulfed the Water-dancer and vanished just in time for the audience to see the ashes of his vest fall to the floor.

Through all this, the dancers were shooting through the air, often colliding, twisting their bodies around each other without touching, back to front, front to back, side to side. In the final movement, the snakes of fire and water gathered every last tongue and drop from the stage, lined up behind their man, and then charged. The men were swept up and pushed towards each other, and everything smashed together in a burst of steam. When it cleared, the two men were on the ground, wrapped in each other's arms, finally touching for the first time.

When the clapping calmed down and the sconces on the walls lit up, Salice stretched. "So, what did you think?" Her grin suggested she already knew the answer.

"If that's what sex in the Coquels is like, I'm glad I came."

"We wish," she said with a laugh. "That was a representation of sex with a Spálorian."

The amusement on Tristys's face disappeared. "Why would anyone glorify Spálorian sex like that? It's slavery."

"Not all sex in Spálor is slavery," Salice said. "Some of it's worship."

Tristys knew that. Tristys didn't care. "This was two men, though. Same-sex worship is forbidden. So that was slavery." The idea of sex-slavery repulsed him. What repulsed him more was the fact that he still found the performance arousing.

"Actually," Salice said with just a slight edge to her voice, "that wasn't slavery. It depicted sex between two men, yes, but a Spálorian and a Coquellian, not two men from Spálor."

Tristys looked skeptical.

"It was! The water represents the quell, and the fire represents Spálorian sex-magic. That's why the water couldn't do anything to the Fire-dancer, but his magic burnt the shirt off the Water-dancer. Our magic isn't sexual, so it's more or less useless in a performance about sex."

Tristys was baffled. "What are you talking about, sex-magic?"

Now it was Salice's turn to look skeptical. "You

were a slave for a few months and you don't know about sex-magic?" Her disbelief was sincere, which agitated Tristys even more.

"Vun'gor never forced me to do anything that I didn't want to do. And he protected me from the people who would have." Tristys sat back in his seat, arms crossed. He didn't look at Salice. "So no, I don't know anything about your sex-magic."

"It's not my sex-magic, Tristys. It's the Spàlorians." She looked sad for some reason. Did she want sex-magic?

"Well, what is it, anyway?"

Salice squirmed a bit, which gave Tristys a little satisfaction. "It's hard to explain, really. Sex feels better for the Spàlorians, and it feels better for the people they're with, too. They say it's a gift from their gods or whatever, but it's just chemicals or technique or something. That's all it is."

Tristys had seen Spàlorians having sex with their slaves. Just one, really, and the slaves never wanted it. But he didn't want to keep arguing with her about it, so he changed the subject. "What about you?" he asked. "What quell Touched you?" He was surprised he didn't know yet.

She hung her head. "None, actually. I have no magic."

"Oh, I didn't—"

"Earth-magic Fingerprinted me once," she continued. "I was really young, just like Calissa was when she was Touched. That's usually a sign of potential, you know? Like it was with Calissa. But with me, I don't know. Maybe I was too young. But at the Altar, nothing. I never got it, you know? That little flicker that says you're ready."

Tristys nodded. He knew it well.

"I kept trying, but it just wasn't there. And then

it was gone." She stopped talking, but she wanted to continue, so Tristys stayed quiet until she did. "It wouldn't have been so bad, you know, if I had never Fingerprinted. I felt it, you know? If I hadn't, I wouldn't know what I lost. But I do. That makes it hard."

Tristys was nodding, touched that Salice opened up so suddenly to him and heartbroken that she had to go through the pain of having her connection taken away. She was right. He couldn't imagine losing his quell now. "Salice, I—"

"It turned out okay. If I had communed, I wouldn't have gone to the Physical Services and met Rami. And if I never met him, I'd have never met Calissa. And Calissa—she's everything."

Tristys caught a little hint of something more there. "You and Calissa aren't—"

"No, of course not!" Salice said at once, almost too quickly. "I mean, I wish, but—no. No." She took a look around her, noticing for the first time that the seats had cleared. "We should probably go. They'll want to start cleaning soon, and they can't 'til we're all gone."

They left the auditorium in silence, that slightly awkward quiet that comes after you've just had an emotional exchange with someone unexpected. As they neared the inn, Tristys asked "Does Calissa know that you..." He trailed off, unsure how to define what Salice felt.

"I don't think so." She'd been kicking a rock along with them since they'd left the Purple Host. "She's too preoccupied with her own life." She kicked the rock again, harder than ever, and it flew off their path. She ran to get it. "I don't mean that in a bad way. She's just—she's very busy, and she doesn't always catch on to what's going on around her. She forgets to look, I think. She sets her mind on something, on one thing, and that's all she can see."

He thought of the Calissa who taught him to use Water-magic so well and the Calissa who stood up to the seyquel's military. "Makes sense," he said.

"I can't believe I told you all this," she said, a strange little half-laugh caught on her face. "Nobody knows but Gawen."

"Gawen knows? And he didn't tell anyone? Not even in an attempt to bang Rami?"

"Nope, he didn't. Gawen's preoccupied with his own life, too. In a bad way."

"That also makes sense."

They walked a bit farther. Tristys spent a lot of time looking up at the sky—the stars were beautiful—and Salice kicked her rock. When they got to the Bellimarin, Salice stopped outside the door. "I'm gonna go to the kitchen and see if they have any of those muffins left." She picked up the rock she'd been kicking and tossed it to Tristys. "Here, keep this."

"What for?"

She had a queer grin on her face. "I may need it later."

"For what?"

She smiled sweetly as she turned to go to the bakery. "To beat you over the head if you tell Calissa what I told you tonight." She waved as she walked away, leaving Tristys standing on the stoop, wondering how serious she was.

She was kidding, of course. She had to be. But he threw the rock as hard as he could, and it landed in a bush near the neighboring inn. Just in case.

CHAPTER FOURTEEN

Everything was ready. Rami'd found the perfect spot, close enough to the shore to see the forest but far enough away to assure privacy. He'd even scouted for the perfect lily pad on the lake. He'd made sure he had a paddle boat reserved, and he'd hidden a cache of food inside it. He'd taken two showers already, three if you included the one when he first woke up. He'd shaved, he'd brushed his teeth, he'd splashed on some cologne. He'd even groomed himself down there, just in case. Everything was ready.

Everything except him, apparently. As soon as night fell, he'd gone to Tristys's door and stood outside for what felt like hours. He'd gone back to his room, then back to Tristys's door, then back to his room, then back to his door, then back to his room. Finally, after the fourth pep talk he gave himself, he'd had it. He could do this! He would do this! He jumped resolutely off his bed, all but stomped to Tristys's door, and promptly froze again. He even had his hand up, fist near his face, ready to knuckle the door. But he couldn't knock, so he stood there, hand up. And when Tristys had finally opened the door, shrieking in surprise to find a person waiting for him, he still hadn't knocked. When Tristys asked what he was doing, Rami played dumb.

"What do you mean?" he asked, trying to look

confused. Tristys wasn't wearing a shirt, and Rami stared intently—probably too intently—at his face, lest his eyes start to wander.

"Did you need something?" His overgrown hair was messed up and wet. He must've just showered.

"No, of course not. Why would you say that?"

"You were about to knock on my door."

"No, I wasn't."

"Rami," Tristys said, looking tired and fed up, "your hand is still in the air."

Rami looked at his hand in shock, as if the hand had betrayed him unexpectedly. Deny, deny, deny! "Oh, no, I was just stretching."

"You were stretching?" Tristys crossed his arms.

"Yeah, stretching. What else would I be doing?"

"Knocking." He grinned then, and it was absolutely adorable.

"No, I wasn't, I—"

"Whatever you say, Rami." He mussed his own hair, to get the wet bangs out of his eyes. "You've been an even odder duck lately, you know that?"

Rami could have said *Because I like you*. He could have said *Because I can't stop thinking about you*. He could have said *Wanna get naked*? Instead, he'd shrugged and scurried to his room, slamming the door as if he were angry. Tristys hadn't come knocking.

Rami had been lying in his bed since, staring at the ceiling, unable to fall asleep and unable to do the only other thing he wanted to do. He couldn't figure out why he still had that paralyzing fear. It wasn't the same, though. It wasn't worry about hurting someone because of his feelings; he didn't think a waterbolt was going to erupt from him and kill Tristys. That part of his life was over. That waterbolt had nothing to do with the kiss he had shared with Tierran. It was just coincidence, bad timing, a nasty Fingerprinting. In the head of a scared, shy twelve-year-old, it became so much more. That made sense. But now, in the head of someone with twelve more years of experience and education, the conflation seemed silly.

This had to do with Tristys, with taking such a huge step forward. He was afraid, just like anyone would be. But now was not the time to be afraid. Now was the time to just do it.

So he did. He jumped out of bed without really realizing where he was going, and he ran to Tristys's door, and before he could stop himself, he knocked three times, loud knocks that echoed through the hall. He hoped he didn't wake anyone else.

After a few seconds, he heard a crash, followed by Tristys's cursing, and then the door opened. Tristys held the remains of a glass in his hand.

"You again." He had one eye shut, the green one. Did he know Rami liked the blue one best? "More stretching?"

"No, not stretching this time. I wasn't stretching before, either, but I couldn't—I want to take you somewhere." The words spilled out too quickly, but Tristys spoke fast, so Rami was sure he'd understand.

"Rami," Tristys said, twisting to look out the window. "It's the middle of the night! Can't you take me tomorrow?"

"Nope. Has to be tonight. Has to be right now. Let's go." He wasn't nervous anymore. It faded as soon as he knocked. Now he was just excited, impatient even. He wanted to get there and get started!

Tristys's one eye was still closed. "Fine, fine." He rubbed his eye, and now both were open. "Let me go put clothes on and wake up Firebird."

Rami gave him a once-over. He had on a faded black shirt, button-front with long sleeves, and a thin pair of sleeping pants. He'd be cold, but he'd survived. "Leave Firebird here. You're fine like that. Let's go."

"I don't even have shoes on!"

"Go put shoes on then!" Rami gave Tristys a little push back into the room. Perhaps he pushed too hard, or perhaps Tristys was still half-asleep and already off balance, but he stumbled backwards a bit more than Rami intended.

"Dammit, Rami! What's the deal? Am I about to get arrested again or something?"

"No, of course not! You're a free man now, you're one of us!" Even he cringed at his over-enthusiasm. "I just—I've wanted to talk to you for a while. It's been a long time coming, and I don't know. I don't want to wait any more, I guess."

For the first time, Tristys didn't look like he was on the verge of going back to sleep. His eyes still looked tired, but he had a hint of his playful grin. "What do you want to talk about?"

Rami considered telling him right there, in his darkened bedroom at the Bellimarin. Then he thought of the lake. "I waited this long. I can wait a few more minutes." Tristys didn't do or say anything, just stood there studying Rami, so Rami shouted, "Shoes, now!" and Tristys disappeared into his closet.

A few seconds later, he came back out with shoes on his feet. Two different shoes. Just as

Rami was about to mention the mismatch, Tristys cut him off.

"It doesn't matter, I'm fine, I can't find the other one." He grabbed Rami's arm and started to drag him to the door. "Let's do this."

Rami followed him out the door and past the bathroom before he stopped. He thought about what he intended to do with Tristys on that lily-pad, and he couldn't do it yet. Not like this.

He grabbed Tristys's shoulder. "Tristys, wait. I can't go with you like this."

Tristys turned around slowly, pivoting on one foot. "Rami, I swear to the two moons, if you even think—"

But Rami couldn't keep a straight face any longer. His smile burst free. "Not until you brush your teeth."

Tristys took a second to process. Then he grinned madly, told Rami he hated him, and ran to the bathroom. He was back in thirty seconds.

~~*

Despite the anticipation boiling in both of them, neither Rami nor Tristys spoke as they walked to the boat. Rami spent the time going over exactly what he wanted to say and how he planned on saying it. Tristys was a bit less focused, bouncing between complete certainty that Rami was and then wasn't going to confess his attraction. By the time they got to the rental hut, both of them were a lot more frazzled than they were when they'd started.

The paddle boat Rami had rented was at the end of the dock, just as he'd left it earlier that evening. The sky was cloudless, a crisp black canvas pierced with stars, and the two moons hung overhead, so close they were almost touching. Their light fell on everything, clear and strong and cool. It was beautiful.

They walked to the edge of the pier. Tristys had that look on his face: wide eyes, open mouth, as if he was about to trip. "You've not seen the water yet, have you?" Rami asked. He felt guilty. The silence had been sacred, a promise he'd just broken.

Silence wasn't sacred to Tristys. "Nope. I saw a glimpse of it on the way into town, but that's it. It looked weird." It looked weird now, too. First, it was purple. It was also changing, patches shifting from transparent to opaque. The patterns echoed across the whole lake like waves. "It's pretty awesome."

"Is this your new favorite shade of purple now?" Rami asked.

"No," Tristys said, bending down for a closer look at the lake. He ran a hand through the water, rippling the surface from transparent to opaque. "I think I'm back to my original, actually."

"Oh yeah?" Rami tried not to squeak.

"Yeah," Tristys said, looking up at him. "You never really give up on your first, I don't think."

Rami hoped he was right. He knelt near the paddle boat he'd rented, grabbing the gunwale to anchor it. "Here, hop in," he said. "I'll hold it so you don't fall and kill yourself."

Tristys scoffed at the exaggeration then blushed when he still managed to lose his balance and stumble even with Rami's added support. He expected a jab or at least a snicker, but Rami just stepped into the boat—fluid, as always—and sat down across from Tristys.

As Rami rowed to the lily-pad, they were quiet again. Rami dedicated his energy to rowing, a thin sheen of sweat forming along his biceps. He'd worn a sleeveless shirt, partly because he'd been warm that day and partly because he knew how good his arms would look while rowing. Tristys was lost in the scenery, gliding his hand along the surface of the lake as the boat moved. The only time he looked away from the forest was to sneak a furtive glimpse at Rami's arms, but since Rami never took his eyes off Tristys, the glimpses were never that furtive. Rami approved.

When the first of the lily pads came into view, Tristys was surprised. They were green! He'd expected purple, like everything else on this island. They were bigger than he'd thought they'd be, too. He reached out to touch the nearest one, but it was just out of his reach. He slipped, his hand grazing the surface.

"I'm sorry," Tristys said, exaggerating his contrition.

"Your almost falling in didn't hurt me at all," Rami said, grinning as he dropped the oars inside the boat to crack his back.

"Not for that." Tristys paused, savoring the confusion on Rami's face. "For this." He flicked the drops of water still on his hand at Rami, who flinched far more than necessary. Tristys burst into laughter.

"Big mistake, kiddo," Rami said as he wiped the drops off his face and arms. "Huge mistake, actually." He picked up the two oars, pushed them far to the front, and then yanked them back and out of the water. Two huge waves of water rushed over the side of the boat, slamming into Tristys and drenching the entire bottom half of his body.

It was Rami's turn to crack up, which he did. Tristys, sopping wet and shivering slightly, sat there as the water drained slowly from the boat. He tried to look mortified, but it was hard.

"I should use my magic to drown you," he said at last. He shook his head violently, spraying Rami with water from his hair. "But I'm going to be the bigger man and just dry myself off with it instead." He shook his head once more, blinked to stars, and was dry.

"Tristys, you will never be the bigger man around me. I'm just bigger than you. In every sense of the word." There was a wink to Rami's word, but even he wasn't quite sure what he meant. All he knew was that he'd never been that suggestive with anyone before, and he liked it.

"Are you serious?" Tristys asked. "I'm taller than you."

"Taller doesn't equal bigger."

"It does in my world!"

Rami pointed at him. "You're not in your world, are you? You're in mine!" He tried his best at a maniacal cackle.

"Blah blah blah," Tristys said. "Are you rowing me out to kill me and leave the body? If so, I think we're far enough."

"We're almost there." Rami rowed a little harder. "Now sit down and shut up." He decided to tease Tristys a little bit more. "You can keep staring at my arms, though." Tristys looked mortified and averted his eyes, which was a peculiar move, since he'd never been shy about his attraction before. "I don't mind." For good measure, he flexed his biceps a little more than necessary on the next stroke. Tristys still looked mortified, but he wasn't averting his eyes now.

A few minutes later, Rami guided the boat to a lily pad within sight of the shore. He pierced the boat's anchor through the pad's fleshy side before stepping onto it. "Do you need my help, or can you manage this on your own? Remember, the lake's pretty deep, so don't fall in."

Tristys could make it on his own, but he lied. "You may as well help me now instead of later. Save us both from getting wet again." He held out his hand, and Rami took it without the slightest bit of hesitation or annoyance. Progress!

The lily pad was smaller than the ones around it, but not uncomfortably so. Rami lay on his back and stretched his arms above his head before using his palms as a pillow. The thought that he should have brought pillows flitted through his mind but only for a second. Tristys was still standing on the pad, staring at the scattering of purple leaves thrown across it. None of the neighboring pads had it. Just theirs.

"Did you do this?" Tristys asked, picking up a leaf and twirling its stem between his fingers. "These are from the trees, aren't they?"

Rami propped himself up on his elbows. "Well, the wind doesn't have this kind of aim, so yeah, I guess I did." He tried not to blush, wondering if he'd gone too far, but Tristys's smile reassured him. He lay back down on his palms.

Tristys followed suit, lying down next to Rami, close but not so close they were touching. They were both staring skyward, Rami trying to figure out how best to phrase what he had to say and Tristys trying not to panic because of how close they were to each other. The slightest motion from Rami ignited Tristys's skin, as if there were some impossible friction between their bodies. His body was so warm, even though the air on the lake was crisp with chill. He could hear every breath Rami took; he could see Rami out of the corner of his eye. Tristys kept waiting, but he had no idea what he was waiting for. A touch, a word, a waterbolt. Something.

The waiting became too much. He turned on his side, propped his head on his hand, and spoke. "So what's up?"

Rami looked at Tristys, but he didn't turn his body, and his gaze lasted only a minute before he redirected it to the stars. "What's up?" Rami repeated. "The sky, the moons, that bat that just flew by." His voice was timid. He knew how cheesy the answer was, even before Tristys said anything.

"Bad joke is bad, Rami. I'm serious. Why are we here?" He threw a leaf at Rami. It landed on his stomach. The thinnest stretch of Rami's abs was showing. Tristys averted his eyes. "The leaves are pretty, but you didn't—"

"Look," Rami said suddenly. He moved his arms to his side, but he stayed straight, his head now resting directly on the lily pad. He didn't turn or even look at Tristys as he spoke. "I've been wrong." He wanted to continue, he had to continue, but he couldn't. His voice had caught in his throat.

"Wrong about what, Rami? Wrong about what? You can't just say—"

"You. Me." He ran a hand through his hair. "Everything. I don't know." Rami felt restless, like he had to move. He sat up. "I thought for so long that the way I am had something to do with what happened to Tierran, maybe even the Altar or who knows, even the War, but—"

"Oh no," Tristys said, sitting up. "None of your

Rami-babbling. I never know what you're talking about when you do it." Rami looked stricken, and Tristys realized perhaps he should try to show a little more compassion. "And I want to know. So just take a breath, calm down, and explain to me exactly what you're talking about. Slowly."

Rami's mouth opened and closed like a fish's, but no words came out. He obviously needed help. Tristys took the lead.

"What way are you, Rami? And what happened to the ferry guy?"

Rami knew what he had to do. "You have to promise something. Nobody knows this, I've never told anyone any of this. You have to promise not to tell."

"Of course," Tristys said. His heart was racing. This was it!

"I met Tierran at the Altar in Quelles. I'd Fingerprinted early, and my parents sent me at once. I was very young, and Tierran was older. He was so... contagious. He was good-looking, and there was something about him. You have to realize, I grew up in Quelles. I was at the Altar of Five Waves. Everything was calm, cool, smooth, fluid. And he was the exact opposite. I was only twelve, and it sounds so stupid, but I felt like I was playing with fire when I was with him. The way you look into a flame, it's just mesmerizing. He was like that. Looking at him was like that." There was a smile on Rami's face, distant and tarnished but still there. Tristys didn't like it.

"We spent so much time together. The more I got to know him, the less I focused on the reason I was there, the magic." Rami twitched, and the smile disappeared. He was looking at Tristys again. "I was so good at it at first, Tristys. You'd have been impressed."

"I'm still impressed. You saved me twice with your magic, remember?"

"I know, but that was nothing compared to what I should be able to do. I spent more and more time with Tierran, and less and less time in the meditation alcoves. It got so bad that we snuck into them together. You don't get it, because you're not from here, but the meditation rooms are the closest thing we have to churches here. They're sacred to a lot of people, and they're intended for one thing and one thing only. And that one thing is: have a splash war with your crush."

Rami paused, obviously waiting for a response, but all Tristys could think was *Did he just admit he likes men*?

"Anyway, one day we were in the alcove, goofing around like always did. I felt eş pulling at me, trying to get me to commune, but I ignored it. That's the scariest thing, I think. I thought that as long as I ignored its call, I'd stay at the Altar, and as long as I stayed at the Altar, I'd have Tierran. But that day I felt it bad, but I didn't care. We were wrestling, rolling around in that water that glows, and he had me pinned against the ground. His face was so close to mine, like this." Rami bent into Tristys, so close that Tristys went cross-eyed trying to focus on Rami's eyes.

"Then he leaned in even further, and he kissed me. It was like... by the quell, I can't even think what it was like." Tristys wanted to ask if it was anything like their kiss in the forest, but he held back. Rami had never spoken about himself this much; Tristys didn't want to ruin it.

"But that's when the Water-magic shot out of

me." He was shaking, shivering really, and he'd wrapped his arms around his legs. "I've never seen anything like it, Tristys. It came from everywhere, my whole body. I felt it leave me, and it walloped Tierran, slamming his body into the ceiling. I can still hear the sound, the cracking and then the thud when he hit the floor, the terrible splash. You know how tall those ceilings are! It was terrible.

"I just sat there. I don't know how long it took, but Liana finally came in. She saw Tierran on the floor, broken, and she started yelling, screaming, cursing. She called me wicked, said I was a murderer. She wanted to hit me, I think, maybe she even tried. She took Tierran and left me in the alcove. I still don't know how long I stayed there. Minutes, hours, days. I don't know.

"Nobody ever told me what happened. She never told me what happened. I thought he died. I thought I killed him. I thought the magic was trying to tell me something, like the burst had been a punishment or protection or... something. I don't know. I just—after that—I couldn't—" He couldn't continue. The tears wouldn't let him.

Tristys wrapped his arms around Rami's shivering frame. He'd never been good at comforting people, but he'd try his damnedest now. All of Rami's hangups suddenly made sense. He'd spent all these years linking his feelings of attraction and his skills with quell to the Tierran trauma. And all his strange behavior since he saw Tierran on that ferry made sense now, too.

"When I saw Tierran," he choked out, "I realized that—"

"It's okay, Rami," Tristys said. "I understand. That's the first time you realized it was okay, that you could be who you are, that—"

Rami jerked. "No, not the first time. That was when I knew for sure it was okay. Don't you remember? I communed with eş to save you, and I used it so much on the way to the Altar with you, I started to think then that perhaps it was okay. I mean, I was so attracted to you, but the magic I used saved you, it didn't hurt you."

"So you admit you were attracted to me?" Tristys was giddy, so he didn't care that he'd interrupted Rami's story. It had stopped his tears, at least. That was a plus.

Rami thought a second as he wiped the last tear off his cheek. "No, of course not." He looked away.

Tristys felt ill. "But you just said—"

"I'm admitting I *am* attracted to you." He feigned resignation, but he wasn't an actor, and the humor showed through. "Probably always will be. Unless you get ugly, I guess, but even then, if you keep those eyes..."

Tristys leaned in for a smack, but Rami caught his wrist and pulled him hard, so hard that he fell into Rami. They fell back onto the lily pad, and Tristys felt a hand on his head, then lips on his lips. He felt all the repressed desire in the push of Rami's hand, all the unbridled attraction in the pull of his body, as if his body itself were lifting off the lily pad to meet Tristys'. Rami's lips opened, tentatively at first, and then Tristys understood what Rami had said about fire.

Even when Rami noticed the balls of firelight dancing around them as they kissed, he said nothing to Tristys. He didn't want to interrupt the moment. He said a little prayer, asking that this Fingerprinting wouldn't make Tristys faint like the other two had, and then he kissed a little bit harder. Just in case.

~~*

"I never thought I'd be the big moon," Tristys said a few hours later. They were still together, lying on the lily pad. Rami had his head on Tristys's chest, with Tristys's arms wrapped around him. Most of his fireflies had gone away, but one or two still danced around them. He'd never fainted.

"What are you talking about?" Rami asked. He was playing with a drawstring on Tristys's shirt, twirling it around his finger and hitting Tristys lightly on the chin with each twirl.

"The moons." He motioned with his head to the sky. The moons were overlapping now, the smaller one in front of the bigger, and Rami realized they did look like they were embracing. "I always thought you'd be the big moon, the one holding me. But look at us now!" He squeezed Rami's shoulder for emphasis.

"Well," Rami said, twirling the string higher so it hit Tristys's cheek, "maybe tomorrow I'll be the big moon. Would you like that?" Tristys wriggled his approval. "I'm just colder than you are tonight. I don't have sleeves."

"I was the big moon in the forest on Quelles, too," Tristys pointed out.

"Right, and I was nearly dead then because of your harebrained attempt to play with the kitty."

"Hey," Tristys argued as he finally grabbed the drawstring from Rami. "I was with Spàlorians right before that, remember? Enormous cats with giant teeth are friendly there!"

"That's true," Rami said, letting the argument

trail off.

"Besides, I wasn't trying to play with the cat. I was trying to find a banana."

"Haven't you been trying to find my banana since you got here?" Rami said. He felt so satisfied, finally being able to use the banana joke he'd been sitting on for weeks.

"Shut up." Tristys was still thinking about Rami's last comment. "Just so we're clear, this isn't a one-night thing, right? We're going to do this again? You're not going to wake up tomorrow and tell me this was a mistake, an accident, you didn't mean to throw purple leaves all over a lily pad and—"

Rami put a finger on Tristys's lips. "I get it, I get it." The last of Tristys's fireflies perched on the tip of Rami's nose, skated up the bridge, and disappeared. "We're going to have to get this Fingerprinting checked out. Looks like we'll be going to Quellus next. Gawen will be happy."

"Actually," Tristys said, "can we not mention the Fingerprinting yet?"

"If those fireflies come back, she'll figure it out."

"I know." He tried to adjust his right arm, which was falling asleep. Rami picked himself up, and Tristys nearly cried out because he didn't want the cuddling to end, but Rami snuggled back down once Tristys rearranged his shoulder. "But maybe that won't happen for a while, and she won't rush us off to Quellus. I like this place."

"I do too." Rami had taken his shoes off earlier and had been rubbing Tristys's instep with his foot. It was driving Tristys crazy. "I won't tell her. I don't like keeping secrets, but I will for you."

Tristys scoffed. It was apparently not the right

move.

"What's that for?"

"Nothing," Tristys said, rubbing back. "It's just funny, since you've been keeping all this from them your whole life."

Rami sat up. He looked hard at Tristys, his face set, and Tristys sat up, too. "I didn't keep it from them because I wanted to. I never told them because I was trying to fix it. It wasn't as easy for me as it was for you. I didn't just—"

"No," Tristys said, trying to contain his indignation. "It wasn't easy for me, either. I may have accepted it more easily than you did, but I had to deal with hatred and abuse and so much more than you can even imagine living here, where nobody cares about anything. So please, don't talk to me about easy." Tristys took a deep breath then tried to lighten the mood. "Besides, I didn't even mean anything when I said that. I know it's been hard for you. I get it."

Rami pouted. Tristys tried to redirect.

"Are you okay now? I mean, do you want to tell everyone when we get back to the inn? Or do you want to wait until you're more comfortable?"

"I want to wait," he said at once. "I made you promise, remember? I don't know how I'm going to tell them. I've been lying about it for so long."

"They'll understand. They love you, Rami. And they know, even if you've never confirmed it. They know."

"I don't know." He trailed off.

"I do. You've been dating Calissa for how long and you've never slept together, right? And Gawen, come on! He tells you to your face that you like men."

"He's kidding. And how did you know Calissa

and I haven't... slept together?"

"Just a hunch. Listen, if you would just trust them, I think—"

He looked directly at Tristys. Their eyes met. "Not yet. They may think they know, but they don't know, and I just—I need to be ready."

Tristys didn't like it, but he wasn't about to argue. "Fine, we'll wait until you're ready. But you've got to let me know when that is, okay?"

"Of course." He put a hand on Tristys's shoulder and pushed him back, gently. "Right now, though, look at the bright side."

Tristys was lying on his back again. "What bright side? It's still pretty dark from down here."

"We just made it through our first fight as a couple."

"Oh yeah?" Tristys said, trying not to giggle like a lunatic. "A couple?"

"Definitely a couple." Rami scooted to Tristys's side and got ready to lie down again, resting his head on Tristys's chest, just as they were earlier.

"Well, just so you know, we're about to have our second fight as a couple."

"Why's that?" Rami asked, yawning. "It's hard to believe someone's chest can be this comfortable."

"Because I want to be the little moon this time."

Rami yawned again and said "Maybe later," but within a few minutes, it was Tristys commenting on the comfort of someone's chest.

CHAPTER FIFTEEN

The next few days were the closest thing to bliss Tristys had known. The day after their first night together, Rami took Tristys on another boat ride. He said he wanted to show him something else, and they went across the entire Amorai, to the far eastern shore. The forest was different. The trees were green, just like in Cyræa, though there were many, many more of them. Rami stopped in a clearing, but Tristys saw nothing special.

"Why are we here?" he'd asked.

"You seemed so tired of all the special stuff here. Blue trees, purple water, cottonblooms. I thought I'd show you something just like stuff you could've seen back home."

They'd had lunch in the plain forest, in the clearing next to a small stream, and when they got back to the Bellimarin, they made up some lie about doing separate things and only accidentally running into each other on the way home. Nobody believed them, but they didn't care.

Rami's birthday was a few days later, and Tristys told him he wanted to be the one in charge for a day. Tristys left Firebird with the others, which elicited a few strange looks, and Rami left a few minutes later. They met up just outside of Anamor. Tristys wanted their destination to be a surprise, so he blindfolded Rami and had to ask lots of people for directions. It took a while, but he managed to find the way to the zoo. Just as Salice had said, Rami knew everything about every animal. The only chance Tristys had to speak was in between exhibits. The only place Rami quit jabbering was the quell-beast enclosure, but Tristys was just as entranced as Rami, so he stayed quiet, too.

They snuck out almost every night. They kissed and cuddled on dozens of different lily pads, on the near and far sides of the Amorai, in two or three different Mauvewood clearings. One night, when the rain was coming down too hard and too cold to stay outside, Rami paid for a room in the Puffball even though he hated cottonblooms, simply because he knew Tristys loved them. They made out, of course, but they talked most of the night away, wrapped in each other's arms, Firebird asleep at their feet. Tristys told Rami about his life back home in Cyræa, about his mother and father, how his older sister had fallen in love with a Spàlorian and moved to the capital to avoid censure, how he'd lost an older brother to war, and how his younger brother hated him when he found out he was diverted. Rami added details to the Tierran tragedy, and he talked about how he'd met Salice and Gawen and even Calissa. They talked about where they'd go next, once they left Anamor and after Tristys attuned to Fire-magic. They talked about bitterberry beer, about the pets they'd always wanted but never had, about their favorite books. They learned more about each other in those few days than they had since Tristys arrived at the islands. And still they wanted to learn more.

Between him and Rami, they'd managed to skirt leaving Anamor twice. First Salice wanted to leave, but Rami convinced her to stay. A few days later, Gawen threatened to leave without them, but Tristys got him to relent via persuasion and more than a bit of flirting. Rami was miffed for about five seconds later that night, but Tristys tickled the anger out of him. The next day, though, there were fireflies all over Tristys, and as soon as Calissa saw them, it was a done deal. They left for Quellus that afternoon.

The plan was to travel along the Riveres, which flowed north out of the eastern end of the Amorai into the mountains of northern Quell. They'd detour from the river to the western shore of Quell and take a ferry from there to Seventh, a city in Quellus near the Altar of Six Plumes. They'd stay there for a day or two and then head to the Altar.

Everything went smoothly until they were crossing the Coquelai to Seventh. They'd just settled onto the ferry. Everybody was lounging around, chatting about nothing in particular. Tristys and Rami were talking to Salice about a book she'd been reading. Calissa was listening to their conversation while petting Firebird, and Gawen had disappeared below deck with a Quellysian he'd met five minutes earlier. Tristys was just about to argue a point with Salice when he suddenly felt very warm.

He groaned. "Did it just get incredibly hot?" He started fanning himself with his right hand. "Is that just because we're getting close to Quellus?"

"No," Salice said. "It's actually a little chilly. Winds from Quellis are in full force today, it seems."

"And we're nowhere near Quellus," Rami said. He was worried, and it showed on his face. He put a hand to Tristys's cheek then moved it to his forehead. If he kept this up, he'd blow their secret. Tristys would have to talk to him about it later.

"Just a hot flash," he said. "I've been having them the past few days. It'll pass. They always have."

Calissa looked worried now, too. "Hot flashes?" she said. "This was before the fireflies happened?"

"Not really," Tristys said. "There were fireflies a few weeks ago, and then—"

"Weeks?" Calissa yelled. "And you didn't tell us? Why didn't you tell us?"

"I didn't think—" Tristys started, but he didn't get a chance to finish. The heat got worse, incredibly worse, and he knew at once he wasn't fine. His eyes refused to focus, and his brain couldn't form a coherent thought to send to his mouth.

Suddenly Rami and Salice jumped away from him. Salice shouted, "By the quell, Tristys, you're on fire!"

He tried to look at her through his daze, but his vision was blacking out, turning to a hazy red screen. He lifted his arm, and he felt the pain before he saw the flames. His entire body was burning, but his skin felt nothing. The pain came from beneath the skin, as if the fire had burnt his veins first and was only now reaching the surface.

The shock lasted only a few seconds. Rami jumped into action, screaming for help. Calissa doused him with Water-magic, and Rami ran to his side, tears tracking his cheeks, mumbling something about burns and scars.

Tristys tried to speak, but he still wore a veil. He was paralyzed. Words took too long to form and even longer to find voice. Calissa was near, and now Gawen was here, too, but Calissa was gone. Gawen looked pinched, as if he was struggling with something, and Rami was there, too, but now he wasn't.

Faces came and went. The sky darkened. The travel grew rougher, harder, his body jolted. There were strangers now, faces he didn't recognize, and a sudden blackness lit up with a dim, otherwordly glare, and then heat overtook him again and everything went cold and black and beautiful.

The Quellusian savanna looked a lot like Cyræa. Tall, thin grasses covered the land, with enormous rock outcroppings punctuating the landscape. There were trees, too, which looked just like the trees in the Cyræan panhandle. They had long, thin trunks that erupted into a tangled mess of branches. Only the farthest ends of the branches nearest the sky had leaves. They were green, just like in Cyræa.

Tristys leaned against one of these trees, his gaze joining the wind as it rolled across the landscape. He worked magic idly, to keep his hands busy: a small river flowed between his palms and a ribbon of fire threaded its way through his fingers. It was like juggling, he thought, only there was no chance he'd ever miss a catch. That took a bit of the fun out of it.

Tristys breathed in deeply. It was still there, that burnt dryness that smelled just like home. There were no wildfires here—the Quellusians maintained strict control over the native element—but even they couldn't get the burning out of the air. The first time he smelled it, coming out of the dormitories the day after he'd arrived, he'd burst into tears, and he cried for what felt like hours.

The scariest part of that whole ordeal had been the way he felt while he cried: he wasn't particularly sad or homesick or upset. The tears came, but they were empty. It was odd and uncomfortable, like trying to swim on land or breathe underwater and realizing you can do it. It had to do with this place, with its familiarity to his homeland, but he'd thought he'd left Cyræa behind him. He'd been so happy the past few weeks with Rami and their friends in Anamor that he'd barely thought of what—or whom—he left behind. He'd just assumed that since he'd stopped thinking about it, he'd finally let it go. He'd been wrong.

So every day since, he'd come out here to the savanna for hours, waiting for something to happen. It was calming, nothing but grasses and trees, rocks and the occasional rodent, but much to his chagrin, his emotions had mimicked that tranquility. There were no more outbursts, no more tears. He'd done everything he could to trigger something—he'd rolled up the legs of his pants so he felt the grasses more easily, he'd run around like a madman during the brief rainstorm just as he and his siblings had done at home, he'd even climbed a tree to read—but nothing happened. Nothing.

He was tired of waiting. He didn't really care at this point if he broke down in tears or finally let it go. Whether he cried from memories of his mother's cooking, his sister's laughter, even his brother's cruelty or whether he forgot about them entirely didn't really matter, as long as he got away from this paradox of numb emotion. He was tired of feeling caught between two countries, loving everything about the Coquels but still feeling drawn to Cyræa. He was tired of that nagging feeling in the back of his mind, that whisper that kept telling him he was shirking some responsibility. He was tired of hearing Tyspal in his head.

The fire through his fingers sputtered out, and Tristys swore. Verilla said practicing would help strengthen his magic, and he'd been Touching Fire virtually non-stop since he woke up, but the magic was still weak. Verilla insisted it wasn't the magic, it was his connection to it, but it all boiled down to the same thing as far as he was concerned: semi-control over a magic that didn't always bend to his will, acting like a fickle lover or an unpredictable child. At least it no longer turned his entire body into flames, though. That was progress.

Tristys remembered very little of the ferry ride from Quell to Quellus, even before the time he Fingerprinted. He remembered nothing after he passed out, just quick flashes hidden behind fog. Verilla had assured him that he'd communed almost as soon as Rami dropped him in a meditation alcove, that only a successful communion would wash away such a dirty Fingerprint, but he didn't remember a second of it.

"Tristys," Verilla said from behind him. He hadn't even heard her approach. "It's getting late. The others will be getting back soon." She put a hand on his shoulder, and for a split second, he wanted to flinch away. He resisted. Verilla had been nothing but kind to him since his arrival, and he didn't want to treat her badly. "You'll want to see them as soon as they get back, I imagine. You must miss them."

The day after Tristys woke up, Rami, Calissa, Salice, Gawen, and Firebird went to Seventh. Gawen's parents were there, and they demanded he show up. Verilla had discouraged Tristys from going, but he didn't really want to go, anyway. Rami offered to stay, and Tristys said no. He'd practically begged in private, but Tristys didn't relent. They'd been gone for a little over four days now, and Tristys wasn't sure he wanted them back so soon. He wasn't going to tell Verilla, though, so he forced a smile. "Thanks, Verilla. I'll head back in a few minutes."

She nodded, her lips pressed in resignation. She turned away, and the moment her back was to Tristys, he shivered off the ghost of her hand on his shoulder, turned his gaze back to the flowing grasses, and kept waiting.

~~*

"I think I'm getting sick," Gawen said, sniffling loudly. "I hate being sick."

"It's just a cold." Rami didn't even bother to look at him. His eyes were focused on the low, brown buildings growing larger with every step they took. He'd only been away from Tristys for a few days, but it felt like an eternity. Maybe it was because of all the chaos before he left, with the dirty Fingerprinting and the miraculous, barely conscious communion. Gawen sniffled again, with even more exaggeration. "You'll live," Rami said.

"It's not about living, though, is it? It's about living well, with the most comfort. That's what quell is for, isn't it? Why suffer even the littlest bit if you can fix it?"

"*Can* you fix it, Gawen?" Rami wasn't smiling. He turned his head slightly, just enough to shoot a challenge at Gawen with his eyes. "Last time I checked, you don't Touch Death-magic."

Gawen looked defeated. "Well, yes, I may not touch Death-magic, but—"

"None of us does," Rami interrupted.

"There may be someone at Six Plumes." His expression belied the fact that he didn't believe that. "And if not, we can go to New Cysal. It's not that far out of the way anyway, if we're going to Zebelli next for Martyrday."

Rami chanced a look to see if Calissa had reacted to the mention of Martyrday. She usually tried to lay low during the festivities in honor of her great-great-great-great-grandmother, and the last thing Rami thought she'd want would be marching into the capital of Quellis with a foreigner in tow right before Martyrday. But she didn't even twitch, so perhaps she'd already resigned herself to it.

"We'll worry about that when we get to it," he said to shut up Gawen. "We're not even back to the Altar yet and you're already talking about leaving it."

"If you want to get to Zebelli in time for Martyrday, Rami, we can't stay long." That confirmed Rami's suspicion that Calissa was okay with their next destination.

"I don't want to stay," he shot back, a bit too cattily. Calissa looked marginally surprised. "I want Tristys to rest. He needs to rest. He needs to get his strength back, in case something else happens." He stumbled over the last few words. Days later, with Tristys totally recovered, and still he got choked up.

"You seem oddly concerned." Gawen's tone dripped with accusation and curiosity. "Any reason in particular?"

Rami figured this question would come up sooner or later. He was surprised it hadn't come up sooner, since he'd been unable to stop obsessing over Tristys the entire time they were in Seventh. Luckily, he'd been practicing casual disinterest. "He's a friend," he said, making sure to shrug his shoulders. "I'd worry about any of my friends, if that happened to them." And now for the clincher, to make sure Gawen stopped pushing. "Even you, Gawen." Rami smiled broadly, though he was surprised to realize he was only half-lying.

When they finally got back to the Altar, Verilla said Tristys had gone to bed early. Rami didn't believe it and took Firebird to find out. Tristys answered the knock quickly, too quickly to have been sleeping. He had been lying down, though: his hair was disheveled, the way it always was after he tried to sleep, and his eyes looked heavy, but not from tiredness. Something was definitely bothering him, and Rami intended to find out what.

As soon as Firebird saw Tristys, he jumped into his arms. Rami wanted to do the same, but instead he asked if he could come in, which was strange, too formal. He'd never done that before. They usually couldn't keep their hands off each other.

Tristys shrugged, not even looking up from scratching Firebird behind the ears. Rami pushed his way into the room, took the few steps to the bed, and waited for Tristys to follow him. After a few moments in the doorway, Tristys put Firebird down and got on the bed. "I've missed you," Rami said as he pulled Tristys into an embrace. He kissed him, tentatively at first, to gauge Tristys's reaction. When he felt Tristys kiss back, he let himself quit worrying, if only for a few moments, and fell back onto the bed, pulling Tristys with him.

A few minutes later, they were all in the bed, Firebird at the foot and Tristys and Rami sitting against the headboard, their bodies pressed against each other, Tristys's head resting on Rami's shoulder. They hadn't said a single word.

"So what's wrong?" Rami couldn't take the silence any longer.

"Hmm?" Tristys mumbled without opening his mouth, although he did shift away from Rami, pulling his knees to his chest and resting his chin on his kneecaps. Rami felt abandoned.

"Something's bothering you."

"It's nothing," Tristys said, shaking his head.

"It wasn't bothering you on the lake. Are you worried about Fingerprinting like that again?" He raised a hand to Tristys's shoulder and nudged him. "You don't need to, you know. Nobody has ever Fingerprinted after they're able to Touch the quell themselves. It doesn't work like that."

"Nobody's ever been able to Touch like I have, either." His tone was light, so Rami knew it wasn't the Fingerprinting bothering him. "It doesn't matter, though. I haven't even thought about that."

Tristys still hadn't turned to look at him, and the lack of eye contact was driving Rami crazy. He pushed off the wall, walked a few steps on his knees, and sat down, legs underneath him, right in front of Tristys. He brought his face just a breath away from Tristys's and said, "Then what's the matter?"

Tristys turned his eyes up to look into Rami's, and a pout spread across his lips. "I just don't know why you don't want to have sex with me," he said.

Rami felt his mouth drop open. In all the time they'd been together, through all the kissing and all the cuddling, they'd never actually talked about sex. He was surprised they hadn't, because he knew they both wanted each other—you only had to look towards their pants whenever they were making out to notice—but neither said anything. Why was he bringing it up so suddenly? And why now of all times?

"Tristys, you can't honestly think I don't want that," he said, his voice almost a whisper. He wasn't afraid of being overheard; he just couldn't believe Tristys felt that way. "I mean, you know when we make out, that I—that my—I mean, you've pointed it out before!" His voice was louder now, and he kept telling himself to calm down, but the more he thought about it, the faster he spoke. And he was still embarrassed, of course. There were no spaces between his words now. "You said you were afraid that if it got any bigger, you'd—"

"Calm down, calm down!" Tristys said, laughing and using his hands to lower Rami's voice—and Rami himself, as he'd started to stand up on the bed. "I'm kidding, I'm kidding." The laughter drained away like rainfall after a storm, and he sobered up. "I was just trying to squirm out of the what's-the-matter conversation. It worked for a little bit."

"Tristys, just tell me." He tried to force his face into a resolute, determined expression, but he still felt a blush in his cheeks.

"I just don't want you to think I'm unhappy," he said, defeat slouching his shoulders and averting his gaze. "I don't want you to think I don't want to be here." He looked up, his eyes pleading with Rami to believe him. "But I miss home. I miss my parents, and I miss my sister." His eyes had filled with tears, and he gave an ironic chuckle as he said, "I even miss my brother." A grin turned the well to a trickle.

Rami's head cocked back in surprise. This was new. He hadn't seemed the least bit homesick, hadn't even mentioned Cyræa the past few weeks. Where had this come from? Rami was afraid of the answer, but he had to ask. "Do you want to go back?"

Tristys hesitated for only a second, but even that second stabbed at Rami. "No, I don't. I miss my family, but I was fine until I came to this stupid island." He looked to the side of the bed and out the small, circular window. Rami could see just one of the two moons in the dark sky. "It looks just like Cyræa."

Rami nodded, but he wasn't sure how to respond. He quaffed the academic in him, which wanted to roll with the comparisons, and he neutralized the acid, which wanted to spit out how much he hated the Quellusian landscape. He opted for the bright side. "We're leaving soon, you know."

Tristys nodded, but he didn't seem convinced.

"We're going to Zebelli, the capital of Quellis, island of Air-magic, for Martyrday."

"What's—"

"It's the biggest holiday in the islands. It's so big, in fact, it takes three days to celebrate. They're called Waves."

"Oh, okay."

"So we'll get off this island, and you'll never have to come here again, if you don't want." Even Rami knew that wasn't enough, knew how feeble and weak his attempt was, but this was something he couldn't control. Every other time Tristys had been unhappy, he'd been able to fix it, usually because he was the cause of the unhappiness. This was entirely outside his powers, and he felt useless and impotent. "How's that sound? Think that'll make it better?"

"Well, it can't make it worse," Tristys said, any trace of his usual light-hearted complaining gone.

"Good, then." Rami's shoulders sagged, and he took a deep breath before getting serious. "You don't have to keep things from me, Tristys." Rami had spent his entire life keeping secrets, and he knew what it could take from a person. "Okay?"

"Yeah, sure," Tristys said, only slightly more genuine than his earlier empty affirmations. He looked at Rami expectantly. "But can we just sit back and forget about all this for a little? I got really tired all of a sudden." He scooted down the bed, preparing to lie down. "I haven't been sleeping much lately, in case you haven't noticed."

"No, I have." How could he not? The dark circles, the change in attitude, the way his eyelids hung slightly closer together than usual. "But there's one more thing first." Rami paused as he repositioned himself to lie down with Tristys. He was planning on being the bigger moon tonight, since he felt like Tristys needed some comfort. As expected, Tristys turned on his side facing away from Rami, and Rami wrapped his arms around Tristys and pulled him close.

"What's that?" he murmured, already half-asleep.

Rami wasn't sure if he should bring this up now, but he couldn't stop thinking about Tristys's initial faux confession. He hesitated for a moment or two, but finally he turned off his mind and charged headfirst. "You know how shy I am, how backwards I am about the whole sex thing." Rami waited, pretended to take a deep breath to see if there was any reaction from Tristys. There wasn't. "But you have to know I want you. All the time I want you, in every way possible. It's just... It's going to take some time." Another faked breath. Still nothing. "And I guess—I mean, I just want—I just want to know that you're going to wait for me."

Rami waited for a response. He needed reassurance, and for the first time in his life, he wasn't ashamed or afraid to ask for it. But Tristys still said nothing, and Rami felt his breath leave his chest until he realized Tristys had been asleep the entire time.

New Cysal stunk, literally. The town was small, composed almost entirely of several families that had decided long ago to corrupt the idea of Death-magic into their own quasi-religion based on death and decay. One of their beliefs involved letting a corpse rot wherever the creature died, so any fallen plant or animal remained where it fell, stinking up the town. Even worse, some of the houses had small altars in their yards, a pedestal to display recently deceased pets or sacrifices or quell-knows-what. Calissa hated this place, hated everything the New Cysalians stood for, and she still had no idea why the seyquel didn't stomp them out.

When Gawen had declared his plans to stop in New Cysal before heading to Quellis, Calissa had done everything she could, other than abject begging, to get them to skip over the town, but Gawen had been insistent. "I don't want to be sick in the frigid, wind-wracked heights of the Pine!" he'd screeched. He wouldn't relent, so she finally gave up.

Now, walking the decaying streets of New Cysal, she'd wished she'd put up more of a fight. They'd been looking for a person to help Gawen for nearly an hour, and most of the New Cysalians wouldn't even speak to them. They got a lot of sneers and a few doors slammed in their faces, but no help. Firebird was getting far too interested in the various piles of decaying whatever, and she was convinced Gawen's cold would run its course naturally before they found someone to fix it with yş.

"Why are we here again?" Tristys asked, kicking aside a decaying fruit. A nearby old man hissed, and Tristys shot him a surprised look. "This place is horrible."

"We won't be here long," Gawen said. "We just have to find someone to fix—to fix," the sneeze never came "—this."

"I don't see how Death-magic is going to fix anything," Tristys whined. "Look at this place!"

"Yş fixes a lot of things," Calissa said. Her loyalty lay with oş, of course, but she had to give credit where credit is due.

"What's the point of Life-magic, then?"

"Oş fixes accidents," Calissa said. "Like what

you did to fix Firebird." She looked at the monkey, which was currently poking at a pile of rubbish. "Speaking of which... Firebird! Firebird!" The monkey looked up, not very pleased to be interrupted. "Get over here! That's garbage!" He didn't look any more pleased, but he listened, hopping over to Calissa, crawling up her leg, and hooking onto her arm. "Figures, you'd come to me of all people after you roll around in filth."

Calissa could tell that Tristys still didn't get it, the confusion and repulsion twisting into an unpleasant grimace. She tried to think of a way to explain it, but talking quell theory always eluded her. She could teach someone how to use it with ease, but that was practical, logical, natural. Talking about it as if it were some abstract, distant notion didn't suit her.

Rami came to her rescue. "Okay, think of it like this. Life-magic fixes things that are broken, and Death-magic gets rid of things that shouldn't be there. Gawen has a cold, so he's not broken, which means we need Death-magic."

Tristys's brow was pinched. "I don't know. I guess you're right. You are the experts, after all. I just don't see how anything good can come from death."

"It's not death," Calissa interjected quickly. "It's yş. This is why I think the layman's terms are detrimental." She directed the last statement at Rami, expecting to incite a heated argument, but all he did was shrug. She remembered he wasn't Fal, which was something she had trouble forgetting lately.

"Whatever," Tristys said, scrunching up his shoulders. "This place gives me the creeps. Let's just fix it and get out of here." He walked quicker, and everyone increased their pace to keep up with his. "Also, just so you know," he looked at Gawen through his bangs, his head lowered, "back in Paru, whenever I got a cold, I sucked it up and dealt with it."

"Luckily, I'm not back in Paru," Gawen said flatly. He stretched his neck, squinting. "I think that's a practitioner's hovel up there, isn't it?"

Gawen's word for the place was perfect. It was a small, squat building, made of a Quellesian softwood, but there was no oş protecting it. The wood was rotting, and insects, mostly grubs and maggots, covered most of it.

"I'm not stepping through that doorway," Tristys said, staring at the frame. "There are bugs everywhere." One bug agreed and fell from the doorway, landing nearby and then scurrying away. Tristys took a step back.

"It'll be fine, Tristys," Calissa said. "I'll prop an air shield above us if we go in."

"What do you mean 'if'?" Tristys said. "I want out of this place. We're going in, fixing Gawen, then getting out." She'd never seen him this insistent. It was just another unexplained change.

"Five seconds ago you refused to go in there," Gawen said. "What changed?"

"Nothing. Death-magic gives me the creeps."

"It's not yş giving you the creeps," Calissa said, tired of his offensive against the quell. "It's this town. Yş is—"

"What do you want?" A person appeared far inside the door, too deep in shadow to see any details. It was a man, which was all the low, breathy voice gave away.

"We require your services," Gawen said after clearing his throat. "I've come down with something, a cold probably, and I'd like it to go away."

"Odd, that is," the man breathed, stepping closer to the door. His dark gray hair was long but thin, and he looked malnourished. "We both want things to go away." As the man stepped into the light, she saw Tristys recoil.

The man was hideous. His pale skin was pocked from sores and blemishes, and his teeth—the few he had left, anyway—were yellow and dead or dying. His left eye looked glazed, and the pupil stared off to the side. He moved quickly, despite his appearance, and within a second he was just a hair's breadth away from Gawen. "Now," he said, exhaling deeply, and Gawen's nose crinkled. Like everything in New Cysal, this man's breath must stink. "How best to get rid of the things we don't want?"

"We'll go," Gawen said, recovering from the stench and getting back in the man's face, "once you work your magic. And not before."

"Perhaps," the man said, stepping back, "but what's to stop me from diseasing you—all of you—right now, on the spot? You'd drop before you had time to cry out."

"You wouldn't dare," Calissa said simply, without aggression or threat. He wouldn't, couldn't, and she knew it. She just had to make him believe she knew it.

His eyes narrowed as he stared at her, but she kept her face impassive. Nobody moved or said anything, which was perfect, and he relented, just as she knew he would. As always, New Cysalians were all bark and no bite.

"Fine." He stepped aside and waited, ushering them in. "I won't do this for free, of course," the man said, "but I will make it quick." He scowled at Tristys, who scowled back, and he added, "You people stink."

"Is he kidding me?" Calissa heard Salice whisper somewhere behind her. Although the man stood aside, nobody made any motion to enter the house.

"I grow impatient," the man said. "Enter now or be gone. You're loitering."

"Shield first, Calissa!" Tristys said quickly, just as Gawen started to move.

Calissa flicked her mind, and small umbrellas of hardened air appeared over their heads. The popping noises scared Firebird, who abandoned Calissa and darted to Tristys. The monkey wrapped his arms around Tristys's neck and dangled, which was his way of saying he wanted held.

The inside of the hovel looked better than the outside. The wood here was cured, Calissa noted with smug satisfaction, and the rooms were free of bugs and beetles. It still stunk, and there were small altars in each corner with the expected sacrifices on them. She couldn't imagine believing in a quell that required sacrifice, still couldn't understand how these New Cysalians developed the way they did, despite all the history classes she'd taken. It was baffling.

He moved quickly through the first few rooms, taking them deep into the deceptively large house. They stopped in a room with ceilings so low Gawen had to stoop. There were no other entrances besides the one they came through, and the only furniture was a large altar in the dead center of the room. It was stone, the black kakenstone iridescing in the torchlight, and the top slab was much larger than the base, a perfect circle and perfectly flat. A deep cavity had been hollowed in the exact middle, and though Calissa couldn't see it, she knew it went deep into the base.

"The tall one is sick, correct?" the man said as he hurried to the other side of the altar.

"Yes, Gawen."

"Your name means nothing to me," the man spat. He pulled out several containers from underneath the slab. He opened the smallest and tossed flower petals across the altar. The petals were, of course, dead. "Sick one, come forward." Gawen took a few steps to the altar, and the man dipped two fingers into the largest container and bent forward, anointing Gawen's cheeks with a deep red liquid.

Calissa rolled her eyes. "Stop with the performance, man," she said. "You don't need any of this. We could've been done in the first room."

His only response was a sneer. He popped the cork on the last container and poured a thick, black liquid into the cavity in the middle of the altar. "Spit here," the man said, pointing into the cavity. "Make it thick."

Gawen looked repulsed. Just as Calissa was about to yell again, Gawen spit. Calissa choked back her protests.

The man peered into the cavity, shutting his bad eye. "That will do," he said begrudgingly. "Now give me the monkey."

Tristys opened his eyes so wide it had to hurt. Firebird squealed as Tristys squeezed him to his chest. "What do you need Firebird for?" His voice was about three octaves higher than normal.

Calissa knew at once that they should have left Tristys outside. This was not going to lessen his hatred for yş at all. In fact, it would probably make it worse. "We assumed you would provide the animal transfer." Her voice left no room for argument.

"That will cost." The man licked his lips. "I am very low on suitable transfers."

"It's fine," Rami said. "Just hurry up."

The man bowed too deeply and hurried out of the room. Tristys turned, still wide-eyed and still clutching Firebird, to Calissa. "What are you talking about? Why did he ask for Firebird? And where did he go?"

"Tristys," Calissa said slowly, trying to stall as she thought of the best way to explain this, but Rami came to her rescue again.

"Whenever a practitioner pulls something out of someone to fix them, he has to put it somewhere, right?"

"No, wrong," Tristys said. "If you gave me a cup of water, I could make it disappear like that." He snapped his fingers.

"Right, but it's not actually disappearing."

"Seems pretty gone to me."

"It's not. It's in the air, sort of. It's like there's some sort of space out there that we can't see or feel or touch that all the quell goes to when we're not Touching it." Rami stopped a second, tried to think of something else to say. "Or something like that. But it's not disappearing, that's for sure." Calissa smiled quietly to herself. Even Rami couldn't explain everything easily.

"So why can't you just send whatever comes out of the people into wherever I send the water?"

"Life- and Death-magic are different," Rami started, but the man re-entered the room, carrying a small box in his hands. Obviously, its contents were still quite alive, because the box jerked angrily in the man's hands.

As the man walked to the altar, he looked at Tristys, directly at him, a twisted grin hanging on his face. "I chose this one especially for you," he said as he set the box inside the cavity, out of their sight. A second later, he removed the box, now empty, and the noise the animal made was unmistakable. It sounded just like Firebird.

The man's smile deepened as the light of recognition bloomed on their faces. "Don't worry," he said. "It's just a baby. He hasn't lived; perhaps he won't miss life much."

Rami was the first to react. "You son-of-a—" he said, moving forward, but Salice caught his arm and held him back.

"Gawen's just got a cold, he's not dying," Tristys said. Calissa cursed his innocence. "The monkey will get better."

"It's not that simple," Rami said quietly, almost a whisper. "The monkey will die. The transfer, it's too much for the little creatures to handle."

"So you're going to kill a baby monkey just to get rid of cold?" His disgust was directed at Gawen, not the man.

"They've never used monkeys before," Gawen said. He was pale, his face drained of color. Calissa had a feeling he'd back out now if she urged him, but she wasn't so sure the man would let them leave so easily. "They use insects back home. Last time I had a cold, they used a beetle."

Tristys turned to the man, who'd been watching their exchange intently, amusement glittering in his one good eye. "Why don't you just use a beetle, then?" Tristys asked. "You've got enough of them on the outside of your house."

"Because," the man said slowly, one eyebrow raised, "the larger the sacrifice, the more I please the Death-quell." He waited a second, then added, "And because it's much more fun this way."

Calissa saw Rami lunge, she was expecting it, but before he got anywhere near the old man, a burst of hardened air pushed Rami back. For a moment, Calissa thought she'd done it instinctively, but then she noticed the man's rictus. He used iş, too? He was more powerful than she thought.

"Now now," he said. "Violence has no place here." Rami was still struggling against the magic as the man walked out from behind the altar and approached the door. "I must insist that you leave now." The moment Rami stopped struggling, the magic holding him lifted, and he sagged. Tristys steadied him with an arm.

"Let's go, Tristys," Rami said. "You don't want to be here for this any more than I do." He took Tristys by the hand and dragged him out of the room.

"Can we finish this, please? I actually envy them for getting out of this degradation already."

"Of course, my lovely darling." The last word dripped venom. "Come closer, sick one, and we will start. This won't hurt at all." He looked into the pit and added, once again with a malicious grin, "For you, anyway."

Gawen went to the altar and set his palms down on the stone. He kept his chin up, eyes high, and Calissa hoped the man would finish this quickly, without a show, but she knew he wouldn't. Just as the man reached out to touch Gawen's hand, Gawen's gaze fell to the pit, his eyes filled with pity, and he recoiled. "I can't," he said, waving his hands in front of him. "I can't. We'll pay you, you'll still get your money." To prove his point, he reached into the pocket of his pants and tossed a few coins onto the altar. "I'll just suck it up and deal, it'll be okay."

"Are you sure?" the man said. He looked disappointed, despite the fee already paid. He clearly wasn't in the profession for the money.

"I'm positive," Gawen said. He turned to Salice. "Let's just go."

"Of course," she said. "Let's go."

Nobody gave the man another glance, but as they were filing out of the small room, he called to them. "One last thing," he said, and the three of them turned around just in time to see the man, clutching the baby taramisk monkey to his chest, snap its neck.

CHAPTER SIXTEEN

Tristys had been too disturbed to stay in New Cysal even a second longer, so the group set up camp just outside of the town, in a lovely green forest that was as pleasant as New Cysal was disgusting. They hadn't planned on roughing it again, so they had just a few blankets. They would have left every blanket back at the Altar of Six Plumes, but Salice had insisted on being prepared, just in case. She was right, and she'd gloated for an hour before bed.

Tristys had his own blanket, though, besides the two they'd brought. He'd kept the blanket he and Rami had shared in the Quellesian woods, after Rami saved his life, mostly for sentimental reasons. He wanted to keep it hidden, didn't want anyone to get any ideas or coo about how cute and sappy he was, but the ground was just too hard. After everyone fell asleep, he sneaked to his knapsack and removed Firebird, who had taken to sleeping inside the bag. He yanked out the tattered blanket and put back the monkey, who could sleep through the end of the world. The blanket didn't help. The ground was still hard. And now there was a rock stabbing his lower back. Lovely.

He started squirming, trying to wriggle the rock free, and when that didn't work, he reached underneath him, trying to contort his body to reach it. It had to be lodged in the most inaccessible spot ever. He was so invested in rock removal, in fact, he didn't hear Rami get up.

"Bug in your britches?" Rami whispered. He was bent over, low to the ground, and he pushed Tristys's shoulder. "Scoot over, I'm coming in."

Tristys nearly shouted, but he stopped himself at the last second. "What are you doing?" he whispered. "What if someone sees you?" His warnings fell on deaf ears; by the time he finished, Rami was already pressed up against Tristys's side, his left hand entangling in Tristys's hair. "You shouldn't be over here." He was only arguing now out of habit. "They're going to catch us."

"So what?" Rami said. "I'm getting tired of hiding how I feel. When that stuff happened on the boat—"

"You hid how you feel for twenty-some years, and now you're finally getting tired of it?" He wanted to sound serious, but it was hard when he was giggling the entire time. "Quit nibbling on my ear, please!" He'd spoken a bit too loudly, and Calissa, the nearest person to them, mumbled in her sleep.

Rami waited a second to see if she'd wake up, but she just rolled to her other side. "Right, and now I want to quit. Why don't we tell them, Tristys? Why don't we?"

Tristys wanted to tell him why. He wanted to say, *Because I like it when it's just you and me.* He wanted to say, *Because I'm scared it'll be different once everyone knows.* He wanted to say, *Because I'm scared if you're open about it, you'll realize you can do better than me.* What he did say, however, was, "What about Calissa? She loves you."

He hated himself for it.

"I love her, too. But she and I, it's a weird relationship. It's not like I'm cheating on her. Our whole thing was so vague and ambiguous. We never did anything, you know. I think she knows."

Tristys didn't understand how such a drastic change could have developed so quickly. A few weeks ago, Rami refused to admit he liked guys. A few days ago, he refused to consider telling everyone else about his relationship with Tristys. Now, he wanted to shout it from the rooftops.

Even more unsettling, however, was the shift in Tristys. He no longer wanted everyone to know. He wasn't even sure why. It had to do with everything he'd just wanted to say, fear of change and preemptive jealousy, but it was more than that. He wasn't sure Rami was as comfortable as he acted, either. Tristys knew from his own experience that wanting to be open about who you are and actually being open are two very different things.

"Can we talk about it in the morning?" he asked finally. "I'm tired."

"Now you're tired? You've been up all night, and now you're tired?"

"I was sleeping before you woke me!" Tristys lied.

"No, you weren't. I can tell when you're sleeping. You breathe differently."

Time to try a new tack. "Fine." They'd been spooning the entire conversation, Tristys tucked snuggly into Rami so their voices could stay quiet, but now Tristys flipped over. "I'm not tired. But less talking, okay?"

"What else can we—"

Before Rami could finish, Tristys pulled Rami into a kiss, more forceful and urgent and needing than he'd ever kissed him before. Rather than fight it, Rami returned the gesture.

The kisses kept coming, and soon their hands joined in. Tristys slipped his hand along Rami's spine, underneath the thin shirt he wore, and when Rami nibbled a bit too roughly, he started to moan but stifled it by scratching lightly on Rami's back. He moved his hands across all of Rami's upper body, along his shoulders and down his biceps, across his chest. He even bent his arms so he could reach his abs. The contortion was painful but worth it. His muscles were amazing, so solid beneath such soft skin.

Tristys had somehow ended up on top of Rami, pinning him down by the biceps. He was kissing his neck, and his hair was tickling Rami's chin. Rami was having a hard time keeping the giggles and the moans under wraps. Calissa had shifted again several times, and even Gawen, who usually slept like a log, had started stirring. "By the two moons," Rami said, breathless, "I wish we were alone right now."

Tristys came up for air. "You and me both," he said. He licked Rami's cheek, which was so unexpected that a giggle did escape. "You and me both."

As their lips met for another deep kiss, the air above them shivered and hardened. The slight pop distracted them long enough to look up and notice the air shield.

"Did you do that?" Tristys asked at once. "You never told me you could use Air-magic, too."

"I can't," Rami said. "Calissa's the only one who can, and she's zonked out over there." He wriggled one arm free from Tristys's grasp and reach up to touch the shield, which was solid but transparent. Tristys shot a glance to the others, but nobody had moved. They were still asleep.

"Can they hear us?" Tristys asked.

Rami's response was to yell as loudly as he could. Tristys freaked out and jumped off Rami so forcefully that he smacked into the shield. He tried to look innocent, but it didn't matter. Nobody had heard a thing. Rami was laughing, and Tristys took the opportunity to smack him as hard as he could. "You stupid jerk!" he said, but he was already examining the shield himself. "If you didn't do this and Calissa didn't do this," Tristys started, already putting the pieces together.

"Then you must be Fingerprinting again." Rami was still on his back, staring at Tristys. "It makes sense. We're close to Quellis, and every time we get close to another island, you go haywire."

For a split second, Tristys panicked. Another Fingerprinting, so fresh after the last traumatic one, was terrifying. But he felt fine. Nothing hurt, he wasn't on fire, he and Rami could breathe. He just needed to relax. "What should we do?"

"Nothing," Rami said. "We're already going to Quellis, and if we wake up Calissa now to get rid of it, she'll see us together."

"I thought you wanted that," Tristys said.

"I do, but I'd like the method of delivery to be a little less traumatic." He pushed against the shield, but it didn't budge. "Besides, that's obviously not what you want, and that matters to me now."

Tristys blushed, but he didn't think Rami could see. "Do you think it'll be gone before they wake up?"

"Probably." Rami reached out again, rapped on

the shield twice. "It's pretty hard right now, but it probably won't stay that way for long."

"Lucky bastard," Tristys said, looking down at his groin.

"About that," Rami said, trailing off. He rolled off his back into a crouch and started slinking towards Tristys. "This time," he cooed, pushing Tristys onto his back and throwing a leg over his hips, "I'm on top."

~~*

Strider was only a day's travel from New Cysal, and since they were ahead of schedule, Calissa had decided to spend a day or two relaxing. She knew Salice liked the location, even if Gawen hated it. But Gawen hated everything if it wasn't covered in fire or seducing him, so she'd grown accustomed to ignoring his complaints. Plus, she hadn't gone water-striding in months, and she missed it.

Part of her felt guilty for making the decision. She kept picturing Ystan in her mind, telling her how important it was to get Tristys to Touch as many quell as he could. She'd written a letter to the Order detailing Ystan's theories and her own observations, but their response was useless, just reassurance that they trusted her judgment and a suggestion she keep doing what she's doing. There was a time when such a letter would have made her so giddy she'd have cried, but now was not that time. Too much had changed.

Ultimately, she'd decided that he'd already communed with three quell, which was one more than anyone else had in generations, so he (and everyone else) deserved a respite. So off they went to Strider.

The day after their arrival, Calissa went to wake Salice and Gawen, but Salice wasn't there. Gawen, still asleep, mumbled that she'd spent the night with an ex that lived in town and that he'd rather mud-wrestle an overgrown windwyrm than stride with her, so she left without saying another word. She went back to her room, but Rami said he was too tired to wake up now and would join her later.

Only slightly daunted, she paraded into Tristys's room, knocking loudly and barging in when nobody answered. He was asleep in bed, still in his clothes. He hadn't even bothered to get under the covers, despite his almost neurotic insistence on having something over him while he slept. Everyone must not have gone to bed quite so quickly last night after all.

Regardless, she wanted to stride. She called his name once, twice, three times, and he didn't respond. She shook him gently, and he batted her hand away. She shook him less gently, and he turned over. She didn't want to drench him, so she did the next best thing: she got on his bed and jumped, just like she did when she was a child. He rocked and rolled and bounced, and a moment later, his eyes opened.

"Why are you always making me get up?" he grunted.

"Today we are going striding," she said simply.

"I'm horrible at striding." He threw himself back down onto the pillow. "I have no idea what it is, but considering I can barely walk without tripping, I'm pretty sure I'll be bad at it."

"You don't have to walk at all." She pulled the blanket off him. "That's the beauty of it. You just float."

"I can't float. Give me that back." He lunged, eyes half shut, at the blanket, but Calissa dodged.

"Oh, come on!" She tried not to whine usually, but desperate times called for desperate measures. "Nobody else will go right now, and I want to get out there. The lake's beautiful in the morning." He opened one eye, his lips pressed together so tightly they thinned to near non-existence. "I will shoot you with ice lances, and you don't want to bruise."

He thought a moment then sighed. She'd won!

"Leave the monkey," she said, "and make it snappy!"

Fifteen minutes later, they were on their way to the Pavilions, a large structure built on a jetty in southern Strider. Inside were small stands and shops, mostly selling food and beverages, though some had silly souvenirs and other tourist traps. Most were closed, but Tristys wandered to one of the stores that was open, the attendant milling through boxes behind the counter. He picked up a stuffed stridus, the small rodent-like quell-beast that lived its entire life floating just above the surface of the lake. He flipped it over a few times, poked it, stared at it face-to-face. He was mystified.

"You'll see the real thing soon," she said, grabbing his arm and pulling him from the stand. "Let's go before she sees us and starts harassing."

At the far back of the Pavilions was the boot rental. That store never closed, and the clerk behind the counter was apparently near the end of his shift. His head was resting on his hand, eyes closed, and he kept almost falling over and jerking back up.

"Excuse me," she said, softly at first so she

didn't startle him. He jumped awake. For a second, she thought he was going to yell. "We need some boots."

"Of course, of course." A blush rose in his cheeks. Guess he wasn't supposed to be sleeping on the job. "What sizes?"

"I'm a six." She looked at Tristys. "Any idea what size shoe you wear?"

He blinked a few times. He probably hadn't heard of shoe sizes back in Paru. "I wear the same size as Rami," he apologized.

"He's a twelve then."

"Sure thing, miss. I'll be right back."

"He's getting us boots, which you need to stride," she explained to Tristys.

"I figured." He was still cranky. He'd get over it.

The clerk returned with the boots. "The water is perfect, and you'll be the only ones out there." Calissa thanked him as she paid and resisted the urge to say sweet dreams or something to that effect. She handed Tristys his pair of boots instead.

"What's in these things, rocks?" he asked, sitting down and hefting them onto his lap. They were heavy leather, tight-laced and high-topped, with thick soles.

"Yes, actually," she said. "They're in the soles. Shake the boots a little. You can hear them."

Tristys shook them. He said nothing, just started laughing wildly. Maybe he'd finally cracked.

"What's so funny?"

"I've seen some crazy, unbelievable things on these islands," he choked out through the peals. He was laughing so hard his eyes were tearing up.

"And I haven't had any trouble accepting them. But if you expect me to believe that I'm about to float thanks to a pair of boots filled with rocks, you're insane."

She rolled her eyes. "The rocks are centering objects for iş, which is why they'll let you float." Tristys was lacing his boots already. "You can get ones where the magic is centered into special blades that let you do fancy tricks, like high jumps and spins and everything. It's beautiful to watch. Like air-dancing."

He stood up, took one step, and faltered. The shoes took some getting used to, which she told him, and after a few more steps he'd had it down. They took more getting used to on the water, and for a good ten minutes Tristys wobbled like a boat about to capsize.

After a few pointers, he got the hang of it, and they started striding across the lake. She loved the motion, the way force became something so graceful and smooth. She loved the union of magical energy and human workmanship, the way that magic alone wasn't enough to stride. It was touching, and she choked up if she thought too deeply about it.

Tristys was enjoying his time on the lake, too. He'd brightened up considerably, and now he was striding circles around Calissa—literally, not metaphorically. He rushed here and there, did awkward twirls, scouted this corner of the lake or chased a stridus until it zigzagged out of range. After chasing one particularly manic stridus, he calmed down a little. Winded, he caught up with Calissa and matched her pace.

"I wish we didn't have to leave tomorrow," she said after a few minutes. "This is my favorite place in the Coquels."

"Yeah, it's nice," Tristys said. "I don't mind if we stay a few more days."

"We can't." To the left was a particularly dense grove of pine trees, several of the trees twisted around each other, and Calissa tried to convince herself she barely registered its presence. She sped up without realizing it. "Rami wants you to see the Martyrday celebrations, so we have to get to Zebelli soon."

"What's up with those trees?" Tristys asked.

"What?" Calissa still didn't look at the grove.

"Those trees over there, with the twisted trunks or whatever. You keep sneaking glances like you're waiting for something to jump out of them."

Ignore him? Deny it outright? Give in? "I used to go there with someone, that's all," she said finally. She stole a glance at the trees. "We should get to Zebelli without any problems."

"With a guy?" Tristys asked, not letting it drop. When she didn't respond, he moved directly in front of her, striding backwards, and grinned wildly. "With a guy?" he said again, exaggerating every syllable.

"Yes, with a guy." She beat down a grin at the memory.

"Not Rami, I assume."

"Not Rami," she said. "I went there with Fal."

"The guy that arrested me?" he said, sounding appalled.

Her refusal to respond was answer enough.

"So that explains why you two got all chummy in that bubble you made." What was he insinuating? Was it that obvious? Did anyone else know?

"No, not like that. We've always just been friends."

"Oh yeah? Just friends? Always?"

Calissa didn't answer right away. She'd never told anyone anything about her relationship with Fal. It had happened before she really knew Rami or Salice or Gawen, and once she found Rami, there was no reason to rock the boat. But, she thought to herself, the boat was already rocking. Perhaps it was time.

"Close friends," she finally said, and the smile they shared said more than any of her words could. He didn't push for more information, and she didn't give any. Perhaps one day she would, but not today. It wasn't time.

Yet.

~~*

The journey from Strider to Zebelli was short – only two days – but rough. The island's terrain was unforgiving, shrouded in a dense fog that never let up. There were evergreen trees covering the land, and what wasn't forested was solid rock, angled and sharp. They had to camp out only once, but once was one too many times. Even with Gawen's Fire-magic heating an insulated wind shield from Calissa, Tristys still felt like he was going to freeze to death that night.

But he woke up still alive. They continued to trek uphill, heading toward Zebelli. Every city Tristys had seen so far in the Coquels knew how to make an entrance, but Zebelli knew how to do it best. Breaking through the dense forest and fog, Tristys saw empty air, crisp and clear all the way across the water to the western peninsula. The land went directly from forest to cliffs. Far below, the Midbay rolled, blue waves and white foam mixing as they crashed against the island's coast.

And above that chaos hung Zebelli, the floating city. Stone platforms radiated out in a sphere from the enormous one in the middle. There was no pattern or symmetry to it. Most were above the cliffs, but as Tristys peered over the edge, he saw several below him. They were shaped similarly, however, their bottoms curving slightly to a rounded apex in the center. Similar decorations hung from the bottom, too: stylized pennants blowing in the wind, three to each platform and configured to form a triangle.

Calissa taxied them via Air-magic. She took them to one of the largest platforms, very near the top of the city, and set them down near the center in a courtyard. Alabaster benches surrounded an enormous fire-pit, a bright blue flame almost as large as Salice burning inside it. The platform's building, crafted from a single piece of pale tan rock, wrapped around its entire perimeter. It had five towers, two near the entrance and the other three spread evenly along the length. The whole thing looked like some of the pottery Tristys had seen back home, as if some giant had thrown a piece of rock onto a wheel and shaped the building out of it. It was even more majestic than the Imidaléan Palace had been. This was an inn?

The wrought-iron double doors of the outer courtyard swung open, and a man and woman emerged. The male innkeeper was plump, and the woman had her blonde hair tied up in a tight bun. They were dressed easily, in loose-fitting clothes that looked comfortable. The closer they got to Tristys and his friends, the faster they moved.

"Calissa, we didn't think you'd be coming!" the man shouted, running the remaining distance and grabbing Calissa in a bear hug. The woman looked put out, her arms still open and empty, but she was smiling.

"Of course I'd be here, Dad," Calissa said. "You know how much we love Martyrday." She tilted her head behind her, in Rami's direction, and Tristys barely registered her sarcasm through his surprise. Dad? Did she say dad? These were her parents? Was this...

"Calissa, do you live here?" he asked, the words rushing out before he could stop them.

She didn't look at him as she answered. "Yeah, I grew up here."

"By the two moons, how rich are you?" he blurted.

"Oh, we're not that rich," the man said, putting an arm around the woman. "Just lucky." Everyone smiled—Calissa didn't—and Tristys felt like he was missing something.

"Calissa is a Temeran," Gawen said, flat.

"I don't—"

"He doesn't know what that means," Calissa said quickly, the first trace of frustration hitting her voice. "He's the only one in all the islands who doesn't, and now we have to go and ruin it." She crossed her arms, her head still down. Was she pouting?

"You must be the foreigner, then," the woman said. She looked him up and down but made no motion to shake his hand or talk to him. "Fascinating."

"Please, Maleen!" the man chuckled. His smile looked just like Calissa's. "He's not a specimen!"

"I know, I know." She looked at Tristys now.

"Please, forgive me. Sometimes I let my curiosity get the better of me." Now she reached out a hand, and he shook it. "I'm not surprised you don't know who the Temerans are, but I must say, I'm a little bit shocked nobody mentioned it to you in your journeys. You've gone all over the Coquels now, haven't you?"

Tristys was about to answer, but Calissa beat him to it. "He's only been to Quelles, Quellos, and Quell," she said. "And Quellus, I suppose, but only Six Plumes." She brushed a stray strand of hair behind her ear. "And we've kept to ourselves for the most part." She took a deep breath, and for the first time, she looked up. "Didn't want to deal with the publicity and all."

"Of course, of course," the woman, Maleen, said. "Let's all go inside. I'll have Valys mix up some of his famous airberry tea, and we'll give Tristys a bit of a history lesson, shall we?"

Valys was one of the Temerans' staff. They had a live-in cook, butler, and maid, as well as several other people who came to help daily. Tristys couldn't figure out what the stablehand was for, considering they lived in the sky, but he didn't ask questions.

Tristys did realize very soon that Calissa's father, Paimal, had been lying through his teeth: The Temerans were very, very rich. Maleen and Paimal were two of the most skilled Air-practitioners in the Coquels, so they did the most difficult, incredible feats with their magic and charged enormous, though justified, fees. They were also as close to royalty as you could get in the Coquels.

Martyrday, Tristys knew, was held in celebration of Clarsi V, the seyan of Quellis during the Great War who sacrificed her life and her city to fatally wound the tyrant Bellimar's army. What he hadn't known, however, was that Calissa was a direct descendant of Clarsi's. And since Quellisian society had been the most stratified, with nobles and underclasses, the Quellisian seyanship was the only one of the seven in the Coquels to be conferred by heredity rather than won by election. That practice had ended when the seven islands unified after the Great War, but the memory hadn't gone, and nearly everyone in the islands treated the Temerans like royalty because of it.

So now Tristys was staying in a palace. As usual after days of travel, they went to bed early. He had an entire tower to himself. An entire tower! Four rooms at the top of a decadent spiral staircase, windows facing out in every direction, and an entire bathroom to himself. There was even a refrigerated box for drinks and light snacks, so he didn't have to walk the whole way to the kitchen for refreshments. It was ridiculous.

Tomorrow was Martyrday, and Maleen told him he'd learn more about Clarsi then, at the vigil. He was only vaguely interested in the history, but he was curious to know why Calissa was so resentful of her past. If he were royalty, he'd milk it.

It was still early, but Tristys wanted to take a shower and a nap. Rami had implied he'd be show up in the middle of the night, and he wanted to be well-rested and well-groomed. He didn't think anything would happen in the royal palace of his boyfriend's girlfriend, but you never could tell with Rami.

CHAPTER SEVENTEEN

The next day was the First Wave of Martyrday; Maleen explained that they were called waves because Clarsi loved the ocean, and there were three of them because Clarsi loved the number three. The First Wave was all about sorrow over Clarsi's tragic end. Huge deep purple drapes had been weighted and hung from the perimeter of every platform, their fabric motionless despite the wind, and every Coquellian citizen stood vigil at various blue flames around the islands to honor her memory. The flame at the Temeran Palace was, not surprisingly, the largest and the most visited. By the end of the day, Tristys had met so many people he fell asleep before Rami even knocked on his door.

The Second Wave had to do with gratitude, showing thanks for Clarsi's sacrifice. Shorter pink drapes, still weighted, had been unfurled in front of the deep purple ones, and any and all work done today was completed without charge. Calissa, her parents, and Gawen flitted around the city, doing everything they could for free, while Tristys, Rami, and Salice lounged around the Palace, playing with Firebird, eating, and talking. It was the most relaxing day Tristys had ever had.

The final Wave celebrated the life that Clarsi had given to her people through her sacrifice. The weighted drapes were gone; in their place were drapes in every color of the rainbow, dancing freely in the wind. The platforms had moved, too, many of them pushed closer to the large central hub, known as the Park, and connected via rope bridges. Salice assured Tristys that, because so many people partied so hard, there were nets of Air-magic to catch anyone who fell off. He didn't plan on testing the theory.

At dusk, the party officially started. One woman rose above everyone else. She had long blonde hair—a trend with most Quellisians, it seemed—and she was thin but curvaceous. When she started to speak, her voiced echoed. Tristys heard every word clearly, despite the distance between them.

"Friends, welcome," she said, opening her arms as if she were embracing everyone. "I, too, am anxious to begin the party, so I'll keep this brief." She dropped her arms, and her body settled lower in the air.

"Who's that?" Tristys whispered to Rami.

"Pari II," he whispered back, never taking his eyes away from the woman. "She's the seyan of Quellis."

Tristys nodded, and Pari II continued. "We are here on this, the Third Wave of Martyrday, to celebrate the most beautiful, the most wonderful, the greatest gift of all: the gift of life. Clarsi V so loved these islands she gave herself, her city, and her people to save it. Without that gift, neither you nor I would be here today. We have already shown our sorrow and our gratitude. Let us now make use of that gift she gave us."

As she spoke the last words, fire shot from the platforms behind her, erupting into the sky and giving birth to thousands of slowly falling stars.

There were several volleys, each one greater than the last, until dozens of fire trails bloomed and then shattered into rain. By the time the last star disappeared, music had started, firelights were strobing across the entire platform, and everyone was dancing. Even Calissa was moving to the music, mostly because Salice had grabbed her wrists and was moving them for her. Calissa was very obviously trying not to smile, but her efforts were in vain, and a few seconds later, she was dancing without Salice's help. Salice hadn't let go.

"They'll be like that all night," Gawen said, leaning in so Tristys could hear him over the music. "Salice is the only thing that can get Calissa to shake like that." Gawen took Tristys by the arm and started to drag him to their dancing friends. "Now it's your turn!" Gawen pulled him close, grabbed his waist, and started grinding.

Tristys was momentarily dumbstruck. He looked at Rami, panicked and pleading, but Rami was just smiling, shaking his head, amused, and Tristys gave in, letting the music fill him until he moved without Gawen's lead. They danced like that for quite a while, shifting partners, and by the time they took a break, Tristys had danced with everyone, even Rami. Rami had been clingy, trying too hard to pull Tristys in closer than even Gawen held him, but Tristys resisted.

After one particularly hectic dance, Salice spoke up. "Let's go get drinks. I'm parched!"

"I can't believe we waited this long to get drinks," Gawen said as they walked over to the refreshment tables. "I mean, what's Third Wave if you're not toasted, right?"

"I'll drink to that," Calissa said. Her cheeks were flushed, and she was breathing heavy. She'd been dancing the most frantically out of everyone. "Liquor's the only thing that gets me through this holiday."

The few times Tristys had been to pubs in the islands, they'd had a huge array of drinks to choose from. Here, though, there was only one option: a fruity, blue blend that tasted like coconuts. It was heinously sweet, and he could barely taste any liquor in it. Tristys had three, Rami and Gawen each had one, Salice took two, and Calissa downed four and took another to the dance floor with her.

They kept at it for hours. The music never stopped, and they all danced until one of them insisted on getting more drinks, and they'd all follow. There were more of the fire trails and sky explosions, which Rami said were called fireworks and handled by the Quellusians. Tristys was exhausted, but the music kept pumping, the drinks kept flowing, and everyone, including Tristys himself, kept dancing.

When the music slowed a bit, the crowd thinned, and Rami decided he had to go to the bathroom. Salice and Gawen agreed, so they left Calissa and Tristys on the dance floor. Tristys had to pee, too, but since he was the last to speak up, he had to babysit Calissa, who had had a few too many drinks. She was still dancing, though her movements were less rhythmic and more rapid. Tristys was too tired to dance, but he stood nearby, one eye on the lookout for renegade limbs.

"Exactly how many drinks did you have, Calissa?" he shouted, loud enough for her to hear. He grabbed her wrists just like Salice had at the start of the night, but now he was trying to calm her down.

"Oh, enough," Calissa slurred. "But this is Martyrday, you know?" She looked around, jerked her head in the direction of the nearest party-goers and shouted. "Celebrate the good times!" She fist-pumped, and the revelers fist-pumped back. "Besides," she said to Tristys, quieter, "this is the only way I can tolerate this shit."

Tristys saw an opening. "Speaking of that," he said, "why do you hate Clarsi so much?"

"Hate Clarsi?" she asked. Her nose was crinkled in confusion, and she was squinting as if she couldn't see. "I don't hate Clarsi. She's an inspiration." It took her a few tries to get the last word out completely.

Now Tristys was the confused one. "If you love Clarsi, why do you hate Martyrday so much?" The song changed, and the music picked up speed, percussion-heavy, and people started pouring out onto the dance floor.

"I hate how everyone knows me," she said. She wasn't struggling to dance anymore, and her eyes were nearly shut. "I hate how I can't be who I am because everyone knows me, and it would be a stain or whatever."

Tristys understood what it meant to feel like you couldn't be who you are, but he was coming up blank on why Calissa felt that way. "I don't understand. Why can't you be who you are? And who are you?"

Anger opened her eyes. "Because you can't worship it anymore! It caused too many problems before the stupid war, and so some dimwit said no more!" She started to walk away, half in anger and half in tears, but Tristys held her wrists tightly. "And now the Orders have to stay hidden, especially me, because the great-great-great-

great—" she took a deep breath—"great-great-great-great-granddaughter of the great Clarsi V couldn't possibly worship oş, no no no!"

Tristys had no idea what she was talking about. Orders? Worship? Was she just babbling? And there were too many greats, weren't there? "Calissa, I don't—"

"Of course you don't!" she said, intuiting what he was about to say. "Nobody does! It's a big secret, just like you and Rami!"

Suddenly the platforms lost their magic and they plummeted... or so Tristys thought. "What are you talking about?"

"Oh, come on," she said. "Everybody knows that Rami doesn't like women. He's diverted, as you'd say." She giggled at the word, then she stopped, caught by a deep thought. "I don't know if everybody knows that you two are banging, though. I'm sure they suspect it."

Tristys said nothing, didn't know what to say, and Calissa just stood there, hiccupping. He felt like they'd stay there forever, just like that, frozen in time for eternity, but then Rami, Gawen, and Salice pushed through the crowd, Gawen already dancing as he moved, and Calissa bounded away.

"Listen to me, guys!" she said, excitement making her frantic. "Tristys and I were just talking, and—"

Panic. What to do? What to do? This wasn't how it was supposed to happen. "Calissa!" he shouted. "Come here! You've had too much to drink and—"

"We were talking," she looked at Rami and pointed, "and we were wondering if you two had figured out yet that Rami and Tristys fool around every night. I mean, you had to know, right? They were so loud!" She started laughing, almost hysterically, and she put a hand on Rami's shoulder. "You know, that one night outside New Cysal, you were so noisy I had to pop a wind shield around you!"

Tristys shut his eyes. He couldn't watch what happened next. He didn't want to see how hurt Rami looked, how angry, how betrayed. He didn't want to see the surprise in Salice's eyes or the jealousy turning to fire on Gawen's face.

Seconds passed, and nobody said a thing. They all just stood there, trapped. Maybe they wouldn't believe her. Maybe they'd just brush it off as the ramblings of a drunk.

"I can't believe you told her," Rami whispered. Tristys opened his eyes, and Rami hadn't moved, but he'd heard the words anyway. Some trick of Air-magic, certainly. He heard them again. "I can't believe it."

"Rami, I didn't—"

He was louder now, but still frightfully calm. "I can't believe this." Tristys expected more yelling, more anger, more something. What he didn't expect was this: Rami's head shaking back and forth as if he were trying to expel the things he'd heard, Rami taking Gawen by the hand, Rami telling him that he wanted to get out of here. Tristys lunged after them, but Salice intervened.

"Let them go," she said, her voice soft and measured. "He'll be there when we go back. He needs to cool down."

"Yeah, let him go!" Calissa shouted. "Who needs them?" She started dancing again, grabbing Salice and forcing her to join in. "Not us! Let's dance!"

Tristys stayed with Calissa and Salice for a few

more hours, though he spent the entire time staring off the edge of the platform, worrying about what Calissa had done and wondering how he could fix it. At the first light of dawn, the drapes beneath every platform were loosed. As they fell to the sea below, flames overtook the fabric, burning them to nothing right before his eyes.

~~*

Rami wasn't there when Tristys got back to the Temeran Palace. Neither was Gawen. The doors to their bedrooms were locked, and nobody had been home all night. Tristys went to bed. He'd have to wait until everyone woke up the next afternoon to see how much damage had been done.

But Rami wasn't there the next afternoon, either. Tristys slept badly, and he jumped out of bed and headed straight to Rami's door. Still locked. Same as Gawen's. Sleep wasn't an option, so he went to the kitchen to eat. He hadn't had any solid food in hours, since the snacks they ate at the party.

Valys was in the kitchen, preparing a breakfast for everyone. He offered Tristys what he'd already finished, and Tristys nibbled on the berry cake as he waited. Valys was a quiet man, older and hard of hearing, so he spoke little, but he was warm and pleasant company anyway. Before Tristys left the kitchen, he asked if Valys had seen Rami or Gawen. He hadn't.

Tristys thought about taking a walk in the courtyard or wandering the house, but he just went back to his tower. He lay in his bed, with his two blankets—one from the Temerans and the one from Rami in the forest—twisted tightly around him. He tried not to replay the night over and over in his head. Usually he failed, and he saw the whole thing in slow motion. He was tired, but he couldn't sleep. Why hadn't he let Rami tell everyone when he wanted to? He was stupid to try and keep it secret. He knew everybody knew Rami liked guys, so how long did he think it'd stay a secret? What was he thinking?

He fell asleep then, somewhere in the transition from memory to regret. He had strange dreams, irrational dreams, that had him riding a jungle cat through the Zebelli sky and shrinking to the size of a bladecutter bug before bursting into flame. When he jolted awake after a dream with Rami and Gawen in a cottonbloom together, he found Calissa sitting in a chair near his bed, watching him.

"Hey there," he said, trying to get the image of Gawen's lips pressed to Rami's out of his mind. "How long have you been there?"

"Not long." Calissa's eyes were puffy, and her hair still had the intricate braids she wore to Third Wave. She had two cups on the nightstand, and she offered one to Tristys. "It was warm when I brought it to you." She shrugged apologetically, as if it were her fault the heat dissipated.

"That's okay," he said. "I can do Fire-magic, remember?" She nodded, but he didn't warm the tea she'd brought. He reached over the bed's side and put it on the floor. "How are you feeling?" he asked at last.

"I should be asking you that." Her brows furrowed. One eye crinkled more than the other when she was upset. "Tristys, I never meant to tell everyone like that."

"I know," he said at once. He never thought for

a second that she had done anything on purpose. She had known for days, hadn't she? "I would never think—"

"I just feel like I've been keeping so many secrets lately. All this stuff is just festering under my tongue, and I couldn't keep it there anymore. I probably shouldn't drink again," she added a few seconds later. She cracked the barest hint of a smile.

"No, probably not," he said. He wanted to say something else, but he wasn't sure what.

She got off the chair and moved to the corner of his bed. "You know, I don't even remember what happened. Not a second of it. The last thing I remember is downing a bunch of drinks dancing around like a maniac, and then waking up in my bed. I had this weird feeling like something bad happened, but I didn't know what. Salice had to tell me."

Tristys knew he should be mad at Calissa, but for some reason, he wasn't. He was more interested in figuring out what exactly Calissa had meant when she'd talked about Orders and worship and hiding who she was. "You said some pretty weird things last night," he ventured.

She looked up, slight alarm clear on her face. "Like what?"

"Well, you were drunk, so it didn't make much sense. Something about not being able to be who you are because of the Order and the War and worshiping it." He stopped, waiting for her to explain, but she didn't. "Care to unravel that for me?"

"See?" she said, tossing her hand in the air. "More secrets under my tongue."

"I won't tell anyone." He held up his hand to

pledge.

Calissa looked more frustrated, though. "I know you won't, and that's the problem. I can't imagine how having to keep you and Rami a secret must have made you feel. You always made it so obvious how much you liked him." She smiled warmly and touched his shoulder. "You probably hadn't realized, but I'd been trying to get you two together since that first day at Five Waves. Just because I have to be alone and unhappy doesn't mean Rami does, right?"

"There you go again!" He wagged his finger in her face, and she pushed it aside, half-laughing. "You're alluding to something, but you don't explain or anything."

"I just don't want to burden you with any—"

"Oh, pig poo," Tristys said. "I'm your friend, Calissa. I'm here to listen, and if you have something bothering you, venting helps. It does for me, at least."

She took a deep breath, squirmed a bit. "It's a long story..."

"More pig poo!"

"Fine!" she said. "But you can't tell anyone."

"I think that's implied by calling it a secret."

She scowled, and then spoke softly, so quietly Tristys had to lean in to hear. "Well, nowadays the quell just sort of exists, like anything else does. A rock, a tree, a quell. It's all the same. We don't do anything special, treat it any different, all that. But a long time ago, it wasn't like that. A long time ago, people worshiped quell, just like your people worship the Two Mothers.

"At first, only oş was worshiped, because that's all there was. Then we discovered the other quell, or they discovered us, and then things changed.

People grew intolerant of the worship, especially since the forces themselves started to change."

"What do you mean?" Tristys asked. He was spellbound. He'd hated history back in Cyræa, but then again Cyræan history didn't have magic.

"Oş, for instance. Everyone thought it was the only quell, the reason for life and the originator of everything. It's easy to worship something when it seems like it's all there is. Back then, oş Touched everyone, not just a few special people. But then the other quell showed up, and oş got shy or whatever and stopped Touching everyone. People got mad. They got tired. They got selfish. Before long, worshiping was forbidden."

He took a leap. "So you worship quell?"

"Not quell," she corrected. "Just oş."

Tristys understood her words but not her rationale. Religious warfare nearly destroyed Cyræa, and even when he left, there were still pockets of unrest. The reason everyone back home hated diverted men was religious. Spàlorian sex-slavery used religion to justify itself. To Tristys, getting rid of religion seemed like a pretty good idea.

"Worship isn't illegal," Calissa added, "but it's highly stigmatized. Random nobodies who get accused of worship find themselves blacklisted, poked and prodded and hated. If people found out a Temeran was a member of the Oşiad... I can't even imagine what they'd do."

"Oşiad?" Tristys asked, having trouble pronouncing the strange 's' sound the first time he tried. He realized then that he hadn't thought about Gawen or Rami for at least three minutes, and he almost smiled... until he realized he'd just thought about them and therefore ruined his streak.

"The Order of the Oṣiad is one of the two societies that work together to sustain quell-worship. The Oṣiad worships oṣ as the prime quell, the only quell, the source of all the others and everything else, but the Yṣiad worships all six quell as distinct and separate forces. Either way, it's not cool nowadays. But Tristys, it's so amazing, the way oṣ makes me feel. I mean, I can't not worship it, you know? It's so beautiful. You have no idea."

But he did have an idea. He thought back to the first time he could control Water-magic, the beauty the quell-stars had made, the awe he had, that feeling that he could do anything in the world, even the impossible. "Eternity in an hour," he mumbled, mostly to himself.

"What?" she asked.

He jumped. He'd forgot she was there, hadn't even realized he'd spoken out loud. "Nothing. Just something I remembered from when I first used Water-magic that day in the forest. Remember? I cried and Rami came back and saw us and he acted like we'd been making out or something."

"I knew then that he was into you," she said. "I knew before, but I really knew then."

"I wish you would have told me. And him, too. It would have saved so much trouble!"

"Yeah, no kidding." She was smiling again, and the gravity in the room had lightened. She was no longer whispering. "But Martyrday makes everything worse, because it's a giant reminder how I can't avoid being the center of attention because of who I am. And having run into Fal for the first time in so long, that just made everything worse. I guess I was a little jealous of you and

Rami together. That's all."

He chose to ignore the suggestion that maybe her letting the cat out of the bag hadn't been entirely accidental. Instead, he shouted, "I knew you were into Fal!" and she nearly hit the roof.

"Be quiet!" she whispered loudly. "All this is secret, remember?"

"Right, right," he whispered back. "Sorry."

"You're right, though. I do love Fal. Or I did. I thought I was over him, but ever since I saw him at Two Souls, I don't know. I haven't been able to stop thinking about him."

He knew that feeling, too. He'd been thinking about Rami since the second he opened his eyes and saw him sitting there in Telia's house. Even now, he wanted to do nothing more than talk about Rami, ask where he'd gone, when he'd be back, but he knew Calissa needed to vent more than he did. "I don't understand, though. Does Fal not like you back?"

"No, he loves me, too." She got the same confused look she had on a second ago. "Or he did. I don't know what he thinks now."

"Then why weren't you with him? Why'd you get with Rami instead, especially if you knew—or suspected, whatever—that Rami liked guys. Wouldn't Fal have been okay with the Oşiad thing?"

Calissa laughed, her first one since he'd woken up, but she wasn't light-hearted or amused. "Oh, he'd be okay with it. He's the one that introduced me to the Order, actually."

"Oh," Tristys said, stumped. "Then why didn't—"

"Worshiping oş isn't just an ideological thing, Tristys." She sounded slightly annoyed, but she reined it in. "It takes over everything. People in the Order are supposed to give everything they have to oş, including their bodies. One of the rules is celibacy." She took a deep breath, obviously not a fan of that rule. "It's a dumb rule, because anybody who truly worships oş shouldn't fall in love with anything or anyone else... or so they say."

"But you and Fal—"

"It was a rough time for me," she said. "I'd been so confused, thinking I was falling in love with Fal and then wondering if I was falling in love with oş instead. I didn't know what to do. He and I spent so much time together, and we talked about our lives and what they'd be like. We were going to live together, pretend to be together, as a cover-up so nobody suspected. But when he found out I wanted more than just pretend, he panicked. I scared him away. He went all the way to Calere to study their magic. He literally fled the country to get away from me."

Suddenly it all made sense. "That's what you did with Rami, then, wasn't it? He was just a cover-up, to keep people off your trail."

"Yeah, pretty much. By then, he was already sort of pretending to date me, and I knew he'd never try anything sexual with me, so I thought, *Perfect!* And it was perfect for a while. I felt bad for Rami, but I figured what's so wrong with dating your best friend? As long as he was okay with celibacy, I figured who was I to complain?"

Tristys nodded, but now that they were talking about Rami, his focus had been redirected. "Where is he, by the way? Rami?"

Calissa's face dropped, and she grimaced. "Oh, Tristys! He left with Gawen last night. They threw their bedroom keys into my parents' room. That's what I came in here to tell you, and then I totally forgot because I was too busy talking about myself."

Tristys sat there, just sat there on the bed, his hands in his lap. He didn't know what to say, how to react. All he felt was blankness, an almost willful refusal to understand or process. Calissa scooted closer, put her hand on his shoulder and embraced him.

"Don't worry," she said. "He just needs some time."

She squeezed, and it kicked whatever silenced him out of the way. "But he's with Gawen," Tristys said, too quickly. "Gawen's been eying him up all over the place, and I had a dream last night they were in a cottonbloom, and they probably are right now, and I screwed everything up, and now it's—"

"Wait wait wait, slow down." She held on to Tristys's shoulders, pushed them together to ground him. "There are no cottonblooms in Quellis, so don't worry about that. And—"

"What do you mean there are no cottonblooms here, Calissa?" Tristys shouted. "We're sitting on one right now!"

"This is a bed, not a bloom!"

"It's still a cottonbloom!"

"Yeah, but were they on a bed in your dream or a wild cottonbloom?"

Tristys's mouth hung open, ready to argue, but he couldn't. "It was a wild one, but—"

"Exactly. There are no wild cottonblooms in Quellis," she said. "And besides, Gawen has been after Rami since they first met, and—"

"Oh, that's very reassuring!"

"And Rami's never done anything about it before."

"It's not the same now! Now he's diverted and he's done it and so there's nothing holding him back like there was before."

"Listen, there's no reason he would—" She stopped. "Wait a minute, did you just say 'done it'? Did you two...?" She trailed off, but her eyebrows finished the question for him.

"No, of course not!" Tristys said, giggling despite himself. "We never quite got there." She nodded as if she expected as much. "But trust me, we've wanted to."

"Who could blame you? You're both so good-looking," she said with a completely straight face. They laughed together, briefly but genuinely, and she stood up to leave. "By the way, you didn't screw anything up. I was the one that let it slip that I knew."

"No, I did screw it up." Tristys felt the guilt wash over him again. "I'm the one who wanted to keep it a secret. He wanted to tell everyone for weeks now, but I kept shushing him. That night you put up the wind shield? He wanted to wake everyone up and tell them then."

Calissa sat back down on the bed. "Why'd you make him keep it a secret?"

"I don't know!" He threw up his hands, shook his head, mimicked a slap on the forehead. "That's a lie. I do know. I was afraid he'd forget about me if he told people, if he got too comfortable being open about what he liked. He's gorgeous, you know?" He looked up at Calissa, and there was compassion in her face. "He could have anyone he wants."

"Oh, Tristys," she said, putting an arm on his shoulder again. He leaned in for the comfort, but she pulled away and slapped the back of his head instead. "He wants you! He could have always had anyone he wanted in the Coquels. But he waited for you."

Time for him to face the truth. "I know, you're right. I told you I screwed it up."

"You're right, you did." He looked up at her devastated, but she was smiling. "I'll still talk to him, though, when he gets back."

"If he gets back."

"He always comes back," she said in that voice that refused argument.

Tristys shrugged. "I hope you're right. I guess I'll just wait here until he does." He perked up a bit. Plans invigorated him. "Not like I have anywhere else to be, after all."

"Actually," Calissa said as she headed to the door, "you do. We need to go to the Altar of Four Winds to see if you can Touch iş." She turned her head to the window. The sky was clear and bright blue. He wished there weren't glass in the windows so he could feel the breeze. "And besides, I hate it here."

"How could you hate it here? It's a floating city, for crying out loud!"

"Well, maybe not hate," she admitted. "But strongly dislike." She opened the door, but she didn't leave. "Everyone here knows my name," she said. "It's annoying."

He didn't want Calissa to be unhappy, and he didn't want her to stay somewhere she didn't like, but he had to stay here, didn't he? This was the first place Rami would come after he cooled off, wasn't it? Tristys had seen so many people back in Paru who acted as if their entire world was their lover—his sister was a good example—and he'd never thought he'd become that person, but here he was, having a hard time imagining the Coquels without Rami. It wasn't the end of the world if Rami never came back, but it sure did put a damper on things.

"Can't we stay here just a few more days?" he asked. He pouted a bit, tried to make his eyes look pathetic and desperate. "He won't stay away too long, right? And he'll come back here first, and if he sees that we've gone, maybe he'll think that we gave up on him."

"Fine," she relented. "A few days." He smiled hugely, like he'd just won a prize, and he bounced a bit on the cottonbloom bed. "But just a few days! I have a theory about you," she said mysteriously, "and if I'm right, you're going to Touch iş, too. I'm surprised you haven't Fingerprinted yet."

"I thought I did," he said, "but it turns out that was just you being sly."

"I did it for you, baby!" she said. "You two enjoyed the privacy, I'm sure."

"It was nice," Tristys admitted, "but it wasn't my doing. So no Fingerprinting yet."

"That's good, I suppose. We can stay a bit, but if you show even the slightest indication of weirdness involving iş, you tell me at once. It's the most dangerous Fingerprint of all six quell." She said the last part too dramatically. "When I Fingerprinted, it took me a few weeks to get control of it, so I had to have practitioners hovering over me at all times, because I kept trying to suffocate everyone within sight."

"Oh, perfect," Tristys said. "So now I'm going to strangle everyone I know?"

"No, usually Fingerprints involve suffocating yourself. I was just a freak."

"Even better!"

"Just let me know if anything strange happens, okay? Also, come down for dinner soon. I saved you some, since you slept through it."

"Will do," Tristys said. "Just let me shower last night off my body. I still feel sticky. I don't know how you can sweat when it's not even hot out."

She was in the doorway now. "All that dancing," she said. She disappeared down the hall, but a second later, her head reappeared. "Even if we didn't know you and Rami were together," she continued, "we would have known by now. You two were all over each other last night!"

"We were not!" Tristys shouted, but a few seconds and a few memories later, he realized she was right again.

CHAPTER EIGHTEEN

Gawen looked utterly miserable. Rami regretted dragging him along, but he needed his Fire-magic to survive the cold of the Quellisian forests. He hated to admit it, even to himself, but he needed the companionship, too. He didn't want to be alone.

But he didn't want to be surrounded by people, either, which was why he and Gawen were trekking through the Pine Forests, far from the manufactured warmth of Zebelli or Zefael. The farther away from the shore you went, the harsher the Pine Forests became, and by now they'd gotten pretty far from the shore. Gawen's Fire-magic was the only reason they weren't freezing to death. He'd been maintaining a bearable temperature in a small bubble since they'd left Zebelli two days ago.

The constant manipulation was starting to take its toll. He looked haggard, like someone who was exhausted but refused to sleep. His eyes were closed slightly, as if the lids had grown too heavy to hold open. But he was an excellent practitioner. He knew when enough was enough, and he could handle this. But perhaps they should start heading out of the forest, if only to give Gawen a night off.

Rami still didn't want to deal with people, but it'd be nice to get away from Gawen. They'd been alone now for two days, which was two days longer than they'd ever been alone before, and Rami was getting tired of fending off Gawen's perpetual attempts at seduction. Last night had been the worst. Rami'd agreed to sleep close to Gawen, so their body heat would allow Gawen to ease up on the Fire-magic. He'd had to swat away invading hands and prodding fingers non-stop for the first hour or so, and even once Gawen had fallen asleep, Rami couldn't doze off, for fear of waking up violated. Definitely, definitely getting to a town by nightfall, Rami thought.

He had no real idea where he was going or why he'd run away from Martyrday. He wasn't even sure what happened. Calissa knew he and Tristys were together, and that was enough to set him off. He couldn't believe Tristys had told his secret. It was his secret, after all, not Tristys's. And hadn't Tristys been the one trying to keep it under wraps anyway? Hadn't Rami been the one wanting to come clean, finally, after all these years of hiding? What right did Tristys have to be Rami's savior?

He reached up and pulled a cone off the nearest pine. It was young, not entirely hardened, and he tossed it to Gawen. "Eat that," he said. "You look like shit."

"You'd look like shit too," Gawen retorted, his teeth chattering for just a second, "if you'd been doing this for two days." He peeled off a scale and ate it. "Speaking of shit, this tastes like it."

"It's not ripe," Rami said, "but it'll give you energy. You need it. Eat."

Two pine cones later, Gawen still looked tired but he had rebegun his attempts at seduction. Rami took that as a good sign, so he increased their pace, backtracking along the path they'd come. By the last of daylight, they'd made it to

Zefael, one of the two towns on the Midbay. Tristys took Gawen immediately to the inn, not even stopping to eat, and they got double beds, even though Gawen tried to insist on a single. They both fell asleep at once, and when Rami woke up hours later, he felt Tristys behind him, holding him tightly in an embrace, and for a brief blissful second, he'd thought everything had been a dream, a long, drawn-out bad dream. But Tristys didn't smell like this.

"Gawen, dammit!" He burst out of Gawen's arms, heaving himself out of the bed despite the fact he was still tired. "What in the name of Water-magic do you think you're doing?"

Gawen feigned sleep for about as long as it took Rami to shoot him a dirty look. "I was sleeping, what's it look like?"

"You know what I mean," Rami said, gritting his teeth. He hid the rage inside. He was tired of the non-stop come-ons, tired of looking at him, tired of being reminded that Gawen wasn't Tristys. That no one was.

"Look, I figured since Tristys and you aren't togeth—"

"We were never together," he said at once without even thinking about it. "He must have been dreaming or—"

"Oh, Rami," Gawen said, his face pinched. Rami wasn't sure if it was pity or revulsion or just being fed up that was doing the pinching. "Are you really going to go back to that?"

Rami crossed his arms. "I don't know what you're talking about."

"Didn't it feel good?" Gawen started to slink across the bed, and Rami prepared to fend off another attack. "Being with Tristys, I mean. Being open about it. Wasn't it a relief? Weren't you happier?"

"I still don't know what you're talking about." His voice was softer now, his resolve cracking. Gawen was right. Everything he said was right.

Gawen had reached the edge of the bed, and he got on his knees to look Rami straight in the eyes. "Aren't you tired of this yet?"

He was. What was he doing? Why was he defaulting back to this, even after he'd begged Tristys to let him open up to everyone?

When Gawen realized Rami was staying silent, he took his hands and pulled him closer. For a second, Rami thought he was about to get a kiss, but Gawen stopped just before their lips touched. Rami averted his eyes. "Look at me, Rami. Listen to me." He looked up. "Everybody knows, Rami," Gawen said slowly, trying to cushion the blow. "Everybody has always known, and nobody has ever cared. Except you."

Gawen had teased Rami at least once a day since they'd met, but this was different. There was no flirtatious lilt in his voice, no hope in his eyes. This was different. This was simple fact, straight truth. Rami couldn't speak.

"I still don't understand what the big deal is," Gawen said. "I've known you for how long now? And as much as I hate to admit this, I've never seen you as happy as you've been since Tristys came along."

Rami felt a smile ghost across his lips. His voice still wouldn't cooperate.

"I've known the whole time, too. I think everyone has, even Calissa. Telia's known since you were a baby, she said. Something about the way you walk."

Rami's voice rushed back to him. "Telia knows?" He felt shock, even though he knew she knew. She was the first person to try and set him up with Tristys, wasn't she?

"Of course," Gawen said. "That's why your parents don't talk to her anymore."

"My parents know?" Rami squeaked.

"Rami, Rami, Rami." Gawen shook his head slowly. "When I said 'everyone', I meant everyone."

"But why wouldn't they talk to her if she knew and they knew and everyone knew? It doesn't make sense."

"You were playing the I-like-girls game, and Telia wanted your parents to confront you about it, help you accept yourself, but they just wanted you to be happy. They didn't want to say anything, so they let it go. Telia got mad. They got mad. Ask them for more details. Or better yet, ask her. She'll be hyped to know she was right."

Rami's mouth hung open as he tried to process everything.

Gawen was looking at him curiously, his head cocked a little to the side and his eyes narrowed. "Why did you hide it, Rami? You had to know we wouldn't care..."

Rami's first instinct was to deny, to refuse, to brush it aside as he'd always done. He opened his mouth to say no, but the entire story came crashing out instead. He told Gawen everything, from his irrational fear of his namesake and Tierran to Tristys's arrival and everything that had happened since. By the time he finished, he was crying, half from the pain of those memories and half from the relief of finally having shed the lies. Gawen held him the entire time, running a hand through his hair, and letting him sob into his shoulder. They stayed that way for a while, until Rami calmed down enough to feel awkward in his arms.

"Thanks, Gawen," he said, pulling his face from the shoulder. It felt like tearing paper. He kept his eyes down and stifled an awkward giggle. The first bit of it escaped, and Gawen smiled softly, amused rather than lascivious.

"So," Gawen said, letting the sound draw out. Rami recognized that gleam, that drawl. It was coming. He knew it would, and somehow in a way, he was glad. Everything was back to normal already. "Should we get naked now," Gawen continued, "or do you want to cuddle a bit more first?"

"How about we sleep instead?"

"That's fine," Gawen said, stretching out on his side and patting the spot directly in front of him. "Scoot on in. Just ignore any pokes from behind."

Rami laughed despite himself. Dealing with Gawen's flirtations was easier when he didn't have to pretend he wasn't at least theoretically interested in them. "No. I sleep here, you sleep there." He motioned to the other bed with his head.

He expected a witty retort, but Gawen said nothing. He stared at Rami, eyes narrowed and fire smoldering through the slits. When he finally spoke, his voice was quiet, unsteady.

"I don't understand. If Tristys is out of the picture, and you aren't pretending to be something you're not, then why—"

"Tristys isn't out of the picture, Gawen," Rami blurted. It surprised him. He had been so angry at Tristys, so ready to drop him, but now... nothing would be the same without him. "You shouldn't—"

"Then why did you do this?" He was no longer quiet, his voice raised and his jaw set in anger. "Why did you make me come with you? I thought you were—"

Rami realized his mistake at once. In all their years as friends, Rami made sure he never led Gawen on, never let him get the wrong idea. Now he'd blown it all with one impulsive mistake. "Gawen, I didn't mean... I just wanted—" He struggled for the words to fix this. "I just didn't want to be alone," he said finally.

"And you needed my magic."

"No, Gawen, I would never use you like that. I—"

"Please, Rami!" Gawen said, his voice steeped in poison. "All you've ever done is use me!"

"When have I ever—"

"You used me to live the life you couldn't. Don't think I never noticed how interested you were in all my affairs. You think I couldn't see the lust in your eyes, the desire, the jealousy?" He had gotten off the bed now, was standing up and bending over his backpack in the corner. "Half the reason I flaunted so much was because I knew you liked it. I thought it'd help you realize there's nothing wrong with the way you are."

"Gawen, I—"

He stopped tossing things into his bag and stood up. His hands were limp at his side as he said, "You know what the funny thing is, Rami? The only person I've ever truly wanted is you." He cinched shut his backpack and slung it over his shoulders.

"Gawen, please don't—"

"I have to go," he said. "I've followed you

around for too long, Rami, waiting for exactly this. For you to be okay with it, for us to be together. I can't sleep another night in the same room with you, knowing now that the only thing keeping us apart is your own disinterest. I just can't."

As he headed for the door, Rami rushed to his side. "Gawen, please just stay." He grabbed his arm. "Please, stay."

"Let go of me," Gawen said, but Rami refused. "Please, just—"

"I said let go!" With that, Gawen's arm flamed, and Rami's fingertips scalded.

"Gawen, I—" Rami said, too stunned by the temporary pain to continue.

"I just have to go," he said again. He repeated it twice more as he left, more softly each time, until Rami was certain he was speaking more to himself than to Rami.

For the first time in a long time, Rami was alone, and though he knew he should chase after Gawen, try to calm him down, get him to stay, all Rami did was the math to know just how long it'd take him to get back to Tristys.

As usual, Calissa got her way. The day after their conversation, Air-magic left its Fingerprint on Tristys. Calissa, along with Salice and Maleen, had him on his way to the Altar within the hour. Upon arrival, several priests escorted him to the meditation alcoves; he stayed awhile, mostly for show. The Trial took even less time than the meditating.

As soon as everyone saw Tristys, they jumped up as if he were a ghost. Firebird scampered up his leg to the usual post, Calissa asked how he was, and Salice looked concerned but stayed silent. Maleen, convinced that he would attune to Death-magic, was mumbling about the quickest way to Quellys.

"I'm fine." Tristys motioned for everyone to sit with his free hand. "Just tired." Everyone sat down, but they still stared at him, as if he were about to suffocate or burst into flame at any second. "Really, you don't have to stare, I'm fine."

Calissa looked away, and Salice blushed a little, but Maleen kept staring. "We know, dear," she said. "I'm just wondering how soon you'll be able to go to Quellys. I really must return to Zebelli soon, but I would like to see what happens at Sole Decay." Her mouth dropped, and she exhaled loudly. "Can you imagine?" She was talking to Calissa now. "Nobody has been able to Touch both Life- and Death-magic in a dozen generations, since far before the Great War."

"We know, Mother."

"I don't," Tristys interjected. Maleen looked as if she were on the verge of another lesson, but he cut her short. "But I'm pretty tired at the moment. I'd like to stay here, I think, at least for the night."

"We can stay here as long as you need," Calissa said, more to her mother than to Tristys. He had a feeling she liked the Altars because they were low-key and everyone minded his or her own business while there. She probably liked the isolation.

"We can go tomorrow, probably. I'd just like to relax a bit."

Maleen was disappointed. "Sadly, I won't be able to accompany you, then." She started to scamper around the room, gathering belongings. Maleen didn't beat around the bush! "I simply must get back to Zebelli by tomorrow night. Your father is utterly incompetent when it comes to catalyzing, and we have a pressing matter to attend to." She leaned in to Salice, who was the closest to her at the time. "You didn't hear this from me, but the Park's centering stones are getting low. I'm surprised the whole thing didn't plummet on Martyrday. It would have been an end to the Zebelli siege all over again!"

Tristys was momentarily panicked at the thought that he could have fallen to his death while partying, but neither Salice nor Calissa seemed worried. Instead, she looked bored. "We'll keep you informed, Mother," Calissa said.

Maleen looked skeptical.

"It's okay, Maleen," Salice said, putting a hand on Calissa's shoulder. "I'll make sure she does."

"Thank you, my dear. Now I can sleep soundly." She set her small bag on the ground and walked to Tristys. She took his hands in her own. "I'm afraid that brings our time together to an end. It really has been a pleasure meeting you, Tristys, and I do hope once you finish your journeys to the Altars, you'll come back to visit us in Zebelli."

"Oh, I imagine that'll happen at some point," he said. Calissa lived there, after all.

"I do hope so." She squeezed his hands, and she squinted, as if she weren't sure she should continue. "I know you probably think I'm only interested in your magic, but you do seem like such a nice boy." She shot a glance at Calissa, then leaned in closer to Tristys and spoke softer. "And it seems like you may finally be able to whip that Rami into shape. Maybe then Calissa will move on and find herself a real man." Her eyes widened a bit at her faux pas and she dropped his hands.

"Not that Rami isn't a real man, of course. He's just not the right man for Calissa, for obvious reasons."

"I know, Maleen. I'm doing what I can."

"Keep up the good work, then." She said goodbyes to Salice and Calissa, and then just as fast as she'd come into Tristys's life, she was gone from it.

~~*

Calissa was not sad to get away from her home island, and the quickest way to get to Quellys from Four Winds was to travel through Windwyrm Way, an undeveloped tract of land between the shore and the Shadowed Ridge, Quellis's western mountain range. Originally, before Quellis had been settled by the Quellosians, windwyrms roamed freely across the island. As the Quellosians spread, the windwyrms were pushed back to Windwyrm Way and contained therein. They hadn't been seen in generations, though, and were thought extinct; nobody knew what happened to them, if they died or disappeared or just vanished into wherever it was iş went.

People crossed Windwyrm Way daily now, but the memories of the beasts hadn't faded. Hundreds of years later, travelers still hurried through it, anxious and afraid, and the closer they got, the more Tristys resisted the impending departure. He seemed to think that the only way he'd get Rami back was by staying on the island, which was ludicrous. Calissa knew Rami, and he was probably back home in Quelles by now, working out in the forest or pouring over piles of books in his bedroom.

When they crested the last hill before the tunnel, Calissa had to reassess her theories about Rami. He wasn't home after all. In fact, he was standing there, right in front of them, leaning against the entrance to the cave, one foot up against the mountain, his knapsack on the ground next to him. Gawen wasn't with him.

For a split second, she panicked. One of the Fingerprints of ysinvolved pulling hallucinogenic poisons out of the air and into nearby people. Was Tristys Fingerprinting, and she was feeling the effects? But a second later, both Tristys and Firebird broke into a sprint, and she knew Rami really was there.

Firebird jumped from the ground straight into Rami's arms, and Calissa thought Tristys intended to do the same, but he skidded to a halt at the last minute, the energy that would have propelled him forward coiled now in his legs. He never looked as young as he did then, like a child who'd found his birthday presents but couldn't open them yet.

But then Rami pushed himself off the mountain and wrapped Tristys in a bear hug, Firebird squeaking his discomfort between them. He kissed Tristys, directly on the lips. *Really, Rami? That simple? That easy?* She couldn't believe it. As she walked the rest of the way up the path, her face must have said everything she was thinking, because Rami looked right at her, his arms still around Tristys, and smiled. "What?" he asked. "You didn't really think I'd let you guys walk through Windwyrm Way alone, with no protection, did you?"

Calissa grinned, fairly certain that no girl had ever been so happy to see her boyfriend kissing another man.

CHAPTER NINETEEN

As Rami had expected, the journey through the Windwyrm Way was uneventful. They didn't see an eagle or a fox let alone a windwyrm. He wasn't sure if Tristys realized what a feeble cover the bodyguard thing had been, but he knew Salice and Calissa understood. He wasn't there to protect them; he was there to be with Tristys.

Rami thought they'd wait for the ferry to take them from Quellis to Quellys, but Calissa was impatient. She also said this would be a perfect chance for Tristys to practice his newly acquired Air-magic, so she had him lift the four of them, plus Firebird, off the ground to ferry them to the Death island. He did well. He dropped Salice once by accident, and he felt so guilty he dunked himself to make amends. He dropped Rami once, too, but that hadn't been an accident.

Rami hated Quellys almost as much as he hated Quellos, for almost the exact opposite reasons. Quellys stank. The trees were twisted, half-dead ghosts missing most of their leaves, and the Death island was the only place where you were more likely to see a walking skeleton than a prowling animal. Add to that the altitude—Quellys was all mountains—and Rami was in hell.

Of course, nobody really liked Quellys, except perhaps the New Cysalians, who didn't even live here. This place wasn't like Quellas, speckled with single-family homesteads across its forests. It wasn't like any of the waterfall islands, with more and more towns beating back the native rainforests. Quellys was virtually uninhabited, except for the few cities across the island. Cysal, Centrespire, Spirescale. If you didn't live in one of those places, you probably didn't live on Quellys.

When they arrived on Quellys, Rami was disappointed. Tristys had overshot, and they were far to the south of where Rami had intended. He'd wanted to go to Spirescale, a smaller, quieter city in the north of the island, but now they'd have to go to Centrespire, the heart of Quellysian night life. There was absolutely nothing to do on Quellys natively, so the Quellysians had developed the wildest night life of the islands. They had the only legal brothels in the Coquels, and their serving-houses served a lot more than just liquor. Consequently, Centrespire was never quiet, never peaceful, and never an intended destination of Rami's.

Despite his distaste for the island, Rami had to admit Centrespire was beautiful. The locals kept the decay clear, and the city had been built in and around the largest kakenstone spire on the island. Kakenstone was unlike any other rock in the world; it absorbed and then reflected virtually everything it could, most notably light, smells, and even quell. The spires were majestic, the endless black of the stone still visible behind the scintillations on the surface, and they almost made Rami forget he was on Quellys. Almost.

They'd found a small room at one of the inns in the spire itself. The fee was exorbitant, but Tristys had been so amazed by the stone that Rami couldn't refuse, even though his funds were getting low. He'd have to stop home soon, though he wasn't sure how much he had left of his Physical Services stipend. He'd worry about it later.

"So," Tristys said once they'd settled into the room, "now what?"

Calissa was in the kitchen—or the corner of the room that substituted for the kitchen. Space in the Spire was tight by design, and so the rooms inside were claustrophobic at best and impossible at worst. "What do you mean?"

"Well, it's so early," Tristys said. He was perched at the sole window in the place—an amenity that cost more than all the clothes Rami'd bought since Tristys got to the islands. "And I'm not tired." He stretched his neck farther out the window, and Rami resisted the urge to rush over and save him from falling out. "And I was just wondering what's going on down there." Even inside their room, they could hear the thumping of the music from the nearest serving-house, as well as the shouts and laughter and camaraderie from the streets. People were wild tonight, probably still riding the Martyrday waves.

"They're just doing what Quellysians do," Salice said.

"And what's that?"

"Oh, a little bit of this, a little bit of that." She joined Tristys at the window and pushed him aside, since it was too small for two to fit.

"Well, can we go do a little bit of this and a little bit of that? It sounds like they're having fun." Someone outside whooped in agreement, and Rami cringed.

"I can't even remember the last time we partied Quellysian-style," Salice said, more to Calissa than to anyone else. She was smiling broadly and looking mischievous. "What do you say?"

"I don't know," Calissa hemmed. "It has been awhile, and this room is way too small to stay in it all night."

"They do that on purpose." Rami tried not to pout. "They make these rooms so small on purpose so it forces you to go out and party."

"So can we go?" Tristys looked at Rami and pleaded with his eyes. "It's not like there's anything we can do together in here," he said, eyebrows raising. Was he suggesting what Rami thought he was suggesting? He got up and took the few steps to get to Rami, who was sitting on one of the beds. He took Rami by the hands and prodded. "Come on, we can dance like we did in Quellis," he said, biting his lower lip. Did he know that drove Rami crazy?

"Yeah, Rami," Salice said. "And this time you can enjoy it openly without having to pretend you're not staring at the way he shakes his ass."

He blushed then brushed an imaginary hair out of his eyes. "So you noticed that, then?"

"Oh, please. Everyone noticed that." Salice got up and headed to her bag. "Also, I hope you don't have any theatrical aspirations, because you're a terrible actor."

"Hey now," Tristys said suddenly, "he can't be that bad an actor. After all, he had all of you thinking he was into Calissa all this time!" Were they really joking about this already?

"Oh, honey," Calissa said, taking the clothes Salice handed to her, "no, he didn't." Yeah, they were joking about it already. Even stranger, Rami was laughing, too.

A little later and they were ready to go. He and

Tristys were wearing virtually the same thing they'd had on earlier—they just changed shirts— but they both fixed their hair. Tristys's was too long, and it kept getting in his eyes, but Rami refused to let him cut it. He liked the way Tristys blew his bangs out of the way. He didn't tell Tristys that, but Tristys didn't really need to know. Salice and Calissa, however, were in full going-out gear, skimpier than he'd seen them wear in a while. Tristys was staring.

"My," Rami said, "you two look like you had this planned from the get-go."

Calissa shot a conspiratorial smile at Salice, who erupted into giggles. "There's a chance we may have," she said, and Rami realized at once that Tristys's misdirection while traveling hadn't been accidental after all.

He turned to Tristys. "Were you in on this, too?" he asked lightly. Tristys had a blank look on his face, his cheeks puffed out with mouthwash. He didn't even have to answer. Rami turned back to the girls. "I can't believe you two took advantage of this poor initiate like that!"

"He wants to go out too," Salice countered. "He'd have done it of his own will if he'd have known what was going on."

"I still have no idea what's going on," he said after he spit and wiped his mouth.

"Never mind," Rami said. "Let's just get the party started."

He wouldn't admit it, but he was looking forward to the night's activities. He'd spent so many years wound tighter than an Elerelacian braid, he wasn't even sure if he'd ever let loose and partied. He had no idea what it'd be like to dance, in public, with someone he truly wanted to dance with.

Leaving Firebird in the room, they decided to start things slowly. The first few serving-houses they went to were light-weight, not much more than the average pub you'd find on any other island. But Rami had left his inhibitions in Quellis. He drank more than any of the other three, and by the time they left the third serving-house, he was feeling pretty good.

The night air was chilly. The cold registered, but Rami didn't feel it. People were huddling around the heated lanterns along the street, arguing about which serving-house or brothel to go to next. A few seconds later, he realized he was also huddling around one of the lanterns, also trying to decide where to go next with his friends.

"No brothels!" he said at once. They looked at him strangely, because none of them had mentioned brothels. But he'd been staring at a tall, well-muscled man who caught his eye, winked, and then strolled into a brothel on the corner, and he didn't want to follow him in.

"Nobody said anything about brothels, Rami," Calissa said.

"And what would you need in a brothel anyway?" Tristys asked. "You have me for that, when it's time."

"True, but you never know," Rami heard himself say slyly, sidling up close to Tristys. "The more the merrier, isn't it?"

Tristys looked flabbergasted, and Salice let out a groan. "Great, he has a few drinks and turns into a slut. Perfect."

"Yeah, Rami." Calissa put a hand on his shoulder. "Baby steps, okay?"

He turned to see what Tristys had to say, but

he wasn't even paying attention, too distracted by an all-male trio making out against a serving-house. Rami had to admit, it was pretty hot. A wind blew; it was cold outside, and inside that serving-house was probably pretty hot, too. "Want to go there?" he asked.

"You really do like to dive right in, don't you?" Salice asked, not making any motion to leave the lantern. Calissa just kept blowing into her hands.

"What's that place?" Tristys asked.

"The Hardening Spire. It's a serving-house that specializes in aphrodisiacs and caters to the same-sex crowd."

"Diverted, as you would say," Rami interjected. "Just like us." He pointed to Tristys and then to himself, to clarify.

Tristys leered at the establishment. "I'd say we should go, but I don't know if he can handle it." He jerked his head in Rami's direction.

"Please!" Rami shouted. He'd show him! He'd be the first to go in! "Let's go!" he shouted as he headed to the Hardening Spire. Tristys followed him at once, but Salice and Calissa hesitated. He didn't care. He kept on going.

The Hardening Spire was very crowded. Most of the men were young and attractive, but Rami tried not to notice. He wondered if perhaps he shouldn't have brought Tristys in here—avoid temptation and all that. He took Tristys's hand, half-afraid he'd pull away, but he didn't. He squeezed it instead.

Rami headed directly for the bar, where he ordered himself and Tristys another drink and bought four shots of the house special, a thick liquid called Pink Passion that had a little pellet of something floating near the bottom. Once Calissa and Salice caught up, he tried to give them the shots, but they refused.

"More for us!" he shouted, and he and Tristys drank their two shots each in quick succession. They both ignored the two girls who were staring at them, heads shaking and arms crossed.

"Come on," Tristys said, dragging Rami away from the bar. "I wanna dance!"

One of the girls mumbled something about being forgotten, but before he could respond Tristys had him on the dance floor. The beat was fast, and Rami felt it more than he heard it—Air-magic in action. Tristys moved in front of him, pushed his body tight against Rami's, and started swinging his hips to the beat. They started dancing in the middle of the song, and before it even ended, Rami knew the Pink Passion pellet was kicking in.

The next song started, and Rami twirled Tristys around so they were facing each other. He pulled him in, and they danced face to face for a few songs. It felt good. Another song started, and Tristys was behind now, and Rami was the one pushing his body into Tristys. It felt even better.

At some point, Calissa and Salice stopped them. They were tired and they wanted to leave. *Have fun*, they said, and *stay out as long as you want*. Tristys can go to the Altar the day after tomorrow, not a big deal. Once they were gone, Tristys and Rami went to the bar for another Pink Passion. He didn't even have to pay this time, thanks to a flirtatious bartender.

Another song danced face to face, then another with Tristys behind and then another with Tristys in front. By this point, they weren't even dancing anymore; they were just throbbing into each other. They'd spent the last few songs kissing wildly, their necks crying out in pain from the strange, stretched contortions required to kiss and still move together. They ignored the pain, of course; if anything, it made the kisses more powerful, more frantic, more scintillating.

Rami lost track of how many drinks they had and how many songs they danced to. As the night turned to morning and the club began to empty out, he pulled away from a particularly slow kiss. A month ago, he thought the idea of kissing to be a bit disgusting, with all the swapped spit and oral violation, but now he hated to pull away, even to suggest what he was about to suggest.

"Listen," he said quietly, whispering into Tristys's ear and nibbling on it in between his words, "you don't have to use the men who work the brothels, you know." He nibbled an earlobe, moved down to Tristys's neck and nipped at it. "We could just use a room."

"Do you mean—"

"Yes, I mean." A month ago, he'd never have thought that he'd be the one propositioning anyone, especially not another man—and a foreign one at that!—but here he was, in a same-sex club, tasting another man's neck. Nothing had ever felt righter.

"Let's go," Tristys said, his eyes alive with anticipation but his eyelids heavy. When Rami finally pulled away from Tristys, it felt like tearing off his own skin. It didn't hurt exactly, but suddenly there was air where there had been no air before, a chill. His skin felt new, like he'd picked at a scab. Rami couldn't imagine what it would feel like later, when they finally broke apart after being more together than he'd ever been before, with anyone. He couldn't wait.

"One more drink," he said, and they both downed one final shot of Pink Passion before leaving the club. The trip to the nearest brothel, just across the street, was a frigid, wind-bitten blur and Rami and Tristys fell over each other as they tried to walk without separating. Rami's world was spinning. He couldn't believe what he was about to do. He had trouble walking a straight line, he was so dizzy. But Tristys's shirt had opened while they were dancing—or Rami had opened it himself, he vaguely remembered now—and his pale chest was like a beacon. Rami couldn't take his eyes off it. It was calling to him.

The clerk at the desk was tall with bad teeth, and he licked his lips when Rami slurred a request for one room, no companion. As they ran to their room, Rami made a note that he'd never gotten his change from the clerk. There'd be time for that later, tomorrow. Right now, he thought as he glanced at Tristys's ass, there were more important things to do.

Tristys barely had time to shut the door before Rami pulled him onto the bed. He was pulling Tristys's shirt the rest of the way off, fumbling at the last few buttons, and Tristys was tearing Rami's off over his head. He bit a nipple, flicked his tongue across it, and Rami heard himself moan. Then Tristys pushed off the bed, pushed Rami onto his back, and started kissing down his bare chest, stopping again at each nipple.

It felt so good Rami could barely keep his eyes open. Tristys got to his navel, and he fumbled at Rami's belt. He started kissing more slowly, more sensuously, and Rami couldn't wait for him to finish removing his belt, which seemed to be taking forever. The last thing Rami remembered before the drugs made him pass out was, *I think that little shit fell asleep!*

~~*

Tristys woke up groggily, certain he'd broken his head the night before. He'd never felt such a sharp, splitting pain in his life, arcing from the base of his skull to just behind his eyes. He used a shaky hand to feel his scalp, but everything seemed in order. He checked his palm. No blood. Just a headache, then. What exactly had he done last night?

There was only one small window in the room, and the meager light from it still too bright. Had the sun exploded? Was something on fire? He squinted as he looked around the strange room. It was red. Very, very red. He looked down at himself. He was half-naked. What in two moons' creation...

Rami stirred next to him, a thin line of drool running to the pillow. He was also half-naked. He saw the half-undone belt buckle, and last night's last few minutes crashed back to him. It made his head hurt even more.

He'd fallen asleep! They'd been about to have sex, and he'd fallen asleep. What was Rami going to think? Would he be hurt, would he be angry, would he be embarrassed? Tristys's head pounded, and all the drinks and all the pellets came flooding back to him. Would Rami even remember?

"Ay, shut off the lights!" Rami said, his voice heavy. He flipped over and buried his face directly into the pillow.

"I know, right?" Tristys said, a little awkwardly. "What do they put in that Pink Passion, anyway?"

As soon as Rami heard 'pink passion,' he jumped up. He looked directly at Tristys, eyes wide. He obviously had no trouble remembering. "I'm sorry!" he said at once. "I'm so sorry, we shouldn't have—"

"What are you apologizing for?" Tristys asked. "I'm the one that fell asleep right as we were—"

"No, the drugs and the liquor. I don't want you to think—"

"I wanted to do it, but I must have passed out and—"

They both started to laugh, realizing that neither was listening to what the other was saying. Tristys nodded to let Rami go first.

"I just don't want you to think I have to be drunk or high to do what we did last night. The dancing and kissing and all that. I can do that without liquor, but—"

Tristys had never even considered that. "I know, Rami. Don't worry about it." Now it was his turn to apologize. "I can't believe I passed out."

Rami looked sheepish. "I didn't notice," he said. "I passed out too." They laughed together again, and then Rami shrugged. "If you want, we can try to do this again tonight, without all the liquor. I want you to know I can do it without all that."

Tristys knew he probably shouldn't tease him right now, but he couldn't resist. "Do what exactly, Rami?"

He was blushing. "You know. It."

"Rami, last night you propositioned me for a threesome, and now you can't even say what *it* is?

You're too cute." Another spasm stabbed him in the eye from the back of his skull. "Do you think this brothel has any drugs that'll help a headache?" he asked as started to get out of bed.

But Rami pulled him back down. "I have the best medicine for that," he said and he started to kiss him. By the time they got up an hour or so later, Tristys felt perfect.

~~*

"What were you two thinking?" Calissa shrieked. She'd already shrieked the same thing at least ten times. Tristys's headache was back. "Salice and I were worried sick! Firebird can't even eat! We thought you two got so messed up you wandered off and were lying for dead somewhere in the mountains!"

"Not me," Salice said, beaming. "I think better of you two, so I knew that didn't happen."

"Thanks, Salice," Tristys said. Sometimes she could be so touching.

"I figured you two probably went home with some crazy hot psychopath, and Calissa and I would have to come back in a few days to identify the bodies."

Tristys changed his smile to a scowl. Salice beamed bigger.

"You never came back last night," Calissa continued. Apparently she had no need of breath when she was angry. Air-magic, perhaps? "You didn't send a message or anything, and then you don't even come back until now! The whole damn day is gone already! It's past dinnertime, for quell's sake!"

"We're sorry," Rami said. He looked so meek

and helpless when he was getting reprimanded, like all those muscles and all that training meant nothing. "We didn't think you'd be worried."

"That's exactly right! You didn't think! We're on Quellys, Rami! We're on Quellys, and Tristys hasn't communed yet! I thought he'd Fingerprinted and poisoned you both! I kept picturing you and him on the floor of some hideous brothel, just a decaying lump of flesh in fancy clothes!"

"We did go to a brothel," Tristys chimed in, ignoring Rami's frantic glances. He knew Calissa, and if she thought she had been right, she might calm down.

"You went to a brothel?" Salice said, suddenly more interested in the conversation. "Was he hot? Did you get one for each of you or did you share?"

"No!" Rami said at once, a blush coloring his cheek just as Tristys expected. "We just rented the room."

It worked. Calissa looked slightly less angry. "We left the club, and we were so caught up in the moment, we just wanted some privacy. We weren't planning on spending the night, I promise."

"Of course they weren't," Salice said. "It never takes men that long. Why would they need the whole night?" She was bored again, so she turned back to Firebird. He was mad at Tristys and Rami, too; he hadn't even greeted them when they returned. Tristys would deal with that later.

"I just hope you two will be a little more considerate the next time you go to the brothel."

"There won't be a next time," Rami said. "You should have seen that place. It was terrible. Never again."

"Everything was red!"

"And it smelled like pleasure oil and feet."

"I mean, everything was red. It was like living in a volasha bloom." Everyone, even Salice, gave him an odd look. Now it was his turn to explain something foreign nobody understood. "Those are these huge flowers that—"

"It doesn't matter." Tristys thought for a second that Calissa was going to launch into another tirade, but she started folding clothes on her bed and Tristys let go of a breath he didn't realize he'd been holding. "That's not the point. I'm just saying, I'm happy for you two, I'm glad you two are together. I've only been trying to make it happen since you got here." She looked at Tristys. "But please, just remember that it's not just you two, okay?"

"Okay," Rami said, tail between his legs. "We won't." He used the plural pronoun, which made Tristys smile just a little.

Her lips were pursed, and she nodded once, forcefully, and that ended the discussion. "Tristys," she said, "you really should go to the Altar as soon as you can, tonight even. I think we should leave at once to get you there." Tristys stared at her. "That's why I've been packing. You're both ready to go."

Tristys wasn't really sure how he felt about having someone else go through his things, but he let it slide. "Are we really in that much of a hurry? I haven't felt even a hint of Death-magic, and I was kinda hoping we could go back to that club tonight." He grinned at Rami, then winked. Rami rolled his eyes. He thought Calissa did too.

"I'd bet the whole Temeran Palace and everything in it, including my parents, that yş will

Touch you sooner or later and you'll commune." Calissa fought with an unruly skirt that wouldn't fold correctly. "I've been living in perpetual fear that it's going to happen before we get there. It's bad, Tristys. There aren't many people out there who can Touch it to save you. None of us can, for instance. So I really think—"

"Fine, fine, fine," Tristys said. He wasn't in the mood to hear another lecture. "We'll go now." He grabbed a towel off the table and shot Calissa a challenging look. "But I'm taking a shower before we go!"

She didn't say a word. Just kept on packing.

~~*

They left as soon as Tristys got out of the shower. Calissa hadn't been lying about the severity of Fingerprinting Death-magic. Sole Decay was high in the Kakenridge, the mountain range that covered most of Quellys. The Coquellians had bored tunnels directly through the mountains to create the most efficient routes, and they'd developed airships that traveled faster than any boat Tristys had ever seen. The trip to the Altar of Sole Decay was so quick, in fact, that his hair was still wet from the shower when they got there.

Calissa warned him about the smell, but he wasn't prepared. He gagged—Salice did, too—as soon as he stepped out of the air-tunnel. He fought back the bile that rose, but it was the worst smell he'd ever experienced. Worse than the Cyræan compost piles. Worse than the waste room on the slave-ship. Calissa promised they'd get used to it, and for the first time since they met, he didn't believe her.

The strength of the smell made sense, once he learned that the Altar of Sole Decay wasn't a man-made building at all but rather the perpetually decaying body of some impossibly large creature. "Nobody knows what it was," Calissa said. "We just know it's been dead for a long time and there aren't any more of them running around."

The place was deserted. It was small for an altar, with no real buildings, just that hollowed out body. They were inside it now. The walls were thin layers of something—he wasn't sure if it was skin or fabric—stretched tight between bones. You couldn't lean on them or they'd rip. The outer walls were thicker, definitely flesh, complete with the expected maggots and beetles. Tristys wanted to run away and never come back. He wasn't even sure he wanted to go back to Centrespire, not even for that dance club. If this was Death-magic, and this whole island was Death-magic, he wanted no part in any of it.

They went immediately to the High Priest, an elderly man named Vilanyth. He was short, smaller than Salice, with no hair on his head and only one working eye. The other had clouded over. Tristys couldn't stop staring at his teeth. They were perfect, absolutely perfect. It was weird.

Vilanyth wasn't a talkative chap. As soon as introductions were finished, he led Tristys to a meditation alcove, which was somewhere near the animal's shoulders, told him to be careful, and then left. Tristys was afraid to push aside the heavy curtain. Every other alcove had some sort of representative of the magic—the luminescent water at Five Waves, hundreds of fireflies at Six Plumes, breezes at Four Winds. The alcove at Two

Souls was practically a jungle. He really didn't want to see what the Death-magic decor was.

He took a deep breath, which was a mistake, since it made him gag. He pushed aside the curtain, its extra fabric pooling on the bare soil beneath it. Blessedly, the room was empty, completely void. Not a thing was inside, not so much as a dead animal, a chair, a bug. Nothing.

He took a step into the room, turned around and fluffed the curtain for some privacy. He took a few more tentative steps, ready to jump aside in case something dead or creepy-crawly fell from the ceiling or jumped from a wall. Nothing happened, and he took a shallow breath, mostly through his mouth. He never knew what to do in these rooms. In all the others, it had taken a few hours at least before anything happened, and he usually spent those hours praying to whatever god would listen to make Rami accept himself. That wouldn't work now, and Tristys couldn't think of anything else to ask for: his life was pretty great.

He sat, crossed his legs, and hunkered down for a few hours of waiting, but it hit him right away, the feeling. Like hundreds of small thousand-leggers crawling just beneath his skin, moving along his arms and down his legs and across his face. His teeth shivered, his eyes skittered, even his tongue squirmed.

He hated it, every second of that feeling. He screamed when it hit his face, crying for help. Nobody came. He tried to think about something else, anything else, something to take his mind off the feeling. Rami. Rami along the Rockaway Trib, bare-chested. Rami on Lake Anamor, surrounded by those purple leaves he scattered. Rami in the club. Rami after the club. But it didn't work.

He thought of everyone else. Calissa striding on the lake, Salice at the Purple Host, even Gawen in the cottonbloom on Quellos. He thought of Vun'gor, his friend and slaver, and Vun'gor's to□, Va'kūnga. He even went back to Cyræa, thought of his family, his parents and his brothers and his sister, Rilyn, even Kitadyn. Nothing helped. The feeling never stopped.

It had been minutes, too many minutes, and nothing helped. He'd focused on everything he could except the feeling, so he gave into that. He fell backwards, lay flat on his back and stared at the ceiling, at the carcass of an animal that should have decayed thousands of years ago. He closed his eyes and sent everything he had to one finger, a single finger, to that feeling there, and he let it go. He followed the feeling as it moved over his body, let it take him and let it fill him, but it never went away. He writhed, twisted and turned like a snake trying to crack its too-tight skin. Would it never go away?

He opened his eyes, and there were stars, black ones, thousands of them, everywhere. Then just as suddenly as it had started, it stopped. It was gone, entirely gone. As he got up to leave, something else was missing: the stench. There was no smell at all. He took a deep breath, then another, then a third. He didn't gag at all, not even once.

CHAPTER TWENTY

Tristys returned to the alcoves twice over the next two days, even though he knew he'd already done what he needed to do there. He didn't tell he was ready; he didn't even tell Calissa. On the second day, when he called on Death-magic the same way he called the other quell, he had that sensation again, the bugs-under-skin feeling he hated.

He knew from both Calissa and Salice that sometimes a quell would forget the person it had Touched, especially if that person took too long to master it. It had happened to Salice, with Earth-magic. He was hoping it would happen to him, too. He wasn't afraid of a bad Fingerprinting; he knew enough now to understand that Death-magic was his, not the other way around. He just wouldn't interact with it, refuse it at every turn, and hopefully it would grow tired and leave, and then Tristys would never have to feel those bugs again.

It wasn't just the horrible crawling sensation. When he'd Touched Death-magic for that split second on the first night, he'd felt... different. Not evil or corrupt. It wasn't that strong, that violent, but he definitely felt some undercurrent of disregard, a wave of morbid curiosity. In that second, he knew what he could do with Death-magic to another person, and in that second he wanted nothing more than to do it. He could poison people, as well as cure them.

Death-magic had changed him for that second, and he didn't like the person he'd become. He remembered that evil man from New Cysal. He remembered stories about the Great War, how the entire thing had started with dead bodies reanimated by the necromancer Bellimar. No, Death-magic wasn't like the others. He wanted no part of it. His mind was made up.

On the fourth day, Rami and Salice were getting antsy. They wanted to leave. So did Tristys. He couldn't bear another day in that barren alcove, doing everything he could not to see black stars. There was absolutely nothing in that room, just him and his mind, and when that happened, his mind had a tendency to wander to things he didn't want to think about. Lately, it kept going back to Cyræa, his family and the war he left. Perhaps now that his issues here in the Coquels were sorted out, the issues he left at home were coming to the fore. Great.

That evening, everyone except Calissa sat in one of the Altar's common rooms, doing their own thing. Salice was slurping up some thick soup, Rami was reading, and Firebird was grooming himself. Tristys was devising ways to get off this damned island. No one knew where Calissa was.

When she finally returned, she was worked up. "Vilanyth seems to think you've had enough time." She was shaking her head indignantly and almost yelling. "I'm not sure why he thinks he knows that, but he's insisting."

Perfect. Thank you, Vilanyth. "Well, I'm sure he knows what he's talking about," Tristys said, trying not to sound too happy about it. "Perhaps we should leave then?" He remembered the stench he hadn't smelled since that first day. "I can't be the only one tired of this stink, right?" He waved a hand in front of his nose for effect.

"Yes, you are," Salice said through a spoonful. "I love this smell. I'm thinking about bottling it, going over to Spälor, and selling it to the perfumers there. They'd love it."

Calissa sat down next to Tristys on the bed. She put a hand on his shoulder and bowed her head. "You want to leave? You don't want to run the Trial?"

"I can't," he said, pushing down the mild panic that threatened to rise in the back of his throat. "Nothing happened in the alcoves. This quell doesn't like me."

Calissa looked as if she were about to cry. "Tristys, I won't believe that. I can't believe that!"

Panic again. Did she know? Could she tell?

"I'll tell Vilanyth," she said, "that you need a few more days. There is no way you can't Touch yş."

Rami put down his book. "Calissa, if he said he felt nothing, then maybe there's nothing here for him to feel."

"No!" she said, standing up. She'd balled her fists, and Tristys thought she was going to hit Rami. "It'll work," she said, not a shred of doubt shaking her voice. "If he just does the Trial, he'll see. It'll happen. It'll be like the Five Waves, Tristys. Remember? Liana and I thought you were going to fail, that we'd have to save you, but then everything clicked and you drenched us and saved yourself. Remember?" Her eyes were wide, and she spoke much faster than she normally did. It was perturbing.

"Yeah, I remember, but I don't think this is—"

"Do the Trial for me, Tristys," she said. Her voice was barely above a whisper, and her eyes had filled with tears. He looked away, looked at Rami and Salice for advice, but they both looked as shocked and confused as he felt.

"Calissa," Rami said, his voice tight with warning, "Trials aren't something to try for fun." He closed his book without even saving his page. Tristys was touched. "Especially Death-magic ones."

She ignored him. "Do the Trial for me, Tristys."

He felt trapped. He didn't know what to do. He didn't want to do the Trial, but it was so important to her. And maybe he was wrong. Maybe the quell wouldn't leave him once he saw the stars, and he'd have it forever regardless. So maybe he should just do it, get it over with, and he could vow never to Touch it then.

"Fine," he said at last, "I'll do it."

"Tristys, you don't have to—"

"It's fine, Rami. It's fine."

"Oh, thank you! Thank you!" She got up, still frantic. "I'll go tell Vilanyth now." She was gone before Tristys could say okay.

Rami leapt from his chair and sat in the same place Calissa had just been. Even Salice came over and sat on Tristys's other side. "Listen to me," Rami said, a hand on his shoulder. "Death-magic is not something you want to play with. This Trial is scary and dangerous, and if you don't think you can do it, you shouldn't even try."

"He's right," Salice said. "It's not fun getting poisoned, even if you can cure it." She smiled weakly. "And you don't even know if you can do that."

"I'll be okay, guys," Tristys said after just a

moment's hesitation. "Even if I can't do it, they won't let me die. They'll stop it way before then, right?"

Rami's head bounced back and forth, and he finally said, "They can try, but usually failure to commune is fatal."

Tristys hadn't been expecting that, but he had faith in the priests. "It's okay, Rami." Tristys took Rami's hand off his shoulder and set it on the bed, where he pet it comfortingly. "I'll be fine. And then we can leave this island. I'm sort of over this place."

"Yeah, me too."

"Me three," Salice said as she got up and returned to the last dregs of her soup. "The food here sucks." For hating it so much, she sure liked to finish it.

When Calissa got back, she barged into the room so forcefully that she knocked half of the curtain off the bone holding it up. "Let's go!" she said, beaming. They were going to a Trial of Death-magic, Tristys wanted to say, not a chocolate shop. Vilanyth was behind her.

"Calissa tells me you feel ready to attempt the Trial," he said. His voice was unpleasant, pinched and too nasal.

Tristys nodded.

"Fine. Let us go." Vilanyth turned around in place and only then started to move forward. It was an unnatural motion, too dramatic, but nobody else seemed to notice.

Vilanyth led the way, Calissa followed, and Tristys followed her. When Rami and Salice came out of the room—Firebird tried to come, too, and Salice had to run him back and appease him with treats—Tristys thought that Vilanyth would forbid them from watching, but he said nothing. They walked through the corpse until they got to a wide room, empty except for a ribbed mass of bones in the middle.

"Is that the heart of this thing?" Tristys asked. It was impossible to hide the revulsion on his face or in his voice.

"It would be," Vilanyth said, "if this creature still had a heart."

Despite it being a ribcage, there was very little space between the ribs; Tristys couldn't see inside, and he doubted anything inside could see out of it. Vilanyth led Tristys to the far side of the cage and pointed at a small opening. "Crawl in," he said, pointing. "The Trial will begin almost as soon as you've fully entered the cage."

"That's it?" Tristys asked. "No instructions, no goodbyes, nothing?"

Vilanyth's only response was a jerk of his finger, still pointing to the cage. Tristys got down on his hands and knees and wiggled through the opening. Inside, the air was so stale and stagnant Tristys had a hard time breathing, though there was no stench. There was no light; he couldn't even see the outline of his hand in front of his face. He sat down. Nothing happened. He took a deep breath. Nothing happened. He touched the wall. Something happened.

The walls changed, turning transparent. Vilanyth was there now, just outside the cage, along with two other men Tristys didn't know. Calissa, Rami, and Salice stood just behind them. Tristys raised his hand to wave, but the Trial started, and he forgot everything.

His skin crawled again, but the bugs burrowed deeper, touching his insides, his heart, his stomach. He panicked, twisted and turned to escape it, and he fell to his back, writhing and beating his arms and legs against the walls. It wasn't pain, but he'd prefer pain to this. He'd prefer anything to this.

He knew what was wrong. He could See it as clearly as he could see Water-magic in a river and Life-magic in a tree. One flick of his mind and he'd be free of it, but he wouldn't do it, couldn't do it, didn't want to feel that thirst for destruction he'd felt earlier.

Somewhere far away, he heard yelling. First a deep voice, unnaturally high from panic, and the torture let up for a second, but a female voice was louder, just as passionate but steadier, surer, determined. The crawling stopped completely now, replaced by pain and an even darker pocket of black stars inside him. Writhing again, but different: not trying to avoid something now but trying to make it stop, trying to make *himself* stop, trying to move because the pain wouldn't let him stand still. He felt his insides swirling around each other, sloshing with every movement. Skin burst into sores and blisters, seeping so much that he felt slick. His tongue fell back in his throat, couldn't breathe. He could stop it all, he knew, but he couldn't breathe, and he didn't want to breathe in a world where something like this existed.

Then everything stopped. He could breathe again. His skin was smooth and dry. Nothing hurt. He lay on the ground, raking in huge gulps of air, as much as his lungs could hold. The small door opened beneath his feet, and Tristys hallucinated, seeing Rami's head appear and then his shoulders and hands. He grabbed Tristys by the legs and pulled him out. It hurt, the ground bunching up his shirt and scraping his skin, but he didn't fight it.

"Tristys!" Rami shouted, his face just inches away. "Tristys, can you hear me?"

"Of course, Rami," Tristys said. His voice was weak but audible. "I'm not deaf."

"I thought you were dead!" he said. Tristys's vision was still blurry, but he thought Rami might have been crying. Rami ignored all the yelling until he knew Tristys was okay. Then he yelled, too. So now Rami was yelling at Calissa, the priests were yelling at Rami, Calissa was yelling at the priests, and then Salice started yelling for everyone to stop yelling. Nobody was really listening to anybody else, and Tristys was still lying on the floor. He wanted up, off the ground, but he was weak, his voice barely audible, and nobody heard him through their shouts. He stayed on the ground, staring up at two faint stars visible through a tear in the ceiling fabric. He fell asleep before they finished.

~~*

When the letter came, nobody was ready for it. It had been less than two days since his failure at the Trial, and he still felt weak, too tired all the time and not hungry enough. The priests had assured him he'd recover fully, and he believed them. Rami didn't. He hadn't spoken to Calissa since that night. Salice kept trying to mediate, using half-baked ploys to get them together, but it never worked. What did they say about unstoppable forces and immovable objects?

Tristys wasn't mad at Calissa, though he didn't understand her actions. He found out that he had been correct: she'd pushed the priests to continue and yelled at them when they'd overrode the Trial. When he and the others had confronted her about it, she'd said she had the utmost faith in him, that she "just knew" he'd be able to Touch every quell, that she couldn't be wrong.

Even after the debacle, an undercurrent of anger still ran through her at the mention of the botched Trial; she never said it, but he had the feeling she wanted him to try again. He knew Calissa cared about him, would never hurt him, but to put that much trust in her own hunches, no matter how strong they seemed, was careless. He'd refuse to try again even if she did ask.

He'd never admit it, but part of the reason he wasn't mad at Calissa was because he felt bad for her. After all, she was right. He would have successfully communed with Death-magic, if he'd let himself. He could Touch those black stars as easily as he touched any of the others. He just didn't want to. So she looked like a homicidal maniac, with Rami refusing to speak to her and Salice holding a grudge, all because of Tristys. He was extra nice to her those two days, which only made Rami standoffish and upset. He wasn't entirely sure how anything would get better, although he knew nothing would change as long as they stayed on this terrible island. He wanted off Quellys, but neither Calissa nor Rami would consider leaving until he was fully recuperated. If that ever even happened, as Rami would say with a scowl in Calissa's direction.

Of course, the letter changed all that. It was unsigned, written in a tight, elaborate cursive. The ink was deep green, the paper pale yellow, and the contents more disturbing than anything that had happened to Tristys yet.

> *Paru has been destroyed, its buildings burnt and its soil salted. Your family has been captured and taken to the slave-breaking capital, Veloxa Tánor, on the western tip of Spálor, to be sold or bred. You must save them. Go now. Return here. There is no time to waste. We need you.*

Nothing, not even Death itself, could keep Tristys on this island now.

~~*

"I have to go," Tristys said for the hundredth time. They were sitting at a large table in one of the common rooms of Sole Decay. The room was larger than any others at the Altar, but it still stunk, that slightly nauseated expression permanently glued to everyone's face. Calissa had suggested they move here to discuss after Rami managed to convince Tristys not to charge single-handedly into Spálor. It hadn't been an easy fight for Rami, but he'd won. "I have to go right now," Tristys said again, more forcefully.

"For the thousandth time, you cannot march into an enemy country, declare war, and then kidnap random people." Calissa rubbed her forehead. She felt like most of her time lately had been spent berating him and Rami.

"Why not?" he shouted back. "That's exactly what they did to my people!"

Calissa knew that, and she commiserated, but

she had no idea how he really felt. She hadn't lived during the Great War; neither had her parents or her grandparents or their parents. To know that your own family had been abducted, to know that the only town you'd had in your entire life had been razed... it had to be horrible.

But it didn't give Tristys the right to sacrifice himself to fix it. She'd never let that happen, even if Rami succumbed to Tristys's determination. She had a duty to Ystan, to the Order, to oş. And most importantly, she had a duty to Tristys.

"That's true," she said, "but you're not going to a foreign country on your own after almost dying from yş." He started to argue, but she raised her hand. "You're not."

"Calissa's right," Rami said. He hesitated at first, presumably so he didn't offend Tristys, but she was thankful for the support anyway, even if it had been late. "Even with your magic, it's too dangerous." Tristys had been raving earlier about magic, about swooping into the Spálorian town and blowing everyone away with his awesome powers, how he'd have no problem against an army of spear-throwing tiger riders. He had a point, but he had grossly overestimated it: even a trained quell-warrior couldn't withstand an entire army on his own forever.

"I can't stay here anymore," Tristys said, his whole body leaning into Rami's. He even took him by the hands. "My family needs me."

This argument again. Calissa didn't understand this at all. "Tristys, your family did not send that letter. There is no way they even know about this place, let alone have the means to get a letter here."

"I know that, obviously," he said. He'd been so

nice to her before this. "But if that letter is true, my family needs me, even if they're not the ones who asked for it."

"Have you ever thought that maybe the letter isn't true?" Salice had said it, and Calissa considered herself lucky. She had been about to say it, but now she wasn't the only bad guy in the room.

"Of course it's true. Why wouldn't it be true? Why would somebody lie about this?" He flicked open the letter and held it up for her to see, as if she hadn't already heard it enough to memorize the words.

Calissa spoke up. "To get you off the island. Just because Ystan likes you doesn't mean everyone else does."

"This place is very xenophobic," Rami said.

"I've never seen one example of a person hating me because I'm a foreigner!"

"We're a subtle people."

"We're sitting in a giant dead carcass at the Altar of Death, Rami. You are not a subtle people."

That was the first time Tristys had joked since he got the letter, so that was a good sign. So good, in fact, Calissa held back the urge to correct his mistake. This was the Altar of Sole Decay, not Death.

"It doesn't matter anyway," Tristys continued. He pushed out from the table and stood up. "I've already decided what I'm doing. Even if there's only one percent chance that letter is true, I have to do something."

Calissa had had it. "Tristys!" She pushed off the table, almost knocking her chair over. "You cannot go storming off to Spàlor! I'm tired of telling you—"

"Calm down," he said, rolling his eyes. He

stood still, arms at his side, and his eyes were half-shut. He looked tired... or sedated. "I'm not storming off anywhere. I'm going to Ystan."

"Ystan?" Calissa asked. Would she understand anything he felt today? "Why Ystan?"

"He's the ruler here, isn't he? And you said yourself I can't do this on my own. But I bet I can do it if I have an army of quell-users behind me."

"I don't think—"

"And if he doesn't," Tristys said, cutting her off, "then I'll storm off into Spàlor on my own." He looked calm, decided, determined. "He doesn't want me leaving the islands, remember? I think when I threaten that, he'll come through."

"And if not?" Rami asked, quietly. His head was bowed.

"Then I'm taking a vacation for a while, and when I come back, I'll have a few more foreigners for the Islanders to fear." Before anyone could say anything else, Tristys left the table. Despite his outward calm, he slammed the door.

~~*

Two days later, and Tristys was still frothing at the mouth. He couldn't let go of the words from the letter, the images they'd put in his brain of his family enslaved. His parents were too old for personal use; they'd be taken to breeding colonies. His younger brother, though, was good-looking and fit. He'd be sold and purchased almost immediately.

Tristys knew from personal experience that the horror stories he'd heard as a kid about Spàlorian slavery were grossly exaggerated, but it was still slavery. And he had been lucky, incredibly lucky.

No slaver in all Spålor could be as kind as Vun'gor had been. No, his family had to be saved, and they had to be saved soon.

Cyræa wouldn't come to their aid, even if the entire town of Paru had been captured. Paru sat on a strategic location—the only entrance to the panhandle—but Cyræa had been slowly ceding control to Spålor for years. There'd be a half-hearted attempt to take it back, nothing serious, and they'd honor the citizens as casualties of war. If his family had any hope, any hope at all, it rested squarely on his shoulders.

He knew this, and he knew his friends knew this, and still they seemed so averse to helping. It stung. They had access to a weapon that Spålor didn't even know about—magic—and still they refused. They told him to let it go, to mourn his family as if they were dead. He barely spoke to anyone during the entire two-day journey from Sole Decay to Imidalé, and Rami and Salice were still mad at Calissa for her actions during his Trial. It had been a quiet trip.

"Tristys," Calissa said, drawing out his name to get his attention. She and he, along with everyone else, were in Ystan's personal suite again, waiting for the seyquel to get out of some official business with the high-priests and chancellors. The room had changed, its color palette lighter now. Still blue, though. "Tristys, you can ignore me until we all die, but there's nothing we can do. We shouldn't even be here."

He ignored her. She turned to Rami, who was sitting next to her, and asked him to talk some serious sense into his boyfriend, but before Rami could response, Ystan came in. Rami looked so relieved Tristys almost laughed.

Ystan was different, too. Last time, he'd been in street clothes. Now, he wore formal regalia, layers of ornamented robes and a ridiculously large headpiece. His face was so lined with worry it looked like a map. He took the hat off at once, but everything else—including the worry—stayed on.

"Sorry about that," he said. "I do apologize for making you wait. My meeting ran longer than expected. Things are a bit bleaker than I expected." He looked strange for a second, unbearably sad, but a brief shake of his head, and it fell away. "Can I get you a drink?"

Everyone refused, but he insisted. "You may not want one," he said as he pulled out five glasses, "but I need one. And I hate drinking alone, it's so uncouth." As he poured, Tristys tried to start his plea—twice—but Ystan shushed him. "Not a word until we've had at least one of these!" he said. Normally Tristys would have found the obsession with liquor endearing, but right now, he just wanted to get everything started.

By the time he finished passing out the drinks, which had twice as much liquor as mixer, and in enormous glasses to boot, Tristys felt as if he were about to explode. Ystan finally sat, crossed his legs, and downed his drink. "Now then, to what do I owe this pleasure?"

"Well, Ystan," Calissa began, "Tristys found out that—"

"I need to go to Spålor to save my family, and you need to help me." Now was not the time to beat around the bush.

Ystan set down his empty cup. "I see," he said, his voice monotone. Tristys expected a more explosive reaction; he was angry at the lack of anything.

Calissa, as it turns out, was the one to explode. "He wants to go and kill himself! To save his abusive family from a life of alleged slavery!" She was so flustered she stood up, knocking her drink over in the process. The liquor bled into the blue carpet.

"Such a waste," Ystan said, shaking his head at the stain.

"Which is ludicrous," Calissa continued, not even fazed by her destruction of Ystan's rug, "because slavery there is not what everyone thinks, right? It's usually not that bad. They're treated like family members, usually, and—"

"And they have to have sex with people they don't want to have sex with!" Tristys shouted back. He'd tried to stay calm, but this was outrageous.

"*Usually* don't want to have sex with!" Calissa retorted. "I've heard stories about slaves who fall in love with their masters, and they—"

"Calissa," Tristys said, his voice steady and soft, "you don't want to hear the stories I've heard."

She hesitated a moment. "Fine. I may not be an expert on Spålorian slavery, but I do know that you don't have an ice-chip's chance in Quellusia of defeating an entire country that's known for its military power. You'll die, Tristys. You'll die." She sat back down, her shoulders hunched, and Tristys finally understood: she was worried about him. Why hadn't he realized that earlier? And why hadn't she said it? "And I just don't understand why you want to save a family you don't even care about."

Now he was mad again. "Where do you get off saying that I don't care about them?"

"You haven't talked about them at all, and you haven't—"

"Look, I may not spend hours a day gushing about my undying love for my mother and father and sister and brother, but I—"

"You told me your brother beat you up daily after he found out you liked guys!"

"That's true, but—"

"And you told me that the rest of your family treated you differently, that they never talked about it or tried to help you get acceptance, that they acted like nothing was going on!"

"Yes, but—"

"So then why, please tell me, would you risk your life—and make no mistake, Tristys, you'll probably die if you do this alone—for a family that treated you like that?" She stopped, debated about adding something else. "Especially when you have people like us here who care about you so much."

Tristys sat in his chair, nonplussed. She was being cruel and insensitive, but she had a point. She wasn't right, but she had a point. "Because they're family," he said at last. "They may not have behaved as well as they could have, but they did a lot for me before they found out I was diverted." He thought of all the struggles his family had gone through after his attraction became public knowledge, all the hateful words and the threats and the destruction. The fire. "And they may not have been as laid back about it as people here are, but they didn't throw me out, they didn't put me to death, they didn't give up on me." The next sentence was hard to get out. "And I guess I haven't given up on them, either."

Calissa looked defeated, but she didn't give up. "Why now, though? You never cared about not giving up on them before."

What an idiotic question! "Because before they were safe behind Paru's walls, not being transported like cattle to some village market to be used or bred?" He wasn't asking a question, but the sheer idiocy of having to answer made him inflect as if he were.

She didn't look convinced, but she stayed quiet.

"Your words are well-spoken and your intention well placed, Tristys, but do you realize what a drastic move this would be, if we attacked Spålor?" He got up to pour himself another drink. "We have spent our entire existence ensuring our complete isolation from outside influence. I mean, as far as those countries are concerned, we don't even exist. You're asking us to throw that away, to charge in and decimate an entire country, just to save one family?"

It was selfish, insane, so out of proportion, but this was his one family. He answered quickly, without hesitation: "Yes."

He looked regretful as he spoke. "I'm afraid I must apologize to you yet again, Tristys. I cannot fulfill your request. Such a display of brute force would destroy everything we have worked to maintain. It would destroy us."

"But Ystan, you have magic, and they don't, and you could—"

"Believe me, Tristys, I know how easy breezing in and conquering our enemies seems, and I don't think you realize how many problems of mine it would solve. But it simply can't be done."

Tristys's breathing sped up. His heart raced. He was angry, very angry. And disgusted. "You have all this power at your disposal," he shouted, "and yet you do nothing with it!" He stood up to continue, but as he stood up, his anger spilled from him like wine from a tipped glass. "I don't want to destroy the country, Ystan. I just want my family to be okay."

Ystan put his cup down and walked to Tristys. He hugged him then held him at arm's length. "I realize that, Tristys, and I want it, too. But unfortunately, there is nothing I can do."

He pulled away again. "Go home, Tristys," he said. His tone had a strange lilt to it, and his gaze was piercing, energetic, almost desperate. Then that all faded away. "You are staying in the Roseate Windwyrm again, yes?"

"We are, Ystan. Same room as before, even." Calissa wasn't smug or victorious; she looked as dejected as Tristys felt.

"Fine, then," he said, leaving Tristys to approach Rami, Calissa, and Salice, who were still sitting. "Take him home."

Ystan walked them out, going as far as the final set of double doors that blockaded the palace from the rest of Imidalé. He stepped out with them, closed the doors behind him. "I wasn't kidding before," he said to Calissa, but he looked at Rami and Salice, too. "Make sure he gets home."

"We will, Seyquel," Rami said. He took Tristys's hand, and though Tristys wanted to pull away, he didn't.

"Take him home," Ystan said again.

Calissa and Salice nodded, and Rami's face looked thoughtful as he nodded assent. The seyquel said goodnight to Tristys, but he snubbed him, which made the seyquel's pleased expression as he shut the double doors that much more infuriating.

~~*

After the meeting with Ystan, Tristys wanted to lie down. Rami went with him, even though he wasn't tired. Within minutes, they were both asleep, and when Rami woke up later that evening, he thought he was still dreaming. After all, Gawen hadn't been with them for days, so how could he be talking to Calissa and Salice in the next room? He turned over to drift back to sleep, but the door was ajar, and sure enough, sitting next to Salice, was Gawen. Rami hopped out of bed.

"What are you doing here?" he asked, rubbing sleep from his eyes.

Gawen stopped halfway through a remark about the temperature in Malatapia and turned to Rami, smiling. "Good to see you, too," he said.

"That's not what I meant." Rami wasn't even sure what he meant. He hadn't thought about Gawen since their fight in Quellis, Rami realized, and that made him feel guilty. Gawen was, after all, his friend, despite or perhaps because of all the flirting.

"I'm sure." Gawen rolled his eyes, but his tone was light-hearted and playful. "To answer your question, I'm catching up. I heard you were in town and staying here again, so I stopped over."

How would Gawen have heard that they were back in town so quickly? They'd been here less than a day. And furthermore, why was Gawen in Imidalé anyway? He tended to Quellus if he could choose. Rami's confusion must have been clear on his face, because Gawen answered the questions without even being asked.

"Ystan had a meeting with the chancellors, and

my sister is an assistant to Pinoda from Malatapian University. I came with her, because as I was telling the girls, the temperatures in Quellus this time of year are terrible."

"I see," Rami said, only half clear on the events that brought Gawen back into their group. Perhaps he was still half-asleep after all.

"Ystan came to see me a little bit ago." He turned to Salice, obviously addressing her now instead of Rami. "I was rather surprised. I didn't think he liked me very much." Back to Rami. "But he came to see me, and he told me that you and Tristys were back in town with Salice and Calissa and that I ought to go catch up, because you may need my help."

"I see," Rami said again, slightly less confused. There had been something about the way Ystan had implored them to stay with Tristys, to keep him safe, to take him home, that made Rami think he had something up his sleeve.

"To make a long story short, I'm here to help you." He flourished, as if he'd just pulled himself from thin air. "So please, do tell me what you need helping with."

"What are you doing here?" Tristys said. He'd woken up and come out of the bedroom during Gawen's speech, but apparently he hadn't heard it.

Gawen sighed and rehashed the entire story again. When he got to Ystan telling Gawen to help, he pointed at Tristys. "You don't look so great, so I'm assuming it's you I need to help."

Gawen was right; Tristys didn't look too great. His eyes were puffy from the crying he'd done, and his hair was in tangles. Since Tristys slept on his side, most of it was pushed to the right. He looked lopsided. His clothes were wrinkled, he was wobbling in place, and one sock had fallen off and he hadn't bothered to put it back on. Rami thought it was adorable, and he started to grin. Perhaps no one would see...

Tristys saw, of course. "What are you grinning at?" He scowled.

"Nothing," Rami answered, ignoring Tristys's crankiness. He really wasn't a morning person, and for Tristys, any time after he just got up was considered morning. "Nothing at all."

"Whatever, you loon." He flopped onto the couch next to Gawen. With everyone else's help, Tristys explained to Gawen the whole story, from the time they left Zebelli through the ordeal at Sole Decay to the letter and the recent rejection of Tristys's plans. Rami couldn't help but notice, and take slight offense, that Tristys left out everything involving him and Rami: nothing about Centrespire, no mention of the make-out sessions, nothing.

"So anyway," Tristys said after detouring through a tirade on the likelihood of a Cyræan intervention to save the former Paruans, "now my parents are probably going to be bred like cattle, my brother will be tied bottom-up to a bed, and there's nothing Ystan can do about it."

Everyone waited for Gawen's response, but he just sat there, nodding, saying nothing, eyes aimed at the ceiling. When he finally did speak, he confirmed what Rami had guessed: Ystan had sent him on purpose. Ystan was up to something, definitely.

"Well," Gawen said, as calmly as if he were suggesting a light snack for dinner, "if Ystan can't help us, why don't we just go and save them ourselves?"

~~*

Tristys had been considering the idea long before Gawen suggested it. He hadn't intended to take anyone with him; he hadn't even intended to tell them he was going. He planned on sneaking out one night, floating himself back to the continent, and winging it from there. He planned it, but he knew he'd never do it. He knew too little about Spälor, knew nothing about wards the Coquellians might have in place to keep people inside the borders. Plus, he was scared. He had magic, but he was still just one person...

Actually saying the plan out loud, though, led to chaos. Calissa started screeching at once, throwing around mockery and hysterics with abandon. Salice took to the idea at once, already talking to Gawen about how best to attack, and Firebird tried to mimic Calissa, screeching himself and jumping in place. Rami was quiet.

They argued for what felt like hours before Tristys had enough. Finally, he told Calissa he was going, no matter what, with or without anyone else. He was bluffing, of course, but Gawen and Salice quickly backed him. When he turned to ask Rami, Rami said nothing, just stood up, stood behind him, and put a hand on his shoulder, for solidarity. Rami was such a drama queen.

Calissa knew when to give up, and she stopped arguing. When Tristys asked her to keep their secret, she laughed in his face.

"If you think I'm letting you four go off alone to die in Spälor, you're even more daft than I thought you were."

"So two practitioners is daft, but three makes

it a no-brainer?" Tristys asked.

"Exactly," Calissa said. She smiled, only slightly, but it was enough.

They decided to leave at once. Calissa knew there were magical barriers preventing entrance and exit from Coquellian waters, but they weren't attended, and she was fairly certain she and Gawen would be able to untangle them. They'd aim for the Spàlorian jungle, and once they landed, they'd head south to Velo□a Tànor. When they got there, they'd find Tristys's family and get the hell out. They'd do everything they could not to hurt anyone. They weren't murderers, after all.

By the time they'd settled on a course of action, the evening had turned to night. They'd only been in Imidalé for less than a day, so they hadn't even unpacked. Calissa had wisely suggested they stock up on supplies, so Salice and Gawen had gone shopping. Luckily, Imidalé was one of the few places in the islands that had all-night groceries. Rami had tried to give Gawen money, but he'd refused. "Consider this an apology," he said. Rami asked him why he was apologizing, and Gawen said, "For suggesting this crazy idea." Then, a second later, he added, "And for other things." Rami debated a second then nodded his head. He put his money away.

While Gawen and Salice shopped, the other three ran around the room, trying to make sure they had everything of theirs and anything not of theirs that they'd be able to use. When somebody knocked at the door, Tristys jumped. He'd been thinking about what they were doing, defying not only unspoken Coquellian laws about isolation but also explicit orders from the leader of the country.

"Why are they knocking?" Calissa snapped.

"Don't they realize we're busy?" She was raiding the refrigerator for something to eat now before they left. Not exactly the most important work in the world, but she had a point.

Rami shrugged as he walked to the door, already yelling at Gawen and Salice as he opened it. But he stopped mid-sentence. When Tristys looked up to see why, all higher thought processes stopped. It wasn't Gawen and Salice. It was Ystan. The seyquel of the Coquels was knocking at his door in the middle of the night just as he was preparing to break every rule in the book. Lovely.

And he wasn't alone. It took a second to process, but the man with him wasn't a guard to escort them to prison. It wasn't even a stranger, though Tristys would have preferred the guard.

"Hello, Ramis," Tierran said. He was smiling strangely, almost cruelly, deriving far too much pleasure from this. When he looked at Tristys, it felt like he slapped him. "Tristys," Tierran said, nodding in his direction. "Calissa. A pleasure to see you both."

He and Ystan were still standing in the hall. Rami had apparently lost all powers of speech, so Tristys jumped up. "What are you doing here, Ystan?"

Ystan wasn't smiling, but he wasn't angry, either. He was, however, looking around the room, appraising things. "May we come in?"

"Of course," Calissa said at once. Her deference to authority could be so frustrating at times.

"Thank you, thank you."

Rami made no motion to close the door behind them, so Tierran said, "Let me get that for you." He put his hand over Rami's, which was still on the doorknob, and he let it sit there for just a second too long. Tristys resisted the urge to pounce. He had more important things to deal with at the moment.

"So, not to be impolite, but what are you doing here? It's the middle of the night." Tristys was starting to sweat, and he felt light-headed. He couldn't faint now; he had no Fingerprinting to blame for it.

Ystan looked at the open backpacks, the haphazard gatherings of food on the table, the piles of folded clothes. "I could ask the same, Tristys. It is the middle of the night, and yet you look as if you're planning a journey. Am I wrong?"

Nobody said anything. They were found out. It was over. *Sorry, Mom.*

"I'm actually rather relieved," Ystan said as he inspected a jar of berries. "I was afraid I'd have to be more direct." He tossed the jar into the sink. "These will spoil soon, no sense wasting the space in the bags."

Even Firebird was stunned, mostly because he liked the berries Ystan just threw out.

The seyquel chuckled. "You seem surprised," he said.

Tristys regained his composure the quickest. "We thought you'd be angry with us."

"Angry? No, quite the contrary. I couldn't be more pleased that you've taken my hints to save your family yourself. I just wish I could do more to help you, send soldiers or something. I'd feel safer that way."

"Don't worry, Ystan," Tierran said. He was still smiling devilishly. He hadn't been this annoying on the ferry to Quellos... but then again, Tristys didn't know about his past with Rami then. "I think I will be able to keep them safe."

"What do you mean you'll keep us safe?" Rami asked. He moved forward, but he stopped himself before it looked too aggressive.

"I'm going with you, of course."

"Not a chance!" Rami said, louder than he'd been in days.

Tierran smiled smugly while Ystan talked. "No, Rami, I'm afraid he is going with you. He's the only thing I can give you, besides the foodstuff he's got with him."

Rami's eyes were narrowed, but he knew when not to fight. "What can he do that we can't? Tristys can Touch four quell, almost five. Can he do that?"

"No," Ystan said casually, "but he can speak Spàloric, which I don't think any of you can do. With the exception of perhaps Tristys."

"Only a little," Tristys admitted, "but most Spàlorians know Cyræan, so..."

"And I can Touch Earth, which I don't think any of you can. With the exception, of course, of Salice. At least a younger version of Salice, anyway."

Salice blanched. Tristys couldn't believe she'd told anyone else about that, least of all Tierran, so how had he known? What else did he know?

Calissa inched forward, obviously hesitant to speak. "It would be good to have as many quell present as possible," she offered. She looked to Rami, judging his response. Did she know about their past, too?

Rami crossed his arms. "Fine." Anger was making him breathe heavily, and his chest strained at the shirt he wore. It turned Tristys on, which was strange, only because of the bad timing. Now was not the time for this! "I won't argue against his accompanying us, but I am curious to know why you, Ystan, are encouraging us. This is illegal, not to mention in direct disregard for what you told us just a few hours ago in your rooms."

"I couldn't say what I wanted to say in the palace. I couldn't risk being overheard, especially with all the chancellors and high-priests here now. They cannot know that I not only gave away confidential reconnaissance information but also encouraged our only hope to risk his life by leaving the islands."

Tristys was floored yet again. There were simply too many strange phrases in that sentence to process. Confidential information? What? Only hope? Who? What future? What? He just stood there, mouth agape, shaking his head jerkily in a botched attempt to understand.

"Ystan, with all due respect," Rami said as he stood next to Tristys and took his hand, "what are you talking about?" Rami gripped his hand a little harder than he should; he was trying to stop the tic.

Ystan steeled himself. "There is no easy way to say this, I'm afraid. I wonder if—"

"So just say it," Calissa said from behind Tristys. Her voice was deadpan, challenging, contorted.

He held out his hands. "Our magic is dying." Tristys felt as if he'd been slapped. "Fewer and fewer people Touch more than a single quell. Older Coquellians lose the Touch, which has never happened before in our recorded history. The window for the Fingerprinted to learn to Touch the quell is getting steadily shorter, with more people failing to transition through it. We have no idea why. We have no idea how to fix it. Tristys.

You are the first person to Touch more than three quell in generations, since the Great War. We have to know why. You are the key."

Tristys looked around, waiting for the others to start laughing so he could join in. This had to be some sort of joke, right? Some last-ditch effort concocted to guilt him into staying? But nobody laughed, and Ystan kept spinning his yarn.

"I have to admit, we were disappointed when you failed to Touch Death-magic." Oh, if only it were that simple, Tristys though. Even now, just the thought of it, and his skin crawled. "We were convinced you were the first person powerful enough in our history to attune to all six quell. This is why I wanted you to speak with our experts. For some reason, quell likes you. It lets you in like no other. We have to find out why."

Nobody said a thing. Calissa had her head bowed. Rami was white as a cottonbloom. Tierran still looked smug, though less smug than he had a few minutes ago. Tristys just stared at Ystan. He had to be wrong. He wasn't a savior. He wasn't powerful. He was just lucky. And if Ystan really thought he was their only hope, why was he having him run away?

"I don't believe you," Tristys said finally, his voice shaking more than he was.

"Tristys, I assure you, the magic is—"

"The magic may be dying," he interrupted, "but that doesn't mean I'm the start of some sort of renaissance. I'm not that special. I'm just some kid from a foreign country. I don't even belong here."

"That's just it, don't you see?" Ystan was nearly shouting now, the most animation he'd shown since he got to the Roseate. "That's exactly why you're so special."

Tristys stared at him blankly. Everybody else—except Calissa—seemed just as clueless.

"You think you are foreign, but you aren't. You are foreign-born. The first foreign-born Coquellian, and the first foreign-born Coquellian who's had such a connection with quell. Our blood in yours allowed the quell to find you, but your foreign blood, I think, is what attracted the quell so deeply. Our blood alone is weak; yours is invigorated because it is mixed. You may not be our rebirth, Tristys, but your blood is."

Tristys was uncomfortable, creeped out. He didn't like all this talk about his blood as if it wasn't in his body at the moment but some separate thing, some entity outside himself. As if he was the only person to have it.

"I'm not the only person with mixed blood," he said. "I have brothers and a sister and parents, and they never—"

"They never stepped foot in the Coquels," Ystan said, usurping Tristys's sentence. It was hard to argue that point. But that point also made things a lot clearer.

"You want me to bring them back here, don't you? You don't care that they're in trouble. You just want them back here." There was distaste in his voice, tempered by disbelief.

"Exactly," Ystan said.

"Can't you just go kidnap some Cyræans like the Spàlorians do?" Salice asked.

Tristys was about to object to that when something else clicked. Instead, he turned to Ystan. "That's why she's here, isn't it? Tyspal. You kidnapped her and you've kept her here all this time hoping she'd Fingerprint! She's decrepit and miserable and unhappy!" The disbelief was gone.

Only disgust remained. "You're no better than the Spålorians!"

Ystan's body, formerly well-postured, sunk. His lips shook, and he fought back tears. "Not quite," he said, "though I understand how you would think that. I've never left the Coquels. The last seyquel did. He brought her over for his own reasons. When he died, I couldn't let her leave, for the same reasons I shouldn't let you leave. There are laws."

Now he looked guilty, ashamed. "But I must confess, I didn't want her to leave. I love her. She is the only person, man or woman, that I have ever truly loved. She wanted nothing more than to leave, and if I had it in my power to let her, I would have, just to see her happy. But I couldn't jeopardize my country by letting her go. And now, I can't jeopardize my country by letting you stay."

Tristys hadn't noticed it before, but there was a sling around Ystan's back. He took it off now, swung it around and opened it up to reveal an urn. "Another confession: I have ulterior motives for sending you back to the continent. I want you to take this to the Cyræan shore. It's slightly out of the way, I realize, but I owe this to her."

"Her?" Tristys croaked, already knowing what he meant but dreading it just the same.

He was stroking the urn now, and Tristys choked up. It was the most pitiful gesture he'd ever seen. "Tyspal died a few days before I wrote that letter to you. I couldn't give her what she wanted while she was alive. At least I can do it for her now. Perhaps, if there is an afterlife, she'll be able to forgive me."

"We'll take it," Tristys said, too choked up to say anything more. He took the urn after Ystan offered it to him, and he set it on the table, next to a pile of their food-stuffs. It was the most bizarre thing he'd ever done, sitting a woman that had scared him half to death just a few weeks ago on a table next to something he intended to eat in the next few days.

"Thank you, thank you," Ystan said, already returning to his less emotional state. He started to fold the sling into a ball, presumably for easier travel. "I was hoping Gawen would have stopped by to see you. I told him not too subtly that you'd be in need of assistance."

"He's here," Rami said. "He and Salice are buying supplies."

"Ah, excellent." He cleared his throat. "I've given Tierran quite a lot of supplies, too. We left them downstairs with the innkeeper. Rami, Calissa, would you mind helping Tierran?"

"Of course," Calissa said. She and Rami followed Tierran out the door.

Ystan stepped closer to Tristys. "I trust you'll take care of my Tyspal?"

"Of course, Ystan."

"She was from Eru. Get her as close to home as you can, okay?"

"Of course."

"One more thing before I go, Tristys. This goes without saying, of course, but I have to say it anyway. Be careful. If anything were to happen to you, I'm afraid I'd be too angry not to do something about it."

"We'll be fine," Tristys lied. He had no idea what they'd be. He had no idea what he was getting into. No one did.

Ystan left then with a goodbye and a hug. A minute later, Rami, Calissa, and Tierran came back, arms full of bags, and Salice and Gawen followed a few minutes after that. They opened the door and rushed into the room, dozens of small bags weighing down their arms, already talking. "They didn't have big bags, so we had to get these little things," Gawen said, huffing as he shut the door. "And I swear to the quell we just saw Ystan walking down the—oh, hello." Tierran had come from the kitchen, a smug smile still on his face.

"What is he doing here?" Salice asked. That seemed to be the first question on everyone's mind when they saw him.

"We'll explain on the way," Calissa said. She'd gone back to commander mode. "Gawen, give me that food. I need to put it in something better than those glorified pockets." As she dumped out the food they'd bought, she shouted at Salice without even looking up. "And you, your clothes are a disaster! Go to the bedroom and try to fit them into a single knapsack. And for quell's sake, woman, fold, fold, fold!"

Within the hour, thanks largely to Calissa the Militant, they'd checked out of the Roseate Windwyrm and were floating across the Coquelai, either to save his family or face certain death. Tristys wasn't sure which was scarier.

ℭHAPTER TWENTY-ONE

Ystan had brought more than just food and an interpreter—he'd brought them a boat. It wasn't a real boat, just a raft, a series of smoothed tree trunks bound together and waterproofed with iş. But even just for that, Calissa was grateful; after all, she'd be doing most of the work to get them across, and this would give her a chance to rest when the wind was blowing.

As she expected, the raft made her job a lot easier. They'd waited to leave Imidalé until daybreak, which was a mistake. As they were rounding Quellas, the sky grew dark and full in the distance. A storm was brewing in the tropical seas off Spálor, and she wasn't the only one who didn't want to weather it on a shoddy raft. She suggested they stop in Quellas, and everyone, even Tristys, agreed. When she suggested they stay a few extra days to see if he could attune to aş, the native Earth-magic, everyone did not agree.

In fact, no one did. Each of them ticked off his or her reasons for the disagreement. Yes, Tristys hadn't shown any signs of Fingerprinting (Salice). Yes, she remembered how bad the last attempt went (Rami). Yes, she knew that every extra second they took would mean they'd have to go farther into Spálor to rescue Tristys's parents (Tierran). And yes, she knew she was being an insensitive jerk (Tristys). She agreed with every one of them.

The last one stung the most. She'd been feeling guilty about the way she'd been treating Tristys anyway, and to have him call her out on it just fueled the fire. She consoled herself with the certainty that she hadn't always been a jerk, that she could blame the stress from having to juggle all her different allegiances vis-à-vis the apparent disappearance of the quell. But even that didn't help as much as it had before Sole Decay. When had her priorities changed? Tristys nearly died, all because she wanted to see if their guesses were right. When had she put her love of oş above her friends, her family, above everything?

When hadn't she?

She pushed thoughts of Fal from her mind. Now was not the time. She could deal with that later—if she had a later. Right now, she had to deal with their trip to Spälor and the issue with quell that led to this adventure. Ystan obviously thought Tristys's bloodlines had something to do with it, but she wasn't so sure. She couldn't imagine a quell that would abandon its chosen people for a stranger from a faraway land, even if his blood did have some of the Coquels in it. No, it had to be something else. She just didn't know what.

But that didn't really matter, did it? The facts were clear: he had a special connection to quell, unlike any connection seen in hundreds of years. She had to find out why. She had to rule out foreigners, which required her to go to Spälor and save Tristys's family. She'd do that, do everything in her power to accomplish what they set out to do, and then she'd get everyone back here, and they'd figure it out. They'd save the quell, no doubt about it.

But first, she had to remember something else. She had to quit being so single-minded, so blinded by her devotion. She loved Rami and Salice, Tristys, even Gawen. They'd been her everything here—at least, everything besides oş—and she couldn't forget that. Just be a little bit more compassionate, she kept telling herself, and maybe they'll stop treating you so differently. The change was subtle at first but impossible to miss now. Tristys and Rami had started spending more time together. That was expected. But now they were actively avoiding her. Even Salice, who normally clung to Calissa, was spending a lot more time alone or with Gawen or even Firebird. She couldn't blame them. She had been a monster that night at Sole Decay, someone even she didn't recognize. She had to keep that in check. She *had* to.

She'd start tonight, she thought as she adjusted the speed of the raft in the wake of a rough wave. Tonight she'd try to get back to the old Calissa, the one who wasn't so panicked by the thought of abandonment that she nearly killed her friend or got so drunk she let every secret she knew out of the bag. Every secret that wasn't hers, anyway. What had happened to the Calissa who spent weeks in a forest trying to get her boyfriend to hook up with the cute blond stranger? Where had she gone?

As the Westerwards came into view, their rounded tops barely visible through the cloud cover, she decided she'd find her again. They were staying in Morningsview that night, a travel destination known for its sunrise vistas. Perhaps tonight she'd make sure Rami and Tristys had a room to themselves, as a first step in her apology.

It wasn't much, but it was a start. And if Calissa knew anything, she knew you had to start somewhere to get started at all.

Their room was enormous. Tristys and Rami were planning on sharing a suite with the others in Morningsview, but Calissa insisted they get a suite for themselves. Tierran didn't like this idea, which made Tristys like it even more. Calissa also insisted on footing the bill, and when Tristys saw the room, he knew she hadn't held back. It was huge! The western wall had more glass than stone, with three large bay windows overflowing with pillows and blankets and cushions. The only bed in the room was directly across from the windows, and it was ridiculously large and lavishly cushioned.

Tristys dropped the two knapsacks he was carrying on one of the chairs before throwing himself on the bed. "I still can't believe we have this room to ourselves," he said, still bouncing. "All six of us could sleep in this bed!" He wasn't very happy about having to sleep in a bed at all instead of continuing their journey, but even he didn't want to brave the storm brewing in the Coquelai. He'd be more use to his family breathing but a day late rather than bobbing dead on the sea.

"True," Rami said. He followed Tristys, dropping his bags and bouncing onto the bed. "But I'd rather it be just the two of us, I think." There was only a hint of mischief in his smile, but Tristys's heart beat faster just in case. They hadn't been alone together since the night of attempted debauchery in Centrespire, and even then, they were alone only for a few minutes before they both passed out. Tristys couldn't even remember the last time they'd been alone before that.

Of course, not being alone hadn't really stopped them. They kissed and cuddled in front of everyone now. Rami had done a complete one-eighty, gone from keeping even the slightest look a secret to shouting his diverted love in any way he could. Tristys made sure not to let the public displays of affection get out of hand—especially the kissing!—but it wasn't always easy. He had needs, too.

"We'll have to thank Calissa again," he said. "Even Firebird likes it." As soon as they got in the room, the monkey had beelined for the middle bay window and burrowed a nest in the blankets. At the moment, he was pulling an overstuffed pillow to his temporary home with his teeth. Tristys hadn't wanted to bring Firebird, but they had no choice. Ystan couldn't take him, partly because he was too busy and partly because the monkey wouldn't unleash from Tristys's arm without throwing a tantrum. Monkey tantrums, as it turned out, were surprisingly unpleasant, considering the claws and the screeching and the spitting. Firebird had become something of a spoiled brat.

"We will. We already told her thanks four hundred times before seeing the place." Rami picked up one of the throw pillows on the bed and tossed it at Firebird, who squealed in outrage before deciding to use the pillow instead. "You're welcome, you ingrate!" Rami was smiling and staring avidly at the monkey, so Tristys took the opportunity to dole out a little bit of justice. He threw a pillow at Rami and hit him squarely in the head.

The only warning Tristys got was a quick "Oh, I don't think so" before Rami grabbed two larger pillows, one in each hand, and started to wail on Tristys. In a few seconds, though, Tristys had beat back the barrage and tackled Rami to the bed, and an all-out tickle-war began. They hadn't played like this since their very first nights together on the Amorai. Much like those early wars, this one involved in-depth making out and some heavy petting.

A knock on their door interrupted them. Tristys jumped out of bed as if he'd been shocked. He straightened his pants, tried to fix his hair, and wiped off his mouth about ten times before Rami said, "Just answer it." He was sprawled in the bed, his shirt half unbuttoned, and the legs of his pants hiked up to his thighs. Tristys had nothing to be ashamed of, nothing to hide, and yet he felt like he'd been caught doing something wrong. He'd get over that, sooner or later... he hoped.

Tierran was at the door. He looked displeased, and that displeasure grew when he noticed the states of Tristys's and Rami's clothing and hair. Among the dirty looks came the news that the group was assembling in one of the finer restaurants in town for a going-away dinner, sponsored once again by Calissa and her bank account. Rami assured Tierran they'd be down in a few moments, then he lunged for Tristys, pulling him back to the bed before Tierran had even left the room. Tristys wanted to die from embarrassment, but a second later and he forgot about everything except the kissing.

~~*

Dinner was decadent, but Rami had trouble enjoying it. He couldn't wait to go to bed. Not to sleep, of course, but to be with Tristys. It had been so long since they'd had any personal time together, and the quick bit before dinner was a nice refresher of what they'd been missing.

Calissa chose to splurge on a traditional dinner, one that hearkened back to the formal ceremonies of high Quellisian culture. That meant there were eight courses. Eight courses! He had to suffer through two appetizers (one warm, one cold), a salad, two meat entrees (one cooked, one raw), a seafood wind-down, and two desserts. They were delicious, of course. Delicious and drawn out. Four and a half hours later, he and Tristys made their way back upstairs to their room. *Thank you, Calissa!* he thought, fully sarcastic and yet fully sincere.

They'd agreed at dinner to leave the inn just after sunrise. Tierran wanted to head out earlier, so that they were already halfway to Cyræa by daybreak, but Calissa insisted they stay to enjoy Morningview's main attraction. Tierran lost the vote 5-1. Rami wasn't even sure Tierran had a vote in the first place.

Back in the room, Firebird beelined for his nest, burrowed into it, and didn't come back out. He'd eaten a big dinner, too, and was too tired to play. "He's got the right idea," Tristys said, his hand on his stomach. "I'm so full I could sleep for days, I think."

"Yeah, me too," Rami agreed. He was lying. He was full, but he wasn't tired. In fact, the last thing on his mind was sleep. Tristys went to the bathroom to change into his pajamas—he was still too shy about his body to change in front of Rami—and Rami changed into his own. He bent down to pick up the clothes he'd tossed, and when he stood back up, Tristys had already climbed into the bed and turned down the covers. He was propped up on one elbow, watching Rami.

"You have a cute butt, you know that?" he said, grinning.

"Yeah, I think so too." He turned around and gave it a few shakes in Tristys's direction.

Tristys threw a pillow.

Rami shot a menacing look back. "Don't you remember the results of that sort of behavior?"

"I remember," Tristys said, still grinning. "That's half the reason I threw it."

That was invitation enough. Rami jumped into bed and he tackled Tristys, who by then had stood up on his knees. They didn't tickle each other, and they didn't make out. They just lay there. Just being in each other's arms was enough. They didn't bother to reposition their heads on the pillows or pull up the blankets. It was a perfect eternity, one of those moments that seemed as if it should last forever, one bubble in time so fragile the slightest movement would break it, but all the more perfect because of that fragility.

Like all bubbles, though, it popped. Tristys twisted to scratch his leg, and that eternity was gone as quickly as it had come. Tristys bent down to yank the covers up, and Rami tossed the small pillow they'd had and grabbed a longer one for their heads. When Tristys snuggled back into Rami's arms, he put a hand on Rami's chest and started playing with the buttons. That's what Tristys did when he was worried about something.

"Are we doing the right thing?" he'd finally

asked after a few minutes. His voice was barely a whisper.

Rami took Tristys's hand, partly to comfort him and partly to save the button. It looked too close to fraying to handle much more worry. "Tristys, we're going to save your family. Of course that's the right thing." He squeezed Tristys's hand.

"I know." Tristys squeezed back. "But at the same time, I don't know. I'm so worried about this."

"We'll be fine, Tristys. We have you and Calissa and Tierran." He hated adding the last name, but Tierran was a huge boon in the situation and it had to be said.

"And you," Tristys said, tilting his head up. "Don't forget you!" He kissed Rami's cheek.

Rami hesitated. He hadn't told anyone else that he could use Water-magic. He'd hid it for so long, just as he'd hidden his same-sex attraction, because the two had become tangled in his mind. Salice and Gawen would be happy for him, but Calissa was going to be angry. He tried not to think about that. "And me," he said.

Tristys played with the button again. "We could die tomorrow, you know that. All of us. You and me, Calissa. Everyone."

"We could die right now. We could have died tonight. You could have choked on that Quellisian nutcake you were scarfing down at dinner." Tristys smacked his chest. "Or my heart could explode right now."

"Not the same," he said, all trace of humor from the nutcake comment gone. "I'm serious, Rami. We could die. This could kill us."

"But it's not going to, Tristys. I promise."

"So you're not worried at all? Not even a little?"

"Of course not. We'll get your parents and get out of there. No heroics, nothing silly. In and out. We'll be fine."

Rami was lying. He was petrified. He had absolutely no idea how this would turn out. In school, he'd focused on physical training and Coquellian history. The little bit of foreign studies he had to take to graduate had been spent on the language of Cyræa. He knew too little about Spålor to know if they really had a shot at saving themselves let alone Tristys's family. All he knew was that this was important to Tristys and therefore he'd do it.

He knew one other thing: he didn't have to do this. He could refuse, tell Tristys he wasn't going, try to keep Tristys here on the islands, but if he wouldn't listen to reason, wave goodbye and wish him luck. Rami had lived twenty-five years now without Tristys, right? He could keep on living without him. The problem, he realized, was that he didn't want to.

"I'm not worried," he said again, though now he wasn't sure to what he was referring, exactly.

"Thank you," Tristys said. He shifted again, pushing up and kissing Rami once more on the cheek. "You're a terrible liar, but thank you for trying." He brought a hand to Rami's face, pushed so that Rami looked down, and kissed him on the lips. He didn't stop. His kisses were greedy, taking as much as they gave. He held Rami's face tightly, his fingers pressing into his cheeks. Soon he was sitting in Rami's lap, his legs straddling Rami's. He was moving in time with his kisses, the rhythmic pressure exciting Rami despite their clothes. Tristys let go of Rami's face, but only long enough to unbutton Rami's shirt, one finger branding a line as it slid down his chest.

Rami gave in to the motion, allowing his shirt to slide off and his whole body to slide down the headboard and sink further into the bed. His arousal hurt. His pants were a prison, and he strained against them, thrusting up into Tristys as Tristys pushed down. Within seconds, Tristys had him free, all his clothes thrown into piles beside the bed. Kissing again, with Rami matching Tristys in urgency and speed. Nothing mattered, nothing was as important as this connection.

Without separating their lips, Tristys lost his shirt. His pants came next. They locked hands, and Tristys moved their arms above their heads, pressed their hands into the bed. He spread Rami's legs apart with his knees. As Tristys lowered himself onto Rami, their bodies touched for the first time. Rami sucked in a deep breath, unprepared for the jolt and the pressure.

They were thrusting together, their desire aching, and when Tristys entered Rami, the pain was sharp and brief. He saw white stars that turned red with pleasure, and heat spread through his body like wildfire. Waves of it, in time with Tristys's rhythm, melting away everything outside of their union. Bed, walls, blankets... gone. Moonlight and sunrise, the islands and the forest, past and future... all gone. Rami's entire world imploded to only Tristys only as he was then, this instant, this eternity: the sweet taste of his tongue, the burning pressure of his cock, the slick touch of his skin, and the motion of the muscles that powered his thrusts.

They spent an hour in that eternity, and as Rami lay beneath Tristys the next morning, still warmed by the night before, his only regret was that nothing, not even eternity, lasted forever.

~~*

Rami was already awake when Tristys woke up. The sun was peeking over the horizon, reflecting off the Coquelai, and trying to blind Tristys in the process. It was beautiful, but too bright.

"Sorry about that," Rami said. He was bent down over their knapsacks, trying to cram the contents of one into the other. He jumped up and pulled a string on the wall, and the heavy drapes above the middle window dropped to the floor. Firebird, who had been sleeping in his nest, squeaked in protest. Tristys quit squinting.

Rami had clothes on, thank the two moons. Tristys wasn't sure what to expect, now that they'd consummated their relationship. He didn't really think Rami would walk around fully nude now, but some small part of him wondered if perhaps he would... and how he'd handle it, if that were the case.

But he wasn't ashamed or embarrassed about the night before. On the contrary, he was glad it finally happened. Hell, he'd been the one to initiate it! But it was such a big deal, his first time, and it had been so amazing. What if it wasn't that good the next time? What if Rami hadn't enjoyed himself? What if Rami went off in search of—what was the Cyræan expression?—new cows since he'd already sampled this milk. Even worse, what if it was Tristys who wanted new cows now?

While one half of his brain stressed over that, the other half wouldn't stop thinking *We had sex we had sex wehadsexwehadsexwehadsex* every time he looked at Rami. Then he'd start to grin like an idiot, and he'd get woozy from excitement and feel as if he was about to faint again for the thirty-seventh time. And he'd only been awake for five minutes.

Rami sat down on the corner of the bed. Why was he sitting so far away? Was he unhappy? Was this it? Was this how you started to break up with someone, sitting far away from them? "How are you feeling?" Rami asked. He reached his hand along the comforter, but he was too far away to touch Tristys.

"I'm okay," Tristys said, uncertain of a better response.

"Just okay?" Rami looked disappointed, and Tristys smacked himself mentally. *What sort of a half-assed answer is that, after what happened last night?*

So he started to babble. "No, I'm great! Stupendous!" Too exaggerated. "I mean, you know, I'm still half-asleep. Groggy or whatever." Too dismissive. "But I'm glad that we—err, you know, I had a good time when—"

Rami's smile turned to laughter. "I know what you mean." He scooted closer to Tristys on the bed and put a hand on his leg. "It's okay if you're feeling a little awkward—"

"I'm not awkward!"

"No, I know. I'm just saying. It's a big deal, our first time and all."

"Oh," Tristys said. He wasn't sure how he was supposed to feel. He wasn't even sure how he actually felt.

"And you are awkward, and it's adorable. But it'll pass." Rami leaned in to kiss him, and Tristys wet his lips before Rami kissed him... on the nose.

He pulled away, smiling like a maniac, and Tristys, who had been expecting more, just sat there, mouth opened, stunned for a second. Rami started laughing, then Tristys joined in, and a second later, Rami was right: awkwardness gone.

They showered together—nothing sexual—and got dressed. Rami had finished packing while Tristys slept in, so they went downstairs to meet up with the rest of the party. Gawen and Salice looked well-rested. Tierran still looked put out, Calissa worried. She lit up when she saw Tristys and Rami, though.

"Had a good night, I hope?" she asked. Her tone was innocent enough, but there was a distinctively suggestive squint to her eyes. Had she planned the whole damn thing this way?

"Oh, we most certainly did," Rami answered. His tone left nothing to the imagination. Dammit. Tierran rolled his eyes as he walked away, Gawen looked uncomfortable but grinned anyway, and Salice snickered. Calissa was pleased, but she didn't press for details. Bless her.

They moved quickly from Morningsview to the beach where they'd left the raft. Tierran had buried it beneath the sand with his magic, and it was still there, untouched. Boarding was a somber occasion. Nobody spoke. Even Firebird, who usually avoided water as if he'd melt, got on without a squeal or a gripe. Tristys assumed everyone, maybe even the monkey, was lost in his or her own thoughts, just as he was. Possible death, wild goose chases, strangers in a strange land. It was easy to get lost in that mess.

The trip across the Coquelai suffered from the same introspective silence. Calissa used her magic to navigate most of the way—Ystan had given them a sail—and Tristys took over every now and then to give her a break. Nobody planned, nobody strategized. The little talking that happened was idle chatter, comments about the weather, a fish they saw jumping. When someone waxed nostalgic, the others would yell; they weren't dying, they didn't want to jinx it.

When they finally landed, they were farther south than Tristys had ever been when he'd lived in Cyræa. The sand was darker, with more vegetation, mostly in the form of larger shrubs and some trees. It didn't really look like his old home—Quellus looked closer—and yet he was mesmerized. He jumped off the raft before they'd even finished coasting onto the beach.

Less than a year ago, this land was everything he'd ever known. It was his life, his vista, his home. But now it was nothing. He had been afraid to see it again, petrified that he'd be unable to leave it a second time, to say goodbye once and for all. But now it was nothing more than sand and a few trees that looked even more out of place than he felt. There was no denying it now: the life he had known, the life he had been born into, was gone. He wasn't a Cyræan anymore; in fact, he might never have been.

He turned around to help his friends pull the raft up the beach, but they'd already finished. They were all standing there, just staring at him, hands behind their backs or on their hips. Calissa and Salice were concerned; Gawen intrigued. Tierran just looked bored.

"Are you okay?" Rami asked.

"Yeah," Tristys said. "Definitely."

"Are you sure?"

"Yes, Rami. I'm sure." He looked over his

shoulder again, at the vast desert that seemed to go on forever, even though he knew it shifted into grasslands and then forests once it passed the Kysim River. "I'm fine." Calissa had Tyspal's urn in her hands, and he motioned for her to bring it over. "Let's get this show on the road, shall we?"

In Cyræa, traditional funerals involved burial. That wasn't possible for Tyspal, of course, so Ystan had decided to start by following the Coquellian rituals of cremation and finish with the burial due her as a Cyræan. He wanted half her ashes thrown out to sea, since she loved the water so much, and the other half buried, with the urn, far beneath the sand. He insisted the burial be so deep that nobody, under any circumstance, would ever find it. He claimed it had to do with the urn itself—it was very obviously not Cyræan or Spàlorian—but Tristys thought it had more to do with making sure Tyspal rested in peace, since her life had been so much the opposite.

They carried out her funeral exactly as he'd asked. Tristys wanted help scattering the ashes, but everybody refused. He wasn't comfortable doing it—he barely knew Tyspal and their one meeting freaked him out—but everyone insisted he should do it, since he was the only Cyræan in the group. He cringed at the label, but he accepted.

He took some ashes from the urn and dipped his hand in the water, letting it rest there until the waves took the ashes to sea. Tierran used his Earth-magic to dig so deep he hit soil, and Tristys lowered the urn gently with his own Air-magic. Tristys said a small prayer to the Two Mothers and Tierran used his magic to bury the urn. When they left, the sand was as smooth as if they'd never been there.

~~*

Since Tierran insisted that the only way to escape a rampaging Spálorian army was by water, they decided to float along the coast as far as they could. Rami would have opted to do pretty much anything else just to spite him, but this was life and death, so he relented.

Rami was in the front of the boat, so he spotted the abandoned camp first. They hadn't left Cyræa yet, but there it was, just a little farther down the coast. They weren't entirely sure if they should approach, but the camp looked deserted, and there was nowhere to hide in ambush, no cover, nothing. So they checked it out.

"Do they really keep their slaves in cages like this?" Gawen walked over and kicked it. The whole thing rattled, threatening to topple. A few sticks even came loose.

"It doesn't need to be very sturdy," Tristys said, his voice twisted. He was hugging himself tightly. He wasn't looking at the cage. This had to be hard on him. Rami walked over and put a hand on his back, which is something he should've done from the beginning. "We were so drugged during transport to the ships it was hard enough to keep our hands off the ground. One of the other slavers had a crush on me, so he kept my doses low. He kept hoping I'd try to escape, so he could override Vun'gor's protection and punish me himself."

"That's horrible," Salice said.

Tristys nodded. "It was worse that way, staying coherent and everything. I heard everything, you know? I saw everything. The crying, the punishment. The rape." His eyes were gone, looking back into his past. "I see those cages and that's all I think about."

"Well," Gawen said. "That's lovely." He snapped his fingers and all the cages burst into brilliant light before falling to the ground, nothing more than ash. "Problem solved!"

A moment later, Rami broke the silence. "Let's go," he said, guiding Tristys back to the raft. "There's nothing here."

They weren't far from Spálor now. Looking south, the horizon was half water and half trees, a rich green that looked similar to the forests of Quelles but different somehow. As the trees grew closer, Rami could feel the raft pick up speed. Probably unintentional on Calissa's part. There was static in the air now, a sizzling impatience. It was infectious.

Once Tierran finally found a suitable spot, they set up camp. They decided to sleep in shifts, with one magic-user and one Untouched staying awake at a time. They wouldn't have to sleep more than one night in Spálor. The coast curved sharply in the distance, and Tierran assured them that the city lay just beyond the bend. One way or another, that city was the end of this journey. They'd either get Tristys's family or they'd get killed. Either way, nothing would be the same after tomorrow.

As he ate his dinner—some disgusting mush that tasted like burnt wood—he had a hard time believing where he was and what he was doing. What were any of them doing here? There was Calissa, so strong-willed and beautiful. So reticent to risk her life, or the lives of her friends, but here she was, planning defensive maneuvers with Tierran.

There was Salice, so dedicated she'd risk her

own life to save a few strangers for a friend even though she was virtually defenseless here.

And Gawen. How many times had Rami mistreated him, led him on even though he tried not to, refused him? Hell, how many times had Tristys done the same thing to him? But here he was, without a second thought.

And then there was Tierran. Now Rami was stumped. He had no idea why Tierran was here. Ystan had obviously asked him to go, but why would he agree? And how did they know each other? Truth be told, it didn't really matter. They'd do what they came to do, and they'd go back to the Coquels, and he'd forget about Tierran, forget about him the way he'd been unable to do for years.

And finally: Tristys, feeding most of his mush to Firebird. His hair was a mess, he had dirt all over his face, and his shirt was ripped along the whole left arm. He was laughing at Firebird, who ate the mush every time Tristys offered it, gagged dramatically, and then asked for more. He was why they were here, all of them, the only link connecting the five, the only reason six young people (and one monkey) were about to attack a fortified city of thousands. It was insane, absolutely insane, and yet Rami knew, just sitting there watching Tristys, that he'd do it all over again if he had to. He had a feeling the other four would, too.

~~*

The night went smoothly, without incident. Calissa and Salice had the last watch, and the only thing that disturbed them was some strange monkey-type creature with huge eyes and extremely long middle fingers. She shot a quick burst of water in its direction and it scurried away, screeching. It didn't come back.

After breakfast, they continued their journey. Nobody spoke much. They knew they were approaching the city, and they had no real idea what to expect. All Tierran had said was that Velo□a Tánor was enormous.

He hadn't been lying. Thick, wooden walls surrounded the entire compound, even along the beach. They'd built watchposts every few feet, and they'd stationed guards on them, two to each post. Both guards carried bows as well as long, thick-bladed swords. The men were big, well-muscled but not well-armored. Gawen was probably having a field day.

"They won't be expecting us," Tierran said. He was right again; they looked more bored than watchful. The city had virtually no external threats; the guards were there to keep slaves in, not foreigners out. "It's best if we can get in without being noticed. The closer we get to the goal before we have to engage, the better."

There were few entrances to the city, which made sense. Calissa had to stop considering it a city. It wasn't. It was a prison, an enormous cage. Cages had one exit—if that. Tierran refused to breach an actual entrance without first scouring the perimeter for a more clandestine way in. They weren't very graceful, six spoiled upperclass people hunched over and walking through an overgrown forest. They weren't very quiet, either. She was pretty sure they were doomed.

"There," Tierran said, nodding to a small stream ahead of them. "That goes right under the wall into the compound."

"I'm sure they have it blocked off," Rami said. "They can't be that stupid."

"The water is moving," Tierran pointed out. "That means we can move, too, even if we have to incinerate a grate or two to do it. That will be less conspicuous than blowing a hole in the wall, don't you think?"

"Or flying over it," Salice added. They'd talked about that option earlier, but they didn't know enough about what to expect on the inside. They could knock off a few guard platforms, jump over, and land in the middle of a phalanx. Tierran's suggestion was the best option.

"Fine," she said, "but we shouldn't all go charging in at once."

"Of course not." Tierran looked past Calissa to Gawen. "You're the strongest Fire here, right?"

Gawen's eyes darted between Tierran and Tristys. "I guess?"

"Then you go under and see what sort of containment they have going on and neutralize it."

Gawen was floored. "You want me to just hop in that water, swim under the wall, blow up whatever I find, come out on the other side and shout "Hey guys, water's fine, come on in?"

Tierran's jaw clenched. They hadn't had a good night together on watch, if all the arguing had been any indication. Calissa had woken up far before her shift started because of them. "No, you nitwit. Get through any barriers, turn around, and we'll all go together."

"I'll go with you now," Tristys said. "I've got Fire-magic, too. And Water and Air, if necessary."

Tierran pointed to the two nearest platforms. "We have to knock out those guards before we do this. Tristys, that's you."

He nodded, and she held her breath. This was it. Once he did this, that was it. They were going. Tristys stared at the guards, and his eyes crossed. The four soldiers fell, almost in unison, the sounds muffled by the soft leather armor. One soldier, though, was too close to the edge of his platform; his sword clattered off the edge, clanging as it hit something metallic below. The noise was ear-splitting to Calissa, and she held her breath again: nothing happened. No calls of alarm, no curious soldiers from nearby platforms, nothing. They were lucky.

A few seconds later, Gawen and Tristys were in the stream, treading water as quietly as they could. "I hate getting wet," Gawen said, but nobody listened.

"Swim as close to the bottom as you can," Tierran advised. "Don't lift your arms above your body, and don't kick your legs too hard. You don't want to make even the slightest splash. I don't know how far through the water their arrows will penetrate, and you don't want one or two in your back."

"Lovely," Gawen said. "Just lovely."

They submerged.

Forever passed before they came back. Calissa kept waiting to hear an alarm, see arrows flying, blood coloring the water. The last one didn't even make sense, since the stream was flowing into the compound, but she couldn't get the image out of her head. When Tristys and Rami finally emerged, a bit closer to the gate than they'd gone, she nearly cried out with relief.

Gawen sizzled, and he was dry. Tristys shook himself like a dog, and he was dry, but Calissa suspected that had more to do with his magic than with his shivering.

"Done," Gawen said quietly once they got closer. "Five gates, each one bigger than before, all gone."

"Wonderful." Tierran seemed bigger, as if their conquering the first obstacle had inflated him. "I'll go through first, with Gawen and Tristys. Then—"

"Why can't I—" Calissa started.

"Because Gawen has Fire-magic, which is good on the offense, and Tristys has Air and Water, which we need to signal you, and I have Earth-magic, which is good for defense." He didn't wait for approval. "Once we're in, we'll signal you through the stream. Then you three—or four, if you insist on bringing that monkey—can come over."

"Fine." Calissa took Firebird from Rami, holding him in her arms like a baby. He was scared, obviously, but he wasn't panicked. Rather amazing for an animal, really. They'd considered knocking him out, but Tristys refused. He said Firebird knew what was happening, and he would help them, not hinder them. She wasn't so sure, but so far, Tristys had been right. She hoped he'd continue being right.

"Once we're over there, we have to move fast. No questions, just do what I say. Low-key is the goal for as long as we can keep it that way. The longer it takes them to start mobilizing, the better. We get in, we find his family, we get out. Assume anyone you see wants to kill you and will do it without a second thought."

Everyone nodded, and Tierran got into the stream along with Tristys and Gawen.

"Remember," he said before taking a deep

breath and diving, "we're not heroes. Don't try to be one." With that, they were gone, and Calissa had to wait for another eternity to pass. The sky was still dark, though light was beginning to show behind them. It wasn't enough light, however, to hide the three flashes of light she saw behind the wall. Rami jerked forward, obviously intending to be the hero, but she stopped him.

"No," she said against every instinct she had. "Wait."

She was right. A moment later, a wave rushed under the surface of the stream, emerging and splashing onto the ground before their feet. That was the signal. This was it. They were going in. Us against the world, she thought.

She looked at Rami and nodded. "Plug your nose, Firebird." She took a deep breath, held on to the monkey, and jumped.

CHAPTER TWENTY-TWO

Velo☐a Tànor looked like a prison. The buildings were the exact same: wooden, single-story rectangles with no ornamentation and small, barred windows near the roofs. They were extremely close together, which proved to be a double-edged sword. Cover was easy to find, but visibility was virtually nil. The area around the stream, however, was open and vulnerable. Tristys wanted to race to a building for cover, but they had to wait for Rami, Calissa, Salice, and Firebird to swim through the wall. It took forever, but all four came through safely.

Tristys helped dry them off while Tierran studied the guard platforms. "We need to capture some guards now," he said.

"We need to what?" Tristys asked. "You said we're supposed to stay low-key. I'm not sure how—"

"We are," Tierran said, frustrated. He apparently thought Tristys should be better at breaking and entering. "But do you really want to run around this entire place, sticking your head in doors and shouting 'Mom! Dad! Where are you?'"

He had a point. He always had a point. It drove Tristys crazy. "I guess not."

"Right. So let's find some guards."

They started maneuvering along the buildings, making sure their bodies were pressed tightly to the structures. So tight, in fact, Tristys had a hard time not hearing the sounds coming from inside: voices, mostly men, having conversations in Spáloric; sobs and cries and moans, pleas in languages he didn't recognize. When he heard slaps, grunts punctuated by another's sobs, it took every ounce of Tristys's willpower not to bust down that building on the spot and stop what he knew was happening inside.

Tierran put his hand out to stop the procession, but it was too late.

Around the corner came a small contingent of soldiers, swords sheathed, bows on their back. There were only three of them, two men and a woman, and they were young, probably younger than Tristys. The taller man looked a lot like Rami, and the other man and the woman were laughing at something he had just said. When they saw a group of six strangers clad in foreign garb, they froze.

It was absolute stillness, a frozen second in time that seemed to rotate so Tristys saw it from every angle, high and low. The Spálorians were quick to react, drawing their swords for hand-to-hand combat, but Tierran was quicker. He yelled—not the best idea, in hindsight—and threw his hands up and apart. The ground beneath the soldiers mimicked that motion, and the soldiers, with no ground beneath them, started to fall. But again, Tierran was quicker. He moved his hands down, and the soil returned to its place, trapping the soldiers in it. They were buried alive, only their heads and necks still above ground.

Tierran and Calissa must have planned this, because almost at once she threw up a windshield to prevent their shouts from being heard. They were yelling, too, in that long, guttural language of theirs.

The female guard was closest to them. Tierran bent low to the ground and took her chin in his hand. She stopped yelling only long enough to spit at him.

He slapped her and yelled as loudly as he could. Tristys wasn't sure of the exact translations, but he had guesses. The taller guard was yelling, too, and the man on the left was sobbing pitifully, his face contorted with fear and wet with tears. The woman asked what they were, but Tierran wouldn't answer, just asked where they kept the slaves from Paru. She spat again, cussed at Tierran.

The sobbing one looked up. He was drooling, and as he spoke, spit flew from his mouth. *If I tell you, will you let me go?*

Tierran's affirmative twisted his smile into a rictus. Tristys hated him so much he was almost rooting for the Spálorians.

The sobbing soldier answered, something about *being new, three walls, many died.*

Tierran said something else in Spáloric, and as Tristys tried to translate, Tierran clenched his fist. The sound was sickening, so horrible that Tristys almost wretched. For a second, Tristys thought Tierran had cracked his knuckles, but the sound was too loud, too grating, too visceral. It was the crushing of three defenseless soldiers, the breaking of hundreds of bones, dusted by the earth itself. It was nightmarish, unbearable, unspeakable. He'd fallen to all fours. He couldn't look at the guards.

"What the fuck do you think you're doing?" Calissa was shouting. "We agreed no deaths! We agreed no deaths!" She kept shouting those words, and by now she was beating on Tierran with her fists, pounding his chest, but he was much taller than she was. He wasn't even flinching—he was still smiling.

She got so caught up in her anger that she'd let the windshield drop. Tristys heard more yelling, but it wasn't coming from Calissa. There were guards ahead of them, running towards them, and one pulled a horn from his back and blew into it, emitting a loud, low sound. They'd been spotted. So much for low-key.

"If you're done now, Calissa," Tierran said, still smiling, "we have to go. Company's coming."

"We agreed no deaths!" she shouted again, still beating.

He wrapped his arms around her body and pulled her off the ground. She was over his shoulder now, beating on his back, still saying something about no deaths, and he turned to the rest of the group. Everyone, even Gawen, was staring at him, still in shock. "Tristys, do something." He ran away. The others followed.

Tristys turned back to the guards. They were so close now, too close, and all he could hear were those bones, those bones, those bones. He refused to look down, but he threw three waves at the rush of soldiers, big enough to knock them over. That would give them time, but not enough. He ignited a line of fire between him and the guards, right through the three fallen soldiers, from one building to another. The buildings might catch, but that would have to be another casualty. Tristys hoped the people inside would have time to get out.

Tristys rushed after the others. He turned the

corner into madness. Tierran was running along the wall, in clear view of every platform. More guards had ascended them, and arrows were cascading through the sky. Gawen was incinerating them before they got too close to their targets, but it was a frightful sight, to see everybody left in the world that Tristys cared about running for their lives because of him. He had to help.

He looked at the guards, twisted his vision until he saw the stars, and let them explode. Wind rushed along the wall, knocking the guards back and off the side. The wall wasn't too high; they'd live. More importantly, so would his friends.

"Let's go, Tristys!" Tierran shouted. By the time he caught up to them, Calissa had stopped trying to beat back Tierran's murders, and he'd set her on the ground.

"I should snuff the breath right out of you," she spat. If she were a cat, she'd be snarling.

"Then you'd be no better than I, would you?" he asked. He wasn't grinning anymore, focused once again on the mission. "We have to get to the center of the city. That's where the guard said the newer prisoners would be." So Tristys had translated correctly. Points for him.

"The last thing the guard told you," Salice said. She looked just as angry as Calissa, though she was better at controlling it.

"These are trained military soldiers," he said, not looking at her. "They knew what they were risking when they signed up."

"They didn't know they would be fighting oş!" Calissa shouted. "They couldn't have known that! And you had no right to use it to take their lives! You're no better than Bellimar!"

That got his attention. Tristys recognized the name from the Great War—he was the dictator who started the whole thing. "I am nothing like Bellimar. I am here to save a family, am I not? Is that something Bellimar would have done?" He waited for Calissa to respond, but she didn't. "I think not. Now, let's get to the center of this maze, so we can get out of this barbaric jungle."

They had been walking as they talked, following Tierran as he guided them farther into the city. They were moving along the stream that they'd hijacked to enter, since it seemed to flow in the direction they needed to go.

They were fending off a seemingly endless supply of small groups of guards, a few here and there, rather than a single reinforced unit. This was a boon, since small numbers were easier to handle. Gawen or Tristys incinerated the arrows. Calissa pushed people aside with her wind or kept them at bay with her water. Even Rami shot a waterbolt; he saved Tierran's life. Calissa was mad, but he wasn't sure what made her angrier, the fact that Rami hadn't told her he could Touch the quell or that he'd saved Tierran's life.

She was yelling at Rami now, something about how he'd kept this a secret for so long, how could he, but when they finally broke through the final wall to the center of the compound, she stopped. The Spälorians had finally decided to mass before they attacked, and they'd brought fighting tòs with them: felines so large that two men could ride comfortably on them. Tristys had trouble viewing them as enemies, since the only one he'd seen before then had been his friend. These, though, were growling, crouched down and fangs bared. These weren't friends.

It started in less than a second. Arrows flew, cats attacked, the front line of soldiers charged, swords raised and battle cries heavy in the air. But even they weren't a match for six men and women—and a monkey—from the Coquels. Whether from water, wind, fire, earth, or Life, they were knocked from their feet and trapped, with melted swords or cracked arrows, before they even registered who was attacking them. It was over before it had even started, really.

"Go ahead," Tierran said, standing over two fallen soldiers, trapped in the same sort of earthen cage that had killed the first three. When Tristys kept staring at the two in the ground, Tierran scoffed. "Don't worry, I won't kill these ones. Go and find your family. We'll take care of any more guards."

"I'm going with you," Rami said, pushing to the front of the group. It wasn't a question, and nobody, not even Tierran, argued.

"Hurry up," Calissa said, her voice calm and steady. "If this is all they've got, we're fine, but I'd rather not dally."

"No worries," Rami said. "I'll make him run."

They ran. They ran from hovel to hovel, peered inside, asked questions when they could, but there was no trace of Tristys's mother, father, or brother. The buildings here were much simpler than the ones in the other rings. They were barely domiciles, just cages with no furniture except straw beds beneath the chains that held slaves in place. It was dreadful. Tristys thanked the stars, once again, that he'd not made it here.

Just as Tristys was beginning to despair—they'd entered dozens of these hovels, and the sheer horror of these people, bruised and battered on the floor, was starting to wear away his no-hero resilience—they came to a bigger building closer to the true center of the city. Before they even entered it, Tristys knew: this was it.

He didn't rush in. He took a deep breath. He was afraid, actually afraid, to go in, to see his family again for the first time in months. To have to explain everything, to merge his two worlds, to change everything. Again.

Shouting in the distance brought him back. He had to do this, and he had to do it now. The time for second-guessing was gone. He burst through the door, and almost at once his eyes fell on his brother, Keltyn, chained to the far wall and crouching in his own waste. He was laughing, hysterical, his eyes distant. Had he lost his mind? Was Tristys too late? But a second later, Keltyn's eyes focused with recognition.

"I knew it was you!" he said through his laughter. "I heard all the sirens, and all the screaming, and I just knew."

Tristys threw himself at his brother's feet, started pawing at the chains, ignored the filth around him.

"Come to save us all, have you?" Keltyn asked. His voice was broken, too throaty and coarse. Tristys nodded rabidly, unable to find his voice, to speak to the brother who hadn't spoken to him in so long. Rami was keeping his distance, staring at the two in what appeared to be mild shock. "I don't know how you got here or where you went." He lowered his head and coughed violently. His whole body shook, and flecks of blood landed on his bare chest. "You won't get those chains off."

"Yes," Tristys finally said. "Yes, I will. And I'll get you out of here, you'll see. Watch."

"You're too late," Keltyn said. He was laughing again, a weak, hollow sound that disturbed Tristys more than the chains. "You're too late!"

"No!" Tristys shouted. He looked at his brother's emaciated form, the blood on his chin, his chest. All the bruises. Had he been used? "You don't understand. We can make you better, we'll fix you up as good as new. We'll get Mama and Papa and—"

Tristys stopped before he finished. Keltyn had raised his head, finally looked at Tristys in the eyes, and there was a cruelty there, a pleasure he'd never seen even when Keltyn abused him for being diverted. "They're dead, you stupid faggot. They're dead. You're too late."

~~*

Rami had stayed back, wanting to give Tristys space with his brother, but when he collapsed to the ground—this time in despair—Rami rushed to his side.

"Are you okay?" he asked.

Tristys was crying, which was a sure sign he wasn't okay.

"What's wrong?" He was rubbing Tristys's back to soothe him. It usually worked, but right now it felt so insignificant.

Tristys sat up. He said nothing and looked vacant, as if his mind had somehow fallen out his body. In any case, Tristys's body had fallen in filth, and Rami Touched Water to rinse what he could. The clothes weren't any better, but it was an improvement.

"What was that?" the boy asked, clearly freaked out. Rami ignored him. Right now, all he cared about was Tristys.

"Tristys, what's wrong? Please, tell me."

He didn't answer. Rami decided to try a different approach. He turned to the chained boy, and said, in Cyræan, "What did you tell him?"

"I told him our parents are dead." His voice was void of any emotion, monotonous and dead. "And I called him a faggot, since that's what he is." He let out a choked laugh that turned to coughs.

Taken aback, Rami doused the boy in water, a quick blast to his face, which only made him laugh harder. *He's not worth it*, he told himself. *Fix Tristys*.

On his knees, he turned to Tristys. He grabbed him by the wrist and started to shake gently. "Listen to me!" he said. "Tristys, listen to me!" He shook a little harder. "You have to wake up, Tristys! Tristys!" Still nothing. He slapped him across the face, but still nothing but an empty stare. He wasn't sure how to revive someone from shock, so he did the only other thing he could think of.

Magic.

Three quick ice daggers, like he'd used in the Bluewood to wake Tristys. It worked. He blinked once, twice, and then gasped when he remembered what had just happened.

"We're too late, Rami," he said through renewed tears. "We're too late." He collapsed again, though this time he landed in Rami's arms.

Even though he kept muttering that it'd be okay, Rami was in a mild state of shock himself. All this to rescue two dead parents and this hateful little vermin? What a cruel twist! It took a moment to register. Even so, he and Tristys couldn't stay like this forever. They had to get out of this bloody town and off this bloody continent. He turned his gaze to the brother, who was still hacking on himself and chuckling in his chains. The worst part of the whole thing was that they had to take the rat with them.

"Hey, little faggot," the brother said. "If you want to say goodbye to your mommy, her body's back there." He tilted his head farther into the hovel. "I bet the butt-fucking sons of bitches haven't even gotten rid of it yet."

Rami didn't want Tristys to see that, so when he jerked in that direction, he held him back. "No, Tristys. There's no point."

He looked down at Rami, his eyes pooling. "I need to, Rami. She was—she is—my mother. I have to say goodbye. Say I'm sorry. For everything."

Rami shook his head, but he disengaged. This was a bad idea, but if Tristys felt like he had to do it, he had to. At least maybe he could get some closure.

Tristys disappeared into the dimly lit innards of the building, leaving Rami with the brother, still chained to the wall, still chuckling on occasion. Rami hadn't seen insanity before, but he was almost certain that this kid was just a few more laughs away from it. He'd be a delight on the raft, no doubt. Perhaps Tristys would let them drag him along behind...

"Rami!" Tristys shouted. "Rami, please! Come here!" Rami forgot about the brother in a second and leaped into the darkness. There were bodies everywhere. He wasn't sure if they were alive or dead or somewhere in between. "Rami, please, where are you?" Tristys shouted again, more frantic. "She's not dead, Rami! My mother's not dead!"

Rami followed the voice and found Tristys bent over a corpse. The cropped hair left on her head was thin and long, caked with dirt. Her body was covered in red, seeping sores. Was that blood? Her eyes were open, but the pupils had rolled to the back of her head. The whites of her eyes were pink. If she was still alive, she wouldn't be much longer.

"Tristys," Rami began, unsure how to continue. How do you tell someone you love—how do you tell anyone, really—that it's too late to save his mother?

"No, Rami, I can save her!" He looked up at Rami, pleading. "I can save her!" He was panicked, but his eyes were clear and lucid.

But what could Tristys do? This woman was obviously on the verge of death, struck down by some blood-curdling disease that had infected everyone in this building. Tristys had Life-magic, yes, but this was a poison in the body, the realm of Death-magic. There was nobody here to help with that, and she wouldn't make it back to the Coquels in time. Ystan should have found them a Death-practioner too.

"Tristys, there isn't anything—"

"Please, Rami," Tristys said. He was sobbing now, his tears splashing onto his mother and leaving a trail as they rolled down her boiling skin. "I can save her."

Well, this is what they came for, wasn't it? No point in giving up now. "Fine, Tristys. I'll get her. Get your brother out of those chains and let's go."

Tristys nodded frantically, his breaths quick and deep, and he ran to do as he was told. Rami bent down, looked for shackles on the woman, but she was so far gone the Spälorians had already unchained her. He took one last breath, fully aware that he was about to cover himself with infected blood. He just hoped Calissa would have enough magic left in her to get the raft to the Coquels at breakneck speed. More lives than just this woman's would depend on it.

As he stood up, he put his arms underneath Tristys's mother and lifted her. He used too much force to pick up such a light woman, and he nearly fell backwards. He could feel the fire in her blood even through the thin shift she had on, and she smelled like shit and dried blood. Her head lolled limply to one side, and he used a hand to push it the other way, so it rested on his bicep. But Tristys was right: she was still alive. She moaned, and there was another noise, a gurgle deep in the back of her throat. She coughed, and Rami tilted her head a little more. Blood dribbled out of her mouth and down his arm. They had to hurry.

Tristys was with his brother. He'd melted the chains off the wall, but his brother hadn't stood up yet. In fact, Rami realized as he got closer, his brother wasn't even conscious.

"He wouldn't come with us," Tristys said as he tried to lift his brother up. "Kept saying he didn't want to get saved by diverted filth. I guess he'd rather just live in it."

"So you—"

"So I knocked him out."

The circumstances were dire—he had a dying woman in his arms, an unconscious teen on the ground, and an entire country out for his blood—but he couldn't help smiling as he said, "I see. Remind me never to say no to you, okay?"

"As if you ever could," Tristys smiled. He tried for a third time to carry his brother, and he couldn't get him off the ground. "We'll do this the easy way, then." A second later, his brother was floating obediently by Tristys's side, and they were moving quickly back to the stream.

More Spàlorians had come to the defense, but Tierran, Gawen, and Calissa were handling them without too much difficulty. They'd bottlenecked the soldiers at the small entrance they'd blown into the inner wall, and Gawen and Tierran took care of the melee coming through while Calissa blew off—literally—the archers on the wall and diverted their arrows. The Spàlorians were persistent, but they weren't that adaptive.

"Let's go, let's go, let's go!" Rami shouted as soon as he had them in his sight. The plan had gone from subterfuge to brute strength. They'd blow their way out of this place, hop on their raft, and get home.

It was a lot easier than they expected. Almost all the Spàlorians had congregated at the bottleneck, so when Gawen blew another hole in a far wall, the area was nearly deserted. But they ran as quickly as they could. There was a bit of resistance—a few melees here, an archer or two there—but getting out was a lot easier than getting in. The Spàlorians, Rami imagined, had a lot more to deal with now than some freak foreigners who were running away—like an entire city of slaves trying to capitalize on the chaos. Oops.

Before they even reached the raft, Tierran had the earth off it. The dirt exploded off the ground, falling in piles to each side, and Calissa floated the raft out of the hole and into the water by the time they'd reached the shore. As they were getting on the boat, Tierran's head jerked up. He had forgotten his bags in the forest, he'd said, and he couldn't leave without them. It took just a few minutes, but again, it felt like hours. The Spålorians had mustered a last-minute force, and Tristys, Gawen, and Calissa had to fend off a few more archers and several soldiers who ran, in vain, after the raft. They even had to pick off a few arrows aimed at Tierran, who was now running back to the boat, both bags in hand.

"There better be something amazing in those bags," Tristys yelled as Tierran jumped aboard the raft that was already floating away from shore.

Tierran didn't answer. In fact, no one spoke as Calissa rocketed the raft away from Velo☐a Tånor and its newly installed fire exits. Once even the smoke had vanished from the sky, Rami turned to Tristys and broke the silence.

"Okay, kiddo," he said, exhaustion quickly catching up with him, "you said you can save your mother, and I hope you weren't lying." He looked down at his arms, which were still covered in blood and filth and pus. "Because you're going to have to save me, too."

CHAPTER TWENTY-THREE

Sitting on his knees at his mother's side, rising and falling at furious speeds with the raft underneath him, Tristys had his eyes closed. He was breathing deeply, consciously, taking in each breath and holding it before exhaling loudly. He was trying to calm down, to find his center, to become one with his inner being, to do all those silly things he'd heard about in the meditation alcoves. He sang an old lullaby to himself, a song with only a single verse that his mother used to repeat until he fell asleep when he was younger.

He was in the middle of the raft, his mother laid out next to him. Calissa and Salice were to his left, both with tears in their eyes. Rami was to his right, close enough to feel but not close enough to touch. Gawen was tending to Keltyn—he wasn't good at sentimental moments—and Tierran was navigating the ship. They'd put up the sails, let the wind do most of the work. For now.

He could do this. He'd done it once. He'd Touched Death-magic. It had Touched him, it would Touch him again, even if he had turned his back on the magic. Quell wasn't bitter or vengeful or vindictive. Quell didn't hold a grudge. Quell would come again. And when it did, he would be ready to grab it, to touch back.

He hoped.

He'd tried twice already to Touch Death, but he

failed both times. The first time, nothing happened at all. Absolutely nothing, like trying to squeeze water from a brick. The second time, they were there, the brown stars, but a second later he felt that crawling on his skin and he recoiled. The stars vanished. He cursed and slammed his hand against the raft. He could stop an entire country's army but he couldn't stomach a single sensation to save the life of the woman who gave him his? And possibly the man who gave it back?

He tried again. More stars, more colors. The scarlet of fire, the deep blue of water, the white and light blue of life and air. No brown. He slammed his fist again.

"Tristys," Calissa said, her voice muffled by her sorrow. "It's not your fault. At the Altar, you didn't—you couldn't—I was wrong to have pushed—"

He shook his head and held out a finger, silencing her. This wasn't about the Altar. This wasn't about her or what she did or didn't do. This was about right now, harnessing something that he knew he could, even if he didn't want to. This was about saving his mother.

He tried again. He concentrated, focused on nothing but Death-magic. He remembered the look of the Altar, its decaying flesh turned into edifice. He remembered the terrible smell, the stench that no longer bothered him after the day in the meditation alcove. He felt in his mind that sensation, that terrible sensation, of crawling skin and insects creeping in waves through his blood.

And then he felt it again, that same terrible sensation. Really felt it. There were brown stars! He didn't recoil, didn't pull away. He held on to them tightly, as tightly as he'd held his mother the day his older brother, Evynn, died. As tightly as he'd held onto the petrified log that floated him safely through the Coquels to Rami. And as tightly as he held onto Rami, as tightly as he was still holding onto Rami. And those stars didn't go anywhere. They stayed.

He opened his eyes. "I can do it!" he shouted. "I can do it!" He was smiling so hard his face hurt, laughing and crying at the same time so that it was hard to talk. "I can save her!"

And then suddenly a single realization wiped all his joy and triumph away. He remembered the Death-magician in New Cysal, saw that little monkey they almost killed just to cure a cold. A transfer. He had no transfer. His mother, and possibly Rami, would die despite everything they'd done to save her.

"We have no transfer," he said, despairing. He wanted to jump off the boat and drown. "We have no transfer!"

"Tristys," Calissa said, her face contorted, "listen, you can transfer a little bit into each of us."

He wasn't an expert on Death-magic, but it couldn't be that easy. "We'll get sick then, won't we?"

She hesitated, "Yes, right away, but not sick enough to die, I don't think. We can get back to the Coquels, we'll rush, and we'll get a proper transfer there."

Risk six people to save one? Again? He couldn't do it. Rami was most likely already infected, already at risk. No, he couldn't do this to them again. Keltyn was right. He was too late after all.

"Open my bags," Tierran said without looking at anyone. He was enraptured with the rigging on the sail, apparently bored with the attempt to save a woman's life.

"Get your own damn bags, Tierran," Rami spat. He was angry, but he had a right to be. His life was in jeopardy, too.

Tierran tore himself away from the rigging, picked up one of his knapsacks, and dumbed it onto the raft. There were plants, dozens of them, pulled up by their roots. Still alive.

"You should be able to use them," he said, his attention back to the rigging. "That way none of us has to risk our lives. Again."

Tristys heard someone shouting "Thank you! Thank you! Thank you!" It was him. He had no idea why Tierran had them, if he were smuggling some sort of special plant back into the Coquels or if he'd known they might need a transfer. Tristys didn't really care.

He grabbed one of the plants—they were cold to the touch and waxy—and put a hand on his mother. He twisted his vision. He willed the darkness out of his mother, moved it into the transfer. The plant withered at once. He tossed it aside, and Rami kicked it off the raft. He grabbed another plant, then another, then another, until there was no blackness left. She was still covered in sores, unconscious and far too thin, but her cough had ceased and her sores were no longer seeping.

"I can help her now," Calissa said. "We brought some medicines. It won't fix her right away, but it'll help her get started. Fix Rami."

There were just a few plants left, but when Tristys looked at Rami, he was clear. No blackness. He hadn't been contaminated. He'd been safe all along. Tristys turned quickly to the back of the raft to look at his brother. Also clean.

"You're fine, Rami," Tristys said. "You didn't get it. There's nothing to fix."

Rami smiled, a big, beautiful grin that lit up his face. "Thank you," he said as he wrapped Tristys in a big embrace. Tristys sagged, collapsing into Rami. He was exhausted. He hadn't felt this fatigued ever, not when he over-exerted with Water-magic, not when he Fingerprinted Fire-magic, nothing. But this wasn't just from the magic, he knew. He was drained, emotionally and physically. He needed to rest, just for a moment.

He fell asleep in Rami's lap, and he didn't wake up until the next day.

~~*

The trip home from Spàlor was rough, even after Tristys and Calissa secured his mother's recovery. Rami had never felt so tired, and though Tristys swore he was clean, Rami still worried about waking up covered in sores for days after the escape. They'd lost a lot of supplies in their getaway, so they had to stop on one of the small islands scattered throughout the Coquelai to replenish. They weren't within the barriers yet, and the island was so small that Rami could walk around the whole perimeter in less than an hour, but it had fruit trees, some edible grasses, and a little bit of wildlife. And it didn't float, which was a huge plus in Rami's book. He loved water, but he didn't like floating on it, apparently.

Tristys's brother, Keltyn, had woken up shortly after they purged his mother. Keltyn looked almost exactly like Tristys. Same hair color, same hairstyle. They even had the same eyes. Rami had joked with Tristys, on the first night on the island, that the only way he could tell Tristys and Keltyn apart was the lust he always saw in Tristys's eyes. He said if Keltyn ever developed a crush on him, there'd be no telling them apart. Tristys had punched him—hard—on the bicep. Rami complained, which led to a massage, which led to more happy memories.

But Keltyn was still incorrigible. He refused to speak to Tristys, since Tristys was a "diverted heathen". He then refused to speak to everyone else, one by one, as he found out they too were heathens. He'd speak only to Calissa and Salice, and he clung to them like a burr.

Salice had even told him about her affairs with women in lurid detail, but diversion in women wasn't a problem in Cyræa, so he just listened attentively and then shared his own (imaginary, Tristys assured him) stories about female worship. Salice was at her wit's end, but there was nothing anyone could do, so she just put up with him. She was the only one, though. Even Firebird disliked him, opting to bite him every time he came too close. Tristys and Rami pretended to discipline the monkey, but Rami, at least, secretly encouraged the behavior. More happy memories.

Tristys's mother was named Tyspal. Rami found the symmetry—leaving the Coquels with one Tyspal and coming back with another—oddly comforting, as if this whole thing was meant to happen exactly as it had. Whether fated or not, she was doing much better. They decided to stay on the island for a few days, to see if the stability would help her recover.

It was a wise choice. By the second morning, she'd regained full consciousness. She ate voraciously, as much and as often as she could, despite the inevitable stomachache food still gave her. When she walked, she'd resist assistance for as long as she could, but she was still weak, so she'd have to take a hand sooner or later. She was a strong, stubborn woman—that was where Tristys had gotten it, obviously—but she had a good sense of humor. Rami liked her. He liked her even more when, after Tristys and Rami accidentally shared a kiss in front of her, her only reaction was a satisfied smile and an offer to leave if they needed more privacy.

They stayed on the island for four days. They were going to stay another, but Salice was afraid they were irrevocably altering the ecosystem there. They'd eaten virtually every fruit off every tree and had scared the wildlife into agoraphobia. Tyspal assured them she could travel, and he liked her even more when she was the one to smack Keltyn when he wouldn't stop yelling to turn the raft around and take him back to Cyræa.

"Don't you think it's time for a little adventure?" she asked.

Tristys had explained everything—their Coquellian heritage, magic, the islands, the time he spent there so far. She had taken it in stride, far better than Rami thought she'd take it. She was tickled when Tristys showed her his quell-work, and she told Salice the first thing she wanted to do on the islands was go to an air-dancing show. Salice hadn't looked so happy in all the time Rami knew her.

As the island of Quelles came into view, Tyspal gasped. "It's beautiful," she said, and Rami had to agree. This wasn't the Bluewood—just green trees, no different to the naked eye than the forests of Spálor—but there was something about the islands, about the colors of the leaves or the smells in the air, that was special. The wind was light, and the raft was coasting smoothly to shore. Tristys was at the front, his legs dangling in the water, watching the beach as it approached. Rami sat next to him, put an arm around his shoulder, and kissed him lightly on the cheek. He was glad to be home.

They washed up very near to Rami's Point, the same stretch of land where Rami had found Tristys, like a beached whale, less than a year ago. Telia's house was nearby, and Rami decided that they'd stay there for a few days to let Tyspal regain more strength before taking her to meet Ystan. Rami and Tristys, along with Calissa, left Tyspal with the others at the raft. Before they even knocked on Telia's door, she was there, throwing it open and running to Rami.

"Oh, you're here! You're here!" she kept saying, the words rushing out of her mouth. She hugged him tightly, so tightly he gasped at first and turned slightly red by the end. "I wasn't sure if you'd come to see me again, and you brought Calissa!" She hugged Calissa next, just as deeply, and she turned to Tristys. "And Tristys! Oh, how exciting!" She hugged him, too, even longer than she'd hugged Rami or Calissa.

Ah, Telia. She'd always been here for him, and he knew she'd always be here in the future, even though he'd treated her so badly the last time they'd seen each other. He'd have to apologize for that at some point, no doubt. He wasn't sure how he'd make it up to her, but he knew how to start. He put an arm around Tristys, pulled him close, and rested his head on Tristys's shoulder. She took the hint.

"Are you—have you finally—oh, thank the quell!" More hugs, all around. "I'm so excited! You'll have to tell me everything. Tristys, how did you finally—Oh! Calissa, are you okay with—well, I suppose you probably knew all along, didn't you? I should have known you would!" Just as they got her settled down, they told her about the previously sick Cyræan on the beach just a little bit away, and she was up again, her words and her feet racing as she ran to get medicine and food and water.

"She's a hoot," Calissa said, still smiling. They waited while Telia gathered whatever she felt like she'd need, Calissa standing next to Rami, his arm still around Tristys. "So," Calissa said unexpectedly, "what are you guys gonna do now?"

"What do you mean?" Tristys asked.

"Well, you can Touch all these magics, you invaded an enemy country and saved your family. What's left?"

"Oh, I don't know. I think we'll—"

"Guys, your presence is requested urgently back at the raft." Gawen had come up behind them so quickly they hadn't even heard his approach.

Tristys's expression dropped. "Is everything okay? Is my mom—"

"Oh, your mom's fine. Everyone's fine," Gawen said, a smile playing just behind his lips. "Your brother appears to have gotten into a little trouble again."

"Oh, by the two moons!" Tristys said, already stomping off. "Did he tease Firebird again? I'm so tired of healing that boy's boo-boos!" Calissa and Rami shrugged at each other and followed.

When they got back to the raft, Keltyn was standing just inside the waves, the water licking his bare feet. His arms were held at his sides, palms down, and the water was reaching up, little fountains all around him, struggling to hit his hands before failing and falling back down. He looked more afraid now than he did in Velo□a Tánor.

"Oh, for the love of—"Tristys said before he ran to help his brother.

"Well, Calissa, I guess that answers your question," Rami said, chuckling to himself.

"I'm sure Liana will be glad to see you again."

"She'll be glad to see you, at least." Rami sighed, but it was a happy one. Content, even. He heard Telia shouting behind him—she must have seen Keltyn —and he started walking to Tristys, to see what he could do to help. "Tristys," he said, putting a hand on his shoulder as he bent down to look at the fountains, "it looks like we're going to the Altar again, and so help me, on the way there, you better stay away from jungle cats."

Fin

ACKNOWLEDGMENTS

I couldn't have finished Eternity without my parents, who have supported me in anything and everything I've ever wanted or needed to do.

I'd like to thank all the people who have read this book in all its many versions: Poppy, Logan, John, and Romina; the members of the now-defunct (*tear*) fcrits; and various readers from critters.org.

I owe a lot to the amazing people at Less Than Three Press: Megan, Sam, Amanda, Raelynn. Amanda needs a special shout-out for putting up with all my neuroses during the editing process.

And this may be uncouth, but I'd like to thank myself, too, for pushing through everything when I didn't believe in anything. Thank you, me, for finally finishing something that mattered to us. Couldn't have done it without you!

I've been wanting to publish a novel for over twenty years, and through every different book I wrote (or tried to), I remember pounding away at the keys, singing at the top of my lungs to music, and thinking, "When this is published, I'll make sure to thank all these songs that got me through!" Now that I'm finally publishing one, I need to make good on my promise.

Thank you to all the artists whose music I've listened to and loved over the years. A few of you deserve special shout-outs: Britney Spears, my first true obsession (in a healthy, gay way), and Anggun, whose voice has carried me since she snowed on the Sahara, and the myriad incarnations of Celtic Woman, my kryptonite to writer's block. Kylie Minogue, your energy keeps me dancing, and Sara Bareilles and Ingrid Michaelson, if I ever need to emote, I come to you first. And a special thank-you to Darren Hayes, who once read my blog and said I was a "vivid and amazing unique bright light" at a time when I really, really, really needed to hear it.

And to you, of course, my readers. (It's still so bizarre to think of myself as having readers!) To all of you: thanks so much for sticking with me through Tristys and Rami's journey. See you in the se*quell*!

About the Author

Matthew Merendo has wanted to write since the first grade, when he wrote a seven-page story about Wormy the Worm's travails during a thunderstorm. (It was supposed to be a single-page assignment. Whoops.) He's done a lot of stuff since then — some college degrees, retail work, web development, college instructor — but he also wrote a novel... and now, thanks to Less Than Three Press, it's getting published! (And there will, he hopes, be more. You can stay in the loop at his website, http://mattmerendo.com, or his twitter, @mamerendo.)

44758049R00275

Made in the USA
Middletown, DE
15 June 2017